CW00683471

VIKING DYNASTY

Gina Dale

Gina Dale Publishing
United Kingdom

Copyright © 2024 Gina Dale Publishing
This work is registered with UK Copyright Service:
Registration 284756106

The right of Gina Dale to be identified as author
of this work has been asserted by her in accordance with the Copyright,
Designs and Patents Act 1988
All rights reserved. This book is sold subject to the condition that no part
of this book is to be reproduced, in any shape or form. Or by way of trade,
stored in a retrieval system or transmitted in any form or by any means,
electronic, mechanical, photocopying, recording, be lent, re-sold, hired out
or otherwise circulated in any form of binding or cover other than that in
which it is published and without a similar condition, including this condition being imposed on the subsequent purchaser, without prior permission
of the copyright holder.

Disclaimer
This novel is entirely a work of fiction. The names, characters and incidents
portrayed in it, while at times are based on historical figures, are the work of
the author's imagination.

Printed by Ingrams UK

A CIP catalogue record for this book is available
from the British Library
978-1-7396031-0-6

Also available as an eBook
ISBN 978-1-7396031-1-3

ACKNOWLEDGEMENTS

I would like to thank the following for their help, expertise and encouragement in producing my third indie novel in the Viking Series 'Viking Dynasty'.

Editor Rachel Gregory, pedanticpolly@gmail.com
Cover designer Jenny Quinlan, USA www.historicaleditorial.com.
Typesetter Catherine Cousins, 2QT Limited.
Marketing & Media, Clancy Walker, Leeds
Photoshoot for cover, Katie Amos, www.equineshoot.com

PHOTOSHOOT ACKNOWLEDGEMENTS

Photography: Katie Amos Photography
www.equineshoot.com, Todmorden.
Hairstyling: Kaye Volante, Zeitgeist Hair, Hebden Bridge,
Models: Ubba - Ben Glynn,

       Torri - Carolyn Eden

       Arne - George Sweeney

       Freya - Maia Brice

Venue and animals courtesy of Alanna and Nathan Douglas-Smith at Blackshaw Royd Equestrian Centre, Hebden Bridge.

Costume Hire: History in the Making Ltd., Portsmouth.
Bridle: Designed and produced by Ryburn Leather, Sowerby Bridge.

Other titles

Viking Series

Viking Wolf (Book 1)
Viking Warrior (Book 2)

Brushstrokes Trilogy

Brushstrokes (Book 1)
Darkness Falls (Book 2)
Drama Unfolds (Book 3)

The author has her own website
www.ginadalepublishing.com
where pictures relating to all these books
can be seen.

Social Media posts for Gina Dale Author are available
on FB, Instagram and LinkedIn.

PROLOGUE

Ubba halted Sleipnir and paused to look across the valley to his farm, which was reflecting the sun through a break in the clouds skimming across the sky, even as the weather threatened an approaching downpour typical of the traditional April weather. He had moved up to Richmond last September and had survived his first winter and lambing season. The farm was in the valley and, although they had experienced some prolonged bursts of snow, it had been relatively mild... considerably warmer than a winter back in Denmark. For once, he had been free to indulge in his favourite pastimes of eating, drinking, sleeping and sex –unconstrained by his previous duties of training troops for battle.

He was no longer a commander and was content that Halfdan was taking on this role now, in preparation for an assault on Durham. He had reluctantly agreed that his eldest son Arne (now 16) could join Halfdan to continue his battle training; Torri had pointed out that Arne needed to become an individual from Ubba. He came back periodically to visit, full of stories of his achievements and occasional failures, inspired by the camaraderie he felt with his fellow troopers. He accepted Halfdan's leadership better than he would his father's, content that he was being treated no differently from the others. He had been punished by Halfdan whenever he failed to toe the line. His occasional overindulgence, causing him to oversleep, had been nipped in the bud too by Halfdan... and Arne knew he would have no special privileges from his uncle.

His athletic skills were being honed, as attacking Durham's high walls would be essential to gaining control of the city. He had his father's perfect balance and climbing skills and was being groomed to be one of the first troopers to break in overnight, before the full-scale attack, and target the gates to gain access for Halfdan's troops when the battle commenced. Arne had suffered a fall and torn the ligaments in his left ankle prior to Yule, so Halfdan had sent him home to his parents to recuperate. He and Torri had enjoyed having him home for a month and Ubba had overseen his recovery. The relationship between the two of them had much improved, as Arne was relieved from the constant comparisons to his father and was now allowed to make his own mistakes. Freya had managed to discover that he had shown an interest in girls – and they in him, though Arne was naturally shy and overawed by women. Ubba had left it to Torri to remind him to avoid getting a girl pregnant and being trapped into marriage too soon. He assured her that marriage and fatherhood were the last things on his mind; he was just enjoying learning the art of flirtation, enjoying sex and trying to avoid any consequences.

The first spots of rain started to fall. Ubba spun

Sleipnir round and cantered down the hill towards home. He had become used to riding alone again, as it brought him closer to nature. He was so attuned to scouting that he was unlikely to miss any movement in the area. He missed Frank being by his side and wished he had not been lost at Jorvik; he felt guilty that Serena had lost both her brother and her husband in his service. She did not blame him, but he blamed himself. Serena and their three children Astrid, Theo and baby Frank (named after his uncle and uncannily like him in looks and temperament) were enjoying spending more time together. It amazed him how hard it was being responsible for a growing young family as he had never experienced it before, having been away for much of his first three children's childhoods. Theo was now six and had formed a strong bond with Torri, who had developed a love of gardening. He spent as much time as he could following her around in the garden, digging and weeding. Torri enjoyed his company and she loved his enthusiasm for birds, flowers and nature.

Torri had enjoyed their extended time together over the winter. However, something was wrong; she was experiencing pains in her stomach, which she had attempted to hide from him. He had noticed her flinch with pain. It was alarming to him that she never discussed it. He could hardly bring himself to admit that there might be something seriously wrong with her health, but when they went to Ireland to visit Ivar, he intended to enlist Sulamain's aid to get to the bottom of the problem. The prospect of losing her was enough to make him cry and he had spent several nights doing just that when she had fallen asleep. She was getting old and had not had an easy life. Her years as a shieldmaiden had taken their toll and bearing six children to three husbands, as well as being a queen, had not made her life any easier. She was mother to two boys from Bjorn, as well as his sons Arne and Viggo and their daughter Freya. He had prayed to both Odin and the Christian God to spare his wife and he knew he would go to the end of the world if there was any hope of a cure. He was saddened she would not admit it to him, but then she had always sacrificed her life for her family.

At least she was no longer a queen, so was free to enjoy her life on her own terms. Knowing how much she loved her garden, Ubba had found an Italian retired gardener and his son Matteo living in Jorvik, who had designed and built some of the ornate palace gardens in Rome and Florence. His father Pedro had compiled a list of flowers and plants Torri should purchase while in Europe. She was overjoyed at the thought of being able to bring more unusual flowers – especially roses – back to Yorkshire. She had been delighted at his thoughtfulness, but if she had known the real reason that Ubba had done it – in the hope she would have chance to see them grow, because he feared for her life – she would have been distraught. Torri had never been one to wallow in sickness or self-pity and she would not want her family to know if she was critically ill. He had also written to Bjorn, suggesting he bring Erik and Refil to Normandie in July to see them and his Uncle Rollo, but he had not revealed there could be an issue with Torri's health. However, he felt her sons needed to see their mother in case it was their last opportunity. He would not tell Torri until he was certain that Bjorn would be at Normandie.

As he turned off the track into his farm, Sleipnir pranced on the spot and whinnied his arrival as top stallion. A chorus of his adoring female fans replied, along with some angry responses from other stallions on the yard. Josh his groom came over, shaking his head.

Ubba said, 'What's the matter now?'

He replied, 'You know I do not like you riding out alone, Ubba; you are still a target for angry Saxons and even Danes who you have fought against in the past. Frank would be spinning in his grave. Even Ivar would forbid it, just as you would if he did it.

Ubba smiled. 'I like being alone. I can appreciate the scenery and wildlife and have time to reflect. Sleipnir is feeling frisky now the breeding season is starting. Do you think the stable staff will cope with the coming season?'

'Yes, of course now you have old Sam coming to supervise whilst we are away; you know he will ensure that everything runs smoothly. It was good of Lady Aethelflaed to give him leave from Jorvik to come here. She seems to have a very high regard for you.'

'Stop digging your grave, Josh; there is nothing to find. She fell in love with a Dane once, but it was definitely NOT me!' He threw Sleipnir's reins to him and smiled, 'Now, if there is any speculation from any of the staff on that subject, you can tell them exactly what I have told you.'

Ubba strode into the house, to be met by Egil, who had been packing wooden chests for their forthcoming journey.

'Don't pack too many clothes for my family. I intend to purchase clothes suitable for the French court when we arrive.'

'Lord, it's very difficult trying to decide what to take when I have never been to a French court.'

'Rollo is a duke, not a king, and it won't be as formal as the palaces in Paris. I have no title or status anymore, so I don't have to dress formally. However, I will treat myself to some up-to-date fashion when I get there. We are visiting family, not royalty. As for Ireland, I would be astonished to find them wearing fashionable clothes. Due to the frequency of fights and squabbles over there, I would imagine they remain permanently dressed for battle. Ivar says it is cold and draughty and rains every day, so make sure there are some fur cloaks packed, even though it will be June. Where is Torri?'

'Out in the garden with Matteo, lord.'

'Then, I will leave them to become more acquainted.' He winked at Egil and headed off in pursuit of Serena.

Egil was shocked. Young Matteo had turned many ladies' heads in the household with his Italian good looks and charm since his arrival, but surely not Torri. What was more surprising was that Ubba appeared to be encouraging it! Why, when the last time she had flirted with a young man he had been jealous and angry with her? He scratched his head. One thing was certain – understanding the mind of a Ragnarsson was impossible; they were just too unpredictable!

That evening as they snuggled up in bed, Ubba said, 'Is Matteo fulfilling his duties, sweetheart? Do you recall what I said when I told you about him?'

'You said, "He is yours to do as you please with darling and be sure to exploit any hidden talents he may have besides gardening." Would you care to explain exactly what you meant?'

Ubba pulled her closer. 'Let's just say that he is a young virile handsome Italian, skilled in the art of charming women; if you want him in your bed, feel free to indulge.'

'What are you saying? Remember how furious you were when I appeared to be flirting with Sigtryggr? Yet, now you are giving me permission to take a lover? What madness is this? I am old enough to be his grandmother, never mind his lover. What possible interest would Matteo have in me?'

'You forget sweetheart, how beautiful you are; age has done nothing to diminish your sex appeal, and your reputation as an indomitable queen and shieldmaiden would stir the loins of any young man to possess you. He is no different from a beautiful rose or a rampant stallion, and if you want him, then have him with my blessing. You forget you are a Dane, free to bestow your favours on any man you fancy. You are not constrained by a vow of fidelity to me; we did both agree that we could take lovers when we were apart. I have loved you all my life and I just want you to be happy. I never thought I would reach this age, but I can't compete with Matteo and if a fling with him will make you feel young again, then how can I deny you when you have let me have Serena in my life as well as you? You have given me three clever beautiful children and Bjorn two impressive sons, too. You are the matriarch of a Ragnarsson dynasty that will continue to flourish long after we have gone.'

She propped herself up in bed and kissed him on his nose. 'You are an inspiration to me and I love the bones of you. You are the bravest, kindest husband and father who ever lived and I count myself to be a very lucky woman to be your wife. If you want to make me happy then make love to me now, then depending on your performance I will consider whether to take the Italian stallion to my bed.'

He looked at her, aghast. 'No pressure then, Torri?'

She smiled. 'None whatsoever, my love! I have total faith in you.

ONE

They had made it to Heysham via the river network between Yorkshire and Lancashire. Ubba was staring out across the calm Irish Sea, offering a prayer to Odin and God to keep the sea calm on the crossing to Dublin as they left the harbour. He did not want a rough crossing and to have his family see him suffer with sea sickness. He and Keir his longboat captain had planned every detail of the journey with this in mind. Ubba had insisted that two longboats were required in case he purchased some horses in Ireland, but he was secretly hoping he might persuade Viggo and Ivar to return to Yorkshire and was determined there would be enough room to bring them back.

His family travel companions consisted of Torri, Freya and a reluctant Arne, who wanted to stay with Halfdan in case his battle for Durham commenced. He was determined to fight in his first battle, anxious to prove his worth, and displeased he had been dragged away to make not just the trip to Ireland, but to Normandie and Spain too. After a prolonged argument with Arne, Ubba had agreed that if when they came back from Ireland, Durham's battle had started early, then he would allow him to join Halfdan and miss the trip abroad. Halfdan had assured him they were in no rush to attack before July, unless political circumstances changed. There was a possibility the Scots might try to take Durham from the sea, but Halfdan considered it unlikely they would succeed without mounting a land attack too, which he himself was planning. The equipment needed to breech the walls of Durham would need a longboat transporting ramps and horses and without it the success rate would be nil. He doubted the Scots would risk that as, like the Irish, they preferred raiding out in the open and making a quick getaway. Sieges of castles as fortified as Durham would not generally appeal to them.

Egil had insisted he go with the family overseas. Ubba was grateful for his organisation skills, his ability to ensure enough food and provisions were available, and that all the necessary equipment was safely packed away and made waterproof. Serena had been happy to remain at home as travelling with baby Frank, Theo and Astrid would have been a hard job. He had allowed Arne to bring his wolf Shadow with him as his ability to sense danger and guard Arne could prove vital in Ireland. He knew the Irish had their enormous wolfhounds to guard their property, but felt they would be unlikely to take on Shadow; his sheer presence and dominance would hopefully prevent any confrontations. Ralf had confirmed that wolfhounds spent the day around the fireside and under the table waiting for scraps of food, not outside chained up and guarding property. Very few were kept purely for hunting and their sheer size did not make it easy for them to cope with Irish bogs and the harsh weather.

Their good friends Ralf, Gytha and Thorin were in the second longboat. Ubba had promised to take them to be present at the birth of their daughter Skye's first baby to Sigtryggr, now King of Dublin. Gytha's excitement had been escalating rapidly as the time came closer. Ubba remembered her delivering Thorin 16 years ago, and the battle he and the midwife had fought to ensure both of them survived the ordeal. He hoped that this birth would be easier, although Skye was very slim and Sigtryggr was over 6 ft 6 inches tall and built like a polar bear, with long curly red hair and a temper to match. Even Ubba would think twice about fighting Sigtryggr as his sword skills were excellent, even though he had limited sight in one eye from an old sword wound. The rest of the crew was made up of sailors and warriors, who could turn their hand to either task.

Ubba's prayers were answered; both longboats rowed into Dublin Bay late in the afternoon on the following day after a calm crossing. They headed to the port and Ubba saw a young man waving and shouting in the distance. Work on unloading and loading cargo stopped on other vessels as the two longboats approached. The young man was at the far end of the jetty, waving frantically.

'Lord Ubba, it is Jed. I am one of Ivar's guards, who came over here with him. I have been instructed to dock your boats in King Sigtryggr's private dockyard. If you sail closer, I will jump across and guide your boats.'

Ubba now recognised Jed and nodded to Keir to let

him on board. He made an impressive leap onto the boat and landed within three feet of Ubba.

'My lord, you look healthy and well. We were all concerned about you in the battle for Jorvik.'

'Jed, I no longer warrant the title "lord". I am merely a retired farmer now.'

Jed laughed. 'Rubbish! Once a warrior, always a warrior.' He ran off to join Keir at the helm, gesticulating at a large building he had spotted on the way in, which appeared to be the only one made of stone. It was three storeys and clearly very new. They pulled out of the port and headed down the coast to the palace. As they drew closer, Ubba realised it was not made of stone but limestone, with marble pillars and huge glass windows catching the sun reflecting off the building. He recalled Freya relating one of her dreams in which she referred to Skye living in a grand palace like the ones in Italy. Had Sigtryggr built a palace during the last year?

Whilst his attention had been on the palace Torri had joined him and said, 'How has Sigtryggr built something as impressive as that and where did he get the materials from?'

'God only knows, or probably Odin, as Sigtryggr is a staunch Norseman. Look, I am sure that's Ivar waving from the top of the steps.'

Torri hurriedly scanned the area and panicked. 'I can't see Viggo! Where is my precious son?'

Ubba hugged her close. 'Calm down sweetheart, he is probably working and hasn't heard of our sighting yet. We may not even recognise him as he is 16 now and will have matured from a boy to an adult over the last two years.'

As they neared the palace, the tall wooden gates swung open, revealing an inlet of water leading to a man-made lake with mooring for four large longboats. Behind was a long two-storey wooden building, which looked like accommodation for the troops and sailors.

Suddenly, they heard distant galloping hoofbeats. Before long, a fine grey stallion came into view, with a young rider wearing full length leather boots, kidskin breeches and a fine scarlet cloak bound in silver thread. His auburn hair was swept up and cascaded down to his shoulders. He continued to urge the stallion to canter down the jetty and reined him to a halt at the end. As the ropes were thrown by the sailors to tie up their longboat, Viggo jumped off his horse and over onto the deck, too impatient to wait for the gangplank.

Both Torri and Ubba were speechless, unable to take in the change in their son. However, neither had noticed Arne joining them and as soon as Viggo approached. Arne strode over to his brother, shaking his finger at him and shouting. 'What the hell were you doing? You could have had that fine beast slipping on wet wooden planks and breaking a leg!'

Viggo pushed Arne aside and flung himself at Torri wrapping her in his arms and hugging her. 'Mother, I have missed you so much. Ireland is a cold harsh country, way behind Jorvik. Why did you bring Arne over here? Surely he should be back home, protecting your land?'

Torri was too emotional to reply. Her long-held

anxiety for the welfare of her favourite son spilled over; tears rolled down her cheeks as she clung to him and her worst fears dissolved. Her beloved son was no longer a boy, but a handsome teenager.

Viggo unwrapped himself from his mother's arms, turned to Ubba and hugged him. 'Father, you cannot imagine how we all worried about your safety, but the gods kept you safe and well.'

Ubba hugged him and said, 'I don't know how much influence the gods had over my welfare; it was more down to a change of attitude towards Danes from King Edward.'

Viggo turned towards Freya and pulled her into his arms. 'Oh, my sweet little sister, you are turning into a beauty the image of our mother.'

They all disembarked the longboat and headed towards the palace. Ralf and Gytha ran ahead, anxious to see their daughter Skye. They were ushered through the reception area and into the King's salon, where Sigtryggr, Skye and Ivar were waiting.

Gytha shrieked at Skye when she saw her and ran over. 'Oh child, you look as if you are going to burst. Are there twins inside you?' She pulled her to her feet. Skye, half laughing and half crying, said, 'No Mama, Sulamain assures me there is only one baby. You forget how tall and strong Sigtryggr is.'

Sigtryggr took Gytha's hand and kissed it. 'Madame, I can assure you that Skye's pregnancy is being closely monitored and the baby is due very soon. She of course wanted you to be here to support her during labour and Sulamain will be in attendance throughout. Ah, of course we also have two more birthing experts in your party, Lord Ubba and Lady Torri.'

Ubba smiled and turned directly to Sigtryggr. 'May I congratulate you on becoming King of Dublin and thank you for extending your hospitality to my family. I trust Viggo has not caused you any headaches, unlike my wicked brother Ivar, who will no doubt have given you much cause for concern.'

He moved to Ivar, who rose to greet him, and they locked eyes and embraced each other. Ivar spoke first. 'Ubba, my big brother. I can't wait to hear how you kept your head in defeat and indeed turned it into a triumph. For someone who professes to loathe politics and who retired to become a farmer, you must have brokered a very competent deal with Edward to still be alive.'

He turned to Torri next and said, 'I can't quite see the role of farmer's wife suiting you, my queen.' She flung her arms around him and kissed his cheek. 'On the contrary, Ivar – I have a new passion for growing flowers, designing clothes and embracing nature.' She whispered in his ear, 'also enjoying my time in Ubba's arms during the long winter nights.'

Ivar shook his head and said quietly, 'And how have you coped with sharing him with Serena?'

She gave him a quizzical look. 'Ivar, you and I both know I hold the key to Ubba's heart. Besides, Serena has been busy breeding and men tend to prefer to bed other women when their partners are reproducing.'

Ivar chuckled. 'How very clever you have been, my dear! Now let me greet my only niece, who is turning

15

into a very beautiful woman. She is destined for greatness. Do not let her stray!'

Ubba and Torri moved across the room to greet Skye.

Ivar pointed to Freya to come to him, as she had been waiting behind with Arne whilst her parents greeted him first.

Freya flung her arms around Ivar and kissed his cheek. 'Oh, you don't know how much I have missed you, Ivar.'

Ivar said quietly, 'Freya, you are no longer a child. Do you know how beautiful you are? You do realise that you must keep men at bay? Your future is mapped out by the gods and you must remain pure until they reveal your husband.'

'But how will I know who is the right one? I may not like the one the gods choose. Oh, don't look so shocked, Ivar – as well as my parents I have a permanent bodyguard in Thorin, plus Arne, who is very difficult to deceive. His tracking skills are the equal of my father's. Besides, I am no longer at court so no men are even going to see me, never mind touch me.'

Ivar smiled. 'I will speak to you privately later my dear; we have a lot of catching up to do. Please send Arne over to me.'

As Arne came over, Ivar was struck by how much he resembled his father when he was of a similar age. Ubba certainly stamped his stock, both in looks and temperament. He sensed Arne was not too pleased to be here. He motioned him to sit next to him on the sofa.

'Well, Arne, you don't look too pleased to be here. Mind telling me why?'

'Because I should have stayed with Halfdan, ready to fight for Durham! I am convinced my father insisted I come over here to avoid getting killed in my first battle.'

'I doubt it, Arne; you look every ounce the warrior your father was at your age. The reason you and your father struggle is because you are too alike. I can understand you find it very irritating, but at least Ubba let you go to fight with Halfdan; that can't have been easy for either of your parents. You must appreciate that our aim is to keep every Ragnarsson alive to take on new challenges in life.'

Arne snapped, 'Well it was obvious that Viggo was the favoured son when they let you take him to Ireland. I am the eldest son, but just because I am not as clever as Viggo, I was left in Yorkshire at risk of being captured and killed while Viggo escaped with you.'

Ivar's temper was rising. 'Now you listen to me, Arne. You were left there as you were battle trained – admittedly not proven yet, but perfectly capable of protecting your mother and siblings, had your father and Halfdan died in battle. It was a tough call, but we knew you would have done your utmost to protect them, and you had the skills to hide them and then leave the country if necessary.'

Arne looked shocked. 'But why did nobody tell me that?'

Ivar sighed and shook his head. 'Because we didn't

think you needed the pressure of being told. Make no mistake, Edward would have killed your mother, father and you if you had been captured in the battle for Jorvik. I would have done the same in his shoes. I might have spared Freya, as she would have been a useful prize in future bargaining power, for her breeding potential. Thankfully, Edward had his own agenda. I intend to find out from Ubba what it was.'

TWO

Ivar invited Ubba to join him out on the balcony of his bedroom for a private chat. The room was on the top floor of the palace and overlooked the bay out to the Irish Sea.

Ubba said, 'It is a beautiful warm summer's evening. How does Dublin suit you?'

Ivar smiled. 'Don't be taken in by today. You are very lucky; it usually rains every day here. The winters are milder but wetter than England; the damp seeps into my bones. The new palace has made a big difference as it is both warmer and easier for me to navigate. I am experiencing problems with my legs again, but it came at the same time Skye was struggling with her mobility due to pregnancy, so I have spent many happy hours chatting with her.'

'Has Sigtryggr proved a worthy husband for her? I know both of us were concerned when she left with him.'

Ivar smiled. 'They do make a good couple. Despite his size and strength, Sigtryggr has many insecurities, but she has few and helps him make difficult decisions. I will say I am impressed with him. He has a natural way of communicating and men follow him like they do you. He knows how to present a difficult strategy and gain their support. He doesn't scream, shout and threaten like me. He has a very calm, quiet demeanour and controls his temper well. However, he is no fool and you underestimate him at your peril. He was very clever to use my reputation to secure him the throne, as ruling the many different nationalities who live here is not easy. The Irish are feudal and highly superstitious. They let imaginary ghosts dictate their daily routine. There are some areas they won't even go to because some dark deed happened years ago and they fear it may happen again. Admittedly, they have bogs to worry about – and until I saw a man and a horse disappear into a bog in less than five minutes, I had not realised just how dangerous they were. The weather here can change in minutes, and when a mist comes down, you can easily stray off the path. Their native horses and ponies have an inbred instinct to avoid bogs.'

'How has Viggo fared over here? His penchant for luxury food and clothing appears to have increased, not decreased.'

Ivar smiled. 'Just because he is not willing to live close to nature like you does not mean he is a lesser person. He is quick witted and can get himself out of trouble when necessary. Yes, he can be precocious, he has a penchant for luxury items including women and he can be lazy, but his desire to learn and experience new environments is to be encouraged. He wants to go back with Sulamain to study medicine and explore Eastern culture. He needs to fly the nest Ubba and seek his own fortune. He may only be 17, but he is ready to go. Sulamain only stayed over the winter because he promised Sigtryggr he would oversee Skye's confinement.'

Ubba sighed. 'I do agree with you, but his mother will find it hard to let go.'

'Then you must prepare her now; she knows he has a fine brain and wants to explore the world. Let him find his own way in life. Whatever he does, he will be successful.'

'For someone who is supposed to be a great communicator I feel I have failed my sons. Viggo can't wait to leave home and Arne and I fight like cat and dog.'

'Only because you and Arne are so alike, Ubba. You have done the right thing by letting him go to Halfdan. He needs to prove himself in battle and if he survives, he will learn that it is tougher than he thought. Remember, Erik was just as anxious to prove himself as a warrior to Bjorn. You know how hard it is to follow a great man who is also your father. No son wants to be found wanting – especially not a Ragnarsson. Now, Freya is blooming into a beautiful woman and you need to concentrate on keeping her safe. I know she has Thorin as her bodyguard, but men will kill to bed her. The gods have a mission for Freya, but unfortunately, we mortals don't get to know what it is in advance.'

'I am well aware of that, Ivar. I have already had Edward asking for her hand for his son, but I am keeping him waiting for an answer. He wanted to take her to Wessex now and convert her to Christianity.'

Ivar gasped in shock. 'Tell me you are not even considering it! She has a link to Odin and you know that. You cannot force her to become Christian; you know she is destined to be a key player in our family's dynasty.'

Ubba laughed. 'I was just jesting as I knew it would infuriate you. You never liked my Christian beliefs, but I can assure you that I would never force Freya to become a Christian. She is a born Norsewoman and nobody will ever overcome that.'

They relaxed and headed down to enjoy a wonderful dinner with the assembled company, in the elevated dining room with huge glass windows overlooking the bay of Dublin. They tasted produce from all over the Mediterranean that they hadn't had the pleasure of eating for many years, combined with excellent French and Italian wine. Afterwards, Ubba excused himself from the table and followed Ivar to his suite of rooms.

'How the hell has Sigtryggr built an Italian marble palace with Roman columns here in Dublin, when he has never ventured further than England and Ireland?'

Ivar smiled as he poured Ubba some more French wine. 'It's all about having the right contacts and finding experts who can build the palace of your dreams. Admittedly, the weather is not as good here, but the Italian architect employed to design it catered for its climate. He installed underfloor heating in the form of a hypocaust, as well as making the walls as thick as a castle to keep out the elements. Your son was part of the team and he certainly has a flair for design.'

'He's never been to Italy, either!'

'Ah, but he has studied Latin and Greek history and language when he was in Jorvik and Sulamain has been all over the Mediterranean.'

'It must have cost a fortune! Where the hell did Sigtryggr find the money to pay for all this?'

'He had a little financial help from me, as I found the climate here cold and depressing in the winter and he needs to keep me here to fulfil his ambitious plans.'

'Which are?'

'He intends to become King of Ireland and wants me to become King of Dublin in his absence, whilst he ousts the Saxons and reclaims Jorvik.'

Ubba knew that Sigtryggr had not come over to Jorvik for a holiday three years ago. His ambitions seemed to be even higher than Ivar's and he had to admire his confidence. However, the first day in Ireland would not be the best time to reveal to Ivar his pact with Edward over protecting Jorvik and he did not fancy having to return home so soon. He would have to pick the right moment. He knew both Ivar and Sigtryggr would be incandescent with rage over the agreement and he had to change the subject quickly.

Ivar intervened, 'What, has the delectable wine addled your brain?'

Ubba grabbed the lifeline with relief. 'I was just mulling over what you said. Do Sigtryggr's lofty ambitions extend to becoming King of England, too?'

'Ultimately, yes, but he is going to need a large army to achieve that. If Halfdan takes Durham and you are close to Jorvik he could push them south again. I know you like to think you have retired as a warrior, but I know you, Ubba; you must be missing the intrigue and plotting battle strategy by now. You have put weight on cavorting in your bed with your wife and mistress and increasing your army of little Ubbas, but I know you are bored.'

Ubba feigned insult to throw Ivar off the scent. 'I have not put any weight on! It is all muscle. I have been digging ditches, fencing, building stables and ploughing fields. Not to mention breeding and breaking horses and farming sheep.'

'Whatever made you take on sheep?'

'My land consists of the valley bottom and gently sloping fields, but it goes right up to the moors at the highest point. I foolishly thought I could breed sheep by grazing them up high in the summer and then bringing them inside during the winter until after lambing.'

'Sounds sensible enough to me.'

'Ah, but like me, you didn't know that sheep have only one ambition in life and that's to die before you can eat them. They don't possess a brain cell; they are the most stubborn and stupid animals that ever walked this earth. You fence them in and if anything frightens them – be it the weather, a wolf on the opposite hillside or even a murder of crows – they take fright and launch themselves over, under or through your precious new fencing in sheer panic. Breaking legs and even falling off cliffs to their death, eating crops of rich grass and dying of bloat, falling into streams and drowning with heavy fleeces. When it snows, instead of coming downhill for shelter, they head back uphill into the snow and die starving, buried in snow drifts when there is shelter and hay available in the valley.'

Ivar roared with laughter. 'Seems like being a farmer has as many drawbacks as being a king!'

Ubba threw his hands up. 'It's not like I went into breeding sheep of my own volition. I employed a Yorkshire shepherd and his son to care for them. I sent them off to Richmond market to buy me a flock of 100 suitable hill sheep and 3-4 rams. They managed to lose 10 of the sheep before they got them back to my farm – and they had two sheepdogs, as well! When it was time to put the rams in with the sheep in the autumn, the best specimen ram who had the best looks and conformation not to mention the biggest balls, whom I had seen getting frisky with the other rams in the stable turned out to be homosexual. When turned out with the ladies, he promptly turned tail, smashed his way out under my precious gate and disappeared up the hillside.'

Ivar rolled about in his chair, screaming with laughter. 'What happened to the homosexual ram?'

'I am sorry to say that the bastard ram possessed one or two brain cells and spent the autumn near the farm, taunting me. I carried a bow and arrow with me for six weeks and tracked him all over. However, not once did I get a clear shot within range; he evaded death. Then, when the first snows were approaching, I went into the rams' pen one morning and there he was. I drew my seax and then a little voice came out of the darkness. 'Daddy, if you kill Freddie, I will never speak to you ever again.' It appears Freya had been feeding him for weeks. What could I do? I swear to God he grins every time I go near him. He knows he won, and no amount of talking it through with Freya about how you can't keep farm animals as pets will change her mind.'

Ivar laughed. 'God forbid when he does die, she will think you have done it. But even I couldn't deny Freya; one look at those sad blue eyes would have done for me, too. In other matters, how productive was the lambing season?'

'Dismal, to say the least. The shepherd had told me that hill sheep are "hefted" to the land they were born on. They should come down to the valley when the weather turned, to shelter, and then go back up the hill in the spring with their new lambs. When we attempted to bring the sheep down in November, I counted them and discovered that there were only 62 pregnant sheep. At my last count there had been 73 ewes. When I questioned where they were, the shepherd's answer was, 'Happen they have gone home.' Then the realisation hit me; the hill sheep bought at Richmond had marched back to where they were born to have their lambs.'

Ivar roared with laughter. 'If only Ragnar was here to listen to your tales of sheep farming, Ubba! He would have some great tales to tell the warriors in Valhalla.'

'Oh, it gets worse! At lambing time the death rate goes off the scale. Even though we had kept them safely indoors and well fed, the number of lambs lost during or within a week of birth was horrendous. We lost six ewes and ended up with only 75 live lambs.

Then there was a further loss of three pregnant ewes at the hands of my dear wife.'

'What on earth was Torri doing slaughtering sheep?'

'Ah, well Torri had become fascinated by the rose and vegetable garden cultivated by the previous owners, and she took on the challenge of maintaining it and developed a passion for gardening. She said it took her back to her childhood days in Denmark, when she was responsible for planting and cultivating the vegetable patch for her family. She also found that Theo soon became fascinated by her passion, as all boys like digging in the mud and they spent many hours together over summer and autumn. However, when we brought the sheep down from the hills to winter, three of them managed to break through the fencing into the garden, enticed by the vegetables. When we drove them into the farm, these three escaped the flock and embarked on their suicide mission.'

Ivar's eyes lit up and he clapped his hands. 'Oh, I do wish I had been there!'

'The first I heard of it was when Egil came running out of the house, screaming that Torri had gone mad as sheep had got into her garden, and she had come running in for her sword. Egil demanded I intervene. Now you know I never lack courage in battle usually, but you have witnessed Torri's prowess as a shieldmaiden when she is in "beserker" mode… and those wretched sheep were effectively mine.'

'I see your point, brother. I think I may have hesitated too!'

'I made my way slowly and carefully round to the

garden, keeping Sleipnir on a tight rein in case I needed to head back up the hill fast. To my consternation, Theo was transfixed and watching Torri's performance in silence. She had killed two of them already with slashes to their throats and they were bleeding out. When I appeared around the corner she despatched the third one, giving me a look that indicated I was next! Freya appeared, snatched up Theo and ran back into the house with him.'

'And then what did you do? Go and calm her down?'

'Don't be stupid! I was going nowhere near her. I valued my life too much! I cantered back to ensure the rest of the flock was safely penned up before she killed any more of them and kept out of the way until dinner time.'

'And what repercussions were there afterwards?'

'Well, she is like you when she's mad, so I knew I would probably suffer, but was hopeful I could appease her in the bedroom. However, she slammed the door in my face and I valiantly withdrew. I went to Serena and had my ears blasted by her sharp tongue as to the damage it could do to Theo to witness such an atrocity at the tender age of five. However, when I asked him about it his only concern was why had his nana slaughtered the sheep in the garden, when I normally slaughter them in the barn? I fabricated a reason to go to Jorvik for supplies to get me out of the way for a few days. The ice maiden thawed and allowed me back into her bed when I returned. Now, I need some sleep after my long journey to get here, so please excuse me.'

THREE

The following morning, Sigtryggr invited Ubba and Arne to join him to see the sights in Dublin. Ubba was grateful, as it delayed him speaking with Ivar and gave him more time to plan what he was going to say about what had happened in England. He knew the outcome would infuriate Ivar. He had never revealed the story of Aethelflaed and Erik to anyone, as his father had insisted on his secrecy after their mission to rescue her.

On the streets of Dublin, he witnessed the respect shown to King Sigtryggr. Several people bowed and curtseyed as they rode past. He also noticed the tension between his two sons and wondered how this rift had occurred. He suspected Arne still felt aggrieved that Viggo had gone to Ireland with Ivar and considered it a slight. He decided he would speak to Torri as it was a mother's job to heal family rifts, especially when Arne took offence so easily.

They went into the harbour. Sigtryggr pointed out the merchant ships and their country of origin. He was very impressed at the variety of the cargo they bore, and appreciated hearing about the bartering that would transpire because of trading. The largest ship in the dock was a Rus ship unloading her cargo of furs, timber and slaves. In a large metal cage, over 20 slaves were awaiting transportation to the slave trader Axel.

Sigtryggr saw the look of sympathy on Ubba's face as he observed the cage. 'You do not approve of capturing slaves from other countries?'

Ubba sighed. 'No, I don't think they should be torn from their homeland and sold like meat to the highest bidder in a strange land and culture. They are human beings and will have suffered enough seeing their families destroyed in battle, and it is mainly women that are exploited in this way. As a father I would be devastated at the prospect it could happen to my own family. Wait until you are a father; you may understand my concern.'

'An unusual concept for a Ragnarsson, my lord, and not a sentiment one would expect.'

'Ah, but my wife briefly became a slave through no fault of her own, resulting from her husband's greed and stupidity. I am a champion of women and appreciate their courage and resilience living in a world ruled by men.'

'Have you met Irina yet? She is now Ivar's companion and is believed to have been a Rus princess captured on her way to marry a prince in Kyiv. Her years as a slave were hard and cruel, leaving her barren and unable to trust men at all. However, she has found a protector and admirer in Ivar; although she struggles with intimacy, he has been extremely patient with her. Perhaps there is a softer side innate in Ragnarsson men after all?'

'I had heard rumours, and if he has found a friend

and confidante to make him happy then I am delighted for him.'

'We shall call in to see Axel and he will fill you in on their relationship. She would never marry him as Axel granted her freedom, and she vows never to be controlled by a man again. I have been surprised and pleased with Ivar's patient courting of her and would like to see their friendship develop for both their sakes.'

Ubba smiled. 'I have yet to find a woman complaining of Ivar as a lover. He usually favours virgins and is a proficient master in teaching them sexual skills. He never forces them, but waits until they are ready. I can understand him seeing Irina as an enjoyable challenge. It has always been a heavy burden for Ivar to bear that he is sterile, too. Hence his morbid curiosity in my sexual exploits.'

'He told me he wanted you to breed an army of little Ubbas. How many offspring have you sired?'

'In my youth I was as proficient as Bjorn at attracting women. I have three legitimate children to Torri and three illegitimate ones to Serena. I have been asked by several husbands or fathers to breed with their wives and daughters and have obliged, but only very occasionally. However, since Torri and I have been together, she has kept me on a tight rein and only approved of Serena breeding more offspring.'

'Well, that's where Viggo gets his sexual appetite from then.'

'Oh dear, what has he been up to?'

'Your son has an enquiring mind and considers a sexual education as important as an academic one. He is just curious; he enjoys flirting and is experimenting with women. Older women find him attractive and want to nurture his skills. He is not looking for a wife, just amusement and knowledge. He is looking forward to going with Sulamain to Arabia and sampling all the different women along the way.'

'Christ, I could not have two more opposite sons as these. Arne won't even discuss sex with me and could still be a virgin at 18. Trust Viggo to throw himself in at the deep end. He has always had a fear of missing out.'

They left the quayside and headed back into Dublin. Sigtryggr led them at a brisk trot to Axel's house. Ubba was again impressed at the two-storey wooden house built overlooking the harbour. Axel appeared at the top of the staircase and surveyed the group. 'Ubba Ragnarsson, you are the image of your father when I last saw him. Welcome to Dublin.'

Ubba noted his imposing size, but his smile was genuine and Ubba responded, 'Well, you look to have spent many years at sea, plying your trade. What made you settle here in Ireland? It can't have been the warm temperatures and ambient weather. My brother informs me it rains daily.'

Axel smiled. 'Ivar finds the cold and damp seeps into his bones in the winter, but Ireland is beautiful, like Denmark and Yorkshire. You will as a farmer appreciate the fertility of this land and the prevalence of horse breeding.'

Ubba turned to Arne and introduced him to Axel.

'Well, your sons are different in both looks and

personality; are you sure they had the same mother?'

Slightly stunned at Axel's question he retorted, 'Absolutely, Viggo looks more like Halfdan and has Ivar's quest for knowledge. However, Arne may look like a Ragnarsson, but he has his mother's and Ivar's quick temper.'

They were ushered into the salon, where servants were bringing in food and drink. Axel ushered Ubba towards a comfy cushioned bench away from the main seating areas, where they could not be overheard.

'So, tell me, is Irina a Rus princess and now Ivar's lover?'

'More a companion and friend. Irina has been traumatised by her kidnap experiences and refuses to engage in sexual activity with any man. However, despite his reputation as a tyrant, your brother displays exceptional patience when it comes to healing damaged souls. If anyone can ever help her overcome her fears, it may well be Ivar.'

'Good. I would like Ivar to have a woman in his life he can trust, and their shared inability to reproduce may be a true healing factor in the relationship.'

'She has no fear of him or his reputation. She gives him her opinion, whether he likes it or not. They enjoy teasing and taunting each other and Ivar does not bear grudges when she disagrees with him. I have witnessed countless heated arguments between them, but he never takes offence as he knows she speaks from the heart. He confided to me that he values your opinion highly and you too have never regarded him as a lesser man because of his disabilities.'

'No, I cannot believe that he can overcome and endure the pain he constantly lives with and achieve what he has done in his life. There is much good as well as some evil in Ivar; deep down he does have a heart.'

'Ah, but what of your opinion of Sigtryggr, our new King of Dublin?'

'A very different character from Ivar, but instinctively he finds a way of doing the right thing, whether it be taking up arms or merely walking away. He is a very deep thinker and does not enforce his decisions, but cleverly communicates with his troops, and they trust and follow him. He does not throw tantrums and inflict cruelty on his aggressors, but respects them as men of valour. Compassion and empathy are very important skills. Combined with his ability to assess the political advantage of being seen to be forgiving to his enemies, it will reap rewards in the future.'

Axel patted him on the shoulder. 'Looks like you don't miss much, like your father. He never said a great deal, but he accomplished a hell of a lot.'

o0o

They returned to the palace and Ubba instinctively knew when he was in the same room as Ivar that he was under his scrutiny.

He approached Torri and drew her to one side. 'What's up with Ivar? He is behaving like he does out hunting. Sizing up his prey ready to kill. We may have been apart for two years, but I know when Ivar is plotting, and it seems I am the centre of his attention.

By the look on your face, you know what he is stressing about, so out with it my dear!'

Torri sighed and hesitated. 'He has been asking questions about your deal with Edward, and is exasperated that nobody will give him a straight answer so as Ivar always does, he fears the worst.'

'Who has he been tackling, besides you?'

'He tried Arne, who claimed he knew nothing of your deal with Edward, but Ivar is no fool and knew he was lying. I tried to wriggle out of it by saying I was not there when you first met. I also pointed out that you were in a difficult situation as you did not know that Edward was in favour of you and Halfdan remaining in the North. You are going to have to confront him soon, as you know how he can make a mountain out of a molehill. He tackled Egil too, who said he should ask you, not him. He has also picked up that something transpired between you and Aethelflaed many years ago, and is seething with anger that you never confided in him.'

Ubba rubbed his hand through his hair. 'Well, I had better tell him the truth. He won't like it, and will be fuming that I have agreed not to fight for Jorvik.'

'Do you want me to be with you?'

'No, sweetheart, this is my problem and I do not intend to drag you into it.'

After dinner Ubba approached Ivar and said, 'May I have a word with you in private?'

Ivar glared at him and said, 'It is going to take more than one word to explain your deal with Edward, not to mention whatever you got up to with Aethelflaed and deliberately avoided telling me about.'

Ubba sighed. 'I had good reasons for both, Ivar, and you would have done exactly the same as me under the circumstances.'

FOUR

Ivar opened a bottle of wine and brought over two tankards to the table in front of their sofa, filled to the brim. 'Now, I want to know exactly what transpired. Let's start with your deal with Edward. It could be a long night!'

Ubba sighed and took a deep breath. 'Have you heard about how Halfdan and I escaped from Jorvik?'

'Yes, if you mean your plan to have Ralf impersonate you while you and Halfdan escaped to longboats hidden upriver. Quite an ingenious plan. I commend your astuteness, but what if Edward was guarding all exits? Then you would have perished.'

'Oh, come on, Ivar; you know I would have checked that out before risking our lives. My main concern was what he would do with Ralf, but he insisted on going ahead regardless.

'We were seen by one of Edward's patrols and forced to fight out in the open, but they were double our number. We lost Frank in the battle, and two more. Frank was protecting my left flank, but was attacked from behind and thrown from his horse by a spear. We made it to the longboats and got away up the Swale. We joined the rest of the family at Terrington and then moved North. Halfdan took one boat and sailed up the Tees. I stayed near Richmond on the Swale, where I had already bought the farm and 30 acres of land.

'Edward first contacted Torri via Ralf. Nobody was more surprised than I at his sudden change of heart. He wanted us to stay in the North to keep the Scots and Danes out. He offered us land to keep the North in Saxon hands, as he could not protect it from Winchester. He intended to make Aethelflaed Queen of Jorvik as well as Lady of Mercia. He hadn't even discussed this with his counsellors.'

'So, if you had your own land, did you swear an oath not to attack Jorvik again? Please tell me you did not Ubba, after all our family has done to establish a base over there.'

'I agreed not to attack Jorvik or Lincoln and to advise Aethelflaed if an attack from any source was aimed at Jorvik. Plus, I offered to remove her to safety and return her to Mercia or Wessex, in the event of an attack.'

Ivar's temper was rising rapidly. 'Ubba, I have in the past looked away when you embraced the Christian religion because you did not turn your back on your Norse religion. I hoped in time you would see the light and turn away from Christ. You know Freya was a gift from the gods, sent here like Thorin on a mission. But this is a step too far, turning your back on your family and your roots.'

'But Ivar, I saw the light. I had never expected to survive either Lincoln or Jorvik's battles, but I realised that suddenly I had a chance to live in peace, harmony and freedom and watch my family grow up. You know

I never craved power or authority; I just wanted to farm like our father. I watched him give up everything to keep his throne when he would rather have walked away and gone back to being the farmer he used to be.'

'Ubba, what hold does Aethelflaed have over you that you would put her above your duty to your family?'

'You know I have the utmost respect for women like her and Torri. They are by no means the weaker sex; they are the real heroes. Both have sacrificed their lives for duty. Torri has reared a Ragnarsson dynasty and Aethelflaed has kept her father's wish to unite England.'

Ivar interrupted angrily, 'What was the mission that you and our father undertook for King Alfred? And why were you sworn to secrecy?'

'Calm down and I will tell you, but no interruptions – just listen.'

'As you wish, but I want you to know that I am very disappointed in you.'

'Ivar, you know that my word is my bond; that is part of my moral code. I had no idea on that night what challenges faced us, as only my father knew what we were intending to do. Aethelflaed had been kidnapped by Dane brothers Siegfried and Erik and demanded a ransom from Alfred. He asked Ragnar to negotiate on his behalf. They demanded a huge ransom that would bankrupt Wessex. It took three weeks to raise the ransom in silver, gold and jewels, but Ragnar received a message from Erik asking him to come and he would hand over Aethelflaed in advance so the ransom would not need to be paid. When we got there under cover of darkness, Siegfried had discovered that Erik and Aethelflaed were lovers and intended to flee the country and leave him without money or princess, aided and abetted by Ragnar. You can imagine his mood on hearing that; he fought Erik and killed him, right in front of Aethelflaed.

'There were only six of us and we were faced with the risk of trying to extract her from a camp of over 1000 Danes. We had one hidden longboat and had swum into the camp. Father screamed at me to get her away. I just grabbed her, headed to the stables and managed to steal two horses while the Danes were fighting fires, stole two wolfskin cloaks and made an escape in the dark without being detected. We headed for the hills and cover, and then I had to stop as she was very emotional. I just hugged her and tried my best to comfort her while working out what I was going to do next. I had no food or water, no idea where I was, in total darkness and surrounded by a Danish army whose trophy I had kidnapped, with no idea whether my father was alive or dead!'

Ivar smiled. 'I sympathise with your dilemma. So, what did you do?'

'Well, exhausted as we both were, we had to keep moving away from the camp and use the darkness to our advantage. I knew that Alfred's army was camped about five miles away, and close to the river we had sailed in on, so I kept moving parallel to the river using any cover available. I also knew Siegfried would attack, so I had to get her back to them as quickly as possible and prepare them for battle.'

Ivar interrupted, 'No qualms that you were a Dane and should have been supporting them?'

'Oh, come on Ivar; you know what would have happened to her if I had done that. Death would have been her only release from torture, just like it was for Irina. You know the physical and mental trauma that Irina suffered. I would never condemn a woman to that.'

'So did you make it back to Alfred before the Danes did?'

'Yes, although she did try to kill herself by galloping off a cliff. Thankfully, I intervened and persuaded her that death would solve nothing... then she revealed she was carrying Erik's child. So now you know why this had to be kept secret. Luckily, Aethelred was in the wrong for having her so close to the Dane camp that she could be kidnapped. Alfred threatened him with death if he ever revealed he was not the father of their daughter Aelfwynn. Yet again, a woman sacrifices her life for the sake of a kingdom.'

'And had you fallen in love with her?'

'No, you know I have only ever loved Torri. I only fell for Serena when we parted for two years; we were both lonely and she was grieving her brother's death. I respect and admire Aethelflaed for her devotion to duty, but was saddened by her sad and lonely life. There never was or will be a sexual relationship between us. I will protect her, as I was asked to do by Edward, because he was courageous to make her Queen of Jorvik. I will join no army intent on removing her as

Queen, so you had better inform Sigtryggr that if he is planning a coup, I will not join him, but will remove her to safety before he lands with his army.'

Ivar sighed. 'Oh, Ubba, you do disappoint me; your loyalty should be to Danes, not Saxons. You have been swayed by your wretched Christian beliefs!'

'No Ivar, my word is my bond. I will stand by it unto death. Twenty years ago, a Dane marrying a Saxon princess would not have been tolerated, but why not now? If it brings peace and prosperity to both sides, then why not? We came here seeking to invade their land and take it from them. They are peace-loving Christians who welcomed settlers from other lands until we came and took not just their land, but their lives, possessions and families too.'

Ivar embraced him. 'Oh Ubba, I am not arguing with you. I know how hard you found it dealing with your conscience after battles. You are not a natural killer; your heart is pure, and you love and respect people. I won't criticise you for honouring your promise to protect Aethelflaed.'

The door opened. Torri came in, took one look at the brothers and said, 'Ivar, do not berate Ubba. He has a right to his opinions and his life is his own now; he is a free man.'

Ivar raised one eyebrow and said, 'You can't surely be content with him becoming more Christian than Norse?'

She nodded her head. 'We both accept that we were lucky to survive. We want to raise our family and see them move on. Surely even you Ivar did not expect to live this long? Surely you have mellowed over the years?'

'Torri, just remember, my father rejected me at birth and left me to die. If it hadn't been for my mother I would have perished.'

Torri replied angrily, 'And was it worth all the pain and suffering you endured to become the tyrant you have? A lot of innocent people died by your hand whilst you were trying to prove that your disability would not prevent you becoming a great King.'

'Peace, Torri. I am not angry with Ubba. I have missed you both considerably since I left Jorvik. Your views my dear were always appreciated by me. You were never afraid to speak your mind or give your valued opinion. I have learnt to appreciate the courage and resilience of women who survive in a hostile environment and protect their offspring. My father saw something very special in you Torri, when he chose you to be the matriarch of the Ragnarsson dynasty. If I had been in his shoes I would have killed you. We owe you a great deal for ensuring the survival of our bloodline. Ubba's endless patience and worship of you from when he was a boy, even when you married his half-brother Bjorn, has ensured there are descendants of Ragnar who will establish their own dynasties all over the world.'

Ubba smiled. 'I knew that eventually she would see the light and marry me. Trouble is, she will never discuss her relationships with her previous husbands – not to mention her fling with our illustrious father.'

'That's because she is a very wise woman. No man

really wants to know about his wife's previous sexual partners, just in case they are found wanting. Women of her calibre are looking for mates to produce strong, healthy sons. Bjorn could certainly do that for her, but she couldn't cope with him pursuing every woman he laid eyes on. Her sons Erik and Refil by Bjorn will leave their mark on history. But then she recognised the exceptional qualities you have; your three children will leave their mark too.'

Torri laughed. 'You are a cheeky bastard, Ivar. I did not weigh up marrying Ubba for his stallion qualities. Remember he was only 12 years old when I first met him. I knew he had a severe crush on me, but I never contemplated marrying him. Even though Lagertha warned me that Bjorn would be unfaithful, he had a zest for life and was a born leader and explorer. Life was never dull living with Bjorn; it was his insatiable desire for women that soured our relationship. No queen wants a king to take other women. It was an insult and not acceptable to me. Ubba was very attractive to women and had no problem bedding any woman he cast his deep blue eyes on as a teenager experimenting with sex, but he was only ever truly interested in me.'

Ubba blushed. 'Was it so obvious? I tried hard not to let it show, as I didn't want to upset Bjorn.'

She replied, 'A woman knows when a man is attracted to her Ubba, but I didn't take it seriously until you were there for me when I went into labour with Refil while Bjorn was chasing another conquest ten miles away; you knew that, but never revealed it. Your kindness, compassion and devotion in my hour of need proved to me just how good a man you are. You may be ten years younger than me, but even back then you had all the qualities of a perfect husband and father. I wasn't going to let another woman have you, and I have never regretted a single moment of being married to you.'

Egil entered. 'I came looking for you to advise Skye has gone into labour and she requests your presence, Torri. Perhaps you should go too Ubba, since you have a successful record of attending difficult deliveries.'

'Ubba shook his head. 'Surely Sulamain, Torri and Gytha have enough expertise to birth the baby?'

Ivar looked worried. 'I have been concerned about Skye throughout the pregnancy; those slender hips are not going to help deliver a baby the size that she is carrying easily. Go, Torri; she will need your reassuring presence and if she has to have a caesarean then she may not be able to have another child. Sigtryggr needs sons and he loves her; if she cannot breed then his crown and his marriage will be in jeopardy.'

Torri left the room at speed. Ubba shouted, 'Torri, if you need me I will come!'

He turned to Ivar and saw a solitary tear running down his cheek. 'Ivar, what do you know? What have you seen in your dreams?'

'I have not had a vision Ubba, but Sulamain and I have talked about the birth. He knows she is only carrying one child, but he needs to be in the right position in the womb for birth. The risk of a breech birth is that if the head is stuck in the pelvis a caesarean is the only outcome. Sulamain knows how to get her in the right position for him to be headfirst. The big danger is if he lies transverse across the womb and there is no room to turn him.'

'How do you know it is a boy?'

'Sulamain told me. I don't know how he knows. If she has a caesarean then she could rupture the scar tissue with the effort of delivering her next child. He has drugs to control the pain, but it can be a fine balance. If he gives her too much, she won't be able to push and he needs her to be able to do that. You will go if you are needed, won't you?

'You can inspire her to fight. You did it with Gytha birthing Thorin, and you can do it with Skye. Sigtryggr will not be as calm as you. He is highly sensitive and will panic if she is in pain and struggling. He fears losing her in childbirth and he does not like to witness a bloodbath. He still has not reconciled killing Kalen Murphy. Like you, he has a conscience when it comes to killing, unlike me.'

FIVE

Ubba had been asleep for three hours when he woke to an urgent knocking on the door. A servant brought a message from Torri, asking him to come to the birthing chamber. He threw some cold water over his face, dressed as quickly as possible and followed the servant with a heavy heart. When he arrived, he found Skye propped up on pillows on the bed. Sigtryggr was sitting on a chair, away from the action, with his head in his hands. Sulamain and Torri approached Ubba, while Gytha held Skye's hand and mopped her sweating brow.

Sulamain looked very serious and explained, 'The baby is coming headfirst but struggling to get his shoulders through her pelvis. We have had to give her some pain relief.'

Ubba replied, 'I have watched mares who were laid down struggling. Get her on her feet, supported by two of us, and gravity may do its work.'

Torri said, 'But she's hardly conscious, Ubba.'

'She doesn't need to be, but when the baby shifts she needs to kneel over the bed and push. Bring her round with smelling salts and get her up quickly.'

Torri and Gytha pulled Skye upright and sat her on the side of the bed while Sulamain found the smelling salts.

Ubba approached her and she said in a slurring voice, 'Ubba, my hero! God, it must be bad if you are here! Have you come to perform the caesarean with your sword?'

Ubba laughed. 'No! There will be no caesarean, Skye; you will birth this child on your own. Now, you need to get up and walk around. Let gravity ease the shoulders through the pelvis.'

'I can't even feel my legs or feet, never mind walk!'

Sulamain wafted the smelling salts under her nose and she coughed and spluttered. When she had come round fully, Ubba pulled her upright and Sulamain supported her on one side and he on the other. It took a while for the feeling in her legs to return, but they kept her moving regardless. After a few laps of the bedroom, she screamed that she wanted to push so they laid her over the side of the bed, on top of several sheets. Ubba had noticed the sheer desperation on Sigtryggr's face and could feel the fear emanating from his body.

Sulamain immediately checked for progress and shouted, 'Well done, Skye; that's his left shoulder through! Now I will turn him to get the right one through.'

They all breathed a sigh of relief that progress had been made, except Skye, who was moaning in agony while the baby's head descended. It was soon obvious that further intervention would be needed to get the head out. Sulamain turned her over and pushed her back onto the bed.

48

Ubba took the decision that Sigtryggr would be better removed from the scene. He strode over, grabbed his hand and pulled him out of the chair. 'Come with me now. It will be over soon, but you don't need to witness this.' They headed into the bathroom. Ubba shut and leant against the door.

'Is she going to die, Ubba?'

'No, of course not. Sulamain is just making a cut to get the head out, but his stitches are finer than any woman's and she will be fit and ready to breed again in no time.'

The look of horror on Sigtryggr's face was shocking. 'No, I can never put her through that again! She may die yet, from a haemorrhage after the birth.'

Ubba hugged him tightly. 'Now you listen to me, young man. Never underestimate the courage and resilience of the female of our species. They seem to be able to forget the horrors of a difficult birth and go right on and produce several more offspring. If they didn't, we would not be able to reproduce.'

He led him to a large sofa and pushed him down. 'You are in shock. Remember, not many men ever see their children born; this is normally female territory. I have only been at the birth of Serena's babies and that was because she insisted I stayed – and boy, did she make a meal of it. She cursed me to hell and back and gave a graphic description of what she would do to me if I ever attempted to bed her again. This was in front of Torri, who found it very amusing. It was Serena's reaction to pain at the time… She was demanding me back in her bed within a few weeks. I was with Torri when she had Refil, and Bjorn had gone off chasing another woman in the next village. She produced him without any fuss or bother, but he was her third baby. It was a turning point for both of us. I must have done something right, as she then took me seriously and divorced Bjorn within months. She did not appreciate sharing him with every woman he met, but Bjorn would never stay faithful to one woman; it was the chase he enjoyed.'

Suddenly, they heard a baby crying. The tension visibly drained from Sigtryggr's body and he relaxed. Torri came through with the baby wrapped in several towels, followed by a servant carrying jugs of hot and cold water.

She took one look at Sigtryggr, noticed he was shaking and gave the baby to Ubba. 'Now, you give him a bath while we patch up Skye. I will have the wet nurse sent in to give him his first feed.'

Ubba looked at the baby, covered in blood, and realised he was going to have to do the bathing as Sigtryggr appeared to have gone white with shock again. The servant filled the baby bath and tested the temperature of the water, then made a hasty exit.

Ubba rolled up his sleeves, unwrapped the baby, held him with one hand and arm, and dunked him in the water. As he washed him, he was relieved to see the blood coming off and a very solemn baby looking him directly in the eyes. Sigtryggr came closer and his face contorted in anguish.

'What's the matter now?'

Sigtryggr stuttered, 'Just look at him! He has a

deformed skull, is as skinny as a starving rabbit, and has a twisted foot.'

'No, he hasn't; he is perfectly normal! The skull of a baby does not close until they are around a year old. He's been through a very narrow gap and that's why it looks pointed. It will fill out within the next few days. If he had more flesh on him, Sulamain would not have got him out. He is all legs, just like you… and his foot has obviously been trapped under Skye's rib. It will right itself very quickly.'

'So, he is not going to be lame? How on earth do you know all this? And you handle him so confidently!'

As Ubba washed the baby's head, a mop of spiky red hair was revealed and he started to kick with his legs. Before he soaked him, he whipped him out of the water, expertly wrapped him in a clean white towel, turned to Sigtryggr and said, 'King Sigtryggr, congratulations on the birth of your first-born son. May there be many more to follow.' He carefully laid the baby in his arms, ensuring the head was supported by his elbow.

'Now, hold him close and talk to him. They are a bit short sighted at birth, but that will change quickly too. He will know your voice already from being in Skye's womb. He will have heard you and can recognise both his parents' voices. Don't worry, they are not as fragile as men think, provided you don't drop them on their head before the skull closes. You will be surprised at how good their lungs are, even from birth; they soon let you know when they are hungry.'

The door opened and a young woman in her

twenties with long red hair came in and bowed to Sigtryggr. 'My lord, I am Frida, the wet nurse your wife appointed to care for your son.' The baby let out a muffled cry. 'Shall I feed him now for you, my lord?' She scooped the baby out of his arms and moved over to a chair on the other side of the room. She undid her dress, exposing her ample breasts. Ubba caught sight of Sigtryggr's startled face and had to refrain from laughing out loud.

He went over to him and whispered quietly, 'Have no fear; he will be as fat as butter in two weeks' time in her care.'

'Does that relieve Skye from feeding him?'

'Absolutely not! It is vital she feeds the baby to bond with him. Her milk will come through soon, but she is going to need time to recover from the birth. It will have taken a lot out of her and Frida will give her chance to regain her strength before she takes over maternal duties.'

'Oh, Ubba, you don't know how grateful I am for your wise advice. Becoming a father is so overwhelming.'

'This is only the beginning; it gets harder as they grow older. Wait for the joy of a daughter. They turn you into devoted slaves from the moment they are born. You are about to experience a whole new world. Nothing can compare to the pride of seeing your beloved wife nursing your child. No crown, gold, silver, land or anything you have coveted before can ever mean as much as that.'

The baby let out a loud belch as Frida was rubbing

his back to wind him before changing sides. They both laughed at the speed of the baby to resume suckling. He was about to scream his displeasure at being interrupted, but as she put him to her other breast he suckled with vigour.

Ubba said, 'You see? He has an instinct to survive and considering the balls on him, he should prove to be extremely fertile too. Have you a name for him yet?'

'Yes, Aralt. It is an old Norse family name, which Skye says Saxons have replaced with Harold.'

Frida came over, having finished feeding and dressing him. 'He is a fine boy, my lord; he will soon fill out and become strong. Shall I give him back to you?'

Sigtryggr looked nervously at Aralt, who was wriggling and full of enthusiasm now his hunger had been sated. 'Yes, I will take him back to Skye now and hope she is recovering.' Frida handed him the baby carefully and left the room.

Ubba came over to them, sympathising with the new father's fear and dilemma. 'Look, hold him with his head on your left arm and cuddle him to your chest. He will be able to hear your heartbeat. Talk to him and he will soon settle down. If he starts crying, put him over your shoulder and walk round the room with him, but watch out because babies often bring back milk all over you.'

'Ubba, I am so useless at this. I would rather fight in a battle.'

Ubba laughed, 'No you wouldn't, because now you are parent you have a son to protect and nurture.

Give it time, Sigtryggr. I know you are not the most demonstrative person, but you will get there in the end. Skye will be a great mother; just copy her. I only learnt about babies with Serena. I was too busy fighting other people's battles when Arne and Viggo were young. That's why I am enjoying my retirement with my second family.'

'Are Serena's children very different from Torri's?'

'Yes. They are less active, more easily placated and don't have the strong will and lust for danger that Ragnarsson children have. I assume it is my father's genes that drive them all into being curious and wanting to excel at everything. I was lucky and got to explore overseas with him and Bjorn while my siblings were back in the eagle's nest, fighting each other for supremacy. When Ivar came along and needed so much care from my mother, Halfdan and Sigurd felt ignored and jealousy caused rifts right across the family.'

Sigtryggr was delighted to find that Aralt was quiet and looked tired. 'Let's get him back in the nursery before he gets lively again.'

As they arrived, Skye was sitting up in bed looking pale and tired, but when she saw Sigtryggr and the baby she became excited. 'Quick, bring him to me. I have not had chance to meet him yet.'

Ubba took Torri to one side, away from the bed. 'How is she?'

'Thankfully, she didn't haemorrhage and the afterbirth came away intact. Sulamain has done a great job of sewing her up and thankfully with all the drugs, she didn't feel too much pain. She will breed again, but needs time to recover.'

'Ah well, the wet nurse will have him thriving in no time. Sigtryggr has taken the birthing process hard and is nervous with the new baby, but it may bring out the best in him. It's amazing how the responsibility of fatherhood alters your entire perspective on life.'

SIX

After the trauma of the previous night, Ubba decided to visit the stables as he knew he would not sleep now dawn had broken. He was intrigued by the native Irish horses that although not tall, were very stocky and capable of carrying weight. They made perfect dual-purpose riding and farm horses. He was determined to buy a couple of mares to cross with Sleipnir, who had the Spanish elegance, to add height and speed to their offspring.

To his surprise, there was plenty of activity on the newly built yard. The stables were bright, airy and each horse could look out onto fields beyond over a split stable door, as well as chatting to their neighbours through the railings in the barn. Horses were herd animals and this was a perfect way of housing them. He marvelled at how much this must have cost to build, but he knew it was a worthy investment. Sigtryggr was determined to make a statement in Dublin and being on a trade route, he had ample opportunity to source materials.

Lost in thought, Ubba had failed to notice a young man coming up behind him and he was startled.

'My lord Ubba, I presume. I am Darragh, the King's stable manager. He gave instructions that you were to have access to any horse on the yard. Your expertise as a horseman and breeder has been widely reported by him.'

Ubba admired the Irish lilt in his voice and said, 'Well, Darragh. I was wondering what it is about Ireland that produces such good horses?'

Well, that would be the temperate climate, ample grass, limestone soil and plentiful rain. One aspect your brother is not too keen on.'

Ubba laughed, 'Yes, he may have mentioned it several times already but Sigtryggr has built him a weatherproof palace and he appreciates the extra warmth.

'How is my son Viggo doing with his riding? I trust he has improved?'

'It depends on whether you are referring to him riding horses or women, my lord?'

Ubba was shocked at his answer, but refrained from reacting. 'Viggo is just 17 now, probably experiencing a rush of hormones and wanting to flirt with girls.'

'Lord Ubba, Viggo's sexual exploits go a great deal further than just trying to kiss the milkmaids. Women seem to have a fascination with him and he has been well tutored in the sexual arts by several women, married, unmarried and harlots.'

Ubba sighed, frantically trying to remain composed and devise a suitable response. 'Viggo has an insatiable desire to learn many subjects. Perhaps he may have overindulged in this particular one. Now, I would like to see the stallions you are using on these mares. I am also looking for a pair of three-year-old fillies

57

to buy as broodmares for my own Spanish stallions.' Inwardly, he was seething with rage that Viggo's sexual exploits were the talk of the court. He was humping every female in Dublin, seemingly at the expense of improving his other skills. Wait till he got his hands on him!'

After the stable tour Ubba decided to pursue a hearty breakfast. He headed to the palace kitchens. As he swept in, all the cooks and kitchen maids stopped what they were doing and stared at him in silence.

A cook came rushing over. 'Lord Ubba, what are you doing in here? Breakfast for guests is in the dining room.'

'Well, I have been having a tour of the stables and thought breakfast might be over now. Besides, I smell of horses and would not wish to offend the King. I thought it would be easier to come here and persuade someone to cook me a hearty breakfast that I can eat in here.'

'If you are sure lord, then I will prepare whatever you wish.'

Ubba gave her a smile and said, 'I am starving, having been up half the night attending to Skye and keeping a very nervous and shocked king company. It was touch and go, but he has a firstborn son and I am sure plenty more will follow.'

'So we have heard. Wonderful news! You have skills in childbirth, my lord?'

'Yes, my experience as a farmer has meant I have been called several times to assist in difficult childbirth cases. I attended Skye's mother Gytha when she had

Thorin many years ago.'

'I will soon whip you up a hearty breakfast, lord. I am Sarah. Just sit down and I will bring you a feast.'

True to her word, she was soon back with a plateful of eggs, bacon and ham, and several pieces of bread dripping with butter. As she put the plates on the table, he touched her hand. 'Stay with me, Sarah. I would like to ask you some questions.'

She blushed and said, 'If you wish, my lord, but I can't imagine that you would want a mere cook's opinion on anything.'

'You would be surprised, Sarah; the kitchen is the hub of the household and anyone working in it will know what is going on.

'But I must remain loyal to my king. I cannot reveal any of his secrets.'

'Oh, have no fear; it is not Sigtryggr I wish to discuss, but my son Viggo.'

She hesitated. 'Master Viggo is a bright boy and wants to experience life to the full, not unlike you at his age, probably.'

'Tell me the truth, Sarah. Is he humping every woman he sees, as has been suggested by others?'

'He is a precocious flirtatious teenager with an eye for beautiful women. If they respond and want to take him under their wing then he is a lucky boy! He has had the occasional knockback, and has been caught in compromising situations by angry husbands, but he has such charm he can talk his way out of trouble. He will calm down as he matures; he is no fool. He never forces himself on a woman. He takes rejection with grace and acceptance.'

'Ah, but he is going east with Sulamain and I know from experience that no Arab sheik will tolerate men taking liberties with their harem. He could end up dead if he pushes his luck.'

'You underestimate him, my lord. Despite his charm and charisma, he has ambition to achieve great things in life, just as his lineage would suggest. He is not stupid enough to compromise that for a tumble in the hay. Have no fear; he will create his own dynasty, wherever it may be.'

'Does Ivar know what he has been doing?'

She threw her hands up in the air. 'Ivar knows everything. Surely you know that! Rumour has it that he spent a lot of time keeping track of your love life in Jorvik.'

Ubba groaned. 'And often got it wrong! I am not the philanderer Ivar depicts. Now, tell me about Ivar and Irina. Has he finally found a woman to share his life with? He seems content.'

'I really cannot say for sure. They share a bed, but Irina has been badly damaged mentally and physically all her life. If something triggers a memory, then she cannot ignore it, and panics. Several times I have found her in the kitchen very early in the morning, having fled Ivar's bed. She maintains he has the patience of a saint in trying to overcome her fears, but her wounds are so deep and Ivar has no idea what triggers these attacks. I believe Ivar has a heart and Irina does not fear him; she gives as good as she gets.'

'I have seen a big change in his condition over the

last two years. I would hope he has found someone to love and comfort him at last.'

'Oh, indeed he has, my lord. He loves Skye as a daughter and supports her marriage to Sigtryggr. He also loves Viggo and sees in him the boy he would have liked to have become. I also know he loves and respects you for having the courage to do your duty.'

'Not anymore I suspect, as I have refused to support Sigtryggr's campaign to invade Jorvik. He did not take that well.'

'Have no fear lord, you have been Ivar's hero since a child; he will not forsake you now.'

'Thank you Sarah, for being so honest. You have saved Viggo a beating, but I intend to remonstrate with him about his sex life. I am a champion of women and I would never encourage my sons to defile a woman. I know from experience they have courage and resilience and will fight to keep their families alive.'

Suddenly, Frida came into the kitchen and Ubba's eyes and attention were immediately diverted.

As Sarah stood up she leant over and whispered to Ubba, 'You cannot blame your son for being attracted to women. You have just proven that you have been doing it all your life.'

Ubba laughed. 'But a wise man learns to look, but not necessarily touch, for fear of the consequences. Believe me, my wife has a temper far worse than Ivar's when roused, and she can handle a sword and seax equally well. I am enjoying my retirement and want it to last a long time!'

He couldn't resist one more look at Frida as he

went out of the kitchen. To his chagrin, she caught him looking and gave him a smile, inviting him to approach.

Christ, he had better get out of here before he got himself into more trouble. As he ascended the stairs, Torri was descending and there was nobody else around. 'Ubba, where have you been? Even Ivar didn't know your whereabouts.'

'I decided to inspect the stables and horses, and then realised I was too late for breakfast, so I went to the kitchen and charmed my way to a full breakfast. I am now replete, but missing my sleep, and intend to have a nap.' He took her hand, kissed it, bowed to her and continued. 'And I would be delighted if you would join me, as I wish to speak with you about Viggo.'

'Are you saying that just to get me into your bed, or are you serious?'

'Well, as you know I would have to do honour and justice to that beautiful body of yours first, and then perhaps we could discuss Viggo afterwards. It's been a while since we had time to enjoy each other, and you must be exhausted too, after being up all night with Skye.'

She threw her hands up in exasperation. 'You are up to something Ubba, and you will need your Christian God to protect you if you are. I suspect you are feeling guilty and desire sex, and of course you don't have Serena on hand here. Very well, husband. I shall accede to your request, but don't even think of falling asleep until I have finished ravaging your body.'

He smiled, knowing he had won. 'When have I ever left a woman unfulfilled in bed, my love?' He grabbed her hand, pulled her up the stairs and marched her into their bedroom. He pushed her back against the door, locked it and kissed her at the same time. He reached behind her to undo her dress and discovered that it was laced across her back, all the way from her neck to her bottom.

'What the hell is this, woman? A dress that needs a maid to get you in and out of it. What's wrong with buttons? It will take me ten minutes to undo that.'

'It's a new dress, designed in Frankia. I bought it for our visit to Normandie so that I fitted in with the court.'

'Well, that says it all and shows just how stupid the Frankians are, choosing fashion over sex. Why isn't it laced at the front? It would make more sense than at the back. I want you naked now, not next week, woman!' He pulled his seax from his swordbelt and its blade reflected in the sunlight.

She fled into the bedroom. 'No, you can't do that! It cost a fortune and it's pure silk. I won't let you take me in the dress either; just be patient and unlace it for me. Besides, there are precious jewels on the bodice and neckline.'

Ubba advanced, his seax still raised, thoroughly enjoying her discomfort. 'So, you expect me to do that to appease your vanity and spendthrift ways? Turn around then, and I will undo the dress.'

She backed away. 'Not until you have removed your swordbelt and replaced your seax.'

He chuckled. 'Madame, I hardly think you are in any position to make such demands of your husband. It would appear you do not trust me. If you keep me waiting any longer, I may forego the sex and go straight to sleep very disgruntled.'

He saw the flicker of anger in her eyes and he knew the battle was won. The ice queen would have to melt if she wanted him. She walked over and turned around. He deliberately hesitated before he started to unlace the dress, slowly and carefully. Finally, she was free and he flung the dress over the back of a chair. She now started undoing his swordbelt and he pulled her chemise over her head.

He looked at her and felt exactly the passion he had when he married her at 18. He ripped the rest of his clothes off, picked her up and carried her into bed.

An hour later, she was begging him to retreat. 'Give me a break, Ubba. I am not as fit as I used to be; my back and knees can't keep up with this onslaught much longer. Even my head is spinning, and I would not be able to stand up unaided.'

He laughed and pulled her close to him, so they were lying sideways but back-to-back. 'This is unusual, my love; you have never called time on our lovemaking before.' He nibbled her neck and wrapped his right arm around her.

'I would dispute the word "lovemaking"; it felt more like I was being pursued by a rampant colt covering his first mare. You have been too long in the stables, husband; this old mare needs a gentler approach... although I appreciate the passion and ardour displayed.'

He laughed. 'Which brings me to the subject of Viggo. I am led to believe he is trying to hump every woman in Dublin. He will end up dead if he intends to go exploring in Arabia with that attitude.'

Torri sat up and turned to face him. 'I cannot believe you just said that. Viggo is pursuing this in a similar vein to when he is interested in any subject he studies. He wants to know the facts and understand the subject, which is precisely what you were doing at a similar age, Ubba. Why would you condemn your own son for doing the same?'

'Because he will end up dead, long before he reaches Arabia. Other races do not treat sex as a pleasure like we do. In some countries, women are kept entirely separate from men, clothed and veiled from head to toe. Arab Sheiks lock their wives in a harem and only castrated eunuchs are allowed anywhere near them.'

'But surely, Sulamain will have acquainted Viggo with this knowledge. Maybe he is just testing the water in case he faces a long period of drought. I think you should leave it to me to speak with him. You will only end up arguing, and are hardly able to berate him on the subject. Remember Ubba, I was ten years older than you and when married to Bjorn I was surrounded by your female conquests during the winter months spent in Jormund. They certainly had tales to tell of your prowess, and their jealousy caused many female fights in the camp.'

'Viggo is hardly going to discuss his sex life with his mother, is he?'

'You may be surprised. Viggo and I have always had a close relationship and he may be more open to discussing it with me than with you. Do not go tearing into him until I have tested the waters. Now, let's get a couple of hours' sleep.'

Ubba decided to do as Torri suggested, but resolved to try and get information from Ivar in the meantime.

SEVEN

That evening after dinner, Ubba saw his chance to speak to Ivar when Torri moved to sit with Gytha after the meal. Sigtryggr was dining with Skye as she was confined to her bed still.

Ivar started the conversation with, 'Where have you been most of today, brother?'

He grinned and tapped his nose. 'Mind your own business Ivar, I don't work for you anymore. I am a free man now.'

'And probably bored to death, too. You are no different from me when it comes to seeking out information. It was either that or sex you were after.'

'You see, you are still obsessed about my sex life, Ivar. I am more concerned that my 17-year-old son has been humping women without you restraining him. You cannot seriously approve of his precociousness, particularly when he is heading East into countries where women are a man's possession and treated as such? He will get himself killed if he pursues his tactics there.'

'Ubba, he is no fool. Learning about sex is no different to him than learning how to play an instrument, wield a sword or speak a foreign language. He is used to being tutored and if he uses older women to teach him the art, then what is wrong with that? You certainly took the same approach at that age, and you survived. I would have intervened if he had been pursuing young girls or using force of any kind to dominate a woman. He has met with some opposition and rejection, and taken it like a man. He has not fallen in love with the first female he humped; he is just doing it for pleasure and to gain experience.'

'Yes, but he needs to know the difference between sex and love – and more importantly, when to back off for his own safety.'

'He reads people well and is aware of his own limits; he is unlikely to court danger. These Irish men have the temper to go with their red hair. He is careful which women he flirts with. Leave the boy alone; he will put his knowledge to good use and achieve whatever ambitions he has in life. This young eagle needs to fly the nest Ubba and he is ready to go.'

Ubba sighed. 'Torri offered to speak to him, but what son would discuss sex with his mother?'

Ivar chuckled. 'Viggo, for one! He worships his mother and he dearly loves and respects you, and would hate to think he had ever let you down. Leave it alone, Ubba. He will make you proud of him whatever path he takes. He knows the difference between sex and love; he has grown up with you and Torri. What better example of true love could he have had?

'Now, where were you this morning? I shall get to the bottom of this. I hear you were in the stables, assessing my stock and enquiring about young fillies to take home. You may have your pick of any of them.

I have become quite a fan of these sturdy Irish horses who can turn their talents to any job. They are sure-footed, even on bad terrain, and have the instinct to detect bogs and inclement weather approaching. I suspect they may have webbed feet to cope with the constant rain.'

Ubba laughed. 'Is it really that bad, both in summer and winter?'

'Not now I have this warm palace to protect me over the winter. It was pretty grim and very draughty before, I can assure you.'

'Ivar, are you sure you can hold Dublin if Sigtryggr sails to take Jorvik? You don't seem as fit as you used to be; what if the chieftains turn against you to claim the throne?'

'I have considered that, but I will introduce you to Donal Murphy, who raised Sigtryggr after he lost both parents. He will put your mind at rest.'

'Wasn't his son responsible for kidnapping Skye?'

'Yes, but he knew nothing of it. His son bullied Sigtryggr in his youth and wanted to deprive him of his future wife out of spite. It ended in a one-to-one challenge. Kalen did not defend himself and poor Sigtryggr was mortified.'

'Strange how the kidnapping news never reached Jorvik, when other news reached us via Viggo's pigeons. I charged you with protecting Viggo, Ivar; what the hell happened?'

'He equipped himself well and posed as Skye's brother, so there was no sign that he was your son. He is proving as adept as you are at disappearing. Anyway, where were you this afternoon?'

'In bed with my beautiful wife, doing what I do best!'

'Ah, so you are missing your mistress, then. There are plenty of women here who would welcome you into their bed. Perhaps you should ask Viggo for an introduction?'

Ubba tried to look angry but could not contain his laughter. 'Maybe I will, to check on his progress! That would stop the little runt in his tracks, wouldn't it? However, Torri would not be in favour of it, and she has ways of making men suffer that even you haven't dreamt up. Both Bjorn and I fell victim to her torture more than once; she is not a woman to cheat on lightly. You know my pain threshold is too low to risk that.'

'I would not approve of you cheating on Torri either, but I can understand your natural sexual desire when you see a tempting woman before you.'

Ubba patted him on his shoulder. 'Brother, I have been so grateful to have had the last two years with my family. I thoroughly expected to die defending Jorvik. Life is precious and every moment spent with my family is a bonus. I have already outlived our father by 10 years.'

'Well, brother, you have certainly done some reflecting on life. At least you will not have as many regrets about your actions as I will. You have always had a pure heart and soul Ubba, and have never craved power or authority, unlike the tyrant I became. You have a natural affinity to inspire others to do great things and they love you for it. You will be remembered as the greatest and most inspirational warrior and commander, beloved by his men.'

'I will settle for that epitaph, Ivar.'

Ivar chuckled. 'Better than "Most prolific Ragnarsson, renowned for siring more offspring than any other Dane due to his charm, charisma and startling blue eyes?"'

'I don't think my family would be too pleased with that one!'

'Before you return home, I have a task for you that I can only entrust to you to carry out for me after my death. Will you do it for me?'

'Of course I will Ivar, as long as it is achievable. Surely Sigtryggr would do the same?'

'I think he may well be away in Jorvik and I would not trust anyone else here to carry out my wishes. I will write it down in Latin for you so you can ask some of your Christian friends if your knowledge of Latin is not up to scratch.'

'On one condition. I will not wage war on your behalf, Ivar. I have had enough blood on my hands already. I wish to die in peace.'

'I would not ask you to do that, Ubba. I have been responsible for enough bloodshed. It is something very personal, and you must promise to keep it a secret even from your own family.'

'You have my word brother, but what if I pre-decease you?'

Ivar placed his hand on his shoulder. 'Trust me, I know you won't.'

'If it is relevant to your funeral, you need to confide

in someone here or you may not achieve your goal. I suggest Skye, in case Sigtryggr is absent overseas. As Queen, she will at least have the authority to insist your last wishes are carried out.'

'Yes, I will think about it as I don't want my resting place to be in Ireland.'

Ubba headed off to seek out Skye, in the hope that Sulamain might be in attendance; he wanted him to examine Torri before they left. It concerned him that Ivar suspected he was on borrowed time. He had always had visions of the future, so he believed him.

He was admitted to Skye's room by a harassed Gytha, due to a screaming baby and a tearful mother.

'Oh, thank God – someone who can help.'

'What is the problem?'

'Skye and breastfeeding.'

'I am a man and know nothing about this subject.'

'I know, but at least you could instil some confidence in Skye to continue, as she is just panicking and being too hard on herself. You talk to her whilst I try and calm the baby down, and persuade her to try again.'

He went over to the bed. Gytha put Aralt over her shoulder and walked him around. Thankfully, the screaming soon ceased.

Skye looked fraught and miserable. Ubba knelt down and hugged her to him reassuringly. 'Now, sweetheart, what is the matter?'

'Oh, I am struggling to feed Aralt because he gets exasperated as I don't have enough milk yet, then he screams his head off and won't feed from me. I am useless at being a mother. I think I should just let Frida feed him permanently.'

He stroked her damp hair. 'Now you listen to me, young lady. Firstly, I have no expertise in this subject at all, but I think you are just having a crisis of confidence that all new mothers go through. Your milk is only just coming through, but it is vital you continue feeding him, as you are passing on immunity against disease and you need to bond with him. Of course he is going to notice the difference in quality and quantity of milk between you and Frida, but you have to persist and the problem will disappear if you give it time and patience.'

Gytha said, 'He has no difficulty latching on to her; he just gets angry when he realises the taste is different.'

Ubba replied, 'You are his mother, Skye. He's been in your womb for nine months. He knows your voice; you just have to coax him and distract him. Talk to him, or even sing to him, and encourage him to continue feeding. He is picking up on your frustration, and that is making him object all the more, because you are worried.'

She replied hesitantly, 'So you are saying exactly what Ivar says to me when I have a crisis of confidence. To grow some balls, stop doubting myself, trust my instincts and get on with the job.'

Ubba kissed her on the nose. 'Bit harsh pet, as you have been through a traumatic birth and you're very vulnerable right now… but essentially, yes.'

'Right then. Mother, give me my baby!' She sat up determinedly and summoned her last bit of strength and courage. She untied her nightgown, put the baby

73

to her right breast and he immediately began suckling. She stroked his head and whispered platitudes to him, and he continued.

'What do I say to him, Ubba?'

'It doesn't matter what you say; it's the tone of your voice that matters. You must not convey anger or fear because he will pick up on it. That's why I suggested singing to him, but if you want to curse him to hell and back then do it in a sweet, quiet voice. I have spent many hours trying to catch sheep, cursing them up hill and down dale, oblivious to the fact that they could detect my anger. Now I wax lyrical and tell them exactly what I am going to do when I get hold them, but in a pleasant voice and with a big smile on my face.'

Both Gytha and Skye laughed loudly. Skye said, 'Father said the only animals you have ever struggled to bond with was sheep.'

'That's because they spend their entire lives trying to kill themselves before I get the pleasure of killing and eating them!'

Gytha said, 'Will you be taking some Irish sheep home with you, then?'

'Not bloody likely; they would surely find a reason to panic and overturn the longboat. Even if they made it home, I would lose them before winter because if they are hefted to Ireland they would pack their bags and march across the Pennines, head to Runkhorn, then launch themselves into the sea and drown.'

They all howled with laughter at the image he portrayed. Nobody had heard the door open and

Sigtryggr enter.

'Well, I am pleased to see my wife laughing again compared to how miserable she was earlier this morning. What has brought about this transformation?'

Skye said, 'Ubba's compassion and wicked sense of humour. He truly knows how to rally his troops. No wonder they loved him so.'

EIGHT

It was a rainy May morning and Freya was bored. She went to see if she could find Ivar, as she wanted to speak to him privately. She discovered him in his office alone and he welcomed her in with a smile.

'What brings you to seek me out, my little princess?'

'I was hoping you knew more about my future. Although I have had visions about Ireland, I cannot seem to glean information about my own future. I want to know what my destiny is, Ivar. Why won't the gods answer my questions?'

Sweetheart, I don't know. The visions we see do not generally relate to our own destiny. I only know that the gods have a special assignment for you, and Thorin is here as your protector and guide.'

'But my father says I may choose my own partner in life. I want to marry for love, not power and authority. I want a marriage like my parents': full of love, happiness and children.'

'Freya, that is what we all want for you. Why do you think the gods will not ensure that is what you receive? You have to remember that your lineage alone makes you a strong candidate to become the wife of any European or Scandinavian king wishing to found a strong dynasty.'

'But I don't want to be married off to some old man just to become his broodmare. I want to be an equal in marriage to my husband and have control over my life.'

'Believe me Freya, you already have that power. You will never allow yourself to become subservient to any man. But you are still only 16 years old and your parents would be devastated if you left home just yet. Patience is a virtue Freya; you must wait and keep yourself chaste until your time comes.'

She turned on him angrily. 'But why is it so important? It is not imperative in our society that a bride has to be a virgin.'

'But it is in Western society and that is why you must remain pure. Have you fallen for someone already, Freya?'

She scowled at him and shouted, 'How is that possible? I don't meet any new people now I am no longer at court. King Edward suggested that I might be a suitable match for one of his sons, but not anymore. He is hardly going to want the daughter of a farmer for his son.'

He snapped back, 'Don't ever say that to your father; he would be mortified and it is untrue. Any king would want Ubba's offspring as a potential mate. He has all the best qualities of a Ragnarsson and your mother is a saint.'

'But tell me why Viggo is encouraged to go rutting like a stag from the age of 12, and yet you are telling me to stay chaste and wait for the gods to find me my mate? It is hardly fair. Why are women treated so badly? Is there nobody here in Ireland I could marry?'

Ivar was horrified. 'There is nobody good enough for you here, pet.'

'Father is taking us to Normandie next; do you think I may find a husband there?'

'If you married one of Rollo's sons you would be second cousins and eligible to marry, although the Catholic Church denies marriage of first cousins, and you would certainly have to become Catholic yourself to marry a future king.'

'I would never change my Norse religion.'

'Then you will have to return to Scandinavia, as the further east you go, you would encounter different religious practices who would demand you convert. You would also be subjected to prove your virginity.'

'How do they do that?'

'Physically examine you to check your hymen is intact.'

'But mother said some girls break their hymen doing physical activities such as riding and fighting. That could have already happened in my case.'

Ivar walked over and hugged her, 'Freya, calm down and be patient. Remember, your parents and the gods will ensure you marry the right man and you will learn to love him as your marriage progresses.'

She threw her hands in the air. 'I know, but it offends me that I should be seen as just a broodmare, rather than being accepted as a queen in my own right.'

'You will have to ensure you rule in the bedchamber; that is where a clever woman influences her king's decisions. Your mother has been doing it for years.

You will learn to find a way to do it, but it must be accomplished with the utmost subtlety. Your husband may plant his seed within your womb, but you have the opportunity to plant your ideas in his head. The secret is, you must guide him to make the right decision, but he must think it was all his own making. I believe Greek, Roman and Egyptian queens were very skilled in the art. You do not want to be in the firing line if your suggestion backfires. You will also have to identify your enemies very quickly and keep a close watch on them. Your enemy could even be your mother-in-law, who perhaps wanted her son to marry someone else. Never assume that your enemies will always be men. Carefully select your friends at court, but do not trust them with your secrets. Beware of spies in your entourage reporting your every move. Several queens have lost their lives for plotting – and don't expect your husband to be able to save you if you are. You will have made him look a fool, however much he loves you.'

'But Ivar, I have not been taught any of these political tactics in which you schooled Erik, Refil, Arne and Viggo. How can I protect myself from these attacks?'

'Use your instincts and your perception of the people around you. Be aware of underlying tension and people's reactions to you. You have Ubba's communication skills and your mother's perception and natural instincts to survive. Make Thorin your bodyguard and keep him by your side permanently.'

There was a knock at the door and Sigtryggr came

in. 'Donal Murphy has arrived. Will you both join us for lunch?'

'Certainly. Now you go and reflect on what I have said, Freya; patience is a virtue and you must wait until destiny calls. I know you will have a long and happy life.'

After she left the room Sigtryggr commented, 'What's wrong with Freya?'

'She is anxious to move on with her life and is finding that being a woman is a little too restrictive.'

'I expect she is missing the excitement of being at court, but she is so beautiful she will have men falling at her feet.'

Ivar smiled. 'Perhaps, but she must wait for the man the gods have chosen.'

Ivar and Sigtryggr set off to the dining room and met Ubba and Torri in the corridor, already making their way there. Donal was in the dining room, chatting to Viggo and being introduced to Arne and Freya, with Thorin in attendance. When Donal saw Ubba and Torri approaching, he remembered the last time he had seen Ragnar; Ubba was the spitting image of him. Torri was, in his opinion, far more beautiful than folk legend had decreed, but Freya was stunning too.

Sigtryggr bore down on them and said, 'Ah, Viggo has introduced his siblings already, I assume. Now, may I introduce Ubba and his wife Torri Ragnarsson.'

Donal held out his hand to Ubba. 'I suspect you hear this often, but you are the image of your father, and so is your son Arne. Viggo has a resemblance to

Ivar and possesses his quick brain and curiosity.' He took Torri's hand and kissed it. 'And you madame, must be the famous shieldmaiden and mother of these exceptional children.'

Torri smiled. 'For my sins I have to admit I am, but keeping these eagles in line is not an easy task.'

Just as this moment, the door was flung open. Skye made a dramatic entrance and headed straight towards them. The servants immediately rushed to set a place for Skye at the table; she obviously hadn't been expected.

Sigtryggr was surprised as she was supposed to be convalescing after the birth and he hadn't even told her that Donal was coming.

'Skye, is this not too soon, my dear? You should be resting.'

Skye gave him an imperious look. 'Certainly not. When we have guests in residence I should be attending to their needs.'

Sigtryggr was just about to object when Ivar leaned over his shoulder and whispered, 'Women know best; back off!'

Donal approached Skye with arms outstretched and hugged her. 'Skye, may I congratulate both of you on the birth of your son. I did as requested and rang the bells of Tara throughout the day to pass on the happy news that our King and Queen have been blessed with a son. Have you a name for him yet?'

'His name will be Aralt after a member of Sigtryggr's family.'

'I have brought you a present and will give it you

later. I am so pleased everything went well at the birth. I would have been devastated if anything had happened as a result of Kalen kidnapping you while you were pregnant.'

They all moved to the table. Skye was sitting next to Sigtryggr, with Donal on her right and Ubba on her left. Donal was delighted to find Torri on his other side. He was fascinated by her because she was the matriarch of the Ragnarsson men and they all worshipped her. Ivar had admitted as much to him. He couldn't help but feel a stab of jealousy that Ubba spent his nights with her in his bed. No wonder he had given up the battlefield to spend more time with her. How he had ever been able to leave her demonstrated Ubba's dedication to duty; had he been in Ubba's shoes, he didn't think he would have been so eager to leave her. He looked down the table at Arne, whom Ivar had said was the image of Ubba and his grandfather in looks, but had Ivar's quick temper.

Viggo however, was a different character entirely. He admired his quick brain, ease of communication and desire to learn. They were qualities that few teenagers possessed, so Donal was not surprised when Ivar declared he would be a future king. He was also a very caring individual and interested in healing, which proved he cared about people more than possessions. He could forgive his love of beautiful clothes and a luxury lifestyle, provided he did not just crave it for himself. Recognising poverty and improving living standards for everyone was important to him and he had demonstrated that in many conversations they'd had.

His attention turned to Freya next, and he had to admit that as well as her outstanding beauty, there was something very special about her. He had been inclined to dismiss Ivar's explanation that she had been sent by the gods to secure the future of their race. However, watching her converse animatedly at the table, he could tell she was no ordinary 16-year-old girl. The serious young man next to her must be Thorin, whom Ivar had said the gods had sent to protect her. To say they were the same age seemed bizarre; Thorin with his impressive build looked as though he had been fighting in a shield war for years. Ivar had told him of the circumstances of his birth but he seemingly bore no resemblance to Gytha or Ralf.

Torri said, 'I see Donal you are admiring my daughter Freya.'

Startled, he replied, 'Forgive me, my lady. Ivar has told me about your daughter Freya, and I thought he was exaggerating until I set eyes on her. May I congratulate you on your beautiful children; you and your husband must be extremely proud of them.'

'We are, but they each have certain Ragnarsson tendencies that cause problems some of the time. Rearing a nest of eaglets has not been an easy task and now I find that another son is about to fly the nest. I was hoping for more time with Viggo, but both Ivar and Ubba think he is ready to go. Having lost my first son in battle already, and Bjorn's sons being with their father in Jormund, I wasn't quite prepared for his departure.'

'My lady, do not think you will never see them again. They will realise as they mature what a significant role model you were in their lives. Ivar assures me that Erik and Refil are explorers intent on heading west. I am sure they will visit you soon. Viggo will carve out a significant future wherever he settles; he is a very quick learner and will succeed.'

'Forgive me Donal, this must be very difficult for you having lost your own son recently under very difficult circumstances.'

'I have no regrets. Kalen was never a son I could be proud of; he was mean, jealous, spiteful and a bully. I should have intervened sooner when he made Sigtryggr's life difficult. You will know how hard it is to accept that your child is not perfect, and you always hope they will alter, but in his case the older he became, the worse he got. However, I have Sigtryggr, whose father would have been so proud of him now, and I adore Skye. She is the perfect wife for him; she knows his weaknesses and guides him through making difficult decisions with the same female intuition you have been applying to your Ragnarsson men all your life.'

Torri laughed. 'Oh dear, is it so obvious Donal? Believe me, persuading a Ragnarsson to change their mind is no easy task. You have to nudge them in the right direction and let them think they came up with the right idea all by themselves.'

Donal took her hand and kissed it. 'Don't ever stop, my lady. You have done an exceptional job.'

oOo

After the meal, Donal accompanied Sigtryggr and Skye to the nursery to meet Aralt. Donal fetched the present he had brought, which was wrapped in a blanket. When they arrived, Frida was feeding Aralt, so Donal gave them his present. To their delight, he had made a small wooden shield with Sigtryggr's snake and axe emblem inscribed on it. Sigtryggr was delighted, but Skye felt a sudden pang of fear at the prospect of her son becoming a warrior. She knew it was inevitable, but realised the burden of continuity would be on her firstborn son forever.

Sigtryggr sensed her mood and hugged her close, whispering, 'Do not be afraid, Skye; you know I will endeavour to rule in peace, not war. Aralt's future may be very different from mine.'

She fought back the tears, worried that her son might have to step into his father's shoes very early if he perished in battle.

Frida had finished feeding, so she took Aralt over to Skye. Skye took her time trying to control the emotions she felt. She thought of Ivar telling her to grow some balls and pull herself together. All very well, but she was not Torri Ragnarsson; she felt utterly overwhelmed and her hormones were all over the place.

She took a deep breath, put a smile on her face and carried Aralt over to Sigtryggr and Donal. As soon as he saw his father, he started wriggling and Sigtryggr could not resist. He took him from her and she was grateful for the reprieve.

Donal said, 'What a shock of red hair he has, and he's so big. How on earth did Skye manage to birth him?'

Sigtryggr replied, 'Not without some difficulty – and intervention by Sulamain and Ubba.'

Donal queried, 'What birthing skills does Ubba have?'

'He assisted Skye's mother Gytha at Thorin's birth and has plenty of experience in birthing foals and lambs.'

Donal remembered how big Thorin was now, and deduced that he must have been a big baby. 'May I hold him?'

'Of course! I consider you his grandfather anyway, as I have no parents alive now.' He carefully handed him to Donal. Aralt stared up at him solemnly with his big blue eyes, then reached for his beard and gave it a pull.

Sigtryggr said, 'Oh, I am sorry; he likes to play with my long plaits and he can be quite rough. Shall I take him back?'

Donal laughed. 'Certainly not! I need to get to know him better. I will sit down and we can have a chat.'

Ralf and Gytha came into the room. Sigtryggr called them over and introduced them to Donal, and they started chatting. Gytha was concerned about Skye as she looked pale and tired. She tapped her on the shoulder and indicated she was to follow.

They moved into the nursery and Gytha said, 'What is wrong, Skye? You look tired. I did recommend you stayed here rather than attending the lunch. It is still only ten days since the birth and you don't realise how much strength you lose coping with such a difficult birth.' To her astonishment, Skye started sobbing. She put her arms around her. 'Skye, whatever is the matter? You are frightening me now.' She ushered her over to the nursing chair and knelt beside her, holding her hand while she cried. All sorts of dire thoughts were going through her mind.

Finally, Skye calmed down and explained her dilemma of Donal giving them a shield for Aralt. It had made her realise that her precious baby would have to go into battle when he grew up – and that if Sigtryggr was killed trying to take Jorvik, then she would lose him and Aralt would become a baby king.

'Oh, Skye, welcome to the world of motherhood and the even more exclusive club of queens. Once you bear a child, you suddenly realise that you are responsible for rearing it and keeping it alive. A mother's love and protection for her child is no different than an animal's love for its offspring. The responsibility can come as a big shock, and you have the added bonus of rearing a future king. Now, I cannot help you reconcile this dilemma – I am an ordinary Saxon woman, but you have your father's genes. You also have one person who has conquered and learnt to live with that threat – Torri. You must speak to her about it… and don't burden Sigtryggr with this revelation. He knows only too well the dangers involved. The decision for you to remain here in Dublin under Ivar's wing has already been made. Plans will have been formulated in the event of Sigtryggr's death.'

'But if so, why have I not been consulted?'

'What husband would even contemplate discussing this with his heavily pregnant wife? Danes never admit defeat; neither must you. Do you want me to approach Ivar about this and ask Torri to speak to you in private? You must keep this from Sigtryggr.'

'But why? Mother, it affects us both!'

'Probably because it is considered bad luck to even contemplate death in case it becomes a reality. You have to accept their rules now, Skye; you are one of them. There is no way you can accompany Sigtryggr to Jorvik with Aralt. You will be perfectly safe here with Ivar.'

'But if Sigtryggr fails, and is captured and killed, the Irish will not wait for a boy king to grow up; they will look elsewhere.'

'They won't need to, with Ivar here.'

'But what if Ivar dies? What will happen to me and Aralt then?'

'Skye, stop panicking and get a grip of yourself. I have no knowledge of Irish politics or being a queen; you must speak to Torri. Knowing Ivar, all morbid eventualities will have been discussed and plans made. Your job is to recover from birth, rear your son and keep quiet.'

Skye wiped away her tears, looked in the mirror, tidied her hair and took a deep breath. 'Right then, Mother. I had better get on with my job, but please ask Torri to come and see me privately; hopefully she will have some wise advice to impart to this very novice queen.'

Gytha touched her arm. 'That's my girl! Now stop

worrying about things that may never happen. You cannot control the future, but you can live for today.'

They both returned to the room just as Aralt decided he wanted his next feed and started crying. Skye waved Frida away and picked him up, and as Sigtryggr and Donal were still chatting on the sofa, she took Aralt back into the nursery to feed him. It gave her an opportunity to reprimand herself and reflect on her mother's wise advice. She knew Torri would help her summon the courage to cope.

NINE

That evening as they returned to their room, Ubba decided it was time to tackle Torri about her health. They were now three weeks in to their visit to Ireland and he had no idea what treatment, if any, Torri would need. If only she had confided in him, he would not have had to be the one to raise it.

It was a still June evening after a hot day. For once, no wind was whipping in from the Irish sea. He opened their balcony door and leant over the rail, looking out to sea. The moon was full and bright and he began to pray to Odin silently in his mind. Perhaps the gods would grant him a reprieve, for surely nobody was more deserving than Torri.

Torri finished in the bathroom and saw he was on the balcony. She thought he was just taking a breath of fresh air. She lay on top of the bed expecting him to join her, but he didn't come. She moved quietly over to the balcony door and saw him leaning on the railings, with his eyes shut but his lips moving. She was in her silk nightgown, but had nothing on her feet; she crept quietly to one side of him and gently placed her hand over his and said, 'What is wrong, my love? You are miles away in thought.'

He was startled, but pulled her into his arms and

hugged her. 'Just reflecting on life my dear, and how happy I am to have you by my side. I never expected to survive Lincoln or Jorvik, but I have relished these last two years being close to you and my children.' He kissed her reverently and touched her chin to make her look up at him. 'You know I am here for you and you mean the world to me. If there was a problem you would tell me, wouldn't you?' Her face was lit by the moonlight and his heart missed a beat as she turned her head away and uttered, 'Of course I would, sweetheart. Now let's to bed!' She moved quickly back into the bedroom.

He steadied himself on the balcony rail and knew she was never going to tell him… but why? Was it possible she did not know she had a lump? Impossible – she had become adept at hiding the problem by initiating the position she wanted when they made love so she had less pressure on one side. Torri was the bravest woman he had ever known and had never lacked courage. Was she trying to convince herself there was no lump, or did she fear what treatment may be necessary? Or worse, was she afraid because she had seen other women die after developing a lump? Was she trying to protect him? Well, this could not wait any longer. Sulamain, having been the doctor for two sheiks' harems, would have much more experience of what was developing, and Ubba was not prepared to let her die before her time. He was not going to let her die on his watch, especially not with a man of Sulamain's experience at hand.

He would make love to her and confront her

afterwards. He was a gentle as possible and allowed her to select the position she wanted. She gave no indication of any pain when he entered her, yet she must have felt some.

After they had parted, he got up and lit the sconces and then went back to the bed. She was still lying naked on her back. He went to her side and surprised her by climbing over her and sitting on her waist.

She looked startled. 'Surely you can't want more sex? And why have you lit the sconces?'

'Because I want to see your eyes when you lie to me, and you are going nowhere until we have had this conversation.'

He saw the panic in her eyes. She tried to twist away from him and he held her hands. She noticed that tears were pouring down his cheek. 'Why are you crying, Ubba?'

'Because I cannot believe my wife would lie to me about the state of her health. I know very well you have a lump that needs investigating and there is possibly the only man who can diagnose and treat the problem, right here. Why would you not seek his advice? Furthermore, why try to pretend there is nothing wrong with you?'

'It's my body Ubba, not yours!'

'Tell me why you are so afraid; it is not like you not to fight when your life is threatened. Why do you think you can ignore something as crucial as this?'

She shouted, 'Ubba, we all have to die sometime. I have seen women develop lumps in their breasts, or in their wombs, which kill them eventually.'

He shouted back, 'And you would rather die in agony than seek treatment. You would leave me and your children when there may be something Sulamain can do. Freya needs your guidance as a mother and a queen, and you should be there for her. I am begging you to let Sulamain examine you and see what the diagnosis is of your own accord, but if you do not agree then I as your husband insist and will force you. I won't let you die if there is any chance of saving you. I love you Torri and you surely cannot refuse me. I won't make you undergo treatment unless there is a chance of recovery. You can see Sulamain on your own, or with me by your side, but don't shut me out Torri; you have carried this burden long enough and fear has driven you to reject help.'

He moved off her waist, gathered her in his arms and wept with her, lying beside her and cuddling her tightly. After about ten minutes, she stopped and whispered in a croaky voice, 'I will see Sulamain and together we will determine the outcome. I should not have kept it from you, but I knew you would be devastated and I wanted to protect you.'

'Torri, I am not your child. I am your devoted husband and have loved you since I was a boy. Did you honestly think I would not notice? I know every inch of your body. The position it is in may make it possible for Sulamain to remove it, so let's see him tomorrow and plan our next move when we have all the information.'

'You sound just like your father! I should not have kept it from you. Will you forgive me?'

'It's a good job I am not my father, as I am pretty sure he would have given you a severe beating for lying to him… and God forbid what Ivar would have done to you. You are the only woman in his life he has ever truly loved. He worships and adores you. Look what he did to me when I thought you had been unfaithful. It frightened me that you tried to hide it from me, but I can understand how terrified you have been. I don't know whether I would have behaved in the same way, but of course I will forgive you. You will not face this alone. I am right here with you.'

oOo

At breakfast the next morning, Ubba took Viggo to one side and asked him to go to Sulamain and ask him if he had time to speak, either at his home or the palace, as soon as possible.

Viggo looked anxious. 'Please tell me you are not trying to stop me going east with Sulamain.'

Ubba smiled. 'No, but your mother has taken some persuading that you are ready to go. I have also heard reports about your provocative sexual encounters, which concern me, and you will surely ensure you lose your head if you continue in that vein out in Arabia, but I will speak to you about that later. Now go, and come straight back and tell me whether Sulamain is coming here or wants us to go to him.'

Viggo left immediately, concerned about what his parents wanted to see Sulamain for; he assumed it must be about one of his many escapades. Although he knew that Ivar would be well aware of his many indiscretions, he had never taken him to task over them. He doubted whether his father would be as lenient.

Sulamain was at home and agreed to come over to the palace. He also assumed it must be about Viggo, who begged him to speak up for him. He returned to the palace and advised his father that Sulamain would be coming later. In an attempt to placate his father, he advised him that he would not be taking risks in Eastern countries and he was well acquainted with the different religions and customs so highly unlikely to offend anybody.

Sulamain arrived promptly. Ubba had already discovered that Sigtryggr and Ivar were in a meeting with counsellors, so hopefully would not be aware of Sulamain's presence. He swept into the salon clothed in bright yellow silk, beaming from ear to ear, and bowed low to kiss Torri's hand, which made her blush a deep red.

Sulamain said, 'I assume you want to speak to me about Viggo and our journey east. We plan to leave straight after you return home.'

Ubba intervened, 'It is not Viggo we want to discuss, but a health matter concerning Torri, which I hope you can help us with.'

Sulamain looked at Torri. 'My lady, how can I be of service to you?'

Noticing her hesitancy, Ubba spoke. 'My wife has a lump on the left-hand side of her vagina, about five inches from the entrance. I first noticed it in October but now it has grown bigger and I am very concerned.'

Sulamain approached Torri, who was looking more embarrassed by the second. 'Torri, come and sit over here by the window. I need to have your permission to discuss this matter with Ubba and obtain your approval before I can examine or treat you.' He led her to an armchair, then went to the sideboard and poured a large glass of red wine and brought it over. 'I understand this will be very difficult for you, but Ubba is right. The cause needs investigating immediately. I can fully understand your reluctance, but I assure you I have significant experience in dealing with these types of problems.'

Torri took a gulp of wine and said, 'I know I should have admitted it sooner, but I have seen women die from lumps in their breast and I just assumed I was going to die. I hadn't the heart to tell him. Of course you have my permission to examine me, but I want the truth, Sulamain. I will decide whether to pursue treatment when you have given me all the facts.'

'Of course, my lady; there is no way I would force unnecessary treatment on you. Let me speak to Ubba first out of earshot, to spare your blushes, and then I will ask you some questions and examine you.' He picked up a fan off the windowsill and handed it to her. 'Now, you just cool down and calm yourself. Fear of the unknown and dealing with an intimate problem can paralyse anybody in your situation. Let me deal with it now and take the stress away from you.'

Tears were pouring down her cheeks and she whispered a thank you. He produced a beautiful silk handkerchief and proffered it, and she smiled.

Ubba had already poured brandy and retired to a large sofa as Sulamain approached.

'I need you to tell me as much as you can about this lump and then we will have to go to your bedroom so I can examine her. You have done the right thing in raising the issue.'

Ubba took a deep breath and told him quietly everything he could. and answered many questions raised by Sulamain. He asked Ubba whether he thought Torri would prefer to have a woman with her when she was examined and whether Ubba would like to be there or not. Ubba suggested Gytha may be the right person if she would not have him, but he would like to be there to hold her hand and give her support.

They adjourned upstairs to their bedroom and met Egil on the landing. Ubba pulled him to one side and instructed him that nobody was to enter their room, especially not Ivar.

Immediately, once they were inside, Sulamain asked whether Torri would prefer a woman in attendance whilst he examined her, or Ubba. She immediately turned to Ubba as he came in and asked him to be there. He hugged her to him and fought back tears.

Sulamain had his medical bag with him. He selected some instruments and laid them out while Torri got undressed. He suggested she put on her nightdress, and he pulled two pillows to the bottom of the bed to raise her hips. He then produced a small bottle of liquid and approached Torri. 'I need you to be as relaxed as possible for this examination, so I want you to drink this liquid, which will make you feel lightheaded and hopefully combined with the red wine you have consumed, will make you feel pleasantly drunk and giddy.'

'Your job Ubba is to keep her as still as possible and anchored to this bed.'

Within a few minutes, Torri needed to lie down as her legs were giving way. Ubba placed her on the bed then knelt beside it, holding her shoulders down. Sulamain knelt down at the bottom of the bed with his tiny thin metal bright light in his hand. He began his examination and Torri was relatively relaxed. When she said Egil must be thinking they were having group sex, both Ubba and Sulamain laughed and Torri giggled. Sulamain finished his examination and went to wash his hands. He came back and gave Torri another potion to counteract the last one, as she still could not stand unaided. He suggested she get into bed until her head stopped spinning. Sulamain pulled up a chair and Ubba sat next to her with a bucket at his side in case she threw up.

Sulamain held Torri's hand. 'You are a brave woman, Torri. My first impression is that we are not dealing with a deadly growth. As Ubba intimated, it is not a solid lump; it is soft and springy to the touch. It is only attached to the vaginal wall by one blood vessel and is not causing complete obstruction. However, they feed on blood and can grow and turn dangerous if left. I want to remove it as soon as possible.'

Ubba sighed with relief, whilst Torri was struggling to take in his words due to her inebriation. 'How are you going to do that when you can't see what you are doing?'

Sulamain smiled. 'By touch and with a very tiny blade. I can see enough with my light if I get your body in the right position, but I will give you a drug to knock you out completely so you feel nothing. It should not take long. I will have to suture the blood vessel to stop the bleeding quickly. It should not take more than half an hour to do. I have performed this operation before on malignant growths and they are far more complicated; often, the cancer may have already spread to other organs.'

Torri mumbled, 'So I am not going to die, Sulamain?'

He replied, 'Not from this cause my lady, but you should have discussed it with Ubba sooner. Are there any other areas of your body where you have felt pain or swelling?'

'Only pain and stiffness in my knees, particularly in cold wet weather.'

'Well, that's quite normal at your age – and after leading such an active life you will notice it more. I can prescribe some herbs to take the edge off that, but I can't give you new knees, I'm afraid. It is nature's way of slowing you down; you have to adjust your activity levels to suit.'

'I just struggle planting and weeding in the garden if I have to kneel for long periods... and my back hurts, too.'

Ubba interrupted, 'Well you will have to sit back and instruct someone else to do the physical work. You have been doing it for years as a queen, so it should come naturally.'

She replied, 'There's something so satisfying about planting a bulb or a seed and then seeing it grow and flourish. I suppose it is the closeness to nature that makes it enjoyable.'

Ubba said, 'I feel the same about breeding horses and sheep; it is the excitement of producing an animal that may be better than the last generation. Will Torri have to rest in bed after the operation, Sulamain?'

'Only for a day or so, to ensure there is no bleeding. And avoid riding for a while. I don't believe in keeping patients immobile; it causes more problems than you started with if you slow down the body's natural rhythm. I found this out working with women in childbirth. Unless they have a serious problem with bleeding or a prolonged delivery, they are better up and about the next day. Remember, most women give birth in the field and then carry on working.'

Ubba said, 'Will you do the operation here, and will you need assistance?'

'Yes, tomorrow morning. I will bring Fyzil to administer the sleeping draught as he has plenty of experience and knows when a patient needs more. I can manage the rest, but if you would like to be around that's fine, too. However, I can fully understand if you would rather be spared. Perhaps Torri would prefer a woman? Maybe Gytha or Skye would act as a nurse? I will leave you to sort that out. I suggest we start at 9.00 am and Torri, you must not eat anything after 9.00 pm tonight. Only drink a glass of water in the morning. This prevents you being sick if you react to the drug; as it is only a minor operation, you should be able to eat again within a few hours afterwards.'

Ubba shook Sulamain's hand. 'Thank you, my friend. You cannot imagine how grateful I am that you are here. You know how much Torri means to me and I want her around for as long as possible. Freya will need her guidance in the future and I want her to see all her children grow up and prosper.'

The two of them went outside for a walk in the formal garden and found a shaded seat surrounded by roses. Neither had spoken, but both were deep in thought.

He took her hand and kissed it. 'Please understand I am not furious that you did not tell me, as under similar circumstances I may have done the same. What I am concerned about is your acceptance that this might have led to death, and your refusal to fight. That is not the attitude of the woman I have known for almost all my life, who has had the courage of a cornered lion in battle.'

She sighed. 'I know, but I think I deluded myself into thinking it was nothing and would go away if left undisturbed. I had thought of asking Sulamain about it when we came over here, but you beat me to it.'

'Are you sure you want to have it removed? I don't want to feel I am forcing you into this.'

'Sulamain has the expertise to remove it. I know there is an outside chance it may return, but he is throwing me a lifeline that many women would never be offered. I intend to take it and thank the gods, and him. It was a case of fear of the unknown, rather than lack of courage.'

He hugged her to him and touched her chin to force her to look up at him. 'Now, tell me if you want me with you during the treatment?'

She smiled. 'That has to be your decision, Ubba. I can imagine how stressful it will be for you, but I will be fast asleep and spared the sordid details. How about you are there at the start and hold my hand until I start to fall asleep, and then you can kiss me and go? As long as you are the last person I see then should anything untoward happen, I will die happy.'

He kissed her forehead and whispered, 'You will not die on my watch, sweetheart. I won't let you!'

TEN

They woke as the sun rose on a beautiful still dawn. Ubba had tossed and turned all night and eventually went outside onto the balcony and imagined what life would be like without his wife. Frankly, it terrified him. He had prayed to the Norse gods and the Christian God, begging them to spare her life. They hadn't told their children about the procedure. Ivar had sensed that something was afoot, but they had managed to avoid detection so far. Torri had slept peacefully, probably because the outcome was out of her hands and relied totally on the skill of Sulamain's hands. Gytha had agreed to assist and had been sworn to secrecy. Viggo was aware that there was a minor health problem with his mother, but had also been silenced.

Torri suggested Ubba went to breakfast prior to the operation, but he refused as the prospect of eating had his stomach doing somersaults. At 8.30 am he heard footsteps and opened the door to allow Sulamain and Fyzal to enter with their equipment. They prepared the bed and he ushered Torri onto the balcony. Egil came next and took up his position guarding the door. Gytha arrived next and he patted her on the shoulder.

He felt there was so much he needed to say to his

wife, but Torri saw his tears and put her arm around him. 'Don't say a word, Ubba. I know how much you love me; it has been demonstrated by you throughout our time together. You are a very special person with the biggest heart I have ever known. I know I failed to notice that your love and devotion was sincere when you were a teenager, and dismissed it as just admiration because of your young age, but when we finally married you proved beyond doubt to be the love of my life as a devoted husband, and father of three very special children. I admire you for never wanting power, wealth and authority as people have always been far more important than material things to you. Never be ashamed of being referred to as "the reluctant king"; you knew what sacrifices had to be made to be successful and chose not to take that path. That took great courage and fortitude, and your devotion to duty and family has never wavered. Now let me fight this battle for you!' She turned and walked into the room like the regal queen she had always been.

He stayed out on the balcony, trying to control his emotions until Sulamain came for him. 'I will do my very best to remove this lump, but I can give you no guarantees of success. Many factors may come into play, but whatever the outcome, its removal is still necessary.'

Egil heard heavy footsteps coming up the stairs and knew who they belonged to. He prepared himself for the ensuing confrontation.

Ivar arrived at the door and said, 'Egil, my old friend and faithful servant. I know you want to deny me access, but allow me one question first. Who is Sulamain treating, Ubba or Torri?'

Egil sighed. 'Torri, my lord.'

'Then I want you to go in there and ask Ubba to come and speak to me as soon as he can. I will wait in this spare room for his answer and will not make a scene.'

'Very well, my lord.' Egil knocked quietly and entered the room, just as Ubba was leaving Torri's bedside as she fell into a deep sleep.

Egil said, 'Your brother wishes to speak to you privately in the room next door at your convenience.'

Ubba hesitated and then said, 'I might as well face him now. If there are any changes Sulamain, send for me immediately.'

He left the room and Egil opened the door. He walked in and found his brother gazing out to sea. Ivar said in a shaky voice, 'Tell me what ails her Ubba, before my imagination runs riot!'

He sighed and suddenly felt weak at the knees, so sat in a chair and told Ivar the whole story. To his surprise, Ivar was very upset and wept at one point. However, he recovered just as Egil appeared bearing a tray of hot coffee, crusty bread and golden butter.

Ubba realised when the aroma hit him just how hungry he was; he helped himself and poured Ivar a coffee.

'You have done the right thing, Ubba. nobody has the experience Sulamain has in treating women's problems and I would back his judgement all the way. I can't quite understand why Torri chose to keep quiet, though. Surely she would know you would not miss a lump in that particular area of her body?'

'She was very adept at hiding it, I can assure you. I too was concerned and challenged her on that point, and it seems there were several factors: fear of the unknown, fear of telling me, mistaken belief that it may miraculously disappear if she ignored it, her fear due to seeing other women die from this type of problem. It wasn't actually lack of courage; she was just paralysed and had actually thought about consulting Sulamain when we came here.'

'You know that I love the bones of Torri. She has always stood up to my excessive temper and told me exactly what she thinks of me, and because of her I made a success of ruling Jorvik.'

Ubba smiled. 'Be honest, Ivar; it was only when you knew Torri and I would be horrified at your actions that you never discussed them in advance. Just remember what you did to the Archbishop of Jorvik in his own church, knowing full well what our opinion of that horrific action would be. The fact they eventually overlooked what you had done was solely due to our efforts to disassociate from your wicked crimes.'

'Trust you to remember that deed, Ubba.'

'There was no way I would ever forget walking into the church and witnessing the aftermath of your excessive cruelty. From what dark passage of your mind did you conjure up such horrendous torture? I witnessed nuns trying to slit their throats with discarded swords, fearing they were going to be raped and tortured. One young girl died in my arms as I

106

tried to save her. That act alone made me turn to the Christian church because I was so ashamed of your atrocities.'

'You know how much time I had to contemplate such deeds when I was left at home and you were overseas with our father. As my brother, you treated me differently than anybody else. You never saw me as a useless cripple; you made time to talk to me and tell me about your exciting adventures. You listened to me and knew how much pain I suffered with my legs and did not denounce me as a madman for my wickedness. You and Torri encouraged me to be a better person and I love you both for that. I love Torri and worship her as the matriarch of the Ragnarsson dynasty. She has achieved more than any of us and the prospect of losing her, or you for that matter, sorely grieves me.'

There was a knock on the door and Egil appeared. Ubba looked concerned.

'My lord, your wife is coming round and the operation was successful.'

Ubba jumped up expectantly. 'Come and see her later Ivar, when she has come round fully. I appreciate your concern and support.' He left the room in a hurry to get back to Torri.

He was pleased to see she was propped up in bed and smiled when he entered. He went over to the bed, took her hand and kissed it. 'You do not know how relieved I am to see you looking so well.' He sat down on the chair beside the bed, but kept hold of her hand. He felt he needed to touch her to convince himself that she was really alive and well.

Sulamain approached, smiling. Ubba jumped up and hugged him. 'What can I say to express my gratitude?'

Sulamain replied, 'Nothing at all. I was just happy to be able to assist you both in your hour of need. The operation went well and there was no excessive bleeding at the site. I am confident it wasn't a cancerous tumour, so there should not be any further repercussions. I want you to take it easy Torri, for the next few days, as you will feel tired and sore – but that does not mean bedrest. I would prefer you on your feet by tomorrow and doing some gentle walking around. No riding, preferably for at least a week. I will come tomorrow to check the dressings and ensure you are not suffering any aftereffects from the sleeping drug. Should you start bleeding heavily then summon me immediately.'

'Sulamain, thank you so much. I was paralysed by fear and not thinking straight.'

'Don't worry, it was perfectly understandable. At least Ubba recognised the seriousness and acted quickly.' He and Fyzal left the room.

Gytha approached and they thanked her profusely. She left to look after her grandson.

Finally, the room was empty.

'How do you feel now, sweetheart?'

'Fine, but I have a headache due to the drug. I would like to sit out on the balcony and see if the air clears my head.'

'Are you sure you are supposed to get up so quickly?'

'Yes, provided you are with me for support.'

'Of course I will be with you. You are going nowhere near the balcony without me, in case you feel dizzy and fall.'

She threw the covers back and he helped her to her feet. He asked her to wait while he fetched her wrap to put over her nightdress. Slowly, she leant on him for support and they made their way out to the balcony. He helped her into the chair and then went inside to bring a blanket to keep her warm, and a pillow for support. He moved the other chair next to her and asked if she needed anything else.

'No, that feels better already, and it is pleasant when the sun is facing this way. I shall sit here until it moves round and then I may have a nap. You go if you have something else to do.'

'What, rather than cosset my brave wife after what she has just been through? I am staying right by your side. I have no jobs to do or people to see; we are on holiday, remember.'

'Gytha said Ivar insisted on speaking to you. Was he upset you hadn't told him?'

'A little, but he did not rant and rave at me. He was more concerned about losing you. He really does love and respect you. He even admitted he loved me, which is most unusual. Perhaps he is reviewing his life and finally admitting he could have handled relationships better.'

'Amazing how a brush with death sharpens your perception on life. I have had time to reflect on mine and although there are some things I regret doing, I can't say I have made any disastrous errors.'

'Rubbish, you put yourself at risk fighting as a shieldmaiden even after you had two children to Bjorn.'

'Ubba, be very careful; if you are declaring that women should stay by the fireside and just rear their children purely because they are women then I shall be very angry with you.'

'Peace, my little firebrand; now is not the time for us to fight. You must rest.'

'Only because you know you will never win!'

'Precisely! I gave up many years ago trying to change your mind, just like I did with Ivar. You have got the colour back in your cheeks now my queen. For two pins I would ravish you, but under the circumstances I expect that is out of the question for a few days!'

She laughed. 'More like weeks! Now remember when you told me that I should enjoy myself with young Matteo when you sent him to sort my garden? Well, I am giving you permission to go and find some young Irish girl to satisfy your sexual appetite. I know you too well, Ubba; when you have no troops to command, spying to do, horses to breed or sheep to chase uphill and down dale – and certainly no Serena in your bed – then you revert to your other favourite pastime, which is chasing women. I have already seen you making eyes at Skye's wet nurse, so go with my blessing and enjoy yourself.'

Ubba's expression was priceless. 'You, my jealous wife, are actually telling me to take a lover. What in God's name has come over you, woman?'

'I am merely trying to salve your conscience because

you will do it anyway and then feel guilty about it afterwards. This way, you have my blessing and can enjoy your favourite sport while I get chance to recover from my operation.'

'You have pierced my heart with an arrow, Torri. How could you cast me aside into the arms of another woman so flippantly? Did you avail yourself of the Italian stallion after I suggested it?'

'No comment. You know I never discuss my sex life with other men, whether they be past husbands or lovers. What is wrong with you? Just get out there and do it. We will be leaving in two weeks. Most men would be delighted with the idea of casual sex with no repercussions and no angry wife.'

Later on, Torri went to bed and insisted Ubba leave her, so he made his way to the kitchen and cajoled Sarah into conjuring him something to eat. She had a very soft spot for this handsome, genial, friendly, charming brother of Ivar. She could hardly believe they were brothers as they had such opposing temperaments. She returned with a tray laden with dishes. Ubba motioned to her to join him.

Sarah laughed. 'I doubt your brother even knows where the kitchen is. He would never turn up out of the blue like you do.'

Ubba smiled. 'To be fair Sarah, it isn't because he is too regal to enter. He does have mobility issues and servants attending to his every need. Ivar knows how important a well-run kitchen is to a household. He may not appear himself, but he will have someone planted here reporting back to him frequently. When he was a boy, he used to spy on everything that was going on and soon learnt that knowledge is power; he used it suppress his enemies.'

'I know that my lord, and thankfully I know who his spy is in my kitchen. I am very careful to keep my true master's secrets as he is responsible for my position here. I have known Sigtryggr since he was a boy and have admired his development. I was glad when he brought Skye over here as she is a perfect match for him. She may not have been born a queen, but she behaves like one. She knows Sigtryggr lacks self-confidence at times, but she supports him and pushes him in the right direction. Rumour has it that Ivar made your wife his Queen Consort in Jorvik, which surprised me.'

'Much as it may be difficult to believe, Ivar adores and respects Torri. She is probably the only woman Ivar has ever loved and taken counsel from.'

'But she is your wife, not his?'

'Don't ever think that Ivar covets her for himself. Neither of them would ever have contemplated a sexual relationship. She is more like the sister he never had, whom has no fear of him and keeps him in line. She knows how to calm him down and persuade him not to react violently when threatened. She has shown him how to court favour with his subjects and not alienate them. I have tried to do so over time, but Torri has been far more successful than I was. She has an exceptional political mindset and knows just how to get a man to do exactly what she wants and persuade him that it was all his own idea. Ivar learnt that he can achieve his goals with positivity, negotiation and guile; his reputation as a tyrant was soon diminished.'

Sarah laughed. 'Isn't it always the way clever women achieve their goal? But to do it without using pillow talk with a man like Ivar is very unusual. He must have a deep respect for her.'

'Believe me, all the Ragnarsson men worship her, but I am the luckiest of all to have her as my wife.'

'Well, be sure you tell her that often.'

As he left the kitchen, he saw Ivar coming his way and they headed outside to sit in the rose garden and chat privately.

Ivar asked, 'How is she doing?'

'Sleeping, I hope.'

'Well, you don't appear very relieved when the outcome has been so positive.'

'It's just that she has fired an arrow at my heart and told me to go and find a woman to appease my sexual appetite. She said when I have no troops to train, fighting or spying to do, horses to breed or farming, she knows I resort to womanising and so she is giving me her permission to do it.'

Ivar laughed. 'Oh, Ubba, you know what your problem is? You have forgotten you're a Dane. You have been brainwashed by the Christian belief that you should remain faithful to your wife forever, and you feel guilty when you cannot do it. Danes know the difference between love and sex, and deep down, so do you. It is impossible to contemplate fidelity to one woman. Variety is the spice of life and Danes indulge when they need sex; it doesn't mean they don't love and respect their wives. Torri is a Dane and she doesn't expect you not to be tempted. Our father could not do it and neither can you. Torri has tolerated Serena all this time, so just accept and enjoy it, and stop feeling guilty! Our father would be laughing his head off – and so would Bjorn – if they could see you now.'

As Ubba made his way back to his room, overwhelmed by tiredness even though it was only 6.00 pm, he contemplated what Ivar had said, and had to admit he might have a point.

He entered the room quietly and discovered Torri fast asleep in bed with just a silk cover over her. He felt the stress of worrying that he may lose her beginning to drain from his mind. He jumped into bed next to her and fell asleep quickly.

ELEVEN

The next morning, Sulamain came and checked Torri over. He announced she could get up and resume normal activities. Ubba told her he wanted to go and look at a horse that had been recommended to him, so she decided to join Gytha, who was looking after Aralt for Skye.

Ubba made his way to the stables and told the groom he needed a horse to deliver a note from Sigtryggr to a tradesman. The groom looked slightly surprised as he did not expect Ubba the "great warrior" to be acting as a messenger for the King. However, his instructions from Sigtryggr had been that Ubba could have any horse he wanted from the stables and was free to come and go as he pleased.

Thankfully, it was relatively quiet when he left through the palace gates, and nobody challenged him. His intention was to deliver the letter he had written to Bjorn, asking him to join them in Normandie during their visit to Rollo. He had not told Torri, because he did not want to raise her hopes of seeing her sons if Bjorn could not make it.

He trotted through the busy streets of Dublin and made his way out to Axel's farm along the coastal track. He was sure of the way as his ability to recall a destination was one of his well-oiled tracking skills. His only concern was that Axel might not be there.

As he approached the driveway, his scent had been picked up by a group of the enormous guard dogs that roamed loose outside the house. They barked loudly and assembled at the gates, alerting the guards. Axel had told him they came from Rus, and were bred as livestock guardians, protecting sheep from wolves and bears.

Even he was intimidated by the size and power of these dogs. However, as their human pack leader appeared and saw him approaching alone on horseback, he called the dogs into a large enclosure, ordered them to be quiet and lie down. Ubba was impressed by their obedience.

One of Axel's guards had already recognised him from his previous visit and opened the gate. He rode through and the guard said, 'Lord Ubba, how can I help you?'

'I was hoping Axel would be here; I have a message for him sent by King Sigtryggr.'

The guard responded, 'He is here in the house, my lord; please follow me.'

A groom appeared at his side to take the horse, which he had felt reluctant to dismount just in case someone let the dogs out of their pen.

Before he had finished climbing the steps up to the house, Axel appeared and said, 'Ubba, what can I do for you?' He looked around and continued, 'What, you have come out here alone?'

Ubba laughed. 'I am not a king, Axel – so why

would I need an escort? I think I could maybe handle most types of unexpected incidents. Besides, I didn't want anyone else to know where I was.'

'Then come in Ubba and take some refreshment. I will give you my full attention. We will go up to my office where I can guarantee we will not be overheard or interrupted.' They climbed up the oak staircase to Axel's office on the top floor, which had a balcony overlooking Dublin Bay. Ubba moved across the room to take in the view. Axel poured them both a brandy and brought them over.

'So, how can I be of service?'

'I want a message taking to my brother Bjorn to arrange a meeting in Normandie in August. My family and I will be visiting Rollo and it seemed sensible to suggest meeting in Frankia to save Bjorn sailing to Jorvik. Any longboats entering most ports are carefully observed and as he will probably have only a small escort; I don't want to risk him being attacked trying to sail inland in Northumbria. King Edward would automatically presume Bjorn may be on a hostile mission. I want you to take another letter to Rollo informing him that Bjorn is coming; he will ensure Frankian ships do not cause him a threat.'

'But what if Bjorn is not at home when I take the message? You never know where Bjorn may turn up next, particularly as his sons Refil and Erik are keen explorers. Now he has been rejected as King of Norway, Bjorn could have departed to conquer new territory.'

'If he is not there and cannot make the trip, then he knows how to communicate with me. You don't have to inform me directly; a family member will know what to do.'

'I have a ship sailing from here tomorrow and returning to Denmark, which I will be going on anyway. I will do my utmost to get your message to Bjorn and I have another ship due to sail through the Mediterranean on Wednesday, which could deliver the letter to Rollo. I assume you don't want your family to know in case it falls through?'

'That's right. I am hoping that Refil and Erik will come with him, as my wife has not seen her sons for four years.' He handed him the two wax sealed parchment envelopes.

'Of course! I had forgotten she was Bjorn's wife before becoming yours. If you don't mind, I have to go and check the loading of the ship. Rest assured I will do my best to get the messages through.'

'Thank you, Axel. I am most grateful for your help.'

oOo

After a farewell feast the night before causing a headache that sounded like Thor was beating his anvil inside his brain, Ubba made his way down to the jetty to board his longboat. Torri was already there, ensuring everybody was present and correct, with Egil by her side. She had given him some stick for coming to bed late as they both knew he would suffer with seasickness on the journey. He blamed Ivar, who he thought in retrospect probably did it on purpose, knowing about his delicate stomach on the water.

He looked around and could not see Arne or

Thorin, and tried to ask Egil quietly. However, Torri had the hearing ability of an eagle and heard him.

'Ubba, they are on the other longboat, seeing to the horses. They cast off ten minutes ago.' She pointed out to the bay and gave him an exasperated look.

They had bade their final farewells to Sigtryggr's family and Ivar at the palace. Ubba had remonstrated with Ivar over the excess alcohol and informed him he couldn't even remember most of their conversation. Ivar had laughed and assured him his memory would return when the alcohol had run its course. He could only recall that when he had hugged Ivar goodnight, a voice in his head told him he would not see his brother alive again. This had terrified him and he could not bring himself to admit to anybody what he had experienced. Visions were usually Ivar's territory, not his. He was not the one with a line of communication to the gods.

As the crew prepared to cast off, he made his way to the stern, found a bearskin rug to lie on and a wolfskin pelt and blanket to cover him. He knew if he did not lie flat and try and sleep once the longboat was out of the bay, he would be incapable of standing up. He had declined any breakfast as he knew it was unlikely to remain in his stomach for long and he detested being sick. He found a bucket, avoided the sympathetic smiles of his crew and settled himself down just as the command to "Row!" was shouted.

Once they had left the shelter of Dublin Bay, hit the Irish Sea and met fresher winds, the boat experienced bigger waves. Sleep was soon banished and he threw up everything remaining in his stomach.

Freya had observed Ubba and did have some sympathy, unlike her mother. It wasn't as though her father regularly overindulged and it had been a party. She couldn't quite appreciate the perils of seasickness as she had never been prone to it. Her mother said she was probably immune because of the rough journey Torri had returning to Jormund in the early stages of pregnancy with her. They had encountered a severe storm, which nearly capsized the longboat. Torri had really suffered from sickness and thought she might lose the baby at one point. She had prayed to Njord (God of the Sea and father of the goddess Freya). The storm had abated and the longboat survived.

Freya went to the freshwater barrel, poured Ubba a flagon of water and took it back to him. 'Here you are Papa, sip some water to rehydrate you.'

Ubba was settling back down under the covers to try and go back to sleep. 'Thank you, sweetheart. I appreciate your concern, but I suppose I have only myself to blame. Had I been sensible and avoided alcohol, I might not be suffering now.'

'Well, don't beat yourself up about it; just try and sleep it off. The wind is receding now and the cloud cover is opening up to sun and blue sky. Just don't eat until your stomach settles down.'

'I will try! If only Thor would stop the hammering in my head.'

She laughed. 'I will ask him to stop. I may have some influence over him, so I will do my best to banish the noise.'

The weather did improve and Ubba slept. He was parched on waking and drank half the flagon of water. His headache had ceased and his stomach was not heaving anymore. He tried standing up and his balance had even returned.

Torri had spotted him and made her way towards the stern. She was carrying a leather pouch and she smiled at him, so he hoped she was not going to give him any grief. 'Are you feeling better for your long sleep?'

'Yes, thankfully, but my stomach thinks my throat has been cut.'

'Well, I can help you with that. I called into the kitchen. Sarah made you a food parcel containing chicken legs, beef pies, pork pies, fresh prawns, cooked plaice and slices of cooked meat. She put in buttered bread, various cakes and fresh oranges, grapes, apples and strawberries with cream.'

Ubba's face lit up. 'The woman is an absolute angel. You should have kidnapped her and brought her home.'

Torri giggled. 'I doubt she would have been too keen, but she certainly has a soft spot for you.'

'Do you wish to join me in this veritable feast, my love?'

'Only if you take it very carefully and don't throw up over me.'

'I shall be guided by you as to what to eat, as I certainly don't want a repeat performance of this morning.'

They both settled down on his makeshift bed and

tucked in ravenously.

After a while, Ubba said, 'I know you were really upset after saying goodbye to Viggo, but you handled it very well in front of him. I know he is young, but he is ready to explore and he could not have a better mentor or travelling companion than Sulamain.'

'I know that, but will he be able to cope in Egypt and Arabia? He can come over as arrogant and cocky and I doubt the Arabs will tolerate that.'

'Have no fear; Sulamain will have him under control. I am more concerned about his sexual overtures to women, which could lead him into far greater trouble. Arabs are very possessive of their women.'

'He surely will be aware of all this... and there is nothing we can do from thousands of miles away. He will either sink or swim, and his future will depend upon his quick wit and understanding.' Torri hesitated, then continued. 'You seemed upset after your drinking bout with Ivar.'

'When I hugged him to go to bed, a voice in my head told me I would never see him alive again and it horrified me.'

'Ubba, we have all outlived our life expectancy and realistically, Ivar should not have made it to adulthood. I had begun to accept that I may be on borrowed time, but maybe Sulamain has given me an extension.'

'I hope so, Torri. I think we both need to be around for the next few years. Our lives may not change too much, but our children need to forge their own paths, preferably with our help and influence.'

TWELVE

They departed on their visit to Normandie. Axel had confirmed his message had reached Bjorn, who'd agreed he would join them. Ubba still kept this a secret from everyone, just in case it did not happen. Torri had been concerned about losing Viggo and he did not want to disappoint her further if for any reason Bjorn could not make it.

He had made some alterations to the crew, substituting in more seasoned warriors, just in case they encountered any trouble. He took two longboats, as he intended to do some trading in Frankia and, if he could reach Andalusia, then some horse trading.

After missing Serena's presence in Ireland, he had contemplated taking her, but leaving their young children at home. However, Serena preferred to remain in Yorkshire. Arne had begged to go to Halfdan in case the fight for Durham was triggered soon. After careful consideration, both he and Torri persuaded him that an opportunity to visit Frankia would be beneficial for his education. Halfdan had also agreed that it was unlikely any battle would commence before September. Arne had been recalcitrant and moody, but recently had become keener to go. Ubba expected that Arne had been listening to the rumours circulating in the alehouse of the beauty of Frankian women and feared missing out. Thorin was going with them as Freya's bodyguard, which would ensure Arne had a companion who could also protect him if they ran into trouble.

Torri had asked to take Matteo on the trip, to help her choose the best roses. Ubba had been a little surprised at her suggestion, fearing her reason might be more personal, but then he had told her she could amuse herself with Matteo if she wanted to. His face had given his thoughts away and she'd laughed at him and accused him of jealousy. The real reason she wanted Matteo there was that he spoke both French and Spanish and had spent his teenage years in the court of Rome. He would be a valuable advisor for them and would be the first to know if there was any discontentment brewing.

Perhaps Matteo would make another excellent bodyguard for Freya, too. Ubba recalled Ivar's warning about protecting her virginity. Having Matteo beside her would ensure no other men could spirit her away. He would of course have a conversation with him after they had sailed, about his role – and advise of the pitfalls of having an intimate relationship with his precious daughter, or allowing anyone else to lead her astray. Thorin, Matteo and himself would surely keep even the bravest young men at bay. If he circulated a court rumour that Matteo was an Italian prince, seeking the hand of Freya himself, this would divert male attention away from her further.

They would soon be out into the North Sea. Ubba

always felt anxious at this point about the potential for rough seas compared to the calm of inland waters. Keir his captain was at the helm, and he smiled at Ubba, recognising his unease. Ubba went to talk to him.

Keir said, 'Don't worry; it's a good sunny day with little wind and I will sail close to the coast so that we can seek shelter inland if a storm brews.'

'I am fine Keir, and if it remains calm, I will even take a turn at rowing to keep my mind and body occupied. I need to find my sea legs. Rowing helps. I was only sick on the return from Ireland because I overindulged the night before, thanks to my wicked little brother.'

The North Sea proved warm and calm, much to Ubba's relief; he relieved one of his crew members and concentrated on getting into the rhythm of rowing just as the sun set. He was captivated by the red and orange colours in the sky and hoped it meant the gods were smiling on them.

As darkness approached and the crew members that were not rowing settled down to sleep, Matteo approached him. 'My lord, I wish to offer my services. I have experience of rowing different types of boats in Italy and would love to row a longboat.'

'Well, Matteo, it is hard graft and requires considerable fitness. Why don't you take Sven's oar across from me and have a go? We shall be ceasing at midnight and resuming at 6.00 am.'

Matteo took Sven's position and Ubba guided him through the stroke for a while. After Sven had left, Ubba took the opportunity to get to know more about the young Roman. He did not mention his plans for him, as there were too many people around.

Keir shouted to reduce speed and head to shore. They had reached The Wash and would shelter there for the night. They anchored in the bay close to the headland, but did not go ashore. Ubba marvelled at Keir's knowledge of the coastline – even in the dark, he knew where to go. He went to the stern and found Torri fast asleep on his makeshift bed, so he removed his outer garments then cuddled up behind her.

oOo

The following morning, the first crew had their breakfast as the sun rose, then took their places. They were doing four-hourly shifts while the weather and sea were calm.

They passed close to their second longboat. Ubba shouted across to Arne to see if everybody was content. He was assured that they had settled down to their confinement and were enjoying their breakfast.

Their next scheduled overnight stop was the Isle of Thanet, where they intended to go ashore for the night before their final push across the Channel to Normandie. This island off the coast of Kent was populated by Danes. His two longboats were flying Ubba's wolf banner with crossed axe and sword, and would alert everyone to his presence well in advance of landing.

They had excellent weather combined with a light summer breeze blowing in the right direction. They arrived at around 6.00 pm and plenty of people had collected in the bay to see the two ships dock. Torri rushed to tidy her hair and Freya untied and re-plaited hers as the wind had blown strands loose. Ubba's hair was now only shoulder length, but the sides were tightly woven into a topknot.

The greeting party consisted of a very tall blond Dane, with three younger men who looked like they were probably his sons, and a group of warriors. The visitors were thrown ropes to tie up to the dock and a portable wooden gantry to help them disembark. Egil was sent to get Arne and Thorin from the other boat. Ubba gathered Egil, Freya, Torri, Thorin, Arne and Matteo around him once they were on dry land.

'Now, listen carefully and follow my lead. We are going to Frankia on a trading mission, then heading down the coast to the Mediterranean to visit Italy and return Matteo to his homeland. Do not mention going to Normandie to see Rollo. I don't want them to know. We are not a raiding party; we are purely trading. Do not reveal we have been to Ireland to see Ivar or Sigtryggr recently. I do not wish them to speculate on our aims. They could be spying for King Edward as well as themselves. I do not want them to think we are an advance war guard or have malevolent intentions.'

Ubba and Torri led them off the boat to the assembled group.

The leader said, 'Welcome Ubba Ragnarsson to Thanet. I am Theobald, the ruler of this island. How can I be of service to you?'

Ubba smiled and replied, 'We are merely seeking

127

overnight shelter as we are on a trading mission through the Mediterranean and returning our honoured guest to Italy. May I introduce my wife Torri, my eldest son Arne, my daughter Freya and Matteo, Prince of Naples.' Everyone's eyes fell on Matteo, and he blushed red.

Theobald replied, 'Well, you are more than welcome to use the accommodation here on the dockside for your crew, but perhaps you and your wife would join us for a meal. I would like to know firsthand what happened at the battles of Jorvik and Lincoln.'

Ubba smiled with relief. 'But of course; we would be delighted.'

Theobald said, 'Well, you get settled in and I will send hot food down here for your crew. You must come and join me when you are ready.'

As soon as they were shown into the accommodation and Theobald had left, Matteo approached Ubba. 'My lord, there is currently no prince of Naples as it is a duchy. The young duke is recently married, but has no children yet!'

Ubba laughed. 'Matteo, Theobald won't even know where Naples is, never mind whether it has a prince or not. It is just a fairytale to cover where I am going. I do not want them to know I am seeing Rollo, as they may conclude we are intending to form an alliance, as we did when all the family joined forces to avenge our father's death. That could have serious repercussions for Rollo and myself. It is not easy to make an innocent family visit; everyone assumes there is an ulterior motive when you are a Ragnarsson. The fact I am just a farmer now, and a retired warrior, does not sit well with the Danes. They still see me as a warrior even though I never became a king.'

'I can understand your problem, lord. And if I can help dispel any rumours then I am pleased to be of service.'

'It may be prudent to use the same tale when we arrive in Normandie, as the Franks are very good at inventing their own stories, too.'

As Matteo left the room, Torri entered. 'Do I need to dress up for this meal?'

'No, don't even change your clothes; we are sailing on a long trading voyage and I want to emphasise that and banish any thoughts of our time in Jorvik. You were Ivar's Queen Consort, so Theobald may ask you questions. You must dismiss it immediately as irrelevant and long ago. Just confirm you are happy being a farmer's wife and breeding horses now. I shall not drink one drop of alcohol tonight; I need to keep my wits about me. Plus, we cross the Channel tomorrow and I don't want to be as seasick as I was when we sailed the North Sea. I shall go and tell Egil, Arne and Thorin to surround Freya and keep any men away from her. I have ordered Keir to post two men on watch duty on each boat, to ensure nobody steals them. As Alfred used to say, "Never trust a Dane." He himself fell victim to Haesten's tricks many times over. I am looking forward to meeting with him again.'

They left to join Theobald for dinner. Ubba announced he would not drink alcohol as he had the responsibility of navigating across the Channel the next day. He was not going to admit his propensity for seasickness.

Ubba gave Theobald a potted version of what happened at Jorvik and emphasised that he was content with his life now and would not be fighting any future wars for anybody. He deflected enquiries about Ivar and Halfdan. He instead tried to prise information about King Edward, which proved easier as his host drank more ale.

Torri thought she would leave the meal on the pretext that she was tired; this would give Ubba a chance to get more information. Ubba insisted on walking her back to the accommodation and checked with Egil what had been going on during their meal. Perhaps he was being overcautious, but old habits die hard and it would be too late if one of them was kidnapped. Thorin had already volunteered to watch over their accommodation throughout the night.

He returned to Theobald, who was now becoming drunk and sleepy. Ubba excused himself within half an hour, citing the early start as a reason for an early night.

oOo

Nothing untoward happened overnight and both longboats left as the sun rose.

As he and Torri ate their breakfast she asked, 'You seemed very anxious about our safety last night?'

'Because we were outnumbered 3-1 by the islanders and only half our men here are seasoned warriors. It is my responsibility to ensure my family's safety and I

130

was taking no chances.'

'But we had the element of surprise, as they did not expect us, and your reputation should have put any Dane off from taking liberties. I am not criticising you, Ubba. I welcome your dedication to duty and your assessment of potential danger. You may no longer be a commander, but your military training remains.'

'We will have to be careful in Normandie to guard Freya from male attention. I trust you have counselled her and insisted she goes nowhere unattended?'

'I have, but she did not like it, as she considers she can take care of herself perfectly adequately. She has become accustomed to Thorin constantly at her side, but if some young Frenchman takes her eye then Thorin will have a difficult job.'

'Ah, but I made the tale up about Matteo being Prince of Naples. I could spin it a bit further and make out that he came over here to take his promised bride home. She could have been betrothed to him since she was a child.'

'But why would we allow the only granddaughter of Ragnar to marry an Italian? Surely, she would receive countless offers from all over Scandinavia? Don't forget, even King Edward has suggested she marry one of his sons.'

Torri, this is just a fictional suggestion to keep potential suitors at bay. I am not suggesting it is true. I have already spoken to Matteo about him being a pretend suitor and he knows his life is in danger if he puts one finger on her.'

'But Freya is already attracted to him; she is not

131

going to accept she can't have sex with him.'

'I don't like where this is leading. Are you saying she would dare to defy us and the gods?'

Torri fumed. 'Only a man could possibly put the responsibility of virginity on a young girl. I don't recall you as a teenage boy even asking whether you could deflower a virgin; it would never have entered your head. As you well know, emotions take over and before you know it, the job is done.'

'She is only 16 years old, Torri; too young for marriage yet.'

'Ubba, I was married at 14 and many girls younger than me were married and having babies at 12 years old. You cannot lock her in a cage until the gods decide her fate; it may never happen. You promised her she could marry for love, and she is strong enough to do it, whatever our opinion may be.'

The conversation ceased as the crew changeover was taking place and Ubba was on the next shift as the sea remained calm. Unfortunately, his head was far from calm as he continued churning over their conversation and eventually, he had to concede that Torri may be right. Just how to control the situation would have to be considered carefully.

THIRTEEN

Two days later, after sailing down the River Seine from the coast at Le Havre, they arrived in Rouen. News had preceded their arrival and a large crowd had assembled at the quayside when the news of Danes approaching had spread. Some of the onlookers were fearful, but when only two longboats appeared, they relaxed. Duc Rollo, Princess Gisela and their courtiers walked down from the palace to greet them.

When Torri saw their elegant clothes, she was ashamed of their travel weary appearance, although Ubba tried to placate her by saying that nobody would expect them to be wearing silks and satin sailing on a longboat crossing the Channel.

As the boat was being tied up, Rollo came aboard and gave Ubba a bear hug. 'Ubba, how pleased I am to see you and your family so well. I feared that all three of my nephews may have been killed during the battles for Lincoln and Jorvik.'

'It was a very close call, and I shall enjoy retelling my story later, but I need to get onto dry land and rest after our long journey.'

Rollo's attention was already on Torri and Freya. He moved over to Torri, took her hand and kissed it. 'Torri, your beauty has increased with the years – and this must be your daughter Freya. News of her beauty has already reached our shores.'

Ubba leant over to Rollo and whispered, 'I am only too aware of the problems of protecting her innocence, so I hope I can rely on your support too.'

Members of the immediate family made their way into the palace, where their rooms had been allocated. Ubba was delighted with the suite of rooms allocated to him, which meant Freya would be sleeping right under his nose. Arne, Thorin and Matteo had been given a large room for all three of them that had previously been occupied by Rollo's sons.

Their personal luggage was already being brought up from the longboats. They were told to prepare to dine at 7.30 pm, which gave them three hours.

Their crew was being housed in a rectangular stone building, with three large dormitories used for housing troops, sailors or personal guards close to the quayside.

Their suite had a bathroom; barrels of hot water were soon being brought up by servants. Torri and Freya were desperate to bathe first, so Ubba removed his dirty clothes, threw on a wrap and lay on the generous canopied bed with a feather mattress that felt like he was floating amongst the clouds. He had not rowed that far for a long time, so his back, shoulders and knees were protesting at their over activity.

Ubba was just drifting off to sleep when Torri came in, having bathed, and reprimanded him for lying on the pristine bedding. He decided a quick withdrawal to the bathroom would be wise to prevent a lecture from his wife.

The metal bath was, to his surprise, very large and sumptuous. He could stretch out and relax with the water lapping over his aching shoulders. He quickly soaped and scrubbed his body clean, washed his hair and then relaxed.

When he ran out of hot water, he slowly rose from the bath and surveyed himself in the full-length mirrors on one wall. He had to admit he had put some weight on since retiring as a warrior. He had always been long, lean, fit and built for speed rather than stamina. However, his building and farming had put some extra muscle on his chest and stomach. His golden hair now had streaks of grey at the sides, but it suited him, just like it did Torri.

Overall, he had been lucky never to take a sword, axe or arrow in a vital organ. He smiled, recollecting how his low pain threshold had driven him to become the ultimate warrior. He had been described as a beserker, but that was never strictly true of him. He concentrated so hard that he appeared to be in a dream world, but it was an amalgamation of all his senses that he needed to keep him alive. He took one last look in the mirror and considered he did not look too bad for a Dane who had survived several brushes with death.

When he returned to his bedroom, Torri and Freya were experimenting with their hair and fussing about what they were going to wear for dinner. He was obviously not going to get a nap. He persuaded Freya to do his hair whilst Torri revealed some of the outfits she had purchased for him from trading ships in Ireland, which she considered suitable for the

Frankian court. He was quite impressed, but dared not ask how much they had cost.

Freya insisted, 'Papa, you must wear the midnight blue tunic decorated in silver thread. You always look lovely in that colour and it will match the silver highlights in your hair.'

'Are you insinuating I am looking old, young lady?'

Freya hastily replied, 'Not at all Papa, but it will make you look elegant and sophisticated. The ladies will be impressed.' She planted a kiss on his head and Ubba looked at her in the mirror.

'Just remember what I said about behaving yourself. If I see or hear of you flirting, I will banish you to your room.'

She lowered her eyes in submission. 'But Papa, I can't help it if young men find me attractive. It is hardly my fault.'

He tried to be angry, but she did have a point. 'Some say Odin sent you here for a reason, but there are times when I see Loki (the God of Mischief) in you, so do not prove me right.'

His hair was finished, so he dressed in clean underwear and put on the new blue and silver tunic. He had to admit it was rather special and did suit him.

Torri said, 'Now you must locate Arne and make sure he bathes and puts on one of the new tunics I purchased for him.'

'Good grief woman, how much have you spent on new clothes? I trust you have not gone too far, because Arne has no interest in dressing up. He is not like Viggo, who dresses like a peacock.'

Torri laughed. 'Only half of what I will spend here in Frankia restocking our wardrobes. You forget, my dear husband –I have amassed my own fortune and will spend it as I please. I think Arne will be just as intent on making an impression on the ladies as Freya is with the men.'

He made a quick exit, intending to explore the palace, and headed down the beautiful sweeping oak staircase.

As luck would have it, he saw Egil as he reached the ground floor, but to his amazement Egil walked straight past him. He shouted out and Egil came scurrying back to him.

'Forgive me, lord. I did not recognise you in such elegant attire; I assumed you were a Frankian lord.'

Ubba laughed. 'It appears my wife has bought new clothes for the entire family to ensure we don't look like peasants among our Frankian cousins.'

'But of course, my lady will always be a queen in my eyes and she knows precisely how to be behave in these elegant surroundings.'

'Rest assured Egil, I know precisely how blessed I am to have her as my wife. She has sent me to ensure Arne is washed and dressed in new clothes, and to ensure that Thorin and Matteo are suitably dressed to dine. Whether we shall make the grade in Princess Gisela's eyes remains to be seen. She has always been unenthusiastic about her husband's heritage. She was appalled at his decision to join us raiding in the Mediterranean, and again when he joined us to find King Aelle.'

'I believe your son is on the second floor, sharing a room with Matteo and Thorin. Would it help if I conveyed Torri's message for you?'

'Perfect, provided you imply the consequences of not reaching the standards required of my beloved queen.'

Ubba explored and then made his way to the sumptuous banqueting room as guests assembled for dinner. Rollo was already there and called him over. 'Well, I am very impressed with your clothes. May I assume your wife acquired them before you left home?'

Ubba chuckled. 'Not as impressed as I am with your silver crown! Do you wear it in bed?'

'As my wife is a princess by birth and duchess by marriage, we both have to wear crowns. This is very plain compared to the jewelled one I was first presented with and flatly refused to wear. I am sure you will have encountered similar differences of opinion with your strong-willed shieldmaiden and queen.'

'Many times, but experience has taught me to only object when I am certain I would win the battle. Besides, my wife still has seaxes, daggers and hunting knives in our bedroom and handles all of them with expertise. Knowing that Bjorn has a vivid scar in a very delicate area after upsetting her once, I know better than to provoke her wrath.'

'Here she comes now. God she is stunning, Ubba. You waited a long time to bed her, but I am sure it was worth it. Look at the children you have produced. Your son is the image of you and Ragnar at the same age, and your daughter is exquisite. Surely, the dark-haired warrior built like a bear is not your son? Is it the other dark haired one?'

'Neither. Viggo is 17 now and has gone east with the Arab doctor who saved Bjorn's life. Viggo has a huge capacity for learning and wants to explore the world. He will make a name for himself. He has Ivar's brain, relishes political intrigue and wants to learn to heal bodies as well as minds.'

Gisela and her family arrived and approached them. Introductions were made. Rollo's eldest son William was 18 and over 6ft tall with long dark curly hair. His nickname was Longsword due to his excellent swordsmanship. Adela was the second daughter of Rollo, aged 16, and Kathlin aged 14, the youngest. Their eldest daughter Crespina had married Grimaldus the Prince of Monaco, last December.

Ubba introduced Arne, Thorin and Matteo to Gisela and explained that his second son Viggo had recently left Ireland to go to Arabia and study. They were seated at the long table. Ubba sat next to Rollo, with Torri on his other side. Sitting opposite were Rollo's children and he studied them intently throughout the meal.

Ubba's minimal grasp of French gave him some insight into their characters. William was bold, confident and very much the pampered heir. He caught him watching Arne and Thorin closely and suspected he was sizing them up as potential combatants. Whilst he knew Thorin would be capable of beating him without a weapon, he did not fancy Arne's chances, as William was built like his father. William was also taking a keen interest in Freya.

Rollo suggested they have a nightcap together, but Ubba made the excuse that the journey had tired him. As they left the dining room, he collared Matteo and asked him to find out as much information as he could about William.

o0o

Ubba woke early the next day and thought his arms, shoulders and legs were recovered from their rowing efforts until he went to the bathroom and experienced stiffness in all his joints. He concluded that age was finally catching up with him.

He disturbed Torri when returning to his bed, but left her alone. She turned back onto her side and he snuggled up behind her. He had made no sexual advances since Sulamain's advice that they should wait for her scar to heal.

On his return to Richmond from Ireland, he had made up for the lack of sex with Serena, who was more than happy to oblige after their four-week absence. His second crop of children was growing up fast. Serena had miscarried at the latter end of pregnancy eighteen months after Theo and they had both been devastated. There had been a long gap where both of them feared that Serena was infertile until two years ago, when they were blessed with Frank. He was named after Serena's brother, who was once one of Ubba's personal bodyguards and had perished during their getaway from Jorvik.

He was wielding a toy sword before he could walk

and had taken over the Shetland pony Sooty, bought to teach Ubba's children to ride. He had witnessed a stand-off between Baby Frank and the pony a few days before they left. Frank had gone into the paddock to catch him to ride him. Sooty knew what was coming. He had let Frank get within a foot of him, but as Frank threw the rope over his neck Sooty galloped off, whinnying with glee. After several failed attempts, Frank was blazing with anger and shouting words he should never have known at Sooty. He stormed out of the paddock and returned two minutes later with the young son of one of his shepherds and two sheep dogs. Frank was not giving up and between the four of them, they soon had Sooty surrounded; Frank triumphed. He watched Frank tie up a disgruntled Sooty and groom him, then fetch his tack. Ponies are far more intelligent than horses and Ubba knew Sooty would be biding his time to break free. If Frank undid the headcollar tying him up before he put his bridle on, Sooty would be off like a shot. As he put the saddle on, Sooty whipped round and tried to nip him, but Frank slapped his nose away and girthed him up regardless. He carefully put the bridle on over the halter, using his thumb to open his mouth, but left him securely tied up to the fence. He let the stirrup down and climbed up into the saddle, shortened the stirrup again and finally unclipped the rope from the halter and told Sooty to walk on. Sooty had finally accepted that this child was the boss.

Torri stirred now. 'Good morning, my love. What are you plotting?'

'I am merely recalling Frank exercising his authority over his pony already. I think I have bred another horseman who will make me and his uncle Frank proud of him.'

'All of your offspring are natural riders; they cannot fail to be, with your genes.'

'Perhaps, but never have I seen a child so young, so determined to impose his authority.' Ubba jumped up. 'Well, I am going to dress for riding, as Rollo promised me a tour of the royal stables after breakfast. Are you going to spend the morning with Gisela?'

Torri moaned. 'No. She doesn't like me; she looks down her nose at me because I am a Dane and as such represent Rollo's heritage, which she despises. The fact I was a shieldmaiden and killed people frightens the life out of her. She is a born princess and has never done a day's manual work in her life. She has only ever had to look beautiful and breed royal children who are raised by others.'

Ubba laughed. 'Torri, don't you dare consider yourself inferior to her. For a start, you have been a queen twice and a jarl's wife. You have ruled in two different countries and have fought alongside your subjects. You have made decisions that enriched their lives and suffered with them when times were hard. You were loved by your people. Can she claim that? And anyway, she can't look down her nose at you, because you are taller than her to start with.'

'I love you, Ubba; you make me a very happy woman. You are so supportive of me and remind me how extremely lucky I am to have you by my side.'

He hugged her. 'And you will be the one remembered for producing kings. I predict that two of your sons will be future kings and your daughter a queen. Feel free to inform her of that if she tries to make you feel subordinate.'

There was a brief knock on the dividing door and Freya bounced into their room. 'Mama, what are we doing today? Father said he would be going to the stables this morning, and I want to go with him, so I will wear my riding breeches.'

'Don't you think a dress is more appropriate?'

Freya threw her hands in the air. 'Mother, you cannot have it both ways. I am not a blood royal princess; I am a farmer's daughter. I will abide by adopting appropriate dress code when necessary, but I draw the line at being forbidden to ride – and neither will I ride side-saddle.'

Ubba scowled at her. 'You will do as you are told, young lady. If we join our hosts on an official visit, you will ride side-saddle. I agree you may wear breeches to ride in the castle precincts and visit the stables, but you will behave like a lady at all times. Do I have your word?'

She hesitated while she pondered her options. Her father had at least granted her request and he looked in no mood to brook any further argument, so she bowed her head in deference, acquiesced and made a quick exit.

Torri countered, 'Where are we going to find a prince capable of coping with her volatile temperament, headstrong ways and wicked tongue?'

'Ivar insists the gods have her future in hand. I just wish we knew their intentions.'

FOURTEEN

After breakfast, Ubba waited in the palatial entrance hall for Arne, Thorin, Matteo and Freya to join him for Rollo's tour of the stables. Rollo descended the grand staircase, with his son William at his side. William was surprised to see Freya there and dressed in breeches. His sisters had been taught to ride as teenagers, but only to cope with quiet palfreys suitable for riding by women side-saddle as a means of short distance travel from A to B. They did not hunt or jump fences, or gallop across country.

When they joined the family William commented, 'Are you here just to observe, Freya, or to take part in riding? We will be showing our stallions' paces in the schooling field, but they are too highly strung to be ridden by ladies. I am sure we can provide a more suitable mount if you wish to take a quiet walk around the grounds.'

The look she gave him should have turned him to stone. 'I have been riding since I could walk. I have been hunting, riding across country and herding sheep on my father's stallions since I was 10 years old. I am pretty sure I can handle any horse in your stable better than you can.'

Thorin and Arne gasped with admiration at her

response and they all looked at Ubba to see whether he would back her or remonstrate with her.

Rollo roared with laughter. 'I did tell you, William; Dane women do not spend their lives in the kitchen and the bedroom. They fight beside their men in battle and have all the skills required to be equally as effective as them. Ubba is renowned as the best horseman in Europe; his son and daughter will undoubtedly have inherited his skills as well as their mother's courage as a shieldmaiden. Never assume size and strength will automatically triumph, especially when it comes to horses. Women are naturally empathetic to horses, as they are to children. They do not use force to impose authority; they command respect without using brute force. It's teamwork, love and trust that binds horse and rider together.'

Ubba intervened, 'Perhaps we should proceed to the stables and have a look at the horses.'

The first stone block in the stables had 10 individual large stallion boxes. Doors were positioned back and front and there were inset grills on both sides between each box set with heavy metal grilles so the stallions could see each other. The floors sloped to a drainage channel in the centre and thick beds of straw had been laid at the front of each stable. Metal hay racks in all four corners and a large, raised feeding and water trough were built into the wall. Looking out to the back was a large sand exercise arena and behind that was another block of 20 wooden loose boxes.

Rollo said, 'I had the stables upgraded to give the stallions more room and comfort. I also built the wooden block for brood mares and youngstock, although actually we are very lucky here, with wind and temperatures that allow us to often winter out our youngstock.'

The first stallion they met was a highly strung dark grey Andalusian, who had been screaming on their approach and leering over the door. A groom put a headcollar on him and tied him up before they were allowed to inspect him. Thorin pulled Freya back and refused to let her go near him. He was rolling his eyes and lashing out with his back legs. They all stayed close to the open door.

Rollo introduced him as Diablo, a six-year-old purchased for William after being fully broken at the Spanish stud. Ubba and Arne exchanged glances, with raised eyebrows. Neither of them considered this horse's behaviour acceptable, but when William announced he was going to ride him they both smiled. They moved on to inspect the other stallions, whilst two grooms and William fought to get Diablo tacked up.

Ubba was taken with a four-year-old grey Percheron stallion who had excellent conformation and an equable temperament. Ubba explained that Halfdan had a Percheron gelding as his warhorse and loved the breed's docile temperament and work ethic.

Rollo had purchased a chestnut Arab stallion to breed with the native horses. Freya insisted on being introduced and he took to her immediately, nuzzling her hand looking for food.

They went to an outdoor arena to await the arrival

of William and Diablo. The horse appeared with a groom on each side of him clinging onto ropes, and he either passaged or bucked every second stride. William kept well back and looked terrified.

Rollo ushered them to an outside seating area. Thorin, Arne and Matteo huddled together at the back, betting on how long William would last. He, Freya and Rollo were in the front row.

Ubba turned to Rollo. 'He seems overexcited; is he normally like this?'

'No, he was probably expecting to cover a mare; he will soon settle down when he realises he isn't getting one.'

Ubba was shocked at the six-inch shanks on the metal bit in Diablo's mouth, and the double reins attached. He knew the reason for this was to give the rider more control and make the horse look engaged with his hindquarters when in fact he wasn't. The severe bit was in fact restricting the horse's forward movement, especially if the rider had rough hands and pulled on the reins. The saddle was high at the wither and cantle and highly decorative, but did not fit the horse properly, causing movement on his back, which Ubba knew would rub him even with the sheepskin pelt underneath.

Eventually, the grooms corralled him close to the five barred fence and legged William into the saddle. They deftly undid the lead reins and ran out of the way as Diablo leapt forward... only to stop short and scream in pain as William pulled back on the reins. After a few minutes, William relaxed his hands and let the horse go forward into trot and did a large circle around the arena. Diablo was so relieved to not have pain in his mouth, he did a happy buck to express his feelings. Unfortunately, William assumed he was misbehaving and he pulled on the reins, forcing him to stop dead.

Rollo sighed heavily. 'When we bought him, he was performing passage, piaffe, pirouette and half pass, but since we got him home William cannot get any of those paces. I have ridden him and he goes slightly better for me.'

Ubba sighed in exasperation. 'Are you telling me you cannot understand why?'

'Yes!'

'Did he have a bit like that on with double reins when you tried him? Was he ridden in a saddle like that?'

'No, but William can't hold him when he tries to bolt.'

Ubba shouted, 'I am not surprised, because he is strangling him with the bit and bouncing heavily in a saddle that is rubbing him. Has he ever been trained to ride a high school horse?'

Rollo shook his head as it finally dawned on him that the problems encountered were not with the horse, but the rider. William had stopped to listen to the altercation between his father and Ubba.

Rollo looked at Ubba and said, 'Show me what you mean?'

'With pleasure.' He called Arne to join him and they went into the paddock. William jumped off sheepishly and handed him the reins, avoiding eye contact. Ubba ordered one of the grooms to fetch a headcollar, overgirth and one rope. Arne undid the saddle and removed it carefully. They examined his back and there were sores where the saddle had pinched his withers and rubbed his back. Ubba insisted Rollo and William both came to look at the damage.

When the groom returned, Arne gently removed the bridle, put him on the leather headcollar, put the rope around his neck, clipped it on one side and knotted it on the other. Ubba put the sheepskin over his back and secured it with the overgirth. Diablo stood very still and quiet as Ubba stroked his neck and rubbed his ears, murmuring platitudes to him. His stiff body relaxed as Ubba hugged him tightly and promised him no more pain. Arne cupped Ubba's left foot in his hand and legged Ubba up. He just sat and rubbed his neck and back, talking quietly to him.

He knotted the rope so it was out of the way, but he didn't pick it up. They set off and Ubba encouraged Diablo to stretch his back and lower his head and increase his stride for several laps of the arena, until the tense muscles on his back were free. He then increased the pace to trot, staying absolutely still on his back as he trotted, and even doing rising trot with no stirrups as his stride lengthened.

William asked, 'How are you steering him without reins?'

'I never use reins to steer a horse. I use my back, my weight, my upper thighs and my heels to instruct him. I am now going to take up a stronger contact with my legs, to control his speed and shorten his outline.'

Sure enough, his trot became shorter and bouncier. Ubba took him to the top of the arena and asked him to half-pass from right to left; he executed it perfectly. He then asked him to do it from left to right, then patted him and told him what a good boy he was. Diablo whickered back at him.

Rollo clapped and shouted, 'Can you ask him to piaffe and passage?'

Ubba grinned. 'I will try, but I don't know what aids were used to train him, so I will have to play about and see.' He halted him with extra pressure from his seat and back, then increased the pressure from his calves until he felt the horse's hind legs come up underneath him. Then Diablo's front legs elevated, and he was trotting on the spot (piaffe). He then nudged him gently forward with both heels. Diablo surged forward, but kept his trot high and elevated. After a full circle in passage, Ubba halted to give Diablo a rest, and allowed him to walk with his head held long and low to stretch his back. To his utter joy, he found he could get him to change the leading leg in canter. He did three strides on one leg, then shifted his weight over the back leg; Diablo changed legs instantly.

Ubba brought him back to the gate and called for Freya to join him. He jumped down and legged Freya up onto Diablo's back, instructing her to walk him round quietly to cool him down.

Rollo shouted, 'Oh, be careful, Ubba! He can bolt from a standstill; he's not suitable for Freya.'

'He is not going to do anything wrong with her on

his back; she knows to stay absolutely still and knows how to ride highly schooled horses.'

Rollo patted him on his shoulder. 'That was the most exquisite display of riding I have ever seen. Will you please teach William how to ride him?'

'Only if you throw that damned bit in the river and find a leather saddle that fits Diablo properly. Did your son learn to ride bareback as a child? You have to be totally balanced and still in the saddle to ride a horse as highly trained as him. Diablo may never trust him again unless he is absolutely determined to retrain. He needs hours being lunged bareback to understand the horse's centre of balance in relation to the rider's.'

'I will speak to him.'

'Rollo, he has got to really want to do it. If he doesn't, you might as well let me buy him off you and take him back to Yorkshire. I do not want to see the horse abused, ruined and wasted.'

William had made a quick exit back to the stables already, knowing he had been made to look a fool by his uncle in front of everybody. It was bad enough to be shamed by him, but to see Freya ride so quietly and confidently without any rein contact was more than his bruised ego could tolerate.

Ubba and Rollo returned to the palace together. He instructed Freya to remain with the boys at all times – especially Thorin.

FIFTEEN

They went to Rollo's luxurious office, settled down on the leather sofas and had morning coffee served with delicious sweet pastries.

Ubba told him first about the fights for Lincoln and Jorvik, and how they'd escaped Jorvik, leaving Ralf to impersonate him. He explained that had he known that Edward was actually in favour of retaining Danes to protect Northumberland from other invaders, and making Aethelflaed Queen, he would have stayed and surrendered Jorvik directly to him. He explained the deal that he had done with Edward to protect his sister and remove her from harm should there be an attempt to invade Jorvik.

He then revealed the story of Aethelflaed, Erik and Ragnar, and his part in saving Aethelflaed. Rollo was surprised and said exactly what Ivar had when he'd told him. 'Did you fall in love with her? Is that why you have given your word to protect her?'

'No, I just felt she had a very raw deal with her first abusive husband, and now she has vowed never to remarry. Being a ruler of any country is lonely enough, but to have to do it all on your own with nobody to advise you and keep you grounded is extremely hard.'

Rollo laughed. 'And did you keep Ivar grounded as

King of Jorvik?'

Ubba smiled. 'No, but I made sure Torri did. I knew he would take her advice, as he has such love and respect for her. After what Ivar did in the church during the battle for Jorvik, I was so repulsed that I threatened to leave him. I still have a recurring nightmare about trying to save a young nun who tried to cut her throat because she thought I intended to rape her. She used a very blunt dagger and plunged it into her throat; it would have taken her hours to die. I will never forget the look in her eyes as I used my sword to finish the job quickly. I have never been able to reconcile raping women. I consider it an abhorrent unforgiveable display of male violence, and as the commander of Ivar's troops, I banned it. I executed two warriors who disobeyed me on that point, then the rest got the message.'

'Hellfire, Ubba! That took some courage on your part. Surely you recognised, as a beserker yourself, that rape was just another way of imposing your supremacy over the enemy?'

'No, I never was a beserker, Rollo. I had to force myself to perform such violence because I was afraid of pain. I trained myself to be the warrior I became, because I had to win to avoid pain and subsequent death. I hated every minute of it but had to overcome it. However, I drew the line at raping women.'

'I remember your first battle; you got a spear in your foot and you were demented. You chopped the guy into pieces and I pulled you away because he had been dead for a while. I know you hated the claustrophobia

154

of shield walls and always opted to go over the top and fight in the open, but I'd assumed it was because of your speed and agility.'

'I feared pain, capture and torture far more than death. When we captured King Aelle, I was terrified that Bjorn might be killed in battle as I was the second son of Ragnar, so in that case, blood eagling Aelle would have fallen to me. I assure you I could not have done it. I remember every detail of Jarl Lund's blood eagling when I was 10 years old, and he never made a sound. I could not have carried it out on a screaming Aelle. Maybe I am just a fraudulent coward.'

Rollo put his hand on his arm. 'Ubba, why didn't you ever tell me? Did Ragnar know? He never discussed it with me.'

'He knew how hard it was for me, but I had to fulfil my role as his son, so failure was not an option. He also knew how seasick I was during stormy weather. Bjorn and Lagertha covered for me as best they could. I have the most perfect balance on land and on horseback, but on rough seas I can hardly stand. But when it is calm, I can beat anybody running the oars. Sulamain said it is due to an ear problem caused by excessive motion's effect on my balance.'

'You have surprised me, Ubba. I remember the day Ragnar put you in an execution line to behead prisoners with an axe. You can't have been more than 14 years old. You were incredibly calm and showed no fear. Floki was at your side, ready to step in if it went wrong, but you performed with such speed and accuracy; it was textbook.'

Ubba groaned. 'I cannot explain to this day. I was terrified of getting it wrong and causing unnecessary suffering, but it was as if I was in a dream; a voice guided me through it and I was convinced Floki was doing it, not me. I actually felt his hands over mine.'

'Ubba, I can assure you Floki never touched your hands. You did look pale and spaced out, and afterwards, you were in shock and could not speak. Perhaps the gods guided you through it because you were so terrified.'

'I still cringe now about having to act as a gothi in animal sacrifices. I make sure I slit their throats as quickly as possible after the axe falls. I cannot perform human sacrifices, so left those to Ivar. I suppose you see me as a weak coward, unworthy of being a Ragnarsson, and lacking ambition for being reluctant to be a king.'

Rollo hugged him and said, 'I have huge respect for how you have conquered your fears all these years and performed your family duty.'

'When we undertook the education of Erik, Refil, Arne and Viggo I learnt a lot, too. Knowledge is power but it can come at a very high price. My father realised too late that it is family that matters, not wealth. I suspect you have regretted some of your own decisions in life. Your slaying of all the Danes that stayed with you in Paris over that first winter was pure treachery, but I can appreciate that you will have been under considerable pressure to prove your loyalty to Frankia by carrying out such a heinous act. I know you wanted to break away from being Ragnar's brother and become a king in your own right. I just hope it has been worth it.'

Rollo smiled. 'You should be called Ubba the Philosopher, because you understand the human mind and its dark intricacies. Money, power, ambition and authority do not compensate for a lack of love, happiness, family or health. You were brave enough to see that as a teenage boy and devote your life to following a strong moral code, where love became your overall priority. Your passion for bonding with nature, animals and people allowed you to refuse to be tempted by power and greed. I hope it has given you the peace and tranquillity you deserve.'

'I do appreciate what I have now, and I know how lucky I am to be alive. I have Torri by my side and three exceptional children to her, and Serena and another younger family of three that I was able to be with from birth. I don't want to return to my birthplace, because I have fallen in love with Yorkshire: its varied landscape and its people. I don't crave wealth and fancy palaces. I have had enough of the politics of war, and do not want to explore and conquer new lands at risk of losing my life.'

'Ah, but you must have ambition for your children and want to see them achieve wealth and recognition.'

'My overriding priority is that they are happy and loved. Arne is like me: bonded to the land, animals and nature. If he wants to become a farmer like me then so be it. Just because he is a Ragnarsson, I won't push him into becoming somebody he does not want to be. Now, Viggo is a different character completely. He has an exceptional capacity for learning and exploring, and Ivar's grit and determination. Whatever he turns his hand to, he will be successful. I have to stand back and let him fulfil his potential. He is young, but he has the choice of either concealing his Ragnarsson background or using it to his advantage. He will make the right choice; of that I am confident.'

'And what about your beautiful daughter Freya? I see you are besotted with her, as fathers often are with girls. I was just the same with my daughters and in many ways, they have to be better educated, more confident and better equipped to rule than boys, as they will be founding dynasties in other countries.'

'I have an added problem with Freya. It appears that like Thorin, she was sent by Odin to promote the Norse gods.'

'But surely not? She is the image of you and her mother, and you stamp your offspring so well.'

'When Torri left after Aelle's death to return to Jormund, she had also lost Guthrun her first son in the ensuing battle. She was distraught as Guthrun gave everything to Ragnar's cause when he could have been murdered as a baby by Ragnar. I had no base here then, and my children were safe in Jormund, with Lagertha protecting them. On the journey home, they hit a massive storm. Torri had no idea she was pregnant and she very nearly miscarried. She prayed to Njord for help. He appeared in a vision and calmed the storm. When she eventually came back when Freya was around two years old, Ivar said straight away that Freya had been sent by the gods.'

'And do you believe him?'

'Yes, I do. Freya has always been older and wiser than her years. She has been on this earth before. Edward has suggested a marriage with one of his sons, but his crown is not solid on his head yet. I do not want to tie her to the wrong man. I just wish the gods would let me in on their plans. That is one of the reasons I asked Bjorn to come here. Perhaps there is a Norse king that may prove more suitable for her, although I foolishly agreed she could marry for love and select her own husband.'

Rollo laughed. 'Big mistake, Ubba! And she doesn't look like the sort of girl who will back down from a fight. Now, tell me about Ireland. What's your opinion of Sigtryggr?'

'I have to say I am concerned about Ivar. He does not look as well as he did when he first left Jorvik. Ireland has a tricky climate, constantly suffering from wind and rain. Ivar proclaims it rains some part of every day in Dublin. Unfortunately, his bones do not respond well to damp, cold conditions. However, Sigtryggr has built him an Italian marble palace that is well protected from the elements. The last thing Sigtryggr needs is Ivar leaving Ireland. He has plans to take Jorvik for himself and to make Ivar temporary King of Dublin whilst he ensures supremacy in Jorvik.

'To understand Sigtryggr, you have to understand the feudal system that ruled in Ireland prior to him becoming King. The Irish born tribes have short tempers to match their flaming red hair, and do not take well to being invaded. They do not take insults readily, are very superstitious, and drink like fish.

159

Mainly because in winter, they stay locked in their wooden forts because it is too cold to go out. They attack on the move as they don't have the manpower or equipment to lay siege.

'Sigtryggr is very tall. He has long curly red hair, is still a fairly young man, and was blinded in his left eye by a sword swipe in his late teens. He looks volatile, but he is quiet and reserved, with a brilliant political brain. He is not a risk taker and uses his brain to outwit his enemies. He can be violent and cruel, but outflanks his opponent by doing the opposite of what is expected. He fought the Welsh successfully and seized Winchester without bloodshed from Edward, after breaking into the palace holding his sons hostage while he was away fighting in Mercia, thereby preventing him from burning or ransacking Winchester.'

'Sounds like a man not to be antagonised!'

'Precisely! Yet he has a soft heart and loves his Saxon wife Skye, whom he met in Jorvik. I helped with the delivery of their son just after we arrived in Dublin.'

'Don't tell me you have turned from a warrior into a midwife now? I could not imagine anything worse than being at the sharp end of childbirth.'

'Well, it can be just as bloody as fighting in a shield wall. My experience with foaling mares and sheep led to me being called in when a birth was complicated. I delivered Thorin, who you can tell by his muscular build now, was an oversized baby to Skye's mother Gytha. It was touch and go, believe me. I have been at the delivery of all of Serena's three babies, which was extremely stressful as she has a low pain threshold like me. I delivered Refil when Torri was struggling and Bjorn was chasing a woman in the next village. Of course, Torri never makes a fuss; she is stoic and resilient, and just gets on with the job.'

'I suppose Torri must have been impressed by your performance, as she soon switched her affections to you.'

'My love and respect for Torri began on the day her first husband was blood eagled by my father when I was only 10 years old. But it wasn't just me who was impressed that day. All my siblings bonded with Torri on that eventful day – including our father. Why kill a beautiful blue-eyed Dane when bedding her would be far more pleasurable? Maybe when he realised that Aslaug would not tolerate him having Torri as a mistress and Bjorn was showing interest in her, he backed off. When Bjorn was ill, our father appeared at his bedside and assured me he would live. He also complimented Torri as the matriarch of his Ragnarsson dynasty. Maybe that was his plan all along.'

'Do you often have visitations from the gods?'

'No. It has always been Ivar who was closest to the gods. I did however have a sobering moment when I left him in Ireland. I suddenly knew I would not see Ivar alive again.'

'Do you still feel anger towards me for turning against my family and preventing Ragnar landing in Normandie?'

'Rollo, what you did shocked me, but now I know what the pressures of being a Ragnarsson are, I can fully understand your need to make your own way in life and not be in your brother's shadow forever. You chose well; you are a duc married to a Frankian princess and have founded your own line. You have land and riches. You came back to avenge Ragnar's death. That confirmed your loyalty to family.'

'Did you know that Bjorn intended to keelhaul me when we went into the Mediterranean exploring?'

Ubba laughed. 'Look, let's put it this way. When you, my father, Bjorn, Halfdan and most of all Ivar planned evil, wicked, heinous crimes you never told a soul because you all knew what you were doing was wrong, and you didn't want to be confronted before you succeeded. Bjorn did not tell me he planned to keelhaul you, but I saw him preparing the ropes and I guessed that might have been his intention.'

'I was told you threw your seax to sever the rope and save me. Why?'

'You had been underwater long enough, and I did not want you to die at the hands of Bjorn. When you and Ragnar fought, neither could kill the other brother. I did not want you to die like that, Rollo; you deserved better. Besides, at the exact moment my seax cut the rope, Bjorn had already ordered you to be hauled back in. He wanted to punish you, not kill you.'

'Well, thanks, Ubba. I have thought about it many times and wondered why you intervened. I suppose you are the only Ragnarsson with a conscience and a moral code. How you managed to become the warrior you did, when you were morally a man of peace, shows the calibre of person you are.'

After her riding demonstration, Freya was feeling rather pleased with herself. Arne, Thorin and Matteo approached her. Thorin said, 'You realise that you have made an enemy of William now? You must stick close to me.'

Freya was surprised. 'I did not intend to offend him. I was purely following father's instructions. He had to point out the problems so that he could understand they were William's fault, not the horse's. If he can't take criticism, then he is not going to make a good duc. Surely he should be ashamed of what he has done to Diablo through ineptitude.'

'Freya, he's a Ragnarsson for one thing, and an arrogant sod for another. He won't want to be shown up by a teenage girl. We can only hope he keeps his distance from you, rather than seeking revenge. Now it is even more important you are never alone with him. You must be with us or your family at all times.'

Arne added, 'Just imagine if he has Ivar's capacity to seek revenge on his enemies. Most of Ivar's enemies ended up dead.'

Freya laughed. 'I think you two are exaggerating. What do you think, Matteo?'

Matteo patted her on the shoulder. 'I think they are probably right. I have noticed him watching you closely – and admiring what he sees, too. Keep well out of his way, Freya.'

Arne said, 'Come on, we are going to look at the kennels. Come with us. I just need to lock Shadow up first, as I don't want him attacked by hunting hounds.'

SIXTEEN

On their first Saturday in Rouen, Rollo had organised a dinner inviting some of the dignitaries from the locality. This had galvanised Torri into a frenzy of ensuring her family were dressed in top quality garments in the latest fashion. She had secured Matteo to advise on what the men should wear and consulted Gisela on the latest trends for women. This meant that Ubba, Arne and Thorin had to endure lengthy trying on sessions of new clothes presented by local merchants. Their lack of enthusiasm was obvious, but none of them were brave enough to defy Torri's demands. Ubba was appalled at the cost incurred but knew when to bow to his wife's superiority. Thankfully, some of the silk ladies' dresses already purchased in Ireland from Italian merchants were used, with adjustments made where necessary.

Ubba looked at himself in the mirror, in his new attire with his hair braided to perfection. He realised he had not been dressed in the height of fashion since his Jorvik days... and although he would have been far happier in breeches and a shirt, schooling Diablo, he did look an imposing figure. He noticed a lot of extra attention from the ladies, which made it worthwhile. Frankian women were renowned for their petite frames, beautiful skin and hair, perfect manners and skilful flirting.

As principal guests, he and Torri were seated at the top table, on a raised dais. His children, Thorin and Matteo were directly below them and although surrounded by Rollo's offspring, he could at least keep a watchful eye on them. He had also seen William's spiteful looks, directed at both him and Freya, and had spoken to the boys about keeping Freya away from him. He ensured the rumour that Freya was the intended bride of Matteo, Prince of Naples had circulated when they arrived, in the hope it would keep predatory males away. He had noticed during the reception before dinner that the majority of men in the room were looking admiringly at both Torri and Freya. The fact his wife still drew so much attention amused him as always. He took great pleasure in knowing that she was his beautiful wife and she resided in his bed only. Freya shone like a bright star even next to Rollo's daughters of a similar age, who were both delicate and pretty, having inherited Gisela's looks. Freya was chatting away to Matteo, totally oblivious of the male attention radiating from around the room.

Rollo nudged him and said quietly, 'I think we both instinctively know which female is causing men's hearts to flutter. You will have an unenviable job as her father, to keep her safe and pure.'

o0o

Freya was not impressed when her father insisted she leave after the dinner and retire to bed with her mother. It was midnight, but things were getting more exciting as the guests were consuming large amounts of alcohol, and she was enjoying some of the bawdier jokes from Arne, Thorin and Matteo. She attempted to protest, but the icy glare from her mother indicated she was not going to win this battle. She decided she would wait until her mother was asleep, then explore the empty room that overlooked the courtyard and had a garden balcony. She would be able to watch the guests departing surrounded by the scent of roses and enjoy the trickle of water from the fountain nearby. She would certainly be glad to take off her silk dress and boned corset that was digging into her waist now she had eaten. She had told her mother that it was a waste of time as she hardly had any breasts to push up and to warrant wearing one.

She returned with her mother to their inter-connecting bedroom and helped her take down her elaborately woven hair. She removed the pins from her own hair, too. The relief was instant and gratifying. She told her mother she could not wait to get her corset off and relax so she could sleep. She went into her own room and changed into her silk nightie and wrap, feeling instantly cooler and less restricted. She knew she would have to wait until her mother was fast asleep before she could even attempt to sneak out. She expected her father would join Rollo for a nightcap; he might just open her door to check she was there. She decided to use the spare pillows to make a shape in the bed, which would hopefully deter him from coming closer.

The thought had crossed her mind that the room may now be occupied by guests staying over, so she would have to be very cautious. She quietly opened the small interconnecting door, and heard the steady breathing of her mother, fast asleep. She closed the door carefully and decided to stay barefoot, as then she could flee quickly and quietly if necessary. She checked the corridor was empty and listened for anybody coming up or down the main staircase.

The room was not far down the corridor. She carefully turned the handle and found it was still unlocked. She went in and there was enough light coming from the elaborate metal sconces placed around the front of the chateau to see the room appeared empty. There was no sign of any baggage and she checked the wardrobes were still unused. The bed still had a large thick cotton cover over it, that she deduced would have been removed if the room was now occupied. She left the door unlocked, in case she had to make a speedy exit.

She went to the balcony and could see that carriages were being assembled around the quadrangle, waiting to take guests home. She settled in a comfy seat, well back from the balcony edge, so she could observe unseen. There was plenty of noise from carriages and horses moving on the loose gravel, grooms from different households chatting to one another, and the background noise from the guests who were leaving.

Suddenly, she heard a male voice from the balcony doorway. 'Well, what do we have here? The ice maiden in her nightgown, spying on proceedings without her bodyguards.'

She jumped up and faced William, careful to show no sign of being intimidated. She drew herself up to her full height, which did not help as he was over six feet tall. His large brown eyes and sardonic smile indicated exactly what was on his mind.

'Where I come from, one knocks on doors before seeking entry.'

He smiled. 'Ah, but mademoiselle this is not your room, is it? Nobody knows you are here: your father is settling down for a nightcap with mine in his study, and your mother is asleep.'

She sized up her only escape route, which meant jumping from this balcony to the next from a standing start. Possibly achievable, but it could prove deadly.

'I couldn't sleep, so I found this empty room and thought I would watch the guests leave and admire the horses.'

She regretted mentioning the horses immediately, as an angry frown spread across his face. 'And you and your father have demonstrated what expert riders you are, and shown me up already.'

'Not intentionally, William; you maybe did not realise that you were harming the horse in the process of trying to control him by using such a severe bit.'

'Very clever Freya, but you don't believe that at all. You think I am an evil cruel bastard, and if I can do that to a horse, what might I do to you now? You have judged my character on one simple mistake. Is that fair?'

She screamed at him. 'You will do absolutely nothing, as the repercussions of raping me would lose you your head. Do you think your father would reconcile with a son who raped his own cousin? Do you think my father or mother would not take their revenge on you for harming me?'

'Freya, peace. I mean you no harm. I was just angry about what happened. I saw you down here from my room across the quadrangle and thought I would try and make my peace with you. You are surrounded by your bodyguards or parents all the rest of the time and I did not want you to think of me as evil.'

She pushed him aside. 'And you thought that frightening me to death was good sport and the action of a future Duc de Normandie? Take a long hard look in the mirror, William; your great uncle Ragnar would be ashamed of you.' She ran for the door, straight back to her bedroom.

She flung herself into bed and could not prevent the shocked tears falling, as she had felt completely bullied and intimidated. He'd let her believe that he might rape her. William's explanation of not intending to harm her seemed implausible. She felt that if she had shown any sign of fear, he would have pounced. Once he realised she was not going to crumple, but would fight back, he'd backed off. She had seen this type of behaviour before, in Ivar. His reputation alone made people fear him and it amused him to set cat and mouse games... but if he wasn't sure of victory, and his potential victim stood their ground, he often stopped.

She contemplated whether she should tell Rollo or her parents about William, but she knew it would cause a huge split in the family. William would claim she was hysterical and making it up. Much as she did not want a bully to triumph, she realised she did now have an advantage. He would not dare threaten her again, as he knew she could tell her story at any time.

So much for being protected by the gods! Their absence in her hour of need spoke volumes. Her father had said many times that men in battle thought their gods would protect them, and he had then seen them frozen in horror when they were mown down by swords, arrows, spears and seaxes. Ubba had also said that the gods considered mere mortals in battle nothing more than playthings to amuse them. It did make her appreciate having Thorin by her side. Perhaps she should ensure she had a weapon on her at all times.

o0o

The next morning, Rollo had arranged for some sport on the training grounds to include long axe and seax throwing, archery, boxing, tug of war and sword fighting to entertain both his and Ubba's troops. Thorin, Arne and Matteo would be taking part. Freya had to stay with her mother, and Rollo's wife and daughters. She had remonstrated with her mother, but had been flatly refused permission to participate, and told to behave like a lady, which did not go down well. Later in the afternoon, the ladies would join the field to see the finals in each section.

Knowing that she would have no male chaperone free to accompany her to watch the early rounds, she persuaded Adela, who was Rollo's second daughter and the same age as her, to go with her. She was a tomboy like Freya and would far rather spend a morning watching men fighting than in the schoolroom or sewing. Adela asked her mother's permission and she agreed, then Freya presented it to her mother as a fait accompli. She wore her breeches and shirt in case there was any chance she could join in some of the games after all.

There was plenty of activity on the training ground; men were thronging all over, anxious to participate. She could see that Thorin and Arne were over at the axe throwing pitch, so they made their way over. The first competition was seax throwing. Two competitors competed, lengthening the distance to the target until one player failed to score. Some of their longboat crew members were matched against Rollo's sailors, and they were taking it very seriously. Luckily for them, most of their sailors were accomplished warriors, and seax throwing was also required to kill game. No Dane liked going hungry. These men knew how to survive both on land and at sea.

The game was being supervised by Rollo's personal bodyguards. Freya flirted with them in the hope of getting her turn. However, Arne spotted her and came over. 'Do not even think about competing, Freya. Father would be furious.'

'I don't see what the problem is! I am not aiming at a live target. You know I have killed many birds and rabbits with a seax, and a bow and arrow.'

'But this is a French court and you are supposed to be a lady, not a poacher.'

'Rubbish! If women can become shieldmaidens and fight men, then I should be allowed to show my skills, too.'

A voice from behind spoke, 'And so you should, my dear.'

William had arrived whilst they were arguing. Freya immediately thought he might be setting up a trap. 'If she has been trained then the lady should at least be allowed to show us her skill. Pierre, she must be allowed to throw, but not to compete against a man.'

Freya knew she had better prove her worth. Arne shook his head in defeat and told her to carry on.

She was handed three seaxes. They were a lot heavier than the hunting seax she was used to. Determined, she took aim from the first marked distance and hit the centre of the circle with all three seaxes parallel across the bullseye.

The crowd gasped and as she moved back for the next distance, they applauded and encouraged her to continue. She finally failed at 50 metres from the target, due to the weight of the seaxes. She received rapturous applause. William bowed and kissed her hand. 'A performance worthy of any Ragnarsson.' He led her away from the crowd and said, 'As your father has not appeared intent on killing me, I assume you have not told anybody about our midnight tete-a-tete last night?'

'No, but consider yourself very lucky. You were completely out of order, and very intimidating.'

'Freya, please believe I do not wish you any harm. I admire your courage and strength of character. You are a breath of fresh air compared to many girls. Do not waste yourself on the Prince of Naples; find a man who has your strength and ambition.'

She laughed. 'Oh, don't worry about me, William. I am determined to make my mark on history, just as my mother did. Finding the right man may take time.'

He laughed. 'And are you prepared to remain a virgin until you do? I doubt it; you are a true Dane. Men will go to war to conquer you, Freya. Be careful.'

Freya and Adela left the training ground. They would have to be back there in the afternoon to watch the finals, looking like the demure young ladies they were supposed to be.

SEVENTEEN

Freya went back to her room and was surprised to find her mother there.

'Mama, are you unwell? It is not like you to be in your room at midday.'

'I came to find a sapphire necklace your father gave me a long time ago, which will complement the dress I intend to wear later. Have you been causing mayhem on the training ground?'

Lying was not easy for Freya and she blushed. 'Well, I did get chance to join in the seax throwing, and I did pretty well... but underestimated the weight of the seax.'

Torri laughed, 'Let that be a lesson to you.'

'Mama, can I ask you some personal questions?'

'You can, but I can't promise I will even know the answers.'

They settled down in the two comfy chairs in the big bay window.

'How did you manage to steer your life the way you wanted?'

'Freya, you have to appreciate that sometimes you don't get a choice. Fate intervenes and you take the path of survival, as there is no alternative. All I can say is that you must trust your basic instincts. Women can sense danger intuitively, but sometimes cannot do anything to avert it. When I was married to Jarl Lund, I knew that his attempt to take Jormund whilst Ragnar was overseas would end in defeat. But I was younger than you are now, and no man will take advice from a wife. Women rarely get input into these matters, so I knew that when Ragnar came back and retook his rightful home, as the wife of an aggressor I would likely die too.'

'So why didn't you run away from him?'

'There was nowhere to go! The nearest village was 20 miles away, over a mountain in the depth of winter. Besides, Jarl Lund would never have let me leave, as I was his wife – and nobody would have sheltered me from my own husband.'

'But why did Ragnar not kill you? I have heard differing opinions from Bjorn, Ubba, Halfdan and Ivar.'

Torri laughed. 'I can't wait to hear them, but remember they ranged in age from 16 to just 8 years old at the time.'

Freya hesitated. 'Well, the consensus was that Ragnar was attracted to you and as his slave, he could take you whenever he wanted. Ivar said he would have killed your son as a baby, to ensure he would be no threat.'

Torri smiled. 'Well, Ivar would think that; his grasp of power and politics was a major factor in his success. Look, Ragnar was attracted to me, but the boys underestimated the power of Aslaug their mother, who was guided by the gods. She was far more of a threat to my survival than Ragnar was. She would not tolerate another woman in her husband's bed.'

'So, did Ragnar take you as his mistress?'

'Yes, but not until six weeks after Guthrun was born – and well away from home. He knew Aslaug would not tolerate my presence, and she had her own spies within the camp.'

'But what if you had become pregnant by Ragnar?'

Ragnar had thought carefully about that. He fabricated a cover that I was the lover of one of his young warriors, in case I became pregnant. However, Aslaug was not convinced.'

'Did you love him?'

'Yes, at the time. Every woman in the camp loved Ragnar; he had an irresistible effect on women. He was not a great communicator like your father, but his eyes did all the talking. One thing you should know is never to compare one lover to another, as it will only ever cause disharmony. Men will not tolerate comparisons when it comes to their sex lives.'

'So, you have never discussed your previous sexual relationships with Ragnar or Bjorn with Father?'

'I told him very early on that the subject was out of bounds. A man never discusses his sexual conquests with anybody, so why should a woman? Men have too fragile an ego to be humiliated. If you inadvertently infer that one partner is better than another, you could destroy that relationship. Remember that; it will stand you in good stead throughout your life.'

'Mama, are Ragnar and my father alike?'

'Yes, in some ways. They both have a strong

connection to the land and nature, and I honestly believe that the nearer you are to nature, the happier you will be in life. Men who have ambition and desire wealth and riches lose their grip on reality. They discover too late that true happiness can only be achieved when surrounded by family and friends. As a result, women have a very difficult life when they are automatically considered to be inferior to men. They are responsible for nurturing their children and keeping them safe. The higher your role in society, the harder that becomes. Your father has been a champion of women all his life. Yet Ragnarsson men cannot be driven; they have to be coaxed into making the right decisions, without realising they are being manipulated by a woman. Believe me, queens are the power behind the throne; you must master this art.'

'But Mama, how did you manage to persuade Ivar as Queen Consort?'

'By taking away from him the tasks he did not like performing as King, and letting him excel in the subjects he was interested in.'

'But I am so confused, Mama. Why do Christian countries insist that girls should be virgins before marriage? We Danes treat sex as a rite of passage to be enjoyed freely, not just within the confines of marriage.'

Torri patted Freya's hand. 'I can understand your confusion entirely, but what you need to understand is the difference between sex and love. We Danes give women a higher status than European women get. In our society, a woman can divorce her husband if he is cruel or beats her. She may also take with her the money and land she brought into the marriage. In Europe, divorce is seldom seen, as the church encourages family union. A woman wanting to flee her husband here would have no dowry, money or land to support her, and her children would remain with their father. She would virtually be thrown out into the street, and only a very brave man would marry a divorcee.'

'So if I was to marry a European prince, I would have fewer rights than if I married a Dane?'

'Probably, sweetheart, but marriages are not just for procreation. They are often an alliance to preserve peace between warring nations. Sometimes they are between young girls and older men, to produce an heir. Love, I am afraid, does not receive consideration in a political marriage. I was only 14 when I first married, and my husband was over 45 years old. His first wife failed to conceive, so he cast her aside. Becoming a queen can be a very precarious lifestyle.'

Freya hugged her mother. 'You must have been very frightened to leave your family home and have to cope in a strange place with a husband you had never even met.'

'Freya, I had no choice; in those situations you just have to reconcile to the inevitable. For all his size and bluster, he was overjoyed to have me as his fertile new wife, and he was very gentle on our wedding night.'

'But Mama, that wasn't right; it was downright cruel. It was just as bad as when you were kidnapped and raped by that Dane in Jorvik.'

'Sweetheart, I was legally Jarl Lund's wife, not his

slave. To be fair, he never physically hurt me. He was overjoyed when I became pregnant within the first month of our marriage, and he treated me like a china doll after that. Why he ever thought he could outwit Ragnar, I don't know, but he never uttered a sound when he was blood eagled. It was hard to witness, knowing my life and my unborn child's could be forfeit too. I showed no fear. My resilience and stoicism had a huge impact on all the Ragnarssons... and ultimately, it saved my life. The kidnapper who raped me received justice by my sword and your father's seax. I had no qualms about killing him.'

'Mama, why did you marry Bjorn before father?'

'Believe it or not, Bjorn was a good man. He just couldn't keep his hands off other women.'

'How come you let Papa keep his mistress and rear a second family in your own home, if you divorced Bjorn for being unfaithful?'

'Freya, I was older when I had you, and both the pregnancy and birth brought massive complications. My breeding days were over. I had given your father two sons, and I was so delighted you were a girl, because I knew how much he wanted a little girl of his own. Your father and I love each other to the moon and back. He is a good father because he has such a capacity for love. I was not going to lose the love of my life and deny him the right to reproduce when he was still young and in his prime. I made the right decision, and I will never regret it. We both know how lucky we have been to survive for as long as we have. We can spend time together, which we never really could when your father was Commander of Jorvik. We have time to be together for the first time in our marriage. It has been wonderful to visit Ireland and come here.'

oOo

They had a quick lunch and then assembled on the training ground to watch the finals. Ubba arrived with Rollo. They were both dressed in leather armour. Torri said to Ubba, 'I hope you are not competing? It's been a while since you were battle fit.'

'Well, Rollo talked me into having a swordfight, just to make sure he can still beat me.'

Ubba was enjoying the different sports. He supported Arne and Thorin in their heats. Arne was third in the seax throwing, and Thorin was narrowly beaten in the long axe throwing. In archery, Arne, who'd inherited the excellent eyesight of his lineage, came second overall – with Thorin in fourth place. It boosted Arne's confidence as he noticed the younger women at court were paying him more attention. Before, it had been Matteo they were all swooning over, but this boosted his popularity above Matteo's.

Torri said to Ubba, 'That's the first real smile we have had out of Arne since we arrived. It appears to have boosted his status amongst the ladies, even above Matteo's.'

Ubba laughed and pretended to be shocked. 'You mean young ladies would prefer a man who can protect them with his seax and arrows, rather than a good looking Roman who can talk them into his bed?'

Torri replied, 'Well, women look towards a male to

'protect them, and one who will produce strong sons.'

'And was that your criteria when selecting me?'

'Yes, because I knew you adored me and would never leave my bed chasing other women.'

'What a lot I have to thank Bjorn for; his infidelity was my pathway to your heart.'

'You repaid him by saving his life, Ubba!'

'Oh come on; Sulamain saved his life. I did nothing but nurse him back to full health.'

Torri sighed. 'I would love to see Bjorn and my sons again before I die.'

Ubba smiled. 'I am sure you will, my dear.' He was delighted that Bjorn would be with them soon, although he still hadn't told her in case it never transpired.

Rollo called him for their friendly fight against each other, and he remembered just how hard Rollo could strike with his sword. He muttered a prayer to Odin, hoping he was fitter than Rollo now. They were at least using blunt-edged metal swords, and he knew that moving fast would be his saving grace. He recalled Rollo's tactics of pushing his opponent off balance and going for their calves and ankles.

Arne helped him with his body armour and fastened the pads on his calves. 'Father, are you sure about this? Rollo does not look unfit, even if he has not been in a battle for a while.'

Ubba snapped, 'Arne, keep your opinions to yourself, son. I thought you knew never to let negative emotions seep into your brain before battle.'

Arne smiled. 'I just thought I had better warn you.'

Arne had done it deliberately, to wind him up. He was secretly looking forward to their fight, and hoped his father would lose. The crew had been putting bets on with Rollo's men, and he did not want to lose his bet.

The square was ready. Egil had been selected as the adjudicator. They were both given their shields and they were allowed one replacement each during the bout. They had one seax for close contact fighting. Ubba was glad it was a lightweight Frankian shield. Egil had braided his hair and made sure the ends were secured under a topknot. Ubba had not forgotten that Rollo deliberately once cut two of his braids off with a sword swipe.

They stood 18 metres apart, facing each other as the horn signalled the start.

Rollo stood stock still and goaded him, 'Come on now, Ubba; let's just see if the apprentice can beat the master.'

Ubba smiled, but knew not to retaliate, as the first rule of combat was to goad your opponent into making mistakes. He held his ground until Rollo advanced slowly and menacingly. Ubba's first sword blow glanced off Rollo's shoulder. He followed this by bending down, turning round and bringing his sword down on Rollo's other shoulder. Rollo charged at him with his shield raised, and made contact, but Ubba whipped round and managed a swipe across Rollo's back, which winded him slightly.

The fight continued, with Rollo advancing and him dancing in and out of range, swiping with his sword. He managed to catch Rollo off balance and aimed his sword at the back of his knees. He smashed his shield into his chest, and down he went. He held the sword at Rollo's throat and shouted, 'Submit!' Rollo roared, 'No way!'

Ubba felt Rollo's hand grab his left foot and saw his sword descending towards his chest. He managed to parry with his shield, but Rollo still had a grip on his foot. Down he went, feeling the impact as Rollo straddled his waist. He was now face down in the mud, with his sword underneath him. Rollo growled in his ear, 'Now you submit, cos you ain't going nowhere!' The crowd was screaming both their names. Ubba released the grip on his sword and felt for his seax. Rollo adjusted his position and in a flash, Ubba turned over and brought the seax menacingly close to Rollo's jugular vein, shouting, 'Submit!'

Egil signalled for the horn to be blown. He told two men to separate them before it escalated into a real fight. He declared it a draw, as both men had scored.

Rollo and Ubba glared at one another. Thankfully, the red mist lifted and they wisely kept quiet and shook hands.

As Ubba returned to his seat after the bout, he received a frosty reception from Torri. 'Was that really necessary? Neither of you should have been competing, and although Rollo is older and should have known better, you should have declined. I wonder sometimes whether Ragnarssons have such an irresistible desire to win that it will be the death of you all. I thought age had mellowed you, and I considered you the most sensible of all of them, but obviously not!'

Ubba recoiled at her tongue lashing, as of course she was right, and he should have resisted the pressure. However, Ubba had spent many hours on the ground eating mud and being overpowered by Rollo when he was a lad. He looked over to Rollo, who was receiving a similar tongue lashing from Gisela. He smiled at the thought of what Ivar would have done in the circumstances. He had never forgiven Rollo's betrayal of Ragnar and would probably have fought to the death.

Arne joined them and said quietly to Ubba, 'Why didn't you insist on continuing? You would have beaten him.'

His mother stood up and gave him a resounding slap on the side of his head. 'Don't you dare encourage him, Arne. He should never have accepted the challenge in the first place, but like all men, he thought he could win and common sense evaporated at the prospect of triumph.'

Arne was slightly dazed after his mother's blow and the whole scene had been witnessed by Thorin, Matteo, Freya and the longboat crew, who could not contain their laughter at Torri's violent reaction.

Matteo whispered to Freya, 'I never knew your mother had such a violent temper!'

Freya giggled. 'Oh yes, we never argue with her when she has her shieldmaiden face on – my father included. We are all terrified of her then, even Ivar. Arne's lucky she didn't have any weapons to hand. Rollo will be wise to keep out of her way too; she is more than capable of giving him a resounding ear bashing!'

As the games finished, Freya managed to catch her father on his own and could not resist giving him a hug. 'Poor Papa, in the doghouse again with Mama. I don't agree that you should not have fought Rollo; I think she should have kept quiet. I imagine there is some history between you and Rollo from when you were growing up. She should have let you test your power against him now. However, she loves you dearly and probably did not want you hurt or beaten. She protects you just like she protects her offspring.'

Ubba smiled. 'True. She knows I can't endure much pain, whereas Rollo feels none when he is in beserker mode. But then, women think very differently when it comes to expressing dominance.'

EIGHTEEN

After dinner, Ubba joined Rollo for a nightcap. He told him what Torri had done to Arne, and how she had chastised him for accepting the challenge in the first place. He warned him to keep his distance from her, as she could throw a punch as hard as any man. Rollo roared with laughter as he just could not believe that Torri could be so dominant.

'Believe me Rollo, she has a temper worse than any man. Ivar loves and respects her totally. If she disagreed with what he was planning as leader of Jorvik, he would always back down. Nobody else could ever control Ivar like Torri. One menacing look from the ice maiden and he bowed to her supremacy. Of course, there were things he did and deliberately didn't tell her about, but she did not hold back when she found out. Bjorn, for all his size and strength, took some severe beatings and torture from her for his womanising, too. He showed me his wounds. When he returned from Africa close to death, Sulamain asked me about the origin of the many healed wounds on his body. When I told him which ones had been inflicted by Torri and not in battle, he was shocked to the core.'

Rollo laughed. 'But it didn't put you off, did it?'

'I had no intention of cheating on her, even though

we agreed to an open marriage when we were separated on different continents for a long time. She was the only woman I wanted in my bed and I was rarely tempted by other women. Only the night before a battle did I have to seek solace in a woman, as it helped me realise how precious life was and made sure I fought to stay alive. Anyway, Gisela looks like she can hold her own; she was giving you some stick today.'

'Believe me, Gisela is one hell of a firecracker and has more courage and determination than any man could realise. She hated me with a vengeance when her father promised her in marriage to me. She thought I was stupid, and an infidel, and refused to marry me. Her father beat the living daylights out of her for daring to voice an opinion. She tried running away before the wedding day. She called me a bear, an ogre and ridiculed me at every point. When I learnt to speak and write French in secret because I had to know what was going on around me and understand the politics of the situation, she did not believe I was intelligent enough to master the language until I proved it. On our wedding day, she cried throughout the ceremony. She was forced to kneel at the altar and her handmaids were made to stand on her veil so she could not escape.'

'Rollo, that must have been so demoralising and embarrassing.'

'Believe me, it got worse. The Catholic Church treats women with contempt. After the three-hour wedding ceremony followed by the wedding feast, there is a "bedding ceremony" – and it bears no resemblance to our ribald festivity. Nobody had told me what to expect, but I soon found out. We were paraded in our nightgowns in front of the clergy and the family, tucked into bed and then endured a ceremony of blessing our union with holy water and praying for children. Gisela was traumatised, as she knew what was meant to come next. The guests and family departed, but the Archbishop and his assistant remained to verify the consummation of the marriage. This meant they had to watch us… and then proof of the bride's virginity was to be confirmed by her bleeding on entry; the sheet removed and displayed to the guests at breakfast the following morning.'

'God Almighty, that is inhuman, Rollo. No wonder Gisela was terrified.'

I forced the Archbishop to tell me what was going on, and then I picked the officious little bastard up and threw him down two flights of stairs. His younger assistant managed to escape, and ran for his life.

'And what did Gisela do?'

'She had concealed a dagger in the bed, which she was about to plunge into her heart. Thankfully, I was quick enough to snatch it from her and she fainted in my arms. When she came round and realised she was still alive, she assumed I was going to rape her. But I spoke to her in fluent French for the first time and reassured her that I would not touch her. She then explained that if we did not provide the bloodied sheet, she would be assumed to not have been a virgin and to have been rejected by me.'

'God, it goes from bad to worse.'

'Precisely, but I told her to go to sleep and that

before dawn, I would supply my blood on the sheet in the appropriate place to save her reputation. She explained that as her husband, I was entitled to do whatever I wanted with her. I told her I don't rape women or take their virginity by force. In Nordic law she had the right to refuse to marry, and she had been forced into it by her father; I should not even have married her in those circumstances.'

'So what happened?'

Well, neither of us slept well for a while. She cried for a long time, still fearing I would take her. In the morning, I used the dagger on my elbow and covered the sheet in blood. I left it outside the bedroom door and then we both had to appear at breakfast and witness it hanging on the wall and pretend we were lovers.'

'Did you love her?'

'I admired her courage and hoped that at some point she might come to accept me as her husband. There was no way I was going to be the beast she made me out to be, but she would have to want me sexually before I laid a finger on her.'

'So how long did you last with her sleeping in your bed and not having sex with her?'

Rollo laughed. 'I don't think you will believe me, but four months.'

'C'mon Rollo, that's just not humanly possible!'

'Funny you should say that – the Pope didn't believe it, either! After the wedding I read up on the Catholic marriage vows and discovered that if the marriage was never consummated then it could be annulled.

Gisela hated me so much, she petitioned the Pope for dissolution of our marriage, but never told her father or me.'

'Christ, she had some guts. Surely her father wanted you as an ally against your own people and to protect Normandie.'

'Oh, it went far deeper than that. Charles III King of France wanted it even more. He did not want Paris raided by us again. He could see the benefits of a Norse alliance. The Pope had to investigate, so he contacted both her father and the King to give evidence. However, for fear of upsetting our alliance, the Pope did not contact me. Of course, her father claimed the marriage was consummated; he even sent the offending sheet to Rome. Unfortunately, my act of deception sealed Gisela's fate. She rightly claimed there was no consummation of the marriage, despite remaining in my bed. Had they asked me, I would have told them the truth – that I agreed to fabricate the evidence to protect her, and that I had never in fact consummated the marriage.'

'Rollo, don't tell me you did not have sex for four months.'

'Oh no, I had a fling with one of her ladies in waiting. French nobility always have mistresses. They only sleep with their wives to procreate. However, when she failed to become pregnant, my father-in-law started asking serious questions as to why I had not impregnated his daughter yet. When the Pope's envoy arrived with her petition, he was apoplectic and went berserk. He would have beaten her to death, so I intervened as her legal husband; she rightly belonged to me. I had to lock her up for her own safety! She had brought shame on her family and her country, and they would have found a way to kill her... probably by poison, their favourite way of disposing of their enemies. They don't like fighting out in the open.

'But Rollo, what did she hope to achieve? Had she a lover she wanted to marry?'

Rollo snapped, 'No, she just hated me because in her eyes I was an uneducated idiot and not worthy to be the husband of a blood princess of France. Look, their women are totally different from ours. They have been born to behave as royalty. They have led a privileged life but are always ruled by men. They have no rights and are forced to become pawns in the politics of men. Gisela had no grasp of reality. She did not know how her poor subjects lived. She was only educated in languages, their potted version of history, music and dancing, and she only read approved books. She had been bred for France to use to expand its territory and form alliances. What she wanted in life did not count. Her own father told me I should kill her, divorce her or despatch her to a monastery for life and remarry. As cruel as they depict us to be, would a Dane ever consider killing his own daughter?'

'But Rollo, Torri had an arranged marriage with Jarl Lund, a man three times her age, and that was to form alliances with neighbours.'

'Yes, but she had the right to refuse and she accepted. I know she was only 14 years old, but she could have refused. He sighed, then continued. 'Don't assume that Gisela was an easy wife to have. French women are not natural mothers; they are groomed to be self-centred and very demanding. However, they are hot in bed and know exactly how to keep their men happy. Her sexual appetite and inventiveness is off the scale. She has no inhibitions either, and when she wants it, she won't be deterred. I think we eventually spent three solid weeks, day and night, having sex. I impregnated her very quickly. We had sex in places I never dreamt of, even as a teenager. She dragged me out of church during important ceremonies. Even at Christmas lunch, she insisted on having sex in the pantry next to the main dining room. She swept all the pans off the table, ripped her dress off and screamed when she climaxed, in full hearing of all the lunch guests. How I didn't die of embarrassment, I'll never know.

'We had a major falling out over breastfeeding. French nobility do not even contemplate it; their babies are handed over at birth and sometimes, they don't even see them until they are approaching puberty. I made her breastfeed them all for at least six months, and she had to be a mother to them. There was no way my children were being raised by strangers. Also, French women sleep separately from their husbands once they have become pregnant, until six weeks after the birth! That's why all the men have mistresses. Needless to say, that was one French tradition Gisela refused to follow; she wanted more sex, not less!'

'How did she cope with the delivery?'

'With difficulty, but she knew she had to breed successfully to establish our line, and that drove her to deliver them. When they are born, their birth has to be witnessed by a priest. Then they are branded on their heel, with the name and date of birth, to prove they are royal children.'

'What on earth for?'

'Believe it or not, to deter impersonation, kidnap, or swapping deformed babies at birth.'

Ubba laughed. 'They have the cheek to consider themselves more civilised than us. Their acts speak for themselves: forced marriages, requiring witnesses be present at consummation and birth, branding regal offspring, removing infants from the family home, infanticide and most of all, a total lack of women's rights. That is not how we behave towards our women. I think they have to be stronger than men to cope with raising a family and surviving in hostile countries. I have huge respect for them.'

'So you understand that my path to becoming Duc de Normandie was not an easy one. Gisela did not want me to join your expedition into the Mediterranean, but she could hardly deny me, after attempting to divorce me when I had saved her from certain death. When I joined the Heathen Army to revenge Ragnar, she was terrified I would not return.'

'I can understand your homesickness and lack of freedom, with the constraints your position imposes. You have more explorer genes than I do. My seasickness keeps me grounded in Northumbria and I am far happier traversing the country by river than by sea. In fact, horseback is my choice of carriage.'

There was a knock at the door and one of Rollo's

men appeared who had obviously ridden hard. 'I am pleased to report that two longboats carrying the flag of a bear and raven have come in from the Channel and are heading down the Seine. Your ship is accompanying them here.'

Ubba shrieked, 'Bjorn has made it and I haven't told any of my family. When will they be here?'

Rollo replied, 'Depends whether he rests overnight. With my boat leading they may be able to navigate through the night. Could be late tomorrow, or the next day. I sent my longboat to escort him, to ensure he is not attacked on the Seine. With only two longboats, he may otherwise have looked an easy target.'

'I don't know whether to tell Torri tonight or wait, as she will be devastated if Erik and Refil are not with him. Last I heard, Erik was planning on exploring the Northwest Passage and Refil was designing and building the boats to do it.'

'I would leave it until they get here, so she is not disappointed. I am sure Bjorn will have brought them if they were at home.'

Ubba turned to Rollo. 'You don't still feel animosity towards Bjorn over the keelhauling?'

'Course not! He made his point and I accepted his punishment gracefully. I joined the Heathen Army, didn't I? And he proved he was a good leader then. I would follow Bjorn any day into battle. I am not certain I would come out alive following Ivar, but there's no doubting his battle strategy, even if it is unorthodox.'

They both laughed and Ubba made his way to his

room with a big grin on his face. Torri was fast asleep, so he kept quiet.

NINETEEN

At breakfast together the next morning, Ubba stood up and banged on the table with a spoon. 'I am delighted to inform you that Bjorn Ironside will be joining us shortly. There are two longboats flying the bear and raven flag, approaching Rouen. I asked Bjorn to come here and bring his sons if he could.'

Torri looked at Ubba in disbelief as he sat down. 'Will he bring Erik and Refil?'

Ubba hugged her. 'He knows how important they are to you, so I hope so, but if they are overseas then perhaps not.'

'Why did you ask him, Ubba? Did you think if Sulamain had not been able to help me I would have died?'

'Sweetheart, I just knew you needed to see them, as you were so distraught when Viggo left Ireland. Besides, I needed to speak with Bjorn about Ivar, as well as Rollo. I wanted his advice on Freya's future, too. We have to appreciate that our time may be limited.'

'Oh, Ubba you are such a caring person. I do love you!'

Freya interrupted, 'Will my big brothers be coming with Bjorn?'

'Hopefully, Freya. We will have to wait and see.

They will both be grown men now and may have gone exploring.'

Torri cried tears of joy at the prospect of seeing her sons. She knew Ubba had noticed how distraught she had been over Viggo going east, as he had always been her favourite. Ubba had never shown any jealousy over her previous marriage to Bjorn and he had never revealed his love for her until after they had divorced. Ubba's devotion to Bjorn and Lagertha for helping him to develop into the warrior he became, had cemented a bond between the two half-brothers stronger than the one he had with his own three siblings.

Rollo came in and saw Torri's emotional reaction to the news. He gave her a hug. 'You are a very lucky woman, Torri. Ubba has the capacity to see into souls, and his love and devotion for you is an example to us all.'

'I know just how lucky I am to have him as my husband and the father of our three children. He may have been called "the reluctant king", but he's always known that love counts far more than ambition and power.'

They went down to the royal dockyard, where the sailors were scrubbing the jetty and hoisting the French flag, plus Rollo's longboat banner depicting two crossed axes in front of a raven. The atmosphere was electric; the French mariners were overjoyed that the legendary Bjorn Ironside was coming to visit.

Ubba turned to Rollo. 'Perhaps if I had brought Ivar with me, I would have warranted this amount of attention myself.'

Rollo laughed. 'I had enough trouble getting King Charles's permission for you and Bjorn to visit. He would never have allowed Ivar the Boneless to sail on the Seine. He has never forgotten our first attack on Paris. It has taken him 20 years to trust me and it was my clemency towards Gisela that convinced him.'

'So why Normandie, Rollo? Why did you settle here?'

Rollo grinned. 'You are sharper than Ivar; you would have made an excellent king. Because I was given a crown, a wife, my own territory, power and authority. All I had to do was keep it protected from Norsemen.'

Ubba gave him a quizzical smile. 'Now tell me the real reason, Rollo. I have lived around Ivar long enough to know that he has ulterior motives for most of the wicked things he does. What's your real goal? King of France, perhaps?'

'Now that is very "Ivaresque" in thought, but pulling that off would be extremely risky. However, since you ask, and as I know I can trust your discretion… You admit you are hefted to Yorkshire. I can fully understand why. When I stand on the beach in Le Havre, I can see the coast of Alfred's proposed united England and I have a fire still burning in my heart for the country. I intend to feature in its future.'

'Wow, now that is ambitious, Rollo. But how are you going to achieve that?'

'If I knew, I would be doing it, but I am just speculating on the number of Norsemen already there, holding land – such as Guthrun in East Anglia, you and Halfdan in the North… Edward's claim to the throne by lineage is not as strong as he thinks. There are other Saxon contenders for England's crown. If Sigtryggr is thinking along the same lines, then he must see it too? Will those Norsemen allow Edward to rule his England when some of them have been ruling their lands longer than he has? I just wish I had the ear of the gods and they would tell me the future, but unfortunately I haven't. However, when I first laid eyes on Freya, I saw her with a crown on her head riding a grey stallion.'

Ubba interrupted, 'Exactly the same vision Ivar had of her when she was barely four years old. Unfortunately, we don't know which country, although she has said she wants to remain in England. She refused to go to Ireland with Ivar.'

News reached them that Bjorn was due in about an hour. Torri refused to leave the dockside, as she wanted to ensure she was there to see them arrive and see if her sons were aboard.

Arne came over to Torri. 'I hope Erik and Refil are coming. I do know that as a mother it must be very hard to let your children fly the nest, and I know you struggled when Viggo decided to go east, but you must remember that you, my father and Ivar have given us the skills to succeed wherever we go in life. Your strength and love has guided us from the start and we will tread our paths wherever they lead.'

Torri hugged him. 'Now you listen to me, Arne; you have your father's love of land and nature, and his moral and ethical code. Do what you want in life, not what other people expect of you. Happiness and contentment are difficult to achieve, but when you find it, stick with it, son.'

Rollo had ordered a picnic to be set up whilst they were waiting. Crowds had gathered now that news had spread of the impending arrival of Bjorn Ironside and although some were concerned this might indicate trouble, others (especially women!) wanted to see these famous warriors and their sons all descended from Ragnar.

William was not amused by the fuss made of his cousins. He realised that as well as Thorin and Arne guarding Freya, there may now be two of Bjorn's sons and half-brothers to protect her. He couldn't quite understand why he felt jealous, but he had found her to be so different and totally the opposite to French women. He wanted to spend more time with her, not less. He was after all the heir apparent to Normandie, a civilised country... and these cousins were practically savages from the North Pole. What possible influence could they have in the future? They couldn't even read or write.

Suddenly, a horn blew in the distance and the first longboat pulled into the dock. Ubba had positioned himself on a boat that was out of the water and being repaired. This gave him height and he spotted Bjorn in the first boat immediately. He was fit and well, and every inch of his frame proclaimed him King. His heart sank when he couldn't see Erik or Refil. Then the second boat came in, with Erik and Refil at the helm. Erik was the image of Bjorn as Ubba remembered him in his twenties. Refil was over six feet tall, but Erik had at least six inches on him in height and he was broader, too. Ubba had always had a soft spot for Refil. Whereas Ubba was an earth worshipper, Refil had been a sea worshipper from birth. He had spent more time in the sea and fjords than on land as a boy. Just like wolves and horses craved his own attention, dolphins, orcas and any sea creatures were Refil's companions.

He climbed back down off the boat and ran to Torri, shouting, 'Erik and Refil are on the second longboat!'

Overcome with emotion, she flung her arms around him and sobbed tears of joy. When she had calmed down, he led her to where the first boat was preparing to dock. Bjorn screamed at him, 'Jump aboard, Ubba! I can't wait.'

He dropped Torri's hand and she shook her head. 'Go on then, but don't kill yourself!'

He sized up the leap, which was a gap of at least six feet, but he knew he had to make it or his credibility would be shattered. Once all the oars were shipped he took a running jump and landed at the feet of Bjorn, whilst his crew clapped and shouted his name.

Bjorn hugged him so tightly he could hardly breathe. 'I was worried about you at Jorvik. I made a sacrifice to the gods to keep you safe and it must have worked as you, your family and Halfdan all survived.'

'I never expected to survive. I just managed to pull off a deception and I escaped upriver by longboat. I can't proclaim it was your plea to the gods, my utter stupidity, or an amazing change in Edward's tactics that spared my life.'

'But don't forget you saved Ivar's life, too. I look forward to hearing the full story. Is Rollo still bearing a grudge against me for keelhauling him? Do I need to watch my back?'

'No, of course not, Bjorn. He was very impressed with you during the revenge we took for our father. We all had a job to do and we succeeded. Remember, his tough love and sword training may just have contributed to us both being alive now.'

Torri came running across the gangplank. Bjorn swept her into his arms and kissed her on her cheek. 'My God, Torri! Age has increased your beauty; you look incredible. I can see Ubba has been looking after you well.'

She laughed. 'I have enjoyed the last two years being a farmer's wife and making up for the years I missed out on being in Ubba's arms.' He set her down as if she weighed nothing.

'Wait until you see Erik now; he has matured beyond our expectations.'

Ubba stepped back to give them chance to talk. He was always mindful that Torri had been Bjorn's wife before, and never forgot that they had been very much in love and had two sons together.

The second longboat had docked. Erik and Refil rushed over to embrace their mother. Erik was indeed a giant, and he threw her up into the air and caught her. 'My beautiful mother, I have missed you so much. Lagertha made sure we never forgot you and sends her greetings to both of you.'

Refil approached Ubba slightly hesitantly, but

Ubba grabbed him and hugged him like he was still the teenage boy that had left Jorvik. 'You are a fine man now, Refil.'

'Only thanks to the time I spent with you Ubba, and your patient coaxing and efforts to make me into a man capable of defending myself. You instilled so much confidence in me and helped me achieve my dreams of becoming a sailor and now a boat builder.'

'I saw so much potential in you as a boy; I knew you would be very special as a man. Besides, I am such a lousy sailor, I had to offer you in my place. I am a landlubber and need my feet on the earth. Why do you think I asked your father to meet us here? There was no way I was sailing across the North Sea to Norway, even in the summer.'

'Erik and I are intending to sail the Northwest Passage and also cross the Atlantic, but we need bigger ships; we would not make it in longboats. I have designed a trading ship with more speed, using oars as well as a sail.'

Erik had finally released Torri. She fell into Refil's arms and they both cried together.

Bjorn pulled Ubba to one side. 'I have a surprise for you, brother. I have brought you someone you love, who when he heard rumours of my sailing to Frankia to meet you, dropped everything and begged to join me. He motioned a figure wearing a deep hooded cloak to come forward.

Ubba stared in astonishment as the figure approached. He stopped in front of him and then pulled back the hood, revealing braided golden hair, bright blue eyes and a tall lithe figure.

He could not believe his eyes and put his hand on the man's shoulder. 'Sigurd my brother, is that you?'

'It is, Ubba. When Axel told me you had gone to Ireland to see Ivar and asked him to try and get Bjorn to meet in Frankia, I was coming, come hell or high water. I wanted to explain why I did not join you all to avenge our father's death; I did not want you thinking I was a coward.'

Ubba grabbed him and hugged him. 'I would never have thought that of you. I suspected it was your animosity towards Ivar that prevented you. I hope you don't bear a grudge against me for supporting Ivar in Jorvik.'

'No, of course not. Like me, you don't crave power and authority; you would rather farm and lead a normal life. We have our father's genes and you learned firsthand what a poisoned chalice a king has to deal with.'

Refil approached his mother. 'Mama, Lagertha sent her apologies that she was not well enough to make the journey. She would have loved to see you all again. However, she insisted that I brought a replacement.'

There was a gap formed by the crew and a young blonde girl moved forward. 'Mama, this is Inga, my betrothed.' She opened her cloak and revealed a baby boy of around six months old, with blonde curly hair. 'This is my son Leif. We think he may be your first grandchild.'

Torri gasped and hugged Inga, then took Leif in her arms and examined him, and kissed his chubby cheeks. 'What can I say, Refil? You have made my day even more special.' She scanned the crowd for Erik and raised her eyebrows, and everybody watched in silence.

Erik smiled in response. 'Correct Mother, I have no wife yet, and no children. Where I intend to go it is not safe to take a family, so I cannot start one until I have made it safely back home. However, Refil has now thrown me an added burden to ensure I return him safely to his wife and son.'

Rollo came on board and made his way over to Bjorn. He held his hand out and said, 'Welcome to Rouen, Bjorn. I hope you have come suitably laden with goods to trade from the land of my birth.'

Bjorn took his hand and shook it vigorously. 'Of course, Rollo; we are traders, not raiders and I handpicked goods that I knew we could exchange with you. Thank you for allowing me safe passage in French waters.'

Rollo stared long and hard at Bjorn. 'Behave yourself, or I will have you eating sand again, with my sword pinning you to the ground like I did when you were a boy learning to wield a sword. Don't think that age has slowed me down, Bjorn; there's plenty of life in this old boar yet.'

Two of Bjorn's sailors approached carrying a wooden crate, which they set down in front of him. 'Ah yes, I nearly forgot, Ubba. I have a second surprise for you. Axel wanted to send you a gift. Apparently, you admired his stock in Ireland and he decided to send you this to protect your farm.'

One of the sailors opened the door of the crate and lifted out a large bundle of fluff with four legs and a tail. He slipped a rope under his collar and the dog sat staring around him.

Ubba bent down and looked him straight in the eye, then stroked his chest.

Bjorn said, 'He is a four-month-old Caucasian Shepherd dog from Rus called Caesar. Axel supplied his feed for the journey and a diet sheet. He eats more meat in a day than we do. Axel says he is not a sheepherding dog, but a guardian dog; you must introduce him to your farm stock carefully so he bonds with them. He will guard sheep, livestock, your family and property, but he needs to be running loose outside, day and night. You must introduce him very carefully to your son's wolf. He has been bred to kill wolves and bears if they attack your flock. Hopefully, the wolf will be the alpha male as he is older than Caesar, but Axel says you must control their relationship carefully as he matures.'

Freya came running over, very excited. 'Is he for us, Papa?' She was about to cuddle him and Ubba stopped her.

'Not yet, Freya; he needs to get to know you and trust you. He is not a lap dog; he is a very large guardian dog that will grow to be taller and heavier than the Irish wolfhounds we met in Ireland.'

Caesar had decided this new human looked good fun. He stood up, wagged his tail and barked. Freya patted him and stroked his big ears. He was blue grey but with fawn legs, and his puppy coat was starting to shed with the increasingly warmer days.

Rollo came over. 'Good God, is that a horse or a dog? You had better take him to my royal kennels and give my grooms instructions on how often and what to feed him. I have a three-month-old deerhound bitch puppy whom he can play with during the day. He needs a kennel to himself the rest of the time. He also needs keeping well away from my French mastiffs.'

Freya said, 'Thorin and I will take him to the kennels and make sure he gets some exercise to stretch his legs after being cramped up in a cage on the voyage over.'

Bjorn added, 'He was an absolute saint on the journey. The sea did not bother him at all, and we let him out on deck before bedtime and he made friends with the crew and persuaded them to give him extra food. There is no nervousness or malice about him at all. He just wants to be your friend.' Bjorn fondled his head before Freya led the dog away.

Bjorn's family started to make their way towards the palace, and the crew to the sailors' quarters. Torri had taken Inga and the baby up to feed and rest before dinner.

Refil and Keir were sitting on a bench discussing ship building. Refil and Erik had spent three summers in Yorkshire as boys, fishing off the coast with Keir as their captain. In a violent North Sea storm off the Scottish coast, the fishing vessel had been thrown onto rocks and Refil had rescued two of the crew by diving to find them within the sunken wreck and securing ropes to pull them out. An amazing feat for such a young boy, but he had always been so confident in the water and could hold his breath for an incredible length of time underwater.

Freya reflected on the amazing change of her half-brothers over the last few years. Erik had been just as surprised at the change in Freya. He told her she was stunningly beautiful and her father had been right to assign Thorin as her bodyguard. Rumour had it that Erik was like Bjorn when it came to women – irresistible, but constantly looking for new experiences and then moving on. She suspected he was being perfectly sensible, as explorers hardly had chance to put down roots, and were at such high risk of death due to navigating uncharted seas and new lands.

When they had all been together in Jorvik, Freya had bonded closely with Refil. There was an innocent vulnerability behind his outward mask, which her father had recognised too. His love for the sea and desire to explore was all-encompassing, but he did not relish the raiding that went with it when they were opposed. Refil was a gentle, peaceful, loyal person who hated confrontation on any level. The fact he had fallen in love with Inga proved he craved love and support. She worried whether it would survive the inevitable separation that exploring required. He could not take a wife and children with him on these expeditions; it was far too dangerous.

She too was amused at Refil producing Torri's first grandchild, because she had followed Viggo's provocative interest in sex from a very early age. She knew Viggo's insatiable desire was fuelled purely by wanting to experience new pleasures. She was certain that Viggo would study sex as avidly as he studied other subjects and would find what suited him best when he had experienced all aspects of the subject. She had heard rumours of Viggo experimenting with homosexuality, when she was in Ireland. However, lack of female partners may have played a part in that, rather than a real desire for the opposite sex.

Admittedly, Halfdan had followed this path, but for entirely different reasons. Halfdan was another who sought a partner for life and had fought hard to overcome the attitude of a male dominated society that insisted on conforming to established tradition. Ubba had supported him, insisting that as long as he had found someone to love, what did it matter if they were same sex partners? She remembered Ivar's indignation that in doing this, Halfdan was failing to reproduce Ragnarsson heirs. This had been resolved by him siring one with Aoife and declaring him – Siegfrid – as his legitimate son and heir. According to Arne, this method had encouraged his partner Stefan to persuade Halfdan to let him do the same, as he was desperate for a daughter. This way, the two men would still have their own family, with each child carrying 50% of their genes.

TWENTY

After dinner Rollo, Ubba and Bjorn retired for a nightcap. Sigurd had been invited, but declined as he was desperate for an unbroken night's sleep in a feather bed after travelling for the last three weeks in such cramped conditions.

Bjorn explained that Sigurd had only arrived with him the day before they were due to sail for Frankia. He had come alone and left his wife and five children to tend the farm and land at Zealand. However, they'd had little time together on the journey to discuss what Sigurd had been doing.

Ubba said, 'I am delighted he has come. Halfdan has always missed him as they had a brotherly bond, which had unfortunately been broken by Ivar's behaviour as a child because he required so much more attention from our mother due to his disabilities. Sigurd was left to fend for himself and he resented it. As I was away with father and you, I did not see what tension was building between them.'

Bjorn said, 'He is very like you: bonded with nature and farming. He had no intention of becoming King of the three islands until they were threatened by other Danes. He realised that unless the islanders banded together from Scania and Halland, they all risked losing their land and livelihoods. They won and insisted Sigurd become King of all three islands. That's as much as I know.'

Rollo said, 'Well, tell us what you are doing now, and where you are living?'

'After becoming runner-up in the election for King of Norway, which Olaf won, I settled close to Uppsala in Sweden. After three years, I ended up as King of Sweden.'

Ubba laughed. 'You see, I told you there is no peace for a Ragnarsson. I thought you wanted to be King of Norway?'

Bjorn laughed. 'Well, as I didn't succeed at my first attempt, I was just biding my time and figuring out how to get rid of Olaf, then a row blew up over the sovereignty of Uppsala and threatened its position as central to Norse religion. As a follower of Odin, I was not prepared to allow that and helped the Swedes to fight to retain it. Like Sigurd, I ended up with a crown on my head. I have not given up on Norway by any means.'

Rollo laughed. 'Well you have always had a big head, but I don't think even you can wear two crowns at once. How the hell can you, born a Dane, rule both Norway and Sweden?'

Ubba roared with laughter. 'Well, I would say you have got yourself in a right pickle. I suspect Ivar would be madly jealous of your dilemma. He intends to become King of Dublin if Sigtryggr succeeds in taking Jorvik from Edward.'

Bjorn laughed too. 'Well Ubba, that leaves you

the only one without a crown, so you had better drag yourself out of retirement and head for Sweden. Erik and Refil are adamant that they are sailing west exploring, and they both think they are too young to be kings yet.'

Ubba's face was a picture of horror. 'No way, Bjorn! I am staying right where I am. It's cold enough in Yorkshire in the winter, never mind Uppsala. Besides, the gods would be angry; they think I have become too Christian. I have been studying Latin and religion, and had to officiate in Ivar's place during Saxon feast days in Jorvik. He was banned from the church by the Archbishop due to the murder and devastation he caused when he invaded.'

Rollo intervened, 'What about your son Arne?'

'God forbid! He's not proven in battle yet, never mind ready to become a king. He wants a quiet life breeding horses on good fertile land.'

Rollo continued, 'Ah, but what about Freya? Marry her to Bjorn's nearest rival, then bump him off when she has bred an heir. The Swedes will be content enough to have a granddaughter of Ragnar as Queen. The gods will be even happier that a true Norse woman is guarding Uppsala.'

'Will you two stop making wild plans for my children? Besides, you think I can be awkward, wait till Torri hears about this idea. My daughter says she is not leaving Northumbria and will not tolerate an arranged marriage. Edward has already been badgering me to betroth her to one of his sons.'

Rollo said, 'But if may not be the atheling she

marries; it may be a younger son. You also said that the gods have plans for her, well, maybe this is their intention. Perhaps that is why Thorin was sent to protect her.'

Ubba exclaimed, 'Right, I am off to bed and I suggest you keep your opinions to yourself. If Torri or Freya get to hear about this then I will have no sympathy for whatever piece of you they decide to chop off!'

oOo

Ubba woke early the next morning, determined to ride Diablo and check on Caesar before breakfast. He made his way over to the kennels first and found a groom feeding Caesar in his spacious kennel.

He said, 'Has he been all right overnight?'

To his surprise when the groom answered, it was apparent she was a girl. 'Yes, my lord; he has eaten and slept well.'

'Good, are you employed by the Duc as a groom? What is your name?'

'Eloise. I have had plenty of experience with horses and dogs since I was a child and he liked the way I worked with his horses, so employed me. Norsemen seem to appreciate people for their skills rather than dismissing them purely on gender. I saw you ride Diablo and I was spellbound. You have such empathy with him and rode him without a bridle. Where did you learn to ride like that?'

Caesar had finished his breakfast and came over to Ubba, who sat down and fussed him. 'I rode bareback as a child and to perform these high school movements you need to be as close to the horse as possible. He responds to the lightest touch or shift of weight and as I don't know exactly what commands he has been taught, it makes it easier to discover without a saddle. I have an Andalucian stallion that I bought in Spain and have trained him as a warhorse. He is brilliant. They have a built-in desire to protect you and will kick any horse who approaches from behind.'

'The young man with the wolf, is he your son?' She blushed and he smiled, knowing that she obviously liked him.

'Yes, Arne is my impatient eldest son, who wants to prove he can be a warrior. He wasn't too pleased to come on this journey; he would rather be back in Northumbria preparing to fight for Durham with my brother Halfdan.'

She looked anxious. 'Will he survive?'

'Only if he remembers what I have taught him when under pressure. He's quick, agile and a good swordsman; he just needs experience. He will be fine when he has his first battle under his belt.'

She looked worried, and he added, 'Don't worry, he won't be too close to the action first time out. We will give him a couple of outings at the back before we put him at the front of a shield wall.'

'Oh, but isn't that the most dangerous place to be in a battle? I have heard the men say it is the most terrifying ordeal to face.'

'I can assure you it is! I prefer to be out in the open, fighting hand to hand.'

Eloise said, 'You are considered the most accomplished Ragnarsson warrior. Ivar the Boneless is considered to be the cruellest and most intimidating.'

'I think Rollo, who was one of my teachers, would still be hard to beat. His strength and experience will see him through any battle. Ivar is not as cruel as people believe, but he does have a very quick temper as he is in pain every day of his life with his legs.

'Can you fetch me a bridle with a soft bit, and a saddlecloth and girth? I will school Diablo in the paddock. Would you also bring Caesar a long lead and bring him over to the arena with you?'

'Certainly, my lord!' She scurried off to do his bidding.

Eloise took Caesar for a walk while Ubba warmed Diablo up and got his muscles stretched and relaxed. As she came back to the paddock, she saw that Arne and his wolf Shadow were there too. She hesitated as Caesar spotted Shadow; his tail went over his back and his body tensed.

Ubba spotted them and told her to keep walking, but to be prepared if he tried to pull on the lead. Arne told Shadow to stay. He came over and took the lead from her. Ubba stopped and came over to the fence to advise. 'Arne, just keep walking over here and then hand him back to Eloise and go back to Shadow. Caesar is young enough to submit to Shadow's age and maturity. Bring Shadow closer, but watch him carefully for any signs of a reaction. Don't you fuss Caesar, or Shadow will be jealous and could attack him. This relationship needs very careful handling. In fact, you come and ride Diablo, and I will make the introduction.'

Arne was delighted to have a chance to ride Diablo, so he jumped over the paddock fence.

Ubba followed suit and Caesar welcomed him back. He took the lead from Eloise, clipped it onto Caesar and walked over to where Shadow was lying down. He sat up as they approached. Ubba told him to sit and stay, talking calmly to him. Caesar did not try to rush forward, but remained on a loose lead at Ubba's side. As they drew level, Shadow stood up. Ubba raised his hand and commanded him to stay. He talked calmly to both animals and neither showed any aggression. However, Caesar opted to lie down submissively to Shadow of his own accord. Ubba patted both of them and turned back to the paddock, leaving Shadow his own space.

Eloise said, 'Impressive control over the wolf!'

'Yes, when Caesar showed submission in front of him that was all I wanted to achieve. Shadow will accept me as pack leader even though he is Arne's wolf, so he will work well for me when necessary. I will keep introducing them until they both accept each other. What I did not want was Shadow threatening him. They will mix fine, but there may be a problem when Caesar hits sexual maturity. By then I will be the pack leader of both of them and tolerate no animosity, though.'

'How do you know so much about wolves' behaviour?'

'You learn by watching them very closely and

observing their behaviour. Shadow is unusual in that he is a lone wolf and left his pack to follow Arne in Jormund. When Arne came back to Jorvik with his mother and brothers, he gave Shadow the option to go back into the forest. However, the wolf chose to get on the longboat as his love for Arne was greater. He could have joined the few wolves there are in Yorkshire, but apart from finding himself a mate and siring a litter, he still remains with Arne.'

Ubba watched Arne attempt half pass at trot with Diablo. He was pleased with his riding. Although he had hold of the reins, Arne had the stallion rounded and balanced with his legs, and allowed him the freedom to place his head at will.

Ubba called him over to the fence. Arne relaxed and let the horse walk and stretch. 'I think he's wonderful. Do you think Rollo might let us buy him? I have heard rumours that William will never forgive the horse for showing him up, and I dread to think what revenge he may take on him. He is not renowned for patience and sympathy towards man or beast.'

Ubba chuckled. 'A true hot tempered Ragnar grandson then. You know you can fly off the handle too quickly sometimes.'

'Maybe with you Father, but never with a horse. I respect them as much as you do.'

'I'll give you that Arne, and the proof is in how well horses respond to you. You understand what makes them tick and they want to perform their best for you. Remember when it comes to battle, you are in a partnership and each one relies on the other to survive.

I will speak to Rollo about Diablo's future. Tomorrow we are going to visit Haesten for a few days. We are riding overland; he lives outside Caen on the coast. Can you and Thorin liaise with Rollo's head groom about how many horses we will need?'

'Sure Father, but how many of us will be going?'

'Well obviously your mother and Freya, as Torri insists on coming rather than being left here. Bjorn, Erik, Refil and Sigurd. Egil, who is a lifelong friend of the wicked old dog Haesten. Thorin and Matteo, as Freya's bodyguards. Keir to talk sailing with Haesten, Erik and Refil. We will need a couple of pack horses to carry equipment and minimal baggage. We won't be attending any society balls I suspect, but your mother will need some changes of clothing. I have one or two items I brought specially for Haesten. It's warm enough to sleep in the open, but we need some waterproof covers in case it rains. Ask if you can take a couple of French grooms to lead the packhorses and care for the horses when we stop.'

'What about weapons? Will Rollo be taking a troop?'

'No, Rollo thinks we will be perfectly safe, and he wants no banners or fuss. William will accompany him and anyone else he wants to take. He just wants to spend time with his Dane family and forget about being a duc. However, it would be wise to have some shields available, plus whatever weapons we normally carry. It is mainly countryside and the farmers are all busy haymaking.'

'Very well, Father. I had better get on with it, then.

I assume you would like to ride Diablo?'

'Yes, and I will speak to Eloise about caring for Caesar. She seems to have a soft spot for you, son.'

Arne blushed. 'Father, do not say another word. Remember how annoyed you used to be when Ivar poked his nose into your sex life? Well, I feel exactly the same, so keep quiet.'

Ubba laughed. 'As you wish son, but I expect you to behave like a gentleman around women, whether they be royalty or servants.'

Arne pirouetted Diablo and cantered off, giving his father a death stare. Ubba was exasperated. Why could he not tolerate advice or discuss sex with his own father? He had been keen to discuss it when he had been in Jorvik with his stepbrothers, as they were going through puberty. Arne was attracting attention from teenage girls as well as older women. His shyness should have left him by now. God forbid, Viggo's appetite had started at 12 years old and had increased rapidly in his efforts to experiment. Perhaps Arne had inherited more of Ragnar's reticence.

He saw Eloise returning with Caesar, so he joined her and asked her to look after him whilst they were away. She asked if Arne was going and looked disappointed when he nodded. Had a relationship forged between them? He refrained from discussing it as he knew Arne would fly into a rage of Ivar-like proportions if he found out, and he needed his co-operation on this trip. He was now feeling hungry, so headed back for a hearty breakfast.

TWENTY-ONE

Ubba intended to speak privately to Sigurd and ask him about his life, as he was fascinated that Sigurd's own attempt to remain a farmer had been derailed. Was he another reluctant king, forced into the limelight due to his bloodline? He asked if anybody had seen Sigurd at breakfast and nobody had. He decided to go and try his room. He knocked on the door and just as he was about to leave, Sigurd opened it wearing just his breeches. 'Oh, it's you Ubba.'

'Sorry, have I just woken you up? Are you still catching up on your sleep?'

Sigurd reddened slightly. 'Not exactly, but come in.'

Ubba walked in to see a woman hastily dressing at the side of the bed. She came quickly past him to the door and scurried out.

'I'm sorry, have I interrupted something?'

'No, I was just enjoying the gift Rollo sent me. He asked me if I needed someone to keep me company at night and when she turned up, I thought it would be rude to my host to turn her away.'

Ubba laughed. 'You thought it was some French tradition, did you?'

'Sort of! I think Rollo thought as I hadn't brought my wife, I perhaps needed some entertainment. Truth is, she would not have joined me even if I had received more notice. Maria is not interested in being a queen; she was brought up on a farm and has no desire to have power or authority. She was horrified when I ended up becoming King, and devoted as she is to me and our five children, she would not have contemplated setting foot on a longboat and travelling to Frankia.'

'I just wanted to chat to you before we go to Haesten's. Come on; let's get some breakfast and then we will find a quiet spot.'

They went down to the dining room and the tables were being cleared. Ubba apologised profusely and charmed the female servants into making them whatever they wanted. Not many women could resist one handsome Ragnarsson, let alone two. Ubba had a coffee and croissant, whilst Sigurd waded through a plate of eggs, bacon, fried potatoes, mushrooms and three thick slices of bread. Sigurd was not talking until his hunger was sated. Ubba searched his pockets for some silver coins with Rollo's head on them, which he had given him. When Sigurd had finished, he gave the girl who had attended them two of the coins and she was delighted. Ubba chuckled as they left the dining room; he had no idea how much money they represented.

The sun was getting hot and Ubba suggested they sit in the shaded rose garden. Sigurd relaxed and started to tell his story. He had stumbled on Zealand by accident when he was travelling, and was able to use silver to purchase a large farmstead, which had very fertile land. He had started with a mixed farm breeding cattle, sheep and horses. He also produced wheat, oats and plenty of hay to feed his stock over winter. Maria was the eldest daughter of a neighbouring farmer and they soon married. They had three daughters: Alof, Tora and Aslaug, and two sons: Helgi and Harthacnut.

Ubba asked, 'You named a daughter after our mother. Why?'

'Only because she has red hair and green eyes like mother, and the same facial features. Alof was born blonde, but went darker as she aged. Tora was blonde from birth. Aslaug has rich chestnut hair and although I should not admit it, she became my favourite child.'

Sigurd explained that everything had been rosy for 10 years and then raiders from Germany were starting to raid in an attempt to conquer their fertile land. At a public meeting called to prevent the invasion, Sigurd suggested their only chance of survival was to unite with Scania and Halland to fight them off. This propelled him into the limelight and he led Zealand into battle. When they succeeded, he was elected King of Zealand. Like his father before him, his life changed dramatically and he began to consider the burden of being King overwhelming.

Ubba exclaimed, 'Well, I saw it happen firsthand with our father. Do you remember when he came back to Jormund after disappearing for the winter and demanding, "Who wants to be King?" Bjorn was already away raiding in the Mediterranean and I was the eldest son left. My head was hammering with the response, "Please God, not me!" But then the burden of our lineage tightened its knot. Thankfully,

Ivar agreed to sail back to Northumbria with him. I felt torn in half, but he told me to stay and defend Jormund, which I was more than happy to do.'

Sigurd said, 'You, me and Father must have soil rather than blood in our veins.'

'Undoubtedly, but neither do I have the sea in my blood. Look at Bjorn, Erik and Refil; they would rather be on the sea than on land. They have that insatiable desire to discover new land and conquer it. I would rather be in a nice warm bed with my wife than rolling around a longboat in a storm. There's one big plus about Alfred's united England. You can navigate its rivers without having to face the North or Irish seas. I lose my sense of balance when it gets rough. Refil and Erik want to cross the Atlantic, exploring. I think I would rather die first.'

Sigurd laughed. 'I am not too bad on the sea, but I don't think I could do it permanently. I love your honesty, Ubba; if only Ivar had been the same, things might have been so different. Rollo told me you only became the warrior you did out of fear of failure and because of having a low pain threshold. Your recent study of the Christian faith has also made you more tolerant of the Saxons' views.'

'Well, the Saxons were a peaceful nation tolerant of outsiders, until we came along and robbed them of their land, possessions and women.'

'But we were short of women too, Ubba. When men are regarded as superior to women then you are always going to have a shortage of women. Whenever there was famine or drought, it was female babies that were discarded when food was scarce. It was only when we started raiding that we lost considerable numbers of men. If we made it back at all, there were always women left without husbands after that.'

'Yes, I know, but surviving warriors took over the responsibility of their wives and children when they returned home, because we were all part of the same community.' Ubba tentatively asked, 'Is your relationship still strong with your wife?'

Sigurd sighed. 'I still respect her and she is a brilliant mother, but as my children have grown up and left home, our relationship has cooled, particularly since I became King. I regret to say I am like Father; when I see a woman I fancy, I have to have her. I have seen your relationship with Torri and it is incredible. You have an invisible bond, which ties you together and your love for each other radiates around the room. You have produced two very different sons, but both will make you proud. Viggo seems to have inherited the explorer gene and Arne has our connection to the land and nature. Your daughter Freya is stunningly beautiful and a lot wiser than her age would suggest.'

'Ah, Freya is my shining light, but I have to keep her surrounded by guards to fend off other men. This European insistence that royal wives have to be virgins is ridiculous. On the one hand they want virgin brides, but on the other they want them to be good breeders. How can you possibly reconcile that? They even want young princes to have sired a child to prove that they are fertile.'

Sigurd laughed. 'Oh come on, Ubba; if some male

lured your daughter into bed you would chop him into pieces. I have the same problem with Aslaug; she is in no rush to embrace marriage or motherhood and I have had to decline her hand in marriage to several suitable matches as she insists she will choose her own husband. But can we honestly trust immature girls to select the right partner for life?'

'Well, I know a twelve-year-old boy who fell in love with a beautiful woman carrying a baby, whose husband my father blood eagled right in front of her. I had to wait patiently for 10 years, while she had a short relationship with my father and then married my older brother and had two more sons.'

'Oh, Ubba it just shows your compassion, sympathy and resilience that you could win her without upsetting Bjorn and causing family friction.'

'I would never have made a move on Torri. Bjorn supported me and helped me become a reasonable warrior, but even he didn't know that I did it out of fear of failure and torture. My greatest fear when we were after King Aelle was Bjorn being killed, as that horrific task would have fallen to me. When I told Halfdan recently he said I should have told him because he would have had no qualms about doing it and neither would Ivar. Would you have been able to do it?'

'Probably not. Like you, I am not generally a hot-tempered violent man who enjoys inflicting pain on man or beast. Neither was our father, but he had to overcome that when he became King, just as I am discovering now. Thankfully, my son Harthacnut has all Ivar's political prowess and evil ways of achieving his own ends. He is clever and when he does something bad, he can always talk his way out of it.'

'Sounds like Haesten, who you have to admire for instigating battles but always having his own personal exit strategy and getting away from danger every time. I thought of him when I devised our escape from Jorvik. It relied on my best friend Ralf impersonating me and could have led to his death had it backfired. I am looking forward to seeing Haesten again, although he was never to be trusted. He would have sold his own mother into slavery if he had the chance.'

As they left the garden, they encountered Rollo and William arguing. It appeared the cause was William wanting to take a troop of warriors with them to visit Haesten, for security.

Rollo roared, 'Have you gone mad, son? We are at peace. What idiot would attack me as ruling Duc of Normandie, as well as three direct sons of Ragnar, four grandsons, a granddaughter with her own bodyguards, and one of the most famous shieldmaidens? We are going on a private visit to Haesten across open countryside, not forming a war band. My men should be out haymaking like everyone else in Frankia.'

William was furious, especially as Ubba and Sigurd had witnessed the exchange. He exploded, 'Very well Father, but don't blame me if we are attacked. Rumour will have spread now that Bjorn Ironside is here, and you never know; somebody may think it worth kidnapping or killing him.'

Rollo laughed. 'The only person who may have contemplated that is Haesten and he is not in any condition to take on Bjorn, never mind the rest of us. You have had somebody protecting your arse since you were born. You have never faced battles like my family have fought in the last 30 years on both land and sea. They are capable of taking on armies that outnumber them 20 to 1 and still winning. I fought the Saxons with Ragnar, Bjorn, Ubba, Floki and Halfdan at my side with 20 men and wiped out an entire army. You would not last a minute facing one of them, so until you have mastered the sword, axe, seax, bow and arrow as well as them, don't argue with me!'

William flounced off.

Rollo turned to the others. 'I am sorry you had to witness that. I should be able to control my temper with my son at my age.'

Ubba responded quickly, 'Oh Rollo, I have been close to strangling Arne many times. They just have this superior attitude, thinking they know it all. The number of good hidings he received as a boy, but when they get to 18 and give you cheek, there's not a lot you can do even though you feel like running them through with a sword. I loved your response to him. I bet it never even crossed your mind about taking armed guards. Don't worry; I told Arne to put shields on a pack horse just in case.'

They all had a hearty laugh at the joy of rearing sons and remembering the beatings they'd had off both parents when they were growing up.

Sigurd said, 'When Harthacnut was a lad, he got so angry we had to lock him in a stable until he calmed down, just like Mother did with Ivar as a boy. He would smash an entire room up if he didn't get his own way. He was so volatile and stubborn, and hated being reprimanded. He is 16 now, going through puberty and discovering women for the first time. He hardly acknowledges my existence and if you try to advise him about sex, he bolts. They don't think we should still be indulging in it at our age.'

Ubba confessed, 'Viggo sired his first child at 12 years old, to one of my warriors' wives. Another reason we sent him to Ireland with Ivar. Don't tell Bjorn, as he thinks Refil's son is Torri's first grandchild.'

Rollo and Sigurd roared with laughter.

Rollo asked, 'So how many children have you sired?'

'I have no idea. Ivar used to keep a record. I discovered a list in his desk headed, "Possible Ubba progeny". He was always encouraging me to breed my own army of little Ubbas. He once asked me to sire one for him with one of his favourite girls.'

Sigurd was shocked. 'What did you say?'

Ubba grinned. 'I didn't say anything. I threw a seax at him and pinned him up against a wooden beam by his ear. Those were the days when my throwing speed and accuracy were 100%. Needless to say, he got the message.'

Sigurd replied, 'But I thought Ivar was only interested in virgins, even though he cannot reproduce with them? He just enjoys teaching them how to keep a man happy.'

Ubba answered, 'Look, I have had the pleasure of several women that Ivar taught and believe me, they are all wonderful in bed. Furthermore, they all adore him and say he never harmed or forced them. He is not the devil people think. It is a crying shame he could not reproduce because potentially, he would have been a great father. He has always had a special relationship with Viggo; they bonded over his raptors. He took his gyrfalcons and eagles to Ireland with him and they are breeding well, despite the constant wind and rain. As a boy, he befriended wild sea eagles, which he taught to fish for him. They were totally free to come and go as they pleased. It was his diligent observation of bird migration that convinced Viggo that if geese can migrate to Yorkshire from the West then there must be land close enough to Iceland to warrant them coming over.'

Rollo asked, 'How did you cope with Ivar as King? He must have been a bastard to work for?'

'No, I only became commander of his troops on my terms. He had his own personal bodyguard of eight men, but even they were under my command. There was no way Ivar was interfering with their training or their loyalty to me. I worked them hard, but they appreciated my efforts and would follow me to hell and back. I insisted on implementing some rules, which Ivar did not approve of and I don't think you would, Rollo.'

'Such as?'

'I forbade any raping of women, hostages or children when on raids. Two men failed to take me seriously. I caught them in the act and then beheaded them in front of the entire troop.'

Sigurd exclaimed, 'Wow, Ubba; that's enforcing

discipline.'

'I have been referred to as a champion of women and you would be surprised to hear that Ivar eventually supported my stance. I also banned the use of sharpened poles hidden under grass to lure warriors into falling into ditches and being impaled – thereby preventing the death of noble horses. They have no choice but to do their masters' bidding, but I will not have them give their lives in that way, whether they are ours or the enemy's. I also ensure that after the battle, mortally wounded horses and men are quickly despatched, not left to suffer for hours before they die. Also, the bodies of our enemies should be dealt with according to their religious beliefs. Moslems and Jews insist on burial within 48 hours of death.'

Sigurd clapped. 'Oh Ubba, I am so proud of you for protecting the horses. It was always an act I deplored. Our father would have been so proud of you!'

Rollo patted him on the shoulder. 'Ragnar would have been very proud of you, Ubba. You may have been a reluctant king, but you have proved you were the ultimate warrior, a man of honour and a friend to all.'

TWENTY-TWO

The courtyard filled up with excited horses, grooms and men preparing for their visit to Haesten.

Arne jumped off his horse and ran up the steps to his mother and Freya. 'Come, you two; I have found you the perfect horses.' He pointed to the groom leading a palomino Palfrey very similar to the mare Blondie, whom Torri had in Jorvik. On his other side, he was leading a skittish Arab grey filly for Freya. Both horses were wearing normal saddles, not side saddles, as Arne knew both of them would want to ride astride.

Ubba had been admiring Rollo's Percheron stallion, who looked sharp and fit. He noted how calm he was surveying the scene around him. They suited the heavier built Danes as they could cope with the weight over long distances. They did not have a great deal of speed, but were excellent mounts on the battlefield. He looked down into the courtyard and spotted the palomino straight away, and Arne legging Torri up. He then saw the young Arab filly and hoped Freya would cope with it.

Bjorn and Erik were presented with Percheron stallions, and Refil and Sigurd a more athletic Percheron-cross Spanish type. He saw a groom approaching with Diablo, who was wearing a bridle with a jointed bit and a lightweight saddle. He went and made a fuss of him, and told him he had better be on his best behaviour. As he mounted and was made to stand still, Diablo was anxious to get going. Ubba rubbed his neck and held him in halt with his legs, deliberately not taking a strong contact on the bit.

Eventually, the grooms and pack horses were brought down and Rollo led them out of the courtyard. He spotted Arne, Thorin, Matteo, Keir and Egil riding in a group with Freya and Torri in the middle.

Most of the horses were probably anticipating a hunting session rather than a 20-mile ride. Bjorn waved Ubba over to join him and he hoped Diablo knew how to behave in other stallions' company, as if not, he knew it could prove an exciting experience for all of them. Satisfied his family was well protected, he trotted over to Bjorn and apart from a slight snort and a twitch of an ear, Diablo settled next to the Percheron stallion quite contentedly. They moved out of earshot of the group.

Bjorn said, 'Christ, he is a flashy mover. How did you manage to bag him?'

Ubba told him about what had transpired.

Bjorn laughed. 'So, not the best introduction to the heir apparent of Normandie, then. That will have pissed him off! Watch your back, Ubba; I hear he is good with a longsword.'

Ubba smiled. 'I am faster and more accurate with a seax than he is. I have already beaten him at that, too. You and I haven't had much chance to talk privately yet, but you and your sons look hale and hearty. They certainly intend to go for broke and be first to cross the Atlantic. I feel seasick just imagining it; rest assured I will be in no hurry to follow them.'

Bjorn grunted, 'To be honest, neither will I. I admit I am too old to take that trial on, even though I am an experienced sailor. It worries me; I could lose both of them at once and not even know how, where or why.'

'Bjorn, it would scare the hell out of me too, but you have to let them forge their own paths. Torri is feeling just the same with Viggo going east, but he does have a survivor's head on him; he has done from a boy.'

'Freya was only around ten when I last saw her, but what a stunner she is now.'

'That's why she has her own bodyguards to protect her from men.'

Bjorn laughed. 'If you take my advice, you need to double them. Remember what you and I were like, chasing women as teenagers. We have our father's gift of being able to charm the ladies into our beds with just our eyes. Can you guarantee she won't let her head be turned by a persistent charming man? The Italian lad, is he really her betrothed? And can you trust Thorin not to step over the line?'

'Thorin would never do that; he knows that he has to protect her at all times. They have grown up together like brother and sister and there is no way Thorin will touch her, or she him. I purposely used young Matteo as a front. He is not a prince, but the son of a gardener who designs palatial gardens for royalty in Italy. His family moved to Yorkshire last year and

I employed him to assist Torri in her new passion for gardening. He is here to collect plants to take home – in particular, roses.'

'But aren't you concerned he may want to do more than gardening with Torri? Age has done little to diminish her beauty; in fact, she looks perfectly happy and content being away from court intrigue.'

'You may rest assured I gave her strict instructions to do whatever she wants with him, including having him in her bed. I think she deserves to have a fling with a young Italian stallion to make her feel young again.'

'You seriously told her to do that? Has she succumbed?'

'I don't know. I gave them plenty of opportunity to get close and I really don't mind. I just want her to be happy.'

'Well, if you wanted her to do it then you should have used an entirely different strategy. You should have employed him as a gardener but told her that there was to be no going any further. Then she would have done it deliberately, because she would not tolerate you forbidding her. You forget that Torri loves you and tolerates your mistress and second family because of that. You are her golden boy Ubba, and yet she would not tolerate my infidelity.'

'Look, she has had a tough ride this last six months; we both feared she might have been failing. Thankfully, Sulamain was able to put our minds at rest and removed a lump, which proved to be benign. I was so delighted and just wanted to make her celebrate a reprieve. I know that she will likely die before me, and it was so hard coming to terms with that, as I thoroughly expected to die in Jorvik.'

Bjorn replied, 'So Sulamain has saved both Torri and me from an early demise. I treasure every moment I have now. I have a special woman in my life and I try to remain faithful. I haven't married again, as I don't need any more offspring. Like you, there are plenty around. I am determined to eventually become King of Norway, but since they turned me down and my sons are departing west, I will have to try and juggle both Sweden and Norway.'

They were now out of the forest and in open country. Rollo decided they would have a sedate canter now there was more room. Diablo had spotted the horses in front speeding up, so he leapt into the air, bucked with delight and for a moment Ubba thought he might even be airborne. He soon had him back under control. They cantered on until they saw a village and started to walk. The whole village was out helping in the fields to make hay, and they passed farm carts laden with stooks of fresh smelling hay. They stopped at the drinking trough in the village centre to water the horses and have a break from being in the saddle. He checked that Freya was surrounded by her team of young men, as several of the farm labourers were admiringly pointing her out.

Rollo and William were chatting to some of the villagers, who were intrigued to know who they were. Rollo told them they were his Danish relatives come to visit. Soon, Ubba heard whispers and noted that himself and Bjorn were being discussed. He was relieved that he could understand enough French to get by, and wondered whether Haesten had mastered the language. He had a cool drink from the trough and then took off his light cloak as it was now approaching midday. He tied it to his saddle. He would not need it now, as the sun was hotting up and there was no breeze.

Rollo ordered a remount and they set off at a steady walking pace. Refil came to join Ubba and they chatted about life in general, and the trials and tribulations Refil would face on his next expedition. Torri joined them, much to Diablo's delight, as he had a very soft spot for the mare she was riding. He tried to get close enough to touch her, but Ubba was on his case immediately.

They rode through idyllic countryside and cool forests until early evening. Rollo decided to use a sheltered field that had been recently cut, to make their camp for the night. Thorin and Arne had spotted some young bucks in the last plantation and asked him if they could go back and try to hunt one as a present for their host. Rollo had no objection and so they departed with their bows and arrows, intending to stalk. They took a spare horse to transport any kill.

Grooms had set up hitching lines for the horses, defined by sex. Mares and geldings could be tethered together provided the mare was not in season. The stallions were kept together but given more room in case a disagreement broke out.

Freya was not in the least bit worried that the boys

had gone. She was attending to her own mare and had taken Torri's too, untacking them, tying them up and fetching water from the small stream that was running through the field. As she came back from the stream and passed a tree, a hand shot out and pinched her bottom. She swung round and threw the water over the perpetrator in one fluid movement.

William was spluttering and coughing as the water ran down his face and arms, and his temper was rising.

'How dare you touch me. I might have expected that behaviour from a groom or my younger siblings, but not from a prince. Don't get angry with me; you deserved a good soaking. Whatever made you do such a ridiculous thing?' She grabbed the bucket and returned to the stream. Luckily, nobody else had witnessed the scene.

William followed her, desperately trying to fabricate a reason for his stupidity. He had expected her to welcome his attention, not throw a bucket of water over his head! He was going to have to apologise, and quickly, before she did it again. 'I am sorry, Freya. It was very childish of me, and certainly out of character for a prince.'

Freya snapped back at him, 'No, William – you were hoping for the response that you normally receive when chasing young women. You expected me to welcome your attention with open arms and even encourage you to go further. Now get out of my way, unless you want another bucket in your face; my horse needs water.' She gave him one of her mother's icy stares and stormed off.

She watered and brushed over the two mares and then went to join her mother to help with the food. One of the grooms had been and fed all the horses on the tether, and put out portions of hay for each horse to eat overnight.

She joined her mother and father who were putting out cooked hams, pheasant and salmon, along with beetroot and lettuce for dinner, using a large boulder as a table with a blanket for a tablecloth. There was ample fresh fruit for pudding. Rollo appeared with a crate of red wine and gave Ubba a bottle, then he went to find the mead, and horns to drink from. Everybody helped themselves and sat around on the grass in small groups eating.

Thorin and Arne returned in triumph, having killed a young buck to give to Haesten. They were hungry and ready for their meal.

As darkness fell, a campfire was lit and they all enjoyed chatting and being out in the balmy July evening.

William kept well out of Freya's way, concerned that she might tell her mother or her brother about his childish prank, which would have yet again made him a laughing stock with his Danish cousins.

They all had a wonderful raucous evening, but by 11.00 pm they were ready for their night under the stars. Ubba ensured that Freya bedded down close to them. There was no way anybody was going to come close enough to ravage his daughter (or wife, for that matter). They were the only females present.

As he and Torri snuggled down on their makeshift

bed, semi-clothed, Torri whimpered, 'Ubba, can you remove your belt? I can feel your seax right up against my backside.'

Ubba laughed. 'Lucky seax!'

She responded vehemently, 'Don't even think about it; behave yourself, or else I will use the damn seax to remove body parts you may miss!'

TWENTY-THREE

Ubba was woken at dawn by horses whinnying for their feeds as the grooms distributed them. He had thoroughly enjoyed connecting with nature again and as he flexed his leg muscles, he was surprised he had no pain as it was a long time since he had spent eight hours in the saddle. Torri was still fast asleep with his body curled around her. She stirred and he kissed the nape of her neck, and let his hands caress her breasts even though she still had her chemise on. She wriggled and turned round quickly, shaking her finger in his face. 'Stop it, Ubba! the entire camp will be up and wanting their breakfast soon. Get up and build a fire, and put the water on for boiling.'

I would much rather ravish you right here and now. Egil will already have the fire burning. I have a much hotter fire burning – for your body.' He pinned her arms to the ground and tried to kiss her. She struggled and bit him on the chest through his shirt.

'Ow, you little vixen; that hurt.'

'I will not be having sex with you for all of your kin to witness.'

'Whyever not? Our children have witnessed several illicit couplings over the years; they won't bat an eyelid. My brothers Bjorn and Sigurd would be cheering me on, as would Rollo. I don't give a damn who sees me humping my wife and declaring to the world that you are mine and mine alone.'

Fearing that Ubba may still be drunk and intending to carry out this fantasy, she retorted, 'Well, I will not partake in such wicked behaviour. Let me get up or you will live to regret it.'

He released her, laughing. 'You actually believed I may carry out my threat. Go and tend to feeding me, wench, if you won't let me have your body.'

She pulled on her shirt and breeches. 'I will see you suffer for this later, my dear. Watch your back!' She gave him a death stare, but when she turned away, she was laughing. She would carry out her threat, but she would wait until he had forgotten. Women know how to bide their time to get the better of their husbands.

Ubba dressed and made his way down to the stream to wash. Bjorn was there too and they agreed they had both enjoyed a night under the stars. He could not resist telling him what had transpired with Torri and he was quite concerned. 'Are you mad, Ubba? She will catch you when you least suspect it – and boy, will it hurt.'

Breakfast was in full swing, with hot bacon rolls and coffee being handed out by Ubba, Torri and Freya as each rider came forward. Arne was on the horse lines ensuring the grooms cleared up any hay on the ground, collected up water and feed buckets and as the group remounted, he dismantled the tethering lines. Arne was also ensuring that they left the field in the condition they had found it, which was a custom always followed in respect of using other people's land. As they started to move off, all that was visible was the blackened grass where the campfire had been lit, which was now thoroughly out.

They expected to arrive late that afternoon, travelling at a leisurely pace. Bjorn commented that he could smell the sea already. Ubba was thankful they were not sailing on it.

Torri and Freya were riding together. There was a sufficient gap in the line for them to have a private conversation.

'Mama, can you give me some advice as to how to respond politely when men attempt to impose themselves on me?'

Torri laughed. 'It depends how persistent they are, and whether you welcome their attention or not.'

'Mama, I am not talking about a young lad with a crush on me. I mean how should I deal with older men who should not be flirting with me at all?'

Torri looked concerned. 'Have you had someone bothering you recently? I thought you had been escorted by Thorin and Arne in public.'

'Yes, I have, but they cannot be my side every minute of every day. I am not revealing who it is because I do not want to cause any trouble. Nothing has happened, but I just felt intimidated.'

'Well, my best advice for dealing with older men who should know better is to humiliate them if they say or do something offensive. Any attempt to touch or kiss you must be dealt with promptly. You have grown up with big brothers, whom you have fought with when necessary. If this approach does not work then you will have to use your seax or dagger, which should be with you at all times. A well-aimed kick in a vulnerable spot should give you time to run away if he attempts to use force, but if you are restrained in any way use your nails, teeth or anything you can reach that may knock him out. You must scream as well, as that will bring help if there is anybody in the vicinity.

'If you are restrained I have to warn you that resisting could make matters worse. A man intent on raping a girl will do the deed but then may kill her to prevent her telling anybody. If you are submissive, you may have an opportunity to break free after the attack: if he thinks he can keep doing it, he may not kill you.

'Do you remember when Skye was kidnapped by Kalen, and Viggo told her that if he came to take her to his bed during the night then she must let him, because she was already carrying Sigtryggr's baby? If she had fought him, both of them could have died.'

'Mother, I don't think I could succumb to being raped. It's my body; how dare a man think he can do what he wants with me just because I am a woman.'

'I completely sympathise with you, but it all depends on the situation. When I was kidnapped from Jorvik I had Arne with me and he was around 12 years old at the time. My captors threatened to bring him into the cabin to watch me being raped and I could not put him through that. Thankfully, your father's timely intervention with a seax in the aggressor's back prevented him succeeding. However, I insisted on killing him and castrating him myself.'

'Mama, I will be careful. I know how dangerous men can be. I am a fair judge of situations, like Viggo, and I will value life over death.'

'Sweetheart, I won't mention this conversation to your father, but you must never be alone with a man. You must keep Thorin at your side and depending on the sleeping arrangements at Haesten's, you may have to sleep in the same room as Thorin and Arne or your father and me. Haesten is not to be trusted and there will be other Danes who will be attracted to you. Stay close to me and your father at all times.'

They came to open country and Rollo halted the troop. 'Those who wish to go across country and are capable of jumping walls, streams and fences may take the scenic route. The rest may follow me on this track, which goes through a shaded forest. We shall meet up in a couple of hours at Harfleur and from there, we only have 30 minutes' ride to Haesten's farm.'

After much discussion the experienced rider group consisted of Ubba, Bjorn, Arne, Erik, Refil, Thorin, Matteo, Sigurd, William and two scouts. As they turned into a mown hay field, the boundaries were solid 3 foot 6 inch walls. Rollo realised those left would want to see if they all survived their first test, and they ventured into the field to watch.

Freya had wanted to go with the lads, but one look from her mother put paid to that idea. She knew her palfrey was only young and may not have been taught to jump anyway, so she did not argue. William's scouts galloped over to the far wall to find the best spot to jump over and check the landing side. The group cantered over and waited patiently for the order to go. All the horses sensed the excitement of their riders and started to prance and jib.

They lined up with the most experienced riders at the front. Ubba and Bjorn were to be the leaders. Ubba was relieved that he had Diablo under control and he hoped he had been jumped before. Bjorn was on a Percheron stallion, who knew his job well. They kept six feet apart from each other and Ubba told Bjorn to go slightly ahead of him. Arne and Thorin were to keep a good gap before following them. They set off and Diablo was bucking, trying to snatch for his head and go at his own pace, but Ubba was not allowing him to win. Bjorn's experienced stallion took off correctly and leapt over, leaving plenty of air. Diablo had Ubba placing him in exactly the right spot to achieve the best landing. He tucked his front legs up and basculed at the perfect angle, and the landing was on firm grass.

Arne and Thorin were in high spirits and competing against each other to be the first to land. Arne won. Erik and Refil did the same and Refil won. Matteo and Sigurd came next, at a more leisurely pace. William and the two scouts then followed and the group moved on.

The two groups met up in Harfleur as planned. The only casualty was Refil, whose horse had stopped dead and spun round on take-off when he saw a stream on the landing side. However, he was unhurt apart from a few scratches.

They were soon at Haesten's farm. It was a typical longhouse construction, but without the need for animals to be accommodated within. There was wooden decking and steps overlooking the yard and drive. Haesten was there to greet them, sitting on a long bench and looking as imposing as ever, but his hair and beard were totally grey now. As he stood up, he used a strong wooden staff to support him.

He stared down at them and addressed Rollo first. 'Welcome, my compatriots, and what a sight I behold: an entire Ragnarsson dynasty before me. Rollo, get them into family groups and introduce them to me.'

They all manoeuvred into some semblance of order and Rollo introduced Bjorn's family first.

'Bjorn Ironside, you look amazing, and these two sons are I believe planning to explore the Northwest Passage. Shame you got beaten by Olaf in the election for King of Norway.'

Bjorn laughed. 'Trust you to mention it, Haesten. I have settled for King of Sweden for now, but I haven't forgotten Norway. I will rule it one day, have no fear.'

Haesten studied each of Ubba's children intently, and his eyes lit up briefly when he saw Freya. 'You stamp your stock well, Ubba – in the image of your father. Where are the rest of your offspring? Aren't half the Danes in Northumbria reported to have been sired by you? But then, you had Torri to breed these excellent Danes and if you can produce girls as pretty as Freya then no wonder you are in demand as a stallion.'

Ubba laughed. 'I left my second family at home and my son Viggo has set off to explore the East as it appears he inherited the explorer gene. I also extend Halfdan's greetings and apologies for not coming, but he is about to make his claim for Durham soon, so he is rather preoccupied at present.'

When Sigurd was introduced, Haesten commented, 'I was looking at you and convinced you must be a bastard son of Ubba. I have never met you in person. So you tried to become a simple Dane farmer and ended up King of Zealand. Quite amazing! You Ragnarssons cannot escape the expectation of your lineage.'

They all joined Haesten in the airy longhouse for cool drinks after their hot journey. Haesten was sitting opposite Torri and Ubba, and he seemed to be paying her a lot of attention.

Ubba said, 'You seem to be enamoured of my wife, Haesten. I hope you aren't falling in love with her, as it will be a road to disaster. She has my name imprinted on her heart, as I have hers on mine.'

'Oh, don't worry Ubba; I was just admiring her and marvelling at how she has produced a dynasty of exceptional heirs.'

'We all appreciate that; Ivar most of all. He is devoted to her and has ensured all her children have been educated ready to fly the nest.'

'How is Ivar coping in Ireland? I hear it's a totally different lifestyle and country compared to Jorvik.'

'Well, as Dublin is such a big trading centre it is possible to import materials from all around Europe. Sigtryggr has built a marble palace in the bay of Dublin, as resplendent as any palace in Italy, with underfloor heating to keep my little brother warm. He swears it rains every day over there, but it also has the most perfect limestone soil for producing top quality grass.'

'Do you miss Jorvik, Ubba?'

'I miss commanding the troops at times, and the camaraderie… but I don't miss the fights, the early mornings, organising training schedules and the responsibility. I enjoy having time with my family and farming. It is very satisfying planning breeding programmes and achieving the results you want. You must enjoy your farming activities, too. You are in a prime location. I love the fact you stuck to your roots and built a traditional longhouse.'

Haesten chuckled. 'Yes, the land is good and the climate better than most. I do enjoy breeding Percherons, and the local Camargue horses make good riding types for this terrain. I will show you around in the morning.'

There were few individual rooms as most of the bedroom accommodation was split into male/female dormitories. There were three guest bedrooms containing a large double and two singles. One was allocated to Rollo and William, one to Bjorn and his sons, the other to Ubba and Torri. This meant Freya was in their room for the duration, which Ubba was quite content with as she would be safe. He chuckled to himself when he saw the look of anger flash across her face, and gave her a raised eyebrow, daring her to object. For once, she kept quiet.

o0o

The next day after breakfast, Haesten showed Rollo, Ubba, Arne, Freya, Thorin, Matteo and Sigurd around the barns and sent his head groom out into the fields to show them the mares, foals and youngstock. Ubba was impressed with the quality of the stock. Rollo was his main customer as he used the purebreds in the field and then used the crossbreds as saddle horses.

When they saw the Camargue horses Ubba commented that they were very similar in height, bone structure and colour to the Irish Draught horses he had seen in Ireland. Light enough to produce some speed under saddle, but with enough strength to work in the field, too. Haesten explained that their natural habitat was low grassland, which was often flooded in the winter. They proved excellent at swimming and coped well in muddy terrain. As cattle herders they were excellent and used to driving through rivers, lakes and marshes. They were brave enough to take on bulls if necessary, despite their small size. They were natural sailors when transported by boat and showed no fear in stormy weather, even on the sea.

Rollo engineered a private chat with Ubba and told him that Diablo would be going home with him to Yorkshire. William had agreed that he should be with an experienced rider so that his full potential could be reached. Whether this was intended to appease Ubba or Freya was unclear. However, Ubba was delighted as Diablo would produce some excellent stock as well as being an asset in battle. If Arne behaved himself he may find Diablo was his, but he needed to learn how to ride him first. He discussed with Rollo about purchasing a young Percheron colt from him and offered to pay for Diablo too. Rollo said Diablo was a gift from him to Ubba and he would not take any money at all.

Ubba contemplated that as he had achieved his purchase of a stallion, he did not need to venture on to Spain now. The two horses would keep each other company as they crossed the Channel back home and depending on whether they were happy on board, he would decide whether they went inland to Repton and north by river, or travelled north by sea to Hull and then up the Ouse. Conscious that Torri wanted to purchase roses and vegetables to grow in her garden, he asked Rollo to advise on how they could obtain them more locally. He promised to look into it.

TWENTY-FOUR

The next day, Bjorn and Erik wanted to have a meeting with all the men to discuss their plans for the design of the boat to tackle the Northwest Passage and ask seasoned sailors what their recommendations were for exploring beyond Iceland. Erik and Refil planned to visit Le Havre early in the morning to look round the port and then have the meeting from 3.00 pm when they returned. Anybody who wanted to go with them was welcome to. Torri suggested that she and Freya went too, to look round some of the shops. Ubba commented that he would accompany them as their escort and paymaster. Freya noted that William had originally declined to come, but when he heard she was going, he changed his mind. She hoped that the presence of her father would keep him away.

It was a beautiful day, warm and sunny but with a slight cool breeze, which was perfect for riding. Freya was pleased she was on the palomino palfrey. Ubba had Diablo, who was feeling fresh and cheeky and wanted to be close to Freya's mare.

Ubba laughed. 'I am the boss here now; you go where I say, not where you want, young man!'

Bjorn was riding behind and overheard him. 'Do you always talk to your horses, Ubba?'

'Yes, of course! My voice is an aid as much as my legs. When I need to react quickly to something my horse does, he soon knows by the tone of my voice whether he is in trouble or not. Sometimes you have to coax them past objects they have never met before. An encouraging voice backed up with a pat on the neck is my first reaction.'

'What has he done wrong?'

'Oh, he just fancies Freya's mare and was hesitant to leave her side, so I put him right and told him I'm the boss. In a powerful stallion like him, if you can correct him quickly before he misbehaves, you save yourself a fight. Basically, the rider must always win, but talking to them often prevents an adverse reaction from the horse. Horses broken by me rarely become difficult or dangerous because I never let them use their strength against the rider. Diablo had been suffering pain for too long from a severe bit and heavy hands. I have already taught him that I will never hurt his mouth, and now he trusts me.'

'Are your young children as well behaved as your horse?'

Ubba laughed. 'If only, Bjorn, then life would be so much easier. I seem to be regarded as an easy target for my daughters to coax to have their own way. My sons see me as someone to attack before I can criticise them. Arne and I are too alike in temperament and Viggo has inherited Ivar's brain and temperament and thinks my opinion counts for nothing.'

'Well, I know exactly what you mean about sons. Erik can be very dismissive of my opinions, but Refil is less arrogant.'

'I think Refil is the most grounded and happiest person when he is at one with the sea. Just like when I am on horseback. He just wants to live a harmonious life. The task he has set himself is overwhelming, but with Erik by his side I can see them achieving their goal.'

'Let's hope so or I could lose both my heirs at once. I know Torri is very conscious of that; she fears for their lives.'

'Well of course she will! She is their mother – and don't think age makes any difference to how a mother feels. The fact they have been away from her does not stop her thinking about them.'

William thought he could take advantage of Ubba riding with Bjorn to get closer to Freya. However, Thorin had seen him attempt to make his move and had deliberately come to her side. Matteo had followed on her other side. God dammit, he would love to have beheaded both of them! He was furious at their obvious intervention.

He contemplated why he was so enamoured of his cousin. Dismissing the fact that she was stunning and so very different in every way from Frankian women, he just found her intriguing, mystifying, unorthodox and so totally dismissive of him that it hurt. Ever since she had arrived, he had dreamt every night about her and felt like a teenager again, with an embarrassing crush on her. Could it be as simple as opposites attracting?

He did not realise that his father had been observing

him and suddenly appeared at his side. 'William, forget it; Freya is linked to the gods and her destiny will be decided by them. Do not try and intervene, or your destiny may be lost. Thorin would kill you and so would her father.'

He was so angry he replied, 'What a load of rubbish you spout – and you are supposed to be a reformed Catholic now, not a Norseman.' He wheeled his horse away and cantered off with a face as black as thunder.

Rollo saw that Thorin had witnessed their argument. He sighed, knowing that William was as hot headed as he himself had been in his youth when he fell for a woman. Hopefully, Freya would be returning home shortly, but would he back off in the meantime? There was a farewell party being held on Saturday after they returned from Haesten's, and he decided to keep a careful watch on his son until Freya had left.

They arrived in Le Havre, where a local ostler was proud to have the privilege of stabling their fine horses. William cleverly approached Torri and suggested he show them around the town as he knew what goods were available where. He was slightly nonplussed that Ubba was going to be with them as well, as this would make it harder still to get Freya on her own. The others set off towards the docks as he enquired of Torri as to what sort of things she was looking for whilst they took refreshment from a local hostelry.

Freya was somewhat amused by William's desire to get close to her, and his obvious disappointment that Ubba was also accompanying them. They headed off to a dress shop where he knew his own mother had bought outfits for his sisters. Ubba said he would wait outside and enjoy the harbour view, as he knew how long and drawn out these sessions could be. William agreed to introduce them to the owner in the hope of being able to speak to Freya alone. Unfortunately, Madame Giron ushered him out of the shop, saying she would send one of her staff members to fetch Ubba when they had selected the garments they wished to purchase.

Ubba was sitting on the harbour wall, admiring the sea view. William had no alternative but to join him.

Ubba said, 'Well William, how are coping with your Danish cousins? Are they what you expected, or can't you wait until we all depart?'

William was slightly concerned by the very direct question and he hesitated. 'I suppose I find it difficult to relate to them in some ways. Despite being Danes, they are all very different. My father was discouraged about divulging his past by my mother, so we never knew what his background was.'

'Your father was a great warrior with the courage of a lion in battle. He taught me sword skills as a teenager.'

'He never taught me when I was learning.'

'That was probably because you didn't ask him, wrongly assuming that your Frankian swordsmen were superior. Rollo followed his own path to live a separate life from his brother because he wasn't prepared to be seen as secondary to Ragnar. I know many consider him a traitor for taking over Ragnar's settlement in Paris, but he paid a high price for it. I have probably been the most lenient to his cause because I appreciate the expectation of his bloodline. I never wanted to be a king because I saw the damage that occurred with both Rollo and my father when they did, and it was not what I wanted. Sigurd was the same, but even he has been dragged into Danish politics because of his lineage. Bjorn has become King of Sweden and is determined to be King of Norway too. How do you feel about what is expected of you?'

'I will try hard to become a good duc and learn from my father. No doubt you think I am as lacking in kingly skills as I am in horse riding. It is probably due to ignorance; I see a horse as a mode of transport just the same as a boat. I don't have your great understanding of what makes each individual horse special.'

'Well at least you acknowledge your weaknesses, which is promising.'

'Is Freya already betrothed to Matteo?'

'Not yet. We are going to visit his family, but no betrothal is in place. Freya will make her own mind up about her future husband. King Edward has expressed a wish to betroth her to one of his sons, but there may be other claimants to his crown.'

'She certainly knows her own mind and has great courage and determination.'

'That's because Danes allow their women to control their own lives and not be subservient to men. If they marry, they keep their lands and dowry, and can divorce their husbands if they are not treated well. We give them respect rather than insisting on dominating them. I have huge respect for women and consider them superior to men. The responsibility of raising children falls directly on them if we die in battle.'

'It is hard to imagine what life was like for my father growing up in Jormund.'

'Well, how about asking him, William? You have led a very sheltered easy life here because of your status. We were peasant farmers originally and only achieved our status through sheer guts, ambition and hard work. Take a look at the poorest people in Normandie and imagine living their lives. What hardships do they have to endure? Consider how you can make life easier for them. You should also ask Rollo about your mother's first reaction to him as a husband and then you will perhaps understand what a difficult time he had when he became Duc.'

A shop assistant came out and invited them back in to pay for the goods. Ubba was delighted to see Torri in her chosen dress. She looked stunning. It was blue silk trimmed with silver thread on the bodice, the same depth of colour as her sparkling eyes. Freya had a lilac dress on, with the bodice covered in small amethyst stones. William flinched when he heard the price and attempted to barter down the cost. However, Ubba did not seem overly worried about it.

He turned to William. 'They deserve dresses for special occasions. Torri still weaves our winter clothing and as she has been Queen I like to ensure she has beautiful clothes for when she needs them. My wife is very special to me. I fell in love with her at 12 years old and although I had to wait to claim her as my wife, she was worth it.'

William was feeling more confident around Ubba.

'Do you not feel jealous of her having been Bjorn's wife too?'

'Not at all. I consider Bjorn my brother and as a teenager, I learnt how to fight in battle at his side. I will always respect that they raised two exceptional children in Erik and Refil, and I am as proud of them as their mother is. She has also blessed me with two sons and a beautiful daughter, whose futures are yet to be determined, but I have no doubt they will excel on whatever path they take.'

William was struggling with his emotions because Ubba had spoken so compassionately and honestly about his feelings for Torri, which many men would never have done. Perhaps his mother had been less than enthusiastic to marry Rollo at first, but he knew they loved each other deeply when their children were born, and to this day. He could never fault Rollo as a father, but he knew his mother had been angry when he'd joined Bjorn and Ubba raiding in the Mediterranean – and again when he'd joined the Heathen Army to avenge Ragnar's death. Having now met more of his Ragnarsson cousins, he was beginning to understand the family bond that tied them together. Perhaps he should climb down from his ivory tower and appreciate what they had achieved instead of considering them as inferior to himself.

He decided he would join the meeting with Erik and Refil to gain an insight into how they were intending to tackle what appeared to him an impossible task because there were so many obstacles to overcome. He thought what he would have done if he had been faced with the same problem. Their chances of survival in his opinion were nil, and yet they still wanted to do it.

o0o

The meeting started on time in the cool of the great hall. Erik, Refil, Bjorn, Haesten, Rollo, Keir and Ubba were at the raised table. Some of Haesten's warriors came, as did William and the remainder of Ubba's men. Torri had declined to sit on the top table as she didn't consider she had enough knowledge of boat management, design, sailing, exploring etc. to be of any use. Bjorn had however persuaded her to attend.

Refil had drawn a charcoal map of their proposed route on the back of a goatskin. It wasn't until you saw the map that you realised just how vast the seas they would be traversing were. A second goatskin had the design and layout of the boat. It was based on a large knarr, with high sides to protect against the massive waves expected. It was capable of carrying 50 tonnes of cargo including the crew. There would be some live animals on board – goats, raptors, lambs, chickens, pigs and two cows – to provide fresh produce during their journey and inhabit any land they found worthy of farming. The remainder of their produce would be salted beef, pork, fish and preserved fruit and vegetables.

Erik talked about the route they would be following. They intended to depart from Dublin the following June. Axel had been instrumental in preparing route maps and advising them of places where it was totally unsafe to attempt to stop. Torri was horrified at the prospect of her two sons being subjected to the fate of previous explorers.

There was some discussion that women would be responsible for cooking and looking after the livestock. Torri was shocked, as reference had been made to them having to dismantle the boat and move it by hand and rebuild it.

Erik noticed her concern. 'Do you have a problem with women being on board, Mother?'

'Well considering you said that you may have to transport the boat overland at some point and that every sailor was vital to ensure success, surely you will be short of manpower for this and for sailing? The cooking will fall to the women… and no doubt keeping the men entertained, as well.'

There were guffaws of laughter. 'Well you can't expect us to go over six months without sex, surely?'

Torri snapped back, 'But if you are going to need strong fit sailors to carry a boat overland and fight if attacked, then women are not suitable for this expedition; it is fraught with danger, could take longer than six months, and could easily end up with them being pregnant. This is not a voyage suitable for women!'

There was a hushed silence and then Erik spoke, 'But surely one of the main reasons we have been successful in conquering new territories is because we (unlike the Romans) took women on our expeditions and populated new land?'

Torri replied in exasperation, 'But this is not about migration to a specific area, as happened when people migrated to Iceland or the small islands surrounding Britain and Ireland. You don't even know whether there is land, never mind the danger of sailing in uncharted waters. This is not a suitable risk for women to take just to appease your sexual appetites. You need all men on this voyage – even then, your chances of survival are minimal.'

She stood up and marched regally out of the room, to total silence from the audience.

Ubba spoke first, 'She has a very valid point of view Erik, and you should consider her opinion carefully. I agree with her wholeheartedly. She has not survived all the traumas in life she has faced without understanding the horrendous pressure you would be exposing these women to on such a dangerous voyage.'

Rollo said, 'I am inclined to agree with Torri on this issue.'

Sigurd added, 'I am not an explorer or sailor by any means, but I don't think women should be on this mission. The risks are just too high.'

Refil responded, 'I would not consider taking Inga and Leif on this journey. We are going to need every ounce of strength and courage to survive this trip. If we find land then families can migrate once we have proven there is a safe place to go to. I think we need to discuss this matter further, Erik.'

There was a surge of men talking to their colleagues and Ubba took the opportunity to leave the room. He knew Torri would be upset as she already knew the chances of her sons' survival were extremely limited, and it must have taken courage to raise the issue.

He looked outside, as he knew she would have gone somewhere quiet to be alone. He asked one of Haesten's men, who pointed to a small paddock in the distance. He could see a lone figure sitting on a bench. He made his way to where she was. As the bench faced the paddock, she had her back to him, but he could tell she was crying quietly.

He leaned over, put his arms around her and kissed the top of her head. 'I knew you would find that meeting upsetting sweetheart, but you were absolutely right. I objected and so did Rollo, Sigurd and Refil, so they will be discussing it more before a final decision is made.'

She patted the bench, too upset to speak. He sat beside her and hugged her tightly. When she had calmed down, she kissed him. 'Thank you, Ubba. You are such a thoughtful compassionate husband. I'm terrified of losing my precious sons, because it is such a dangerous route they are taking and I know their chances of survival are so very low, but I don't want to argue with them and cause a rift before they go.'

'Sweetheart, you are not doing that. Refil agrees with you – as do I.'

Suddenly, they heard voices. Bjorn and Erik were approaching.

Ubba stood up and kissed her hand. 'This is between you and Bjorn as parents, and is not any of my business, so I shall leave you to talk freely. I will be in our room if you need some comfort afterwards, but you did the right thing to point it out. Ivar would have agreed with you too.'

As he drew level with them, Bjorn asked, 'How is she, Ubba?'

'It is hard for her to stand back and encourage her sons to go on a dangerous mission with all the uncertainties that entails, and then cause conflict by raising this issue. As a father, your opinion must be the same, but she was right to say this is no venture for women. However, she does not want to cause a rift between herself and her sons.' He carried on walking and left them to it.

TWENTY-FIVE

It was their last day with Haesten and they were having a party to celebrate their final evening together. This would be no grand ball, but a typical Dane celebration. Ubba was adamant that he and Torri would keep a watchful eye on Freya, especially around the younger members of their group, not to mention Haesten's men, who had all been bowled over by her beauty.

To his astonishment, William came to him and asked if he could speak to Freya alone. Ubba immediately said that would depend on Freya, but if this was in any way a proposal of marriage, he would not allow it. William said he understood his concern as her father, but he had no intention of asking for Freya's hand in marriage. He just wanted to apologise to her for his overbearing arrogant attitude towards her and he also wanted to assure her that if she ever needed help in the future, she could always rely on him for sanctuary or rescue, should she need it. If she married in Europe then he would be able to reach her before Ubba if she ever needed it. Ubba thanked him, but assured William that as far as he was concerned, Thorin would be her protector wherever she was. He sent Egil to fetch her. She was slightly bemused when she saw her father and William together.

Ubba understood and said, 'Do not be concerned, sweetheart. William has asked to speak to you privately before you return to Rouen. He has assured me he is not about to ask for your hand in marriage; he just wants to apologise for his behaviour when he first met you. It is entirely your choice whether you wish to speak with him.'

Freya looked relieved and smiled. 'Yes, I will speak with you, William. We did rather get off to a bad start, but I think your opinion may have changed a little about your heathen Dane family now.'

Ubba said, 'I will be right outside the door Freya, should you need me.' He turned to William and said, 'And I will expect you to behave as a gentleman and a prince towards my precious innocent daughter.'

William said, 'You have my word, sir.'

Ubba left the room and gave Freya a kiss on her head as he passed.

Freya said, 'Well shall we sit down with the prescribed distance between us and confess why you wish to speak to me? It must be important if you went straight to my father to demand an audience.'

William approached and they sat on the bench together.

He hesitated slightly. 'Freya, I am so sorry I was such an arrogant bastard and made you feel threatened. I had a long conversation with your father in Le Havre and I admit I had preconceived ideas about all of you, which were very wrong. It is only since being with you that I have realised just how wrong I was to assume that you were inferior in any shape or form to my Frankian family. My only excuse is that I was probably influenced in my youth by my mother and others around me. I want to apologise sincerely for my bad judgement as I have seen a totally different side to my Dane family, which has made me realise my grievous error.

'I think your mother and father are wonderful; their relationship is so unbelievably strong, and the respect they have for each other is a joy to behold. Your father never wanted to be King and was brave enough to follow his own destiny. He perfectly understands the expectations of being the son of a famous father, and has balanced that against his devotion to his family.'

She put her hand on William's knee. 'You don't need to tell me how very special my parents are; I know it already. We may not be royalty now, but I don't regret leaving that lifestyle. One day I may return to it and I am impatient to know what the future holds for me. I hope I can be as brave and courageous as my parents have been.'

'I went to Erik's talk yesterday about his expedition and I was totally overawed at them taking on a near impossible task with such grit and determination. If my father said to me, "Go find new land and conquer it!" I would be terrified.'

'But your father did it, William; somewhere deep down you will have that resilience. All three of my brothers have followed their own paths and I will do the same. But we all know that love and compassion matter more than crowns, power and authority. We are not motivated by greed but by an inner drive to explore, discover and raise our own families.'

William said, 'That brings me to what I wanted you to know, Freya. If you do marry in Europe then I will be closer to you than the rest of your family will be. If you ever need my help then I will be here for you.' He pulled a gold signet ring off his finger and placed it in her hand. If you send me this ring I will know it is definitely from you and will come to your rescue.'

Freya smiled benevolently at him. 'Whatever makes you think I am not capable of finding my own way out of trouble? Besides, the gods have given me Thorin for protection and he has done an admirable job so far.'

'But Freya, men take advantage of women. Queens in particular can have a very rough ride and often a loveless existence.'

She leant forward and put her hand over his mouth. 'William, trust me, that will not happen to me. I am my mother's daughter and a Ragnarsson too; I have been well trained for my future role. You concentrate on building bridges with your father and learning how to be a future duc.' She brushed his cheek with her finger and gently kissed the tip of his nose. 'I forgive you, but next time do not judge people until you have met them.'

oOo

Ubba realised that the preparations for the farewell party were going to be noisy and boozy. He did not want Freya assailing with drunken young men trying to court her. He also knew the younger men were likely to go overboard with challenges. He went in search of Torri, who was with Freya, helping with the food preparations. Torri was supervising the presentation of a roasted boar's head as a table centrepiece. Freya was decorating an enormous pudding with cream.

He spoke quietly to Torri, asking if he could have a word. She did not look overjoyed to be interrupted, but moved away from the table so they could have some privacy.

'Darling, it is likely to get out of hand later on and I am concerned about Freya's safety. I think Thorin deserves a night off from guarding her to enjoy the festivities. Do you think we can oversee her safety tonight?'

Torri laughed. 'I am assuming that "we" includes you, but I know as well as you do that you are likely to be drunk long before the majority of these men, as you have a low level of alcohol resistance anyway. Not to mention your natural way with any woman once inebriated.'

Ubba feigned offence. 'Torri, that is not really true. I am not a philanderer when drunk. You know I generally end up falling asleep long before I can bed any female.'

She tried not to smile as he looked just like a scolded naughty teenager. 'What makes you think Freya cannot cope with defending her own honour? Remember, she has been here in a previous life and is no innocent teenager.'

'I am worried about William paying her too much attention... and although Matteo seems more enamoured of you than her, drink can make any man act out of character.'

'So, what you really mean is you want me to be the bodyguard whilst you indulge yourself however you please.'

There was a pause whilst Ubba realised he had been sussed out once again by his queen. He could not prevent a smile forming and his blue eyes sparkled. 'Yes, sweetheart if you don't mind, because I may fall asleep on the job.'

'Odin help me, you are just like a little boy Ubba, but I cannot resist your Ragnarsson charm. I will look after our daughter, but you will promise to keep an eye on your son and my two sons and see they don't do anything stupid.'

Ubba hugged and kissed her. 'I will do my best, but Erik is as hot headed as Bjorn was at his age and I wasn't able to prevent Bjorn from doing crazy things, so what makes you think Erik will even listen to me?'

'Ubba, just do your best and get out from under my feet!'

He escaped with a big grin across his face, knowing that he had achieved his objective although it was impossible to outwit his clever wife.

oOo

The evening started with a feast. A roasted deer was the principal meat, with several other meats and fish in evidence. The noise was loud and bawdy as the drinking increased. Freya was annoyed she was made to sit next to her parents rather than being on the same table as Thorin, Arne, Matteo, Erik, Refil, William and the younger men. Rollo had warned Ubba that he had a crate of French wine hidden and as he knew Ubba preferred wine to mead, he suggested they just top up their horns with wine, then nobody would know. Ubba was delighted but knew he could get drunk and sleepy just as easily on wine as on mead.

During the meal Haesten, Rollo, Ubba and Sigurd were asked to speak about their favourite adventure or battle. Rollo kept well away from describing his battle against Ragnar, for fear of causing upset. He opted to tell of a battle he led against the Saxons whilst chasing Aelle across Northumbria. Ubba was asked to describe Aelle's blood eagling and death. Sigurd described the battle on land and sea for Zealand, and his part in it. Torri was asked to tell them about Ivar and Sigtryggr's life in Ireland, and to share some battle tales of her own.

The toasts were long and became even more bawdy as the alcohol intake increased. This was followed by some arm wrestling and various other games to test male prowess. Torri made sure she had a word with Erik, suggesting how painful it would be rowing across the North Sea with a broken arm, which did curtail him partaking in some of the antics.

By midnight some of them had passed out and were fast asleep. Others disappeared with the few women present. Bjorn was next to Torri, with Ubba on his other side. He chatted away to Torri as Ubba's eyes started to close. Freya kept quiet and listened carefully to her mother and Bjorn's reminiscences of their time

271

together. She had developed a fondness for her Uncle Bjorn as nothing seemed to faze him. He met every obstacle with a solution, and just kept ploughing on, showing his total belief in his own survival.

Sigurd was sitting opposite her and did not seem in the least bit drunk. She was fascinated by his physical likeness to her father. He was shyer than Ubba, but he leant forward to talk to her. 'Freya, I know that your father thinks the gods have your future in mind, but have you considered that you have a higher status as a Ragnarsson granddaughter in Denmark because of your background? There would be many offers for your hand in marriage over there, perhaps even more prestigious than marrying a European prince.'

'I am aware of that as Bjorn discussed it with my father, but the visions that I have had of my future have always been in Yorkshire. I know that Sigtryggr intends to try and retake Jorvik and of course he has a Saxon queen already, in Skye. I love Yorkshire and I know King Edward would like me to marry one of his sons. I do not have any desire to marry soon, as I want to be sure to marry the right man. My father says I have to be patient and wait until the gods reveal my future. I have been blessed to have my parents and Ivar as role models and to educate me in politics. My brothers are now forging their own futures and my turn will come.'

'You have a very sensible attitude to life, Freya – and wisdom far beyond your years.'

'Well, my mother always says that I have been here before. I intend to make the most of this life. I have my mother's example to follow, and I will do my best to make my mark in the future, just like my brothers. I am just not a very patient person. I will have Thorin to rely on; I won't go anywhere without him.'

'You may find that difficult to enforce in a marriage, Freya. Men do not trust other men around their wives. Think carefully about your actions or both you and Thorin could end up dead.'

'Sigurd, that is a bit harsh! I believe my father has displayed a perfect example of tolerating my mother's past husbands and trusting her to remain faithful to him. He strives to stand back when she is with Bjorn as although they are divorced, they are parents to Erik and Refil. He never questions her past relationships and never shows any jealousy. Their bond is as strong a marriage as I have ever seen, but I do admit my father is very different to most men.'

Sigurd smiled. 'Perhaps because he was blessed with the perfect wife who was worth waiting for, lucky man… and he certainly deserves it.'

o0o

The next morning there were some very sore-headed Danes coming round from their drunken slumber.

Ubba woke and discovered he was alone in the overhead haybarn above the stables, completely astounded as to how or why he was there. When he sat up, his hammering head reminded him how much he must have consumed to feel as bad as this. He made his way down the loft ladder very gingerly, and to the amusement of two grooms mucking out the horses. As he reached ground level, he shook off some of the hay sticking to his cloak and hair and then headed outside.

He headed for the longhouse, sat down and asked one of the women to bring him food he hoped might stay in his stomach.

As he was eating, a very drunk Bjorn and Erik appeared and joined him at the table. To his amusement, Bjorn said quietly, 'I have no recollection after eating my meal to waking up in bed this morning.'

Ubba replied, 'Neither have I, so let's just eat in silence, shall we? At least you made it to your bed! I woke up in the hayloft.'

Erik burst out laughing until his father Bjorn put his hand over his mouth. 'Shush! Keep quiet son, or I swear I will knock you senseless!'

Erik recoiled in shock. He was surprised but knew to keep quiet. Antagonising Bjorn "the bear" was never a good idea.

Freya came over and Erik was quick to say, in a quiet voice, 'Freya, be careful; these two are suffering with a deserved hangover from hell. No scolding or raising your voice girl, or you could live to regret it.'

Freya giggled. 'Well spill the beans, Erik! What did they get up to last night after mother spirited me away at midnight and locked us both in our room?'

Erik grinned. 'How should I know? To my knowledge they didn't partake in the outdoor sports I was watching. Although, I can't remember much except everyone being beaten by young Thorin at arm wrestling. He has extreme strength in his arms and upper body.'

'I know, nobody can escape Thorin's grasp, me included.'

Ubba, who had appeared to be nodding off, suddenly exclaimed, 'And exactly what do you mean by that remark, young lady?'

'Oh Father, go back to sleep. There is nothing salacious in that remark. I was just trying to hide something from him years ago and he grabbed me. I couldn't get away even when kicking and biting him. He has a very high pain threshold, unlike you.' She hugged him and told him not to be so grumpy.

Egil appeared and announced, 'Rollo says we shall be leaving at noon to return to Rouen.' There were groans from the audience at the prospect, but Egil continued, laughing, 'Nothing like a good ride out in the country to clear your head.'

Twenty-Eight

Ubba stood on the masthead with Torri in front of him, waving as their two longboats peeled left away from Bjorn's pair and headed in towards the Humber Estuary, while Bjorn sailed north for Sweden. They were both crying at the realisation that they may not see any of them again. Both of them were fearing for the lives of her two explorer sons Erik and Refil, and also Bjorn, who was on a dangerous mission to retain his Swedish crown.

At Ubba's feet sat Caesar, who had already become his devoted guardian. He looked up at his master, whimpered knowing that he was hurting, and licked his hand to assure him everything would be all right. Ubba bent down and hugged him. 'It's all right, boy; sometimes we men have to let our feelings flow when parting from our family – just like when you left your mother and siblings in Ireland.'

He was conscious of Torri still sobbing and he hugged her to him and said, 'I know you must be feeling devastated to see your sons sail north, but they will have the gods with them and all our family praying for their lives as they explore uncharted lands. You must not let fear of the unknown frighten you, my darling – they certainly won't! You and Bjorn have given them your drive and determination. Remember what successful role models you two have been. They will make their mark in our family history; I have no doubt about that.'

'I know Ubba, but as a mother, it is very difficult to stand back when you have no idea of the dangers that lie ahead. They are my babies and it's a mother's job to protect her offspring. You will have it to face with Freya and it won't be easy. Arne and Viggo have their own paths to tread now too, and it is difficult to find a balance between interfering and letting them make their own decisions. I know I am being emotional, but I think I have just cause.'

He laughed. 'Some people would be surprised to see the ice maiden in meltdown, but I know how much your public exterior differs from the kind, considerate loving mother behind the mask. I am glad to be heading back to Richmond to continue our quiet farming existence. However, I don't expect peace to last much longer in Jorvik and Durham. I fear I will be back on the battlefield with Arne before long.'

About four miles before they reached Jorvik, approaching a bridge, they saw an old man leaning over the parapet. He was holding his horse and waving. As they got closer, Ubba ordered the rowers to slow down as the man had put his hand up for them to stop. He had also pulled back his hood on his cloak. Egil shouted, 'That is Sam the groom, my lord.'

They pulled up directly below him. Sam had a metal box tied with rope, which he lowered down to the boat. 'Greetings, my lord. I have a message for you from Ireland, which I think you need to see.'

Ubba's face fell as he knew instantly that Sigtryggr must have sailed from Dublin to take Jorvik.

Sam shouted, 'It arrived two days ago, but your longboats had already been spotted in Hull and we knew you were heading home. I decided to meet you personally to deliver it. May Odin keep you and your family safe, my lord. I see you have two new horses on the other boat – and a dog the size of a pony, too.'

Ubba shouted, 'Thank you, Sam… and keep yourself safe and well.'

He took the box back to Torri and they opened it to find the message written by Ivar in Latin, informing him that Sigtryggr was intending to set sail immediately.

'Sweetheart, I am going to get you home and then I will have to leave and honour my vow to Edward to remove Aethelflaed to safety, which probably means escorting her south to Mercia.'

Torri groaned. 'So soon? I was hoping for a peaceful few months after our journey, but that is not going to happen is it, my love?'

'Sweetheart, you are not in any danger. Sigtryggr will not harm you and I shall leave half my men to protect the farm and send the others with Arne to support Halfdan.'

'It's not my safety; it's yours I am concerned about. You will be heading south through Saxon territory with their Queen and you are a Dane with a price on your head. What if you are attacked?'

'Then the Queen will repay my kindness and

protect me. The Jorvik troops will be needed to fight Sigtryggr. I expect Lord Aldhelm will stay as their commander. The essential objective is to remove Aethelflaed to Mercia and then I will return to assist Halfdan if necessary.'

'But surely not alone, Ubba?'

'Yes, the two of us travelling together will attract a lot less attention than taking a troop. I am sure Aethelflaed will be happy to disguise herself as a man to ensure her safety – and sleeping rough in August is no trial for her.'

They moored at the riverbank and Arne and Thorin came over. Ubba and Torri moved away from the boats.

Arne was excited. 'Was that a message that Sigtryggr has sailed?'

'Yes son, it was… but as you know I have a duty to honour my promise to Edward first, so you and Thorin and half the men are to leave for Durham without me. In fact, it may be sensible for us to swap boats and for you to sail straight up to Durham. I can send men after you with horses unless you think Halfdan can provide you all with suitable mounts.'

Arne replied, 'To be honest, I would rather have our own horses; we have trained them for battle and I would rather put my trust in them than new horses.'

'Very well, son. I will send you what I can, but I need to ensure there are enough horses left to provide escape from home, should anybody launch an attack on the farm or intend to kidnap or take your mother or Freya as hostages. Egil will be in charge of their safety and the farm. I think Thorin needs to accompany you, as you are both untried in battle and I cannot be there. I will join you as soon as I have discharged my duties to Aethelflaed.'

Ubba climbed onto the mainsail platform and shouted, 'Men, can all those selected to fight for Durham ensure they and their possessions are in this longboat and the others move to the second longboat carrying the horses and bound for Richmond. Sigtryggr has probably landed in Runkhorn and will be sailing to Jorvik by river. I will have your horses sent to Durham as soon as I get home. May Odin keep you safe and well. I will join you as soon as I can.'

There was a lot of activity as the men changed boats. Freya took the opportunity to speak to Ubba. 'Father, may I be one of the riders taking the horses up to Durham?'

Ubba sighed, shaking his head in frustration. 'Freya, your mother has just seen her two eldest sons depart on an exploration across the Atlantic Sea with no known destination, her third son Arne is embarking on his first battle and her fourth son Viggo has gone east. I am also departing on a dangerous mission. Do you really think this is a good time to put your own life in danger?'

Freya blushed and muttered, 'Perhaps not, Father. I had not considered it in that context. I will look after her and keep the farm safe for your return. I will also look after and train Caesar; he will sorely miss you and is too young to accompany you on such a mission.'

'Good, but you must also promise to keep well

away from Jorvik and may I suggest you read some of the Latin texts about Rome and Greece Ivar gave you to improve your language skills. You are a queen in waiting and need to understand the politics of war.'

'I will do my best to keep out of trouble and devote time to expanding my education.'

'As Thorin is needed in Durham you will not have your faithful shadow protecting you. I have asked Matteo to stay on the farm for as long as he can, to protect you and your mother, along with Egil. Do not indulge in any impropriety with any man as your virginity must not be compromised. That is one area of your education you will promise me faithfully not to explore.' He pulled her chin up and looked into her deep blue eyes. 'Do I have your word, Freya? The future of the Ragnarsson dynasty relies on you. We could all be killed in battle or drowned in an angry sea. You may be the only one left.'

'Yes, I promise to remain pure. The gods are as insistent as you are, but I would appreciate an indication of where my destiny lies. I am ready for marriage, but I want time to select my own husband. I hope they do not leave it too late and waste my fertile breeding years.' She jumped down and collected her bags to swap to the other longboat.

As Ubba joined Torri to collect his bags and equipment she asked, 'That looked like a heated exchange, Ubba?'

'I was merely reminding her of her duties as a granddaughter of Ragnar. I suggested she spent time expanding her knowledge of politics and war, and reminded her of her duty to remain pure and innocent.'

Torri spluttered, 'No wonder she looked angry. Freya may be young in age, but she has been here on this earth before and knows exactly what she is missing.'

Ubba snapped, 'I have asked Matteo to remain at the farm for as long as he can, for added protection. I have already given you permission to indulge your pleasure with him in my absence, but I do not wish to extend that privilege to my precious daughter Freya. So please ensure she remains safe and secure.'

Torri gasped and shouted, 'So I have to protect my daughter's innocence whilst you gallop across England with the Saxon Queen of Jorvik and Mercia, doing what comes most naturally to you – humping her every night, no doubt!'

There was total silence as all the men had heard every word Torri said.

Ubba stared at her in total shock, devastated. Egil pulled him away and muttered about changing boats.

Torri was horrified as she had no idea where that ugly thought had come from. She had no reason to suspect that Ubba or Aethelflaed had ever been lovers. Ubba had given his word on that and she suspected jealousy had reared its ugly head in her mind out of nowhere. Why had she responded so angrily? The look Ubba gave her as he followed Egil made her cringe in fear and tears slowly ran down her face.

She rushed over to Arne to wish him a safe journey. Luckily, he had been too preoccupied to hear what she had said. He assumed the tears were because of him.

He hugged her tightly and said, 'Don't worry, Mama. I will be fine. I have been taught by experts to fight and survive. I need to do this for myself, to prove I have the courage and skills. I will have Halfdan and Stefan watching my back.'

'Be careful, son, remember it may not be the person you are fighting that is the threat; it may be a spear, axe or an arrow from someone else.' Conscious that she should not unsettle him, she kissed him on his cheek and whispered, 'May the gods protect you and give you strength and courage. My thoughts will be with you.'

The first longboat bound for Durham moved off and Ubba turned to Egil.

'I need to speak to my wife alone. Can you release Caesar from his crate and we will walk and give him some exercise. Tell Keir to stand down the men and take some refreshment. I intend to leave late tonight to go to Jorvik and remove Aethelflaed.'

'Why so soon, Ubba?'

'I suspect Sigtryggr will have sent an advance party over here before he sails. Although we were in total agreement that Aethelflaed would be allowed to leave under my protection, I would feel happier the sooner we depart.'

Egil replied, 'You don't suspect Sigtryggr would try to stop you, do you?'

'No, but I think we should leave as quickly as possible with no armed guards. We should just appear to be two travellers on the road so we are less likely to attract attention. I will go via Roche Abbey and then travel through Lincolnshire and on to Mercia, keeping off the road as much as possible. I need to be up in Durham as soon as possible, to help Halfdan. I leave the protection of Torri and both my families in your hands. I do not expect an attack by Sigtryggr, but who knows who else may be in the area and fancy their chances of attacking the farm to steal my horses or my family? Keep a spy in Jorvik who will report back what is happening. You will have the longboat; use it if you need to escape north.'

'You know I will do my best to protect them all and I will have Ralf to turn to if necessary. As Sigtryggr's father-in-law, his word should carry some impact. I understand your need for haste my lord, but you will have to be very alert on both journeys.'

'Egil, I have just had three months of pleasure visiting Ireland and Normandie. I am well rested and fit to go on this mission alone. I know I risk Aethelflaed's safety as well as my own, but I think travelling incognito is the safest and quickest way to achieve my objective. The Saxons will be looking for Danes heading north to attack them, and we will be heading south.'

'May you have a safe journey, my lord.' Egil turned and hurried over to the longboat to find Torri and release Caesar.

Caesar was delighted to be let out and had already spotted Ubba on the riverbank. He launched himself off the boat and headed straight to his master at full speed. Ubba found a convenient fallen log to sit on, to brace himself for his enthusiastic arrival. He was now 10 months old and the size and build of a Shetland pony. He launched himself at Ubba and jumped up onto his shoulders, covering his face in sloppy kisses.

Ubba laughed and tried to fend him off. 'Caesar, this is not the way to greet your master; you must learn to behave properly and not endanger my life. I know you love me, but you will double in size soon and I cannot withstand such an onslaught. Caesar jumped down and went for an urgent call of nature. Then he saw Torri approaching and went back to his master, barking at the approaching figure. Ubba shouted at him to 'Sit and be quiet!' His body relaxed when he saw it was Torri.

Torri looked concerned. 'Egil said you wanted to speak to me in private. If it is about my outburst, I apologise profusely for what I said and beg your forgiveness.'

'Come here, sweetheart. I am not angry; I just want to know why you doubt my sincerity when I have sworn to you that I have never had a sexual relationship with Aethelflaed.'

'I don't know. I just feel jealous of you wanting to spend time alone with her rather than me, and ultimately putting your life in danger to protect her rather than me. I have been so stressed about losing all my sons at once, and worried about my own health, before Sulamain sorted me out. I seriously thought that my life was ending.'

Ubba pulled her close and hugged her, kissing the top of her head. 'Torri, have I not loved you since I was a boy? Where is the triple queen and fierce shieldmaiden who fought like a lion at my side and produced a dynasty of Ragnarssons whose names will fill the history books for years to come?'

He tipped her chin up and saw tears in her eyes. She replied defensively. 'Just feeling old, vulnerable and frightened that you may find younger women more attractive. Aethelflaed is 12 years younger than me!'

He smiled. 'But she is not the woman I love! I shall merely be escorting her to Mercia and galloping hotfoot back up north to support Halfdan's cause to take Durham.'

She raised her hand to his cheek and touched him tenderly. 'But you could still die doing that and I cannot contemplate life without you by my side. You are everything to me and you have no idea how much I pray to the gods to keep you safe every time you go on dangerous missions. I have had to bear losing my sons to forge their new lives, but I can't and won't lose you!'

'It is in the hands of the gods. I promise I will do my very best to stay alive.'

She rounded on him angrily. 'If you dare to die, I will come and drag you back out of Valhalla personally!'

He had never seen her so animated and laughed. 'But how do you know I will go to Valhalla in the first place? The Valkyries may not consider I am brave and courageous enough to warrant entry?'

She punched him hard on the chest. 'Don't be ridiculous. What woman could ever resist you? One flash of those blue eyes and they would whisk you to Valhalla to play war games all day and feast, booze and womanise all night.'

He bowed his head to her. 'Dearest Torri, I am flattered you would consider me worthy of a place in Valhalla. However, I would rather have you stay on this earth and protect our children and grandchildren and guide them through their lives.'

'Typical bloody man! Yet again you renege on your responsibilities and leave me alone to raise your heirs. When am I going to have some peace, quiet and fun?'

'Torri, cease fretting, woman! I am not going to be fighting on the frontline; I am going to be protecting Aethelflaed on a journey south.'

Torri stood up, her eyes flashing, and scowled at him. 'As long as that is all you are doing!' She stomped off back towards the longboat and he called Caesar and followed her.

Ubba had no idea why she suddenly felt this way. He had never courted Aethelflaed. He admired her for what she had achieved, but there was no way he had ever considered her as a potential conquest.

As the boat pulled away, he watched Torri chatting and laughing with Freya. He had assumed that the older he got, his knowledge of how women's minds work would become better. Obviously this was not the case; he vowed that before he left Richmond he would make love to her and try to dispel these unrealistic ideas from her mind.

TWENTY-NINE

As they docked at home, Serena and their children Astrid, Theo and Frank were at the jetty to greet them. They hadn't seen each other for three months, since he'd left for Ireland and then on to Normandie. Serena appeared, warning Frank to stay close by her side, as he had only just mastered walking. Ubba jumped across to the jetty and hugged them tightly. He watched Torri's reaction. She was smiling and there was no sign of jealousy. He ushered them over to a wall and picked seven-year-old Theo up, sat him on the wall, kissed Astrid's cheek and ruffled her blonde hair.

'Serena, I am delighted you are all fit and well, but I have to leave tonight on a mission and after that I intend to go straight to Durham to support Halfdan. I have sent one longboat full of men straight up to him now.'

Serena looked shocked. 'Has Sigtryggr arrived already?'

'I don't know, but he will be coming soon. I have had news of his departure.'

'Oh, Ubba, I had hoped we would have more time together.'

'I am sorry love, but I can't delay.'

As the boat was being unloaded, Ubba grabbed his

personal possessions and took them up to his room to select the clothes he would need for his journey. Thankfully, all his riding gear had been washed before they left Normandie and he would not be needing court dress on this trip. He had already asked Egil to prepare Sleipnir as his mount and settle Diablo into his new abode. He was going to sneak into the palace in Jorvik at midnight and remove Aethelflaed with as little fuss as possible.

Torri appeared with her bags and as she was about to put them on the bed to unpack he said, 'Do not put them on the bed; they will have to wait.'

He tilted her head up to look at him. 'I don't know why you don't believe me about there being no sexual relationship with Aethelflaed in the past, but I am going to let my body prove to you now that you are the woman I have loved all my life and honour as the mother of my children. You did not show any jealousy towards Serena when I greeted her just now. I know you have welcomed Serena and our children as fixtures in your life because you know that you are my true wife and nobody will ever take your place. As you are well aware, since I was a teenager, I have always found it necessary to have sex before I go into battle. It sharpens my senses so that I understand what I would be missing, should I die. Like you, I want more time on this earth with you by my side and I promise I will return.'

For the next hour, he paid homage to his wife and swept her up on a journey of love and enlightenment. It was not all one sided either, as she became the instigator ensuring that she reciprocated his intense passion and desire on his willing body.

oOo

Ubba left Sleipnir munching a net of hay in the royal stables at Jorvik at midnight. He had slipped through the walls by an unlocked gate he knew of that was well hidden and in a quiet area of the city. He had wrapped sacks around Sleipnir's front hooves so his shoes would not resound on the cobbles, which made his approach to the stables unseen and unchallenged.

His next challenge was to scale the three-storey stone palace to gain access to Aethelflaed's bedroom. The warm weather on a hot August night meant that bedroom windows were open enough for him to use a grapple iron on the gargoyles extending out from the roof above the windows to secure a rope. He expected that Aethelflaed as Queen would be occupying the same bedroom suite that Ivar once had. He had used this room for training his troops to climb battlements in preparation for a surprise invasion. He checked the area and found the concealed thick rope that had been used for this exercise was actually still attached. Now he had to decide whether the rope was sound enough for him to risk ascending, or whether he should use the new rope he had brought with him. If he used the new rope and missed the gargoyle, it could clatter down the outside of the building or could hit a window and wake others up. He tested the strength of the old rope by climbing up it a short way and noticed that the position it was in was well protected from rain and avoided any rainwater run-off.

Everything was quiet and the moon came out from behind cloud and he opted to risk the original rope. He climbed slowly and carefully, using the wall to support him at a 45-degree angle from the building. Thankfully, the window was wide open and as he got nearer he could hear voices indicating that there was a man and a woman in the room. He quietly pulled himself up so he was kneeling on the windowsill.

What he saw nearly sent him toppling back down to the ground. A couple was engaging in sex inflagrante, totally nude on the bed. Neither were facing the window and so he could not identify them. His instinct was to try and climb back down the rope, but he desperately wanted to know who they were. He was frozen in time, unsure whether to flee or stay quiet. They were making a fair bit of noise so he prayed they would not hear him.

Eventually, the excitement reached its peak and both slumped back on the bed, wrapped in each other's arms. It was Aethelflaed and Lord Aldhelm, Commander of her personal bodyguard. Ubba's knees were suffering on the sill so he coughed politely and said, 'My lady, I apologise profusely for my untimely intrusion.'

Aldhelm leapt out of the bed, grabbed his sword from his belt and ran to the window.

Ubba shouted, 'My lord Aldhelm, it is only me attempting to make a quiet and unscheduled visit to the Queen of Jorvik's bedchamber with a message.'

Aldhelm brandished his sword and swore. 'Ubba

bloody Ragnarsson, what in God's name are you doing here, and how often have these trysts been going on?'

Aethelflaed burst out laughing. 'No, Aldhelm, nothing has been going on between us. If Ubba is here then it can only mean one thing. Sigtryggr's army is marching to take Jorvik.'

Ubba relaxed slightly as Aldhelm put down his sword and offered his hand to pull him up over the windowsill and help him jump down into the room.

Aldhelm said, 'So have you come to kill or kidnap the Queen?'

'Remove her to safety, as requested by King Edward.'

'And you expect me to believe that and hand her over to you? Aethelflaed, is this true? You cannot seriously intend to go with Ubba when he will be in league with Sigtryggr to retake Jorvik. Once a Dane, always a Dane.' Aldhelm continued, whilst dressing himself, 'Do you really intend to go with him? He will cut your throat or hand you over to Sigtryggr to dispose of.'

'No he won't, Aldhelm! Ubba rescued me many years ago when I was a hostage of East Anglian Danes. He returned me safely to my family. Ragnar was working for my father, trying to extract me before a huge ransom was paid. Ubba took me to safety and risked being killed in the process.'

Ubba said, 'My lady, I came at this particular time to extract you under cover of darkness so we can be many miles away from Jorvik before dawn.'

Aldhelm said, 'Is your escort waiting outside the gates?'

'No, we will travel together and attract less attention by keeping off the usual routes and using lesser known paths, which I know extremely well.'

Aethelflaed jumped up from the bed and went to her wardrobe. 'So, do you want me to travel as a man or a woman, Ubba?'

'A man, my lady, with the minimum of baggage and no attendants.'

Aldhelm exploded. 'No bloody way is she travelling alone with you!'

Aethelflaed was pulling on breeches and a plain white shirt. 'Peace, Aldhelm, this was arranged between Edward, Ubba and me two years ago. You forget that Ubba has fought bravely at your side against Danes and I will not have you question his integrity now. You will remain here and face Sigtryggr and either fight for Jorvik or sue for peace. Edward has always known the risks of defending Jorvik so far from Winchester. I know this leaves you in an untenable situation, but at least if God allows, we may both survive.'

Ubba added, 'I swore to Edward that I would not fight for Jorvik for myself. Once I have safely delivered the Queen to Mercia, I will be coming back north to help Halfdan in Durham. Sigtryggr is a clever man; he won't want the infrastructure of Jorvik damaged and he has brokered peace settlements at Winchester in the past. Before you provoke him, you must recall the terror and slaughter he inflicted on Wales when their king tried to double cross him. You must trust I will protect your queen with my life. I have given you my word.'

Aldhelm threw his hands in the air and sighed. 'So, nothing I say will persuade you to stay, Aethelflaed? I can see the point in leaving to ensure your survival, but I pray your trust is not misplaced. Come, let us make our way to the stables and get you on your way.'

Ubba sighed in relief as he had been contemplating what to do with Aldhelm if he became obstructive. He pulled the hood of his lightweight cloak over his head to prevent easy recognition. As they came out of the palace, two guards challenged them. Aldhelm told them to relax and the darkness shielded Ubba from recognition.

When they reached the stables, Sleipnir whickered a quiet greeting.

Aldhelm was shocked. 'How the hell did you get into the palace grounds and put your horse in the stables without being challenged? Christ, I will have some strong words for my guards tomorrow.'

Ubba chuckled. 'Well, if I had left him tied up outside then somebody may have spotted him and you did not have a groom sleeping at the stables in case of an emergency overnight.'

They tacked up their horses quietly. Ubba saw Aethelflaed and Aldhelm embrace and witnessed the love and deep affection they had for each other. It could not have been easy for either of them, facing the likelihood of separation and potential death. He understood the difficult situation Aldhelm was facing and wondered what he would do in his shoes.

Ubba followed a track north as he did not wish them

to be seen leaving the city gates, then he turned south on farm tracks, avoiding the city centre. They kept up a slow canter, helped by the moon and guided by the stone walls of the fields around them, and Ubba's knowledge of their whereabouts.

Two miles from Jorvik they headed into the forest to avoid meeting anybody on the Roman road. They slowed to a walk as there was reduced vision. He began to feel unsettled as he heard a noise in the forest of an animal fleeing their presence. He paused and listened to the sound of it crashing through the undergrowth away from them. His tracking instincts surfaced and the hairs on his back were raised just like a wolf sensing danger. He heard the crack of a twig and he called to Aethelflaed to head back out onto the road. Instinct told him they were being followed.

As they cantered out of the trees he saw three riders spanning the road. He knew whoever had been in the forest was following them, but he had no idea how many there were. As he looked back, three more riders were breaking cover, halting to span the road and stop them turning back. He drew his sword and called to Aethelflaed to stop. One of the riders came forward on a big grey Percheron stallion and raised his hand. Ubba knew that taking six men on was likely to be impossible, so he did as he was bade.

The leader shouted as he got nearer. 'Ubba, peace, I mean neither you nor the Queen any harm.'

Relief flooded through Ubba as he recognised the Irish lilt. He said, 'My lady, it is Sigtryggr; have no fear.'

Sigtryggr rode up to them. 'Greetings Ubba and my lady, rest assured I will not imprison you. I gave my word to Ubba that I would allow you to leave in his care, but I wanted to say something before you go.'

Ubba said, 'How long have you been following me?'

'Since you entered Jorvik. You are not the only one to have scouting and spying skills. I came over with a small advance party to familiarise myself with the layout.' He turned to Aethelflaed. 'My lady of Mercia, do you relinquish the rule of Jorvik to me in exchange for your life and freedom?'

Aethelflaed gave him an imperious look and replied, 'It grieves me that I am not leading my people into battle, but my removal from Jorvik was orchestrated by my brother two years ago. I am not a coward and it concerns me that my people may think that, but I do not wish the city to burn or the people to lose their livelihoods and homes, so I agreed to do as Edward wished. I will relinquish my crown of Jorvik, but only if you promise to treat my people fairly and with respect. I have no idea whether they will accept you as King or will fight to prevent you from taking their city.'

Sigtryggr smiled. 'My lady I appreciate that, but by removing yourself voluntarily you have effectively made the first move. I want you to know that I will do my best to take over without bloodshed and I have no intention of threatening your rule further south. I hope that there can be peace between Saxons and Danes as it will mutually benefit all of us. I send my good wishes to King Edward and hope that we can reach a mutual understanding in the future. Go with Ubba, my lady; you could not have better protection.'

Ubba replied, 'I will call in on my way north to see how things fare, and may the gods keep you safe.'

'And you too, my friend. Your brother sends his wishes for your good fortune, too. I will be forever grateful for your skill and kindness during Aralt's birth. Without you and Sulamain, I could have lost my precious wife and child. You are a very wise and special friend Ubba, and I will be forever in your debt.'

He signalled to his men to leave, but Aethelflaed moved her horse closer to Sigtryggr. 'I would be grateful if you could spare Lord Aldhelm if there is a fight for Jorvik. He has been my counsellor and protector since I became Queen of Mercia.'

Sigtryggr looked surprised at this request and glanced over to Ubba, whose eyes were fixed firmly on the ground. 'I cannot ensure my own safety, never mind Lord Aldhelm's if we end up fighting, but I will do my best to return him to your service, my lady.' He looked at Ubba, who was now smiling at him directly and even proffered a wink. Sigtryggr smiled as he realised that Aethelflaed "the virgin queen" who had vowed to remain celibate and not remarry was not quite as pure as her reputation suggested.

Aethelflaed spoke as they watched the Danes leave. 'So that is the infamous Sigtryggr of Ireland. He is a very imposing man and has such self-confidence. Rumour has it that he is feared more than Ivar.'

THIRTY

They rode off as dawn was breaking. Ubba wanted to put as much distance as possible between themselves and Jorvik. Once the road started getting busier with travellers, he intended to rejoin it so their cover as merchants looked genuine. Aethelflaed had made a good job of braiding her long hair and pinning it in a net underneath under her existing hair. He had unbraided his hair and left it loose, falling from a ponytail on top of his head.

They stopped several times to rest and water the horses, and even risked lunch at a roadside tavern, sitting at an isolated table so nobody could overhear them.

Ubba explained that he had been returning to Richmond after his trip to Normandie when he had received news from Ivar that Sigtryggr had sailed. He had gone home and come straight back to Jorvik. He expected that Sigtryggr would send a small troop over in advance to assess the layout of the area to plan their assault, and he had wanted to reach her before that, but obviously Sigtryggr had decided to come over early himself.

They continued making good progress as the weather was not too hot and gave them a cool breeze. They stopped for the night in a forest clearing by a stream. They had purchased some pies and cooked meats for their supper, which did not require cooking. Ubba had intended making separate sleeping arrangements for them, but Aethelflaed told him in no uncertain terms.

'Ubba, surely we can lie next to each other under the same canopy. It isn't cold and I don't think it will rain. I trust you implicitly to behave as the true gentleman I know that you are. I would prefer to sleep next to you knowing that you will protect me, rather than sleeping alone.'

He laughed. 'Well, perhaps you would reveal that to Torri; she was not best pleased when I told her we were travelling unaccompanied.'

'Well, you can hardly blame her for that. She knows very well how attractive you are to women.'

'But why won't she believe in my undying love and loyalty to her? Why does she assume that I would crave other women sexually just because we are apart?'

She smiled and patted his shoulder. 'Oh Ubba, I suspect she feels like most older women married to a younger sex symbol, that there will always be younger women prepared to try and steal her husband now she is getting older. It just may be a sudden lack of self-confidence.'

'Well, to be fair she has had some recent health issues, which frightened both of us. Thankfully when we visited Ivar, Sulamain was able to save the day. She has been particularly anxious about me escorting you to safety and going to fight for Durham for Halfdan, which is so unlike her.'

'That's completely understandable – now she has stared death in the face, the last thing she wants is to lose her beloved husband in battle. Nobody is invincible – not even you, the great warrior Ubba.'

'You don't know how hard it was for me to kill. The fear of pain, capture and death drove me to hone my skills to such a high level so I could avoid death. I am not a natural killer Aethelflaed, and I do regret being responsible for so many deaths. I still have nightmares about some of the incidents I was involved in, both on and off the battlefield.'

She gave him a hug. 'That's because you are a decent human being Ubba, reflecting on past deeds that your conscience knew were morally wrong. I don't expect Ivar ever considers his wicked deeds – the desecration, rape and slaughter of nuns and clergy in Jorvik, for one.'

Ubba put his head in his hands. 'Oh, that incident recurs frequently in my dreams. I knew nothing in advance of Ivar's intentions; my remit was to gain entry to the city over the walls, but when I walked into the church and witnessed the devastation, I thought I was in hell.'

Aethelflaed hugged him tightly. 'That must have been devastating for you, Ubba. I know you are a champion of women. It wasn't your fault, but I can understand totally why it still haunts you. There are many things that I look back on in my life and wish had taken a different path.'

'Such as, my lady?'

'I regret my naivety in falling in love with Erik my

captor. I was too young to appreciate that a love match between a Saxon princess and a Dane would never have been tolerated by my parents or the elders, and I regret the shame I brought on them. We would both have been a target and even when Aethelred died, I would not have been allowed to marry Erik. We would have had to flee the country immediately and would be forever hunted by Alfred's enemies, especially if we had produced a male child instead of Aelfwynn. It would appear that Danes are more prolific at breeding male offspring than Saxons are. Your record proves it.'

Ubba blushed and said, 'If that is in fact true, it is probably due to our high levels of testosterone. However, I am blessed with two daughters who mean the world to me. Freya is my reason to stay alive as she still needs guidance from us. However, it would appear that the gods have a vested interest in her future too. Does it sadden you that you have no other children?'

'No, not really. My decision to remain chaste and never marry was purely political as if I had remarried, I would have had to bow to my husband's rule and I wasn't prepared to do that.'

'Forgive my impertinence, but what made you take Aldhelm as your lover?'

She laughed. 'Surprisingly, a conversation with your wife, who advised me that being a single queen is a very lonely life and not a path she would want to follow. She praised you very highly as the husband who had always been her rock and was the perfect father to all her children. She admires you for not wanting to be King because you saw firsthand the devastation it can bring to a marriage. However, she admitted that she could never have achieved founding a dynasty without you at her side. High praise indeed Ubba, and testament to the love and respect you have for each other.

'I soon came to realise what a lonely existence I had. Perhaps God will punish me for being weak and submitting to temptation of the flesh, but I needed the comfort and support of a partner. Do you consider me a fallen woman? I was unfortunately never lucky enough to have a man like you around.'

'Never would I condemn you for taking a lover. Being a single woman alone in a man's world must have been a very dark place to be. We Danes consider a sexual relationship very important. We need to fulfil our needs emotionally and sexually to remain healthy. Your God would surely not want you to sacrifice your life, purely for political reasons. We all need to have someone at our side to feel loved and wanted. Odin would not want us to suffer, so why would your God?'

'Thank you, Ubba; you make me feel less guilty, but I will have to make my peace with God and the Church and they may not be quite so understanding.'

They settled down on the waterproof sheet topped with sheepskins and blankets. Ubba lay on his side and reached out to pull her closer to him. 'I prefer to protect the back of the woman I am sleeping with, my lady. I promise to behave; I just need the comfort of physical connection to another human being.'

She giggled. 'Well after the view you had of me and Aldhelm at play, I cannot deny your polite request. To have a warrior of your stature and renown guarding my back will be an honour and will make me relax and sleep soundly.'

Ubba smiled; he certainly had witnessed an astonishing sight that he would likely remember until he died. Best never to reveal this episode to anybody –especially not Torri. He settled down to sleep, leaving one ear open for any impending threat.

oOo

They resumed their journey as the dawn welcomed the sun and calmed the wind. Today looked like it would be hot and humid, so a steadier pace would be required across open country to Roche Abbey. They stopped at midday to lunch at a wayside tavern and give the horses a rest during the heat of the day. The teenage groom raised an eyebrow at the high quality of their horses, but took them into the cool stables, untacked them, washed them down and provided fresh water, small feed and a net of good hay. Sleipnir appreciated his efforts and nuzzled his pockets looking for treats. He went to the feed room and returned with a handful of chopped carrots, which he shared between them. Ubba observed his dedication and rewarded him with silver coins before they left.

They opted to eat inside, out of the way of the sun, flies and heat. They chatted amicably about his trip to Normandie and Aethelflaed appeared to be convinced he had been plotting with Rollo and Bjorn to enlist their help in a Dane war against the Saxons on the south coast. He assured her that apart from helping

Halfdan with Durham, his extended family was far too busy protecting their own domains to risk taking on any extra battles. Bjorn had asked him to join him in Sweden, but he had declined.

They arrived at Roche Abbey at 6.00 pm and their old friend Father Raymond greeted them effusively, delighted to see them. 'My lady of Mercia and Queen of Jorvik, how can I be of assistance to you and my favourite Dane Ubba? Your presence together does not bode well; I hope you are not being kidnapped.'

Ubba laughed. 'I am acting purely as her guardian and removing her from Jorvik before Sigtryggr attempts to take it, thereby honouring my vow to Edward to get her out before any fighting begins. We are on our way to Mercia to ensure she survives.'

'Oh, well I am glad about that, but saddened that once again Jorvik's peace is threatened. Come, you must eat and have one night indoors before you continue your journey. My grooms will see to your horses and give them a comfortable stable.'

He ushered them into his study and ordered food for them. 'I am surprised Ubba you took on this challenge, as I can't see Sigtryggr being pleased at you removing his potential hostage.'

'My guardianship of Aethelflaed goes back many years to when she was kidnapped by Danes in East Anglia and my father was charged with retrieving her by Alfred before he paid the ransom. Thankfully, I managed to escape with her whilst my father created a diversion. I successfully returned her to her family.'

Aethelflaed added, 'An experience which changed

304

my life, thanks to the intervention of Ubba, who prevented me from doing something reckless whilst consumed with grief.'

Father Raymond replied, 'I can understand that. I consider Ubba to be one of the kindest, most sympathetic men I have ever met. His ability to understand the intricacies of the mind and encourage people to conquer their fears is better than any clergyman. This may be at odds with his warrior status, but his compassionate and caring nature is one reason why we all love him.'

Ubba shook his head. 'I am a country man at heart and just want to be left in peace while I still have my wife and children around me.'

Before Ubba retired to his room, he felt an overwhelming need to go and pray in the abbey's church. Last time he had been here, he had participated in compline and thoroughly enjoyed it. There was something spiritually comforting about being surrounded by the monks praying and responding to the ancient Christian texts. He loved when they sang or chanted in unison and he had studied Latin so he could fully understand the ceremony. He was a doubly baptised Christian and Father Raymond had always allowed him to pray there.

The candles were still burning two hours after compline and the sun was setting outside. This projected rays of red and orange light through the abbey's rose window, which had produced a myriad of rainbow colours in front of the altar. He took a seat on a front row pew next to the aisle and just watched the shimmering light flicker like flames. Was this a warning of battles to come? He hoped not, but could not help cringing at the thought of Arne possibly already fighting at Durham. He prayed silently that Arne, Thorin, Halfdan and Stefan would survive. He was heading into his twilight years now and he did not pray for his own life to be spared. He was contemplating this when his highly charged senses told him somebody was watching him. His hand went instinctively to his seax and he leapt into the aisle and looked towards the church door. A novice monk was staring angrily at him. 'You are a heathen and should not be in God's house! You have killed many Saxons and are certainly not a Christian.'

Ubba relaxed his grip on the seax tucked into his belt and replied, 'Actually, I am a Christian and have in fact been baptised twice. I have also killed Danes when the need arose. Father Raymond let me join your services when I was here last.'

He pulled the silver cross out of his shirt, along with a silver Thor's hammer on a separate chain.

The young monk pointed. 'See, you still wear the hammer and you cannot belong to two religions at once.'

Ubba smiled. 'Why not? I have studied your Bible and never came across any such reference.'

But you are Ubba Ragnarsson, brother to Ivar the Boneless who ransacked the church at Jorvik and killed monks and nuns!'

'I knew nothing about my brother's plans prior to invasion and I did what I could to stop it when I reached the church. It haunts me to this day.'

'Liar, someone who was there saw you kill a young novice nun!'

'I was trying to stop her plunging a blunt knife into her heart. I couldn't stop her, but knew that she would have an agonising prolonged death, so I cut her throat to end her life quickly.'

Suddenly, Father Raymond came marching up the aisle. 'Josef, cease questioning Ubba at once! He is a Christian and welcome here at any time.'

Ubba intervened, 'Father, don't chastise the young man; he is only reacting to an understandable hatred for Danes. We have been responsible for many cruel and evil acts and regrettably, we deserve the hatred we receive.'

Father Raymond turned to Josef and said, 'Now, you apologise to Ubba and you will remain here for the next hour to contemplate your misdemeanour before God.'

Josef went red with embarrassment and turned to Ubba. 'I am sorry if I misjudged you sir, but you can understand how it looked.'

Ubba bade Father Raymond goodnight and went to his room.

THIRTY-ONE

The next morning, they left after eating a hearty breakfast and being supplied with food to keep them going. Sleipnir was rested and full of energy, putting in the odd buck as they cantered off from the abbey. Ubba wondered whether that was to impress Aethelflaed's mare rather than him. Still, he would ignore it unless he became too cheeky. All day, they travelled parallel to the road, keeping out of sight when necessary. They both wore lightweight cloaks and hoods to cover themselves with, should they meet anybody.

Ubba found a quiet cool spot to camp for the night, with the added advantage of a clearing in the wood that had been fenced to hold sheep and cattle. This would be ideal for the horses to have some freedom to graze and rest overnight. However, when he unsaddled Sleipnir tethered next to Aethelflaed's mare, she whipped her head round and bit Sleipnir on the neck and stamped her front leg in anger. Realisation suddenly dawned on him and he moved Sleipnir further along on the hitching rail. He carefully examined the mare and sure enough, she was coming into season.

He called Aethelflaed over. 'Your mare is coming into season. I wrongly assumed she was already mated and in foal.'

Aethelflaed replied, 'Well, last year she was covered in May and appeared to be in foal, but in September she was back in season again. I assumed that at 10 years old her fertility was deteriorating, and she has produced me four good foals, so I decided not to cover her this season. Is there a problem?'

'Well, Sleipnir is not going to just ignore her; he is a full blooded stallion. We have at least two more days and nights before we reach Tettenhall and he is not going to like not having his way with her.'

'Well, I am more than happy to have a foal sired by Sleipnir, so why don't you just throw them into the paddock and let them get on with it?'

'Because she is not ready for covering yet; she could kick and bite Sleipnir and lame him.'

'Ubba, are you telling me your stallion is no gentleman and incapable of courting her sweetly until she is ready?' She howled with laughter as Ubba went bright red.

'It is not something I would normally allow Sleipnir to do. He has been taught that there is a time for covering mares – when running free with a herd or covering a mare in hand – but not to pursue them when ridden under saddle. I am only concerned for your safety my lady, as your mare could be difficult to ride when her mind is on other things.'

'Ubba, I promise you that I can keep Trixie under control under saddle and I am sure you already have Sleipnir's respect for your authority.'

'I just don't want him kicked and lamed, especially

as I have to ride back to Durham at some speed to assist Halfdan. We have another two days to reach Mercia and by then your mare should be fully in season and covered by Sleipnir. As there is a suitable paddock, I suggest we turn them loose and if your mare does not consent to his attention yet, he knows to bide his time.'

They turned them into the paddock and Sleipnir had a canter around, bucking and rearing to impress Trixie, who flattened her ears back and attacked him when he came too close. They eventually settled down and Sleipnir kept his distance from the mare. Apart from a few squeals and running around, they both settled down to eat the luscious grass.

Ubba checked them as dawn broke. They were standing within six feet of each other, although any attempt by Sleipnir to approach her from behind was firmly being rebuffed by Trixie. He was relieved that neither of them appeared lame or injured. He hoped there would be no problem on their journey as the mare came fully into season.

There was an amusing bucking incident from Sleipnir as they set off, which Ubba quelled with an angry shout so loud that it spooked Trixie as well.

Aethelflaed calmed Trixie and said, 'Christ Almighty Ubba, you frightened the living daylights out of me and both horses. I have never heard you raise your voice to that level before.'

Ubba laughed. 'I am sorry, my lady. I resorted to my troop commander voice used in battle.' Sleipnir was snorting and passaging on the spot, wondering why his beloved master had shouted at him. Ubba calmed him with a quiet voice and stroked his neck and said, 'Now behave yourself; work comes before pleasure, so keep your mind on the job!'

Aethelflaed giggled. 'I trust you always put work before pleasure.' She smiled and winked at him.

'I try my best my lady, but it is difficult when you are tempted by a beautiful lady.' He returned the wink and cantered off before he did something he might regret.

The road was getting busier as they approached the next town and Ubba decided to buy a cold lunch and a chicken to cook over the fire for their evening meal. He was not prepared to risk separating Sleipnir from Trixie and leaving them in stables. Trixie was well into season now and Sleipnir was getting more anxious. They paused briefly to eat their lunch in a pretty little copse next to a stream. Ubba was taking no chances and made Sleipnir stand quietly behind the fallen tree they were sitting on, keeping hold of his reins so he could not get close to Trixie, who was now equally enamoured with Sleipnir.

Aethelflaed laughed. 'Ubba Ragnarsson, you are like a fussy mother hen worrying over your baby.'

Ubba flushed red. 'With good reason, my lady. We have here two horses intent on mating and for all of our welfare I intend to impose my authority over Sleipnir and ensure it does not happen until I give permission. We shall ride for the next couple of hours and as soon as I find a safe paddock, I will release them to do what nature intends… whilst you, my lady, are safely out of sight and mind.'

'Are you telling me I am not allowed to witness this epic mating of my mare?'

'Absolutely not, you are a Saxon queen and will never have witnessed such scenes; it would be entirely inappropriate for you to be there. Besides, I have no time to be tending to you if you faint with shock.'

She roared with laughter. 'Peace, Ubba, I am only teasing you because I am enjoying your discomfort. My father brought back a Spanish mare and stallion when he visited the Pope as a teenager. Whilst royal children were banned from the royal stud, we were not entirely innocent of what took place in the covering yard.'

'My lady, my promise to your brother was to escort you safely back to Mercia and whilst I appreciate you would wish to oversee your mare's covering, I must insist you observe from a safe distance and respect my wishes.'

'Oh Ubba, what an absolute gentleman you are! I will abide by your wishes but can assure you there will be no histrionics from me.'

They mounted up and Trixie was not impressed to be ridden again when all she wanted was to be left alone with Sleipnir. They were soon within a few miles of Tettenhall.

Aethelflaed said, 'There is a farm within a mile that supplies the palace with beef, pork and chickens. I know the family well. I am sure they will have a small paddock where we can turn them out and let nature take its course.'

'That would be ideal, my lady. Please show me the way.'

It took a few twists and turns, but they were soon trotting up a long drive with cows and sheep grazing on either side. As they approached the large farmhouse, an older lady was just coming from the dairy with a jug of milk. At the sound of hoofbeats, she stopped and waited for them to come nearer, slightly mystified as to what they wanted.

Aethelflaed shouted, 'Florence it's me, Aethelflaed of Mercia. May I ask you a favour?' She pulled back the hood of her cloak and Florence stared in amazement. She put the jug down on a table and came towards them.

'My lady, how can I be of service? I thought you were based in Jorvik now?'

'I have returned to Mercia on urgent business.'

An older man came striding over from the barn. Florence informed him, 'Sam, my lady of Mercia requests a favour.'

Aethelflaed hesitated and said, 'Please speak to my escort, Sam; he will explain my situation.'

Sam approached Ubba. Ubba said, 'I wonder if you have a small paddock we could turn our horses into. My lady's mare is in season and she wishes to use my stallion's services before I go back north.'

Sam stuttered, 'I am sure I can oblige, but let the ladies go into the house first. I would not wish to offend Queen Aethelflaed.'

Aethelflaed shouted over to them, 'No, I wish to witness the covering Sam, to ensure the safety of my mare.'

Florence stuttered, 'Surely not, my lady? It would be obscene for a lady to attend the covering yard. Leave it to Sam and your man to deal with and come with me for refreshment.'

Aethelflaed replied quickly, 'No honestly, Florence. I do need to be there, but I have promised to keep my distance and I know from my father's stud what to expect.'

Sam shook his head and reluctantly said, 'As you wish, my lady; please follow me. I have an ideal paddock behind the barn over there.'

He turned to Ubba and appraised Sleipnir for the first time, who by now was getting fractious. 'Well at least my lady has an eye for good horseflesh and obviously her mare is besotted with him.'

Ubba replied, 'If you would untack her mare and turn her into the paddock, I will deal with Sleipnir. He is an experienced stallion used to running with mares and covering in hand. I will ensure the mare is safe.'

Sam untacked Trixie, put a headcollar on her and led her to the paddock gate. Ubba unsaddled Sleipnir but kept his bridle on. As the mare was led away, he whinnied to her and lunged to follow, but Ubba was quicker than him and raised his hand in front of his nose and shouted 'Stop!'. As Trixie was released, the stallion snorted and pawed the ground in anticipation of what was to come. He walked quietly to the paddock, obeying his master as expected.

Sam opened the gate. Trixie was cantering around, bucking and calling to Sleipnir. Ubba led him in through the gate, commanded him to wait and removed the reins from the bridle, leaving it on his head. He released him and he chased after Trixie until she stopped and whickered to him. He approached gingerly to confirm she was compliant; she stood like a rock and Sleipnir performed the deed.

Aethelflaed clapped and shouted, 'Just like his master! A true gentleman. My compliments Ubba, on the trust and training you have put into your stallion; this is the greatest gift you could give me.'

Sam stuttered, 'Did you say "Ubba", my lady? Is he Ubba Ragnarsson?'

Aethelflaed laughed. 'He certainly is – my closest friend and confidante. Don't worry; he is not kidnapping me, but escorting me safely back to Mercia.'

Ubba summoned Sleipnir to his side and he came over obediently. Ubba removed the bridle, rummaged in his pocket for a carrot, patted his neck, ruffled his ears and turned round to exit the paddock. Sam decided to leave them after inviting them to go in for refreshment and to see their guest rooms.

Aethelflaed hugged Ubba and said, 'Shall we leave them out together overnight? Will he cover her again?'

'He will repeat the mating as often as he wants until she goes out of season. It's been a while since his last mare. I suggest we leave them overnight and then move to the palace tomorrow. I will let him cover her again if she is still willing before I go, to ensure she has the best chance of conceiving, but I have to get back to Durham to support Halfdan and my son.'

'I know that Ubba, and I pray that your family is safe and sound. Please don't take any risks; they need you for guidance in the future. Torri must be terrified for you, especially after what she has been through recently. If you go into Jorvik, please try and find out what has befallen Aldhelm.'

'Aethelflaed, do not worry; Sigtryggr will not harm him. He will likely keep him as a hostage because he knows he means a lot to you. I will do my best to persuade him to release him, but I have to go to Halfdan in Durham first.'

'I appreciate that and I will do everything I can to get you there as fast as possible. It would be quicker if we could find a merchant going north to sail up to Durham.'

'Thank you, my lady; that would be much appreciated.'

'May I ask you one last favour? Florence says she has put you in a bedroom overlooking Sleipnir's paddock so you can keep an eye on them. Would you mind if I joined you later tonight? I have so enjoyed your company and I will sleep far better not worrying about Trixie.'

Ubba was startled – was Aethelflaed making a pass at him and using this as an excuse?

'As long as you are certain that Florence will keep quiet. I know from experience that women always know what is going on in their household, as my wife was an expert at detecting trysts, even under the palace roof. If Florence notices and reports it back to your clergy and elders, you could be in trouble. I certainly do not need the ignominy of being classed as your lover. There are enough Saxons after my head as it is.'

'Fear not, Ubba. Florence would never do that; she is a model of discreetness. We have managed to lie together for four nights on the way here without ravaging each other, we can surely manage another.' She hugged him and made a hasty exit from the room.

He plonked himself in an armchair and tried to unravel whether Aethelflaed was flirting with him or just being friendly. He had to admit he had been tempted when he woke and found her curled up behind him, because in his dreamy state he was used to having his wife sleeping beside him. There had been many occasions over the years when he had woken her from her slumber by making sexual overtures. Especially recently, after the cancer scare, as they had resumed lovemaking. She was so precious and he was overjoyed that he wasn't going to lose her imminently. What if Aethelflaed touched him? He was certain that his body would react instinctively and then he would be in dire straits.

Florence came to show him to his room, assuming he would like a bath before dinner after four days on the road. He soaked himself and washed his hair then very nearly fell asleep in the bath, exhausted after their escape from Jorvik. He woke with a jolt, jumped out of the bath and scrabbled in his bag for clean clothes. He headed down to dinner with wet hair, but at least it was clean.

He was overwhelmed by the taste of a delicious beef stew and complimented Florence. She went red but was delighted. He felt like he hadn't eaten for days and the return to indoor living was more than welcome. Aethelflaed chatted away about her childhood, when Florence had been her nanny, and kept the conversation light and humorous. Ubba tucked in to a delicious peach sponge cake and let the conversation flow over him. Soon, sleep was catching up with him and even though it was a warm June night and darkness would not come for three hours, he excused himself and made his way up to his room.

He checked on the horses. They seemed to have settled into a pattern of grazing close together; hopefully, their passion had abated. He could not resist the tempting double bed any longer, so stripped off naked, intending to have a quick nap before Aethelflaed arrived.

Relieved of his duty to escort Aethelflaed back to Mercia, his mind and body relaxed and he fully switched off, exhausted. Normally, he would have woken immediately if someone approached his bedroom, but the first he knew of Aethelflaed's arrival was when she slipped into bed next to him. However, he was still asleep and he thought he was in bed with his wife.

Ubba woke before dawn as the birds started singing and he heard Sleipnir calling. He felt movement next to him and turned over to see a stark naked Aethelflaed curled up next to him, followed by the realisation that he was naked too. He saw her nightdress laid over the chair on the other side of the bed. Panic set in. He had no recollection of Aethelflaed coming to his room. He lay still, racking his brain, trying to recall what might have happened.

Suddenly, she moved again and he quickly said, 'My lady, you must get back to your room for your own safety. I apologise profusely that I did not recall you coming in and must have fallen heavily asleep.'

She sat up, smiling. 'Really, Ubba. You were pleased to see me when I climbed into your bed and as it was so warm, I decided to discard my nightdress and sleep naked like you.'

Ubba's heart sank. 'My lady, have I done anything to offend you?'

Her eyes sparkled as she replied, 'How could you do anything to offend me if you were hard and fast asleep?' She threw the sheet off, jumped up, retrieved her nightdress and put it on. 'I will see you at breakfast, my handsome Dane hero.' With a coy wave and a smile, she skipped out of the room, giggling.

Oh God, what had he done? He threw himself out of bed and ran to the bathroom to see if he had any marks on his body, but could find none. He then rushed back to the bed to check for any signs of sexual activity on the sheets, but again found no evidence. He thought back to what she had said and remembered the phrase "hard and fast asleep". This was an often used Saxon and Dane expression and he knew that he had been exhausted. She had also referred to him being pleased to see her, though. Was she teasing him, or had they had sex while he was half-asleep? Surely he'd remember?

He knew that she admired him and had flirted with

him on many occasions… all of which he had ignored, due to her status as Queen and his fear for his neck if he fell for her charms. Perhaps she had found him in a vulnerable position and capitalised on it.

He recalled a conversation with Torri in Ireland after her treatment. She said she had always feared that Aethelflaed was physically attracted to him. He had reassured her that there was never any sexual relationship between them. But now he was not so sure. The question was, would Aethelflaed keep quiet? Should he tackle her, or keep quiet himself? The last thing he wanted to do was upset Torri, but he was reliant on Aethelflaed. He would wait and see if she raised the issue on the way to their final stop – the palace.

THIRTY-TWO

Ubba breathed a sigh of relief as the merchant ship pulled into the docks at Jorvik. He had managed to negotiate passage with a Dane trader to Jorvik, then on to Richmond so he could see his family briefly, and then up to Durham. He unloaded Sleipnir, who was anxious for some exercise after being cooped up on board for two days.

News had reached them on their journey that Sigtryggr had taken Jorvik peacefully and was now installed as King. Certainly, he could see no sign of any opposition on the way to the palace. He approached the gates and asked to see Sigtryggr. The guard recognised him and allowed him through. He trotted down to the stables and was greeted by Alwin, the stable manager who had been in charge during his own time in Jorvik.

While they settled Sleipnir into a turnout paddock, Alwin explained that once the elders realised that Aethelflaed had left Jorvik, they invited Sigtryggr to parley and negotiated a peaceful settlement. Sigtryggr had taken Lord Aldhelm and two more elders as hostages. Should there be any resistance, their lives would be forfeited.

Sigtryggr had obviously been informed of his arrival and was on his way to meet him. They were close to the ornamental fountain and garden. Sigtryggr ushered him over to a bench so they could have a private conversation.

Ubba hugged him and said, 'Congratulations! I am delighted you have taken Jorvik without a fight or siege. The last thing Jorvik needed was to be ransacked and pillaged yet again.'

'Well, your removal of their queen helped me achieve a peaceful settlement. Unfortunately, they assume she knew of the attack and abandoned the city to save her own neck. Nobody is aware of your involvement except Lord Aldhelm, and he will not reveal what happened, to keep his own neck.'

'Aethelflaed did ask me to try and persuade you to release him without harm.'

Sigtryggr laughed. 'I thought a few nights with you would have made her forget about him.'

Ubba was shocked at his comment. 'Look, I was fulfilling my oath to Edward to remove her to safety and I have too much respect for her and my own wife to consider it. Whatever gave you the impression that I would do such a thing? I have been her friend for a long time, but there has never been any sexual relationship between us.' To his utter consternation he heard Ivar's distinctive laugh in his head and knew he was mocking him, too.

Sigtryggr patted him on the shoulder and said, 'My apologies if I have offended you, Ubba. Several people here have mentioned that you were a frequent visitor of the Queen and I assumed there was something between you.'

Ubba was disgruntled to hear this, as if word reached Torri, he knew she might doubt him unnecessarily.

'Look, if you can release him as a favour it would look good and show both Aethelflaed and Edward that you granted her request. You never know when you may need a favour from them.' He had planted the seed and knew it was best left for Sigtryggr to germinate. He changed the subject completely. 'What news of Durham?'

'I heard only yesterday that after a short battle, Halfdan was installed as King. I hope that means your son survived too.'

Ubba groaned, 'So do I. He was determined to be on the frontline, but he is young and inexperienced.'

'Rubbish, you trained him. Besides, Halfdan would not risk losing your son.'

'I do hope not, but I won't be content until I have seen him with my own eyes, so I shall still travel on to Durham after a brief stop to inform my family I am safe.'

'Ivar sends his good wishes, as does Skye. I will be fetching her and the children over when I think it is safe to do so. Edward may want to fight to regain Jorvik.'

'I would doubt it. Jorvik is too far from Winchester for him to control and he knew it when he asked me to remove Aethelflaed. Not that he would admit it, but Edward was impressed with Ivar's reign over Jorvik. It is now one of the most sought-after trading ports in the country. The population has expanded and Ivar left the settling of fallouts between citizens and families to Torri to govern, and the command of his troops to me.'

Sigtryggr smiled. 'Skye has been a huge help to me as Queen of Dublin. She has always managed to cope with the feudal barons who are extremely volatile one minute and then as quiet as lambs when left to work their land.'

'Women have a completely different perspective than men because they have to live with the consequences. Take it from me, women are courageous and resilient and used to coping with the fallout of war. They sacrifice their husbands and sons to war and when they die, the women are left to pick up the pieces. Skye helped Torri in the family court cases. She may not have been raised as a queen, but then neither was Torri! You can always run your ideas past her if you need her advice. Ivar was genuinely in awe of Torri. When Saxon women knew she was dealing with family court business they were overjoyed, because at last they had someone who would fight for them.'

'So what did Ivar do while you and Torri were governing Jorvik?'

Ubba laughed. 'Whatever he wanted, of course! Hunting, hawking and breeding raptors. Dabbling and frolicking with young women. Planning his next conquest and educating himself. Thankfully, he extended this to his nephews and sought out the best tutors in languages, history, maths, science and geography to prepare them for becoming kings. It was a great shame Ivar could never reproduce, because he would have made an excellent father.'

'And which of your children and nephews do you consider future kings?'

Ubba thought for a moment and said, 'I would doubt Arne would want the role as he is bonded to the land and animals, like me. Viggo has the brains and potential to do whatever he wants in life, which is why I encouraged him to go east with Sulamain. Freya will be a queen as the gods have already decreed. She is determined to stay in this country. Bjorn's son Erik is the explorer and has all the qualities to become a great king. His second son Refil is the consummate sailor and boat builder, but it is unlikely he would want to become a king. However, Rollo's eldest son William has been raised to rule. He is clever, determined and believes in himself just like his father... and he has learnt from his mother's knee how to influence other people. He will not be satisfied just inheriting Rollo's title of Duc of Normandie; he wants to be King of France and it would not surprise me to see him achieve it.'

He had a refreshing meal with Sigtryggr and then returned to the stables for Sleipnir, who had enjoyed his freedom in the field. He rode him back to the docks and loaded him onto the merchant's ship to continue their journey. He had agreed to stop briefly at Richmond so he could see his family for a day and then they would go north to Durham, or as far as they could get. Halfdan would likely have blocked the Wear north and south while he took control of Durham, to counteract an attack by boat whilst he was fighting to take the city. Hopefully, it would have been reopened by the time they got there.

He settled down to sleep on the deck close to Sleipnir and eventually fell into a fitful sleep. He kept waking and visualising Ivar admonishing him for his behaviour. He woke up with a start, shouting, 'I did not do anything!' Thankfully, nobody heard him and he lay awake for some time contemplating what he was going to do. He was not admitting to something that he was convinced never happened. Torri would be devastated and he was not upsetting her for nothing. He could just be imagining it – after all, he had managed four nights previously sleeping next to Aethelflaed and was absolutely certain nothing untoward had happened.

oOo

Two days later they were pulling into Ubba's concealed moorings at Richmond. To his utter delight, Freya and Egil were awaiting his arrival. However, he soon saw Torri running from the house to the dock and his heart missed a beat. Thank the gods she was alive and well and he had taken the decision to go to Ireland hoping that Sulamain was still there. The prospect of losing his beloved wife still made him emotional. Although he had always known she would probably die before him as she was 15 years older than him, it had frightened him as he would have been lost without her wise judgement.

As they were trying to unload Sleipnir, he heard voices approaching and knew his second family was coming to greet him. Serena appeared carrying Frank to ensure he did not fall into the water. Astrid and Theo were dying to get closer, but he told them to stay back until Sleipnir was unloaded and he would come to them. Serena looked relieved to see him.

A groom took charge of Sleipnir coming off the boat and Ubba said, 'As Sleipnir has done enough work and Durham appears to have been vanquished by Halfdan, I will take Diablo with me and leave Sleipnir to rest. Turn him out with his mares and he will catch any that may have slipped their foals. Diablo needs some experience in troop riding without full battle engagement; it will be an ideal opportunity to introduce him to this experience. Has he successfully covered the three mares I allocated?'

The groom laughed. 'With great enthusiasm and they all held to their first mating. He had to be reminded about his manners a few times, but he behaved himself. You were wise to select experienced brood mares who once covered, would not let him repeat it unnecessarily. He was too excitable for maiden mares in his first season.'

'Have him ready before dawn; we will be sailing early to get there as quickly as possible.'

He felt a tug at his hand and Theo was staring up at him. 'Mama and Torri have been concerned for your safety. I told them I should have gone with you. Will you take me to Durham?'

'No young man, not just yet, it is too dangerous... but when I get back I promise I will give you more riding tuition on your pony and if you are doing well I will buy you your first horse.'

Theo's face was a picture of joy. 'Oh, really? I promise I am ready; ask Freya. She has let me school her filly in the paddock and I have not fallen off. I have jumped her too, and she can be excitable.'

Astrid shouted, 'Why are you letting Theo have a horse before me, Father? I am two years older than him!'

Ubba hugged her. 'Age is not a consideration Astrid, but experience of riding is and you have not spent the hours in the saddle that Theo has to move on to a horse yet. Now let me hug your mother and Frank.'

Astrid glared at him and flounced off towards the house, aggrieved.

Serena flung one arm around him and stood on her tiptoes to give him a kiss, with Frank in her arms. He kissed her and took Frank off her, who was wriggling to get down. He threw him up in the air and caught him. 'Now, my little warrior, what naughty things have you been up to in my absence?'

Serena laughed. 'Oh Ubba, he is impossible to watch as he is determined to kill himself before he reaches his fourth birthday. The falls he has had off the hay cart, in the barn, climbing trees and playing with the foals have been horrendous. The only person who he obeys instantly is Torri, and she says he is just like Erik and Arne were at the same age. He will never make it into his teens, that's for sure – especially when he starts riding. Do you know he climbed up a tree then onto Diablo's back when he was out in the field with his mares? He could have been killed!'

Ubba smiled. 'Did he manage to stay on Diablo

bareback?'

'Yes, even when he galloped off round the field with him.'

'Well, that's very promising; his balance must be good.'

Finally, they had reached Torri. Serena ushered her children into the house while Torri led Ubba round to her rose garden and ushered him onto the garden seat, where he gave her a long lingering kiss, which she returned enthusiastically.

She said, 'I worried about you being alone with Aethelflaed and getting caught by Saxon troops who would have killed you.'

Ubba stroked her nearly white blonde hair and said, 'Do you not have faith in my tracking skills to avoid such a disaster? My hearing and eyesight are still very sharp. I am not in my dotage yet. Have you had confirmation that Arne is alive and well?'

'Yes. Halfdan sent a message via pigeon to assure me Arne was fine. He was one of the first over the battlements and he fought well, slaying three Saxons. Out scouting with Stefan, he saved him from death by barging into his stallion; the arrow skimmed his shoulder blade instead of hitting his heart. His hearing and sight under battle conditions appear to be as sharp as yours.'

Ubba sighed with relief. 'I told him instinct and training would automatically kick in once he was in battle mode. He is not a violent person, but he knew it was either kill or be killed and he triumphed. I am so pleased for him, as he will never doubt his abilities again. The pressure of emulating his half-brothers Erik and Refil, and also fulfilling his Ragnarsson role, hung heavy in his heart and mind.'

Torri sighed. 'I am also pleased for him because he has always considered himself inferior to Erik and Refil, which was untrue; he was just younger than them and had to bide his time until he was truly tested in battle. He may have no interest in becoming a warrior, but his talents as a farmer and a horseman will give him a living on the land.'

Torri rushed off to oversee preparation of the evening meal to include the six men from the merchant ship while Ubba decided to go and check on the farm. Egil was in the barn, checking a newly born filly foal who'd had difficulty birthing. He explained it was to one of his maiden mares who had been covered by Sleipnir. She had panicked when foaling and when she was trying to lie down, she hit the foal's head on the wall. Thankfully, apart from the foal being slow to come round due to the blow on her head, the filly was now up and suckling well.

Ubba said, 'Poor girl. I have never seen that happen before, but then maiden mares can be unpredictable. You did well to spot it and get there quickly to birth her, or she could have died.'

'I was just glad I was there and saw what happened, or she could have suffocated in the bag.'

Ubba patted him on the back. 'Egil, birthing horses is a far cry from being Ivar's Master of the Palace in Jorvik, but I am grateful for your skills.'

Egil laughed. 'You know as well as I do that old

warriors have to be adaptable and serve where needed. I have enjoyed my time on the farm, although I must say birthing horses is easier than sheep. They give up at the slightest thing and have no desire to stay alive.'

Ubba said, 'Does that mean lambing has been a disaster this year? I am sorry I had to leave you coping in my absence.'

'No, not really lord; it's just that sheep have no stamina or desire to live. They do the most incomprehensible things and die on you in minutes.'

'Egil, I am not your lord anymore. You were one of my father's best warriors and were responsible for teaching me to swordfight as a boy. You did a brilliant job and it is probably why we are both still alive now.'

'Your father would have been so proud of you, Ubba. And now Arne has followed you onto the battlefield and triumphed, too. Do take time to speak to him about it when you get to Durham; it won't have been easy for him.'

'I will, Egil. I know how hard living up to the expectation of being a Ragnarsson is and we all have different ways of coping with it. Now, has Freya been behaving herself?'

Egil laughed. 'Lord, it's not her fault she is so wise and beautiful. You were enamoured of her mother as a boy.'

'And has my wife indulged her passion for Matteo? I gave her my permission to do whatever she wished with him. He can't help being so good looking and attractive to women. I want her to feel young and carefree again and she will enjoy teaching him.'

331

Egil stared at him. 'You sanctioned this, my lord? But are you not jealous?'

'How can I be jealous when she has allowed me to rear a second family with Serena and allowed them to share our house? Is that not the act of a woman who loves her husband and wants him to be content? I just want her to be happy and if having a young man in her bed makes her feel young and virile, then why would I deny her? I am getting older too, you know, and soon women won't be falling at my feet anymore.'

Egil roared with laughter. 'That will never happen. You have the same effect on women as your father did and can tempt them into your bed without saying a word. Those blue eyes do it all for you.'

He laughed and said, 'Remember I have to live with the fact that my father and brother Bjorn were previous lovers of my wife. Bjorn was her husband, to whom she bore two sons. Do you know she has never revealed anything about her sexual relationships with either of them?'

Egil smiled. 'Torri is a very wise woman and knows how difficult it is for men to accept that their wives have had previous relationships. You should be delighted that she has been a devoted wife to you and produced your three outstanding children.'

'Exactly, and I would do anything to keep her happy, so if she wants to flirt with Matteo, why should I worry? I am confident that she loves me as much as I love her. I am going to be in Durham for a while. I know she will be safe here with you looking after the farm and Matteo will keep her amused in my absence.'

Egil smiled. 'One skill you have over any other Ragnarsson is your understanding of women. You know what they are thinking, you know what they want and you give it them, then stand back and reap the rewards. A very clever strategy, my lord. If only Ivar had done the same he would not have been as hated as he was. His desire for total dominance and submission could not be contained.'

Later, when Ubba was tucked up in bed with his soulmate, she asked him if Aethelflaed had made any overtures to him. He reassured her that keeping his head on his body was more important than risking losing it for ten minutes of sex. He was able to distract her by telling her the intimate details of how he found Aethelflaed and Aldhelm in flagrante when he climbed up to their bedroom window.

oOo

Ubba arrived in Durham on the merchant boat and offloaded Diablo in the busy port. He set off to find Halfdan and found some of the narrow streets blocked by houses that had succumbed to fire, but on the whole the city had received minimal damage. He had to ask where the King's residence was and as he approached, he was stopped by guards blocking the entrance. When they realised who he was, he was welcomed in and told Halfdan was inside, but that Arne was out on patrol with Stefan.

He walked round to the stables to find a groom he could trust with Diablo who was overexcited and really needed a good stretch of his legs. Thankfully, he found a groom he recognised who agreed to put Diablo in the stallion paddock for an hour.

He went back to find Halfdan and found him in a big office surrounded by elders, clergy and officials poring over documents with his advisors. When Ubba came in, Halfdan hugged him.

Ubba said quietly, 'Well done, brother; you achieved your target quickly and easily. I am sorry I could not be with you for the battle.'

Halfdan patted him on the back and said to everybody present, 'Gentlemen, this is my brother Ubba Ragnarsson. He is here to assist me with forming governance over Durham after his years supporting Ivar in Jorvik.'

One of the clergy commented, 'Well, I know Ubba was in charge of dealing with the clergy there and they had nothing but praise for him. His wife was also instrumental in presiding over the petty court disputes and proved a fair and conscientious judge.'

After the meeting, Ubba and Halfdan retired to his office and took lunch there.

Ubba said, 'Thank you for sending word to Richmond that Arne was safe. Now tell me, truthfully, how he performed in battle.'

'He was like a seasoned warrior. Nobody would ever have known it was his first battle. Your training provided him with the confidence to do what was necessary to win. He was first over the battlements and killed three soldiers within ten minutes. His ability to attack one soldier, yet be totally aware of what is happening around him, is outstanding. As a scout he is exceptional. When out with Stefan they came under attack in the woods. He heard an arrow coming and deliberately cannoned his horse into Stefan's and deflected the arrow. It was remarkable.'

'It takes a great deal of practice. You have to train your brain to be alert for any danger and mentally block out any background noise. Hunting trains you to stalk prey and strike at exactly the right time. Arne is grounded to the land like me and can actually feel the disturbance in the air as the arrow is flying.'

'I am so grateful that he saved Stefan's life. The arrow winged his shoulder but did not enter his flesh and cause any real damage. How much time can you spare me to set up government here? Have you to return to Richmond soon, or has Sigtryggr asked you for help?'

Ubba chuckled. 'Sigtryggr neither wants nor needs my input. He will follow his own path, just as Ivar did. You have to drop little seeds of information for him to germinate if you have a better solution than him. I left him with one of those, suggesting he frees Lord Aldhelm as a gesture that may reap rewards in the future with King Edward and Aethelflaed. As for my time in Richmond, the stud season is nearly over and they have managed without me so far. Egil has found, as I did, that breeding sheep compared to horses is far more stressful and uneconomic.'

'I would be grateful if you could give me a few weeks to get sorted... and can I keep my best scout, too?'

At this point, the door was flung open and Arne charged in, closely followed by Stefan. Arne ran over and Ubba hugged him tightly. 'My son, I am so proud of you. Halfdan has been telling me of your exploits and I am delighted you equipped yourself with such courage and valour.'

'It wasn't easy Father, but like you found, it was a case of staying alive and I knew I had to strike first.'

'Your mother is delighted for you and your sister is angry that she couldn't be on the battlements with you.'

Arne laughed. 'Well nobody would attack her; she is too beautiful to kill!'

THIRTY-THREE

Sulamain heard a horse cantering into his drive and went to the window expecting it to be Viggo back from the hospital, although he did not usually finish his shift until 6.00 pm. To his surprise it was an Arab sheikh, Abdul Habib, who was one of the most influential men in Egypt. He was surprised to see the sheikh alone; he would have expected him to have an escort, riding into the city. Sulamain went to the door as his groom was taking the grey Arab stallion round to his stables.

'Your excellency, welcome to my humble abode. How may I be of service to you?'

Abdul replied, 'I had a private errand in the city and I heard you had returned from the West accompanied by a young Dane. I wonder if he may be able to help me with a problem.'

Sulamain ushered him in and sent his servant for refreshments. He was concerned as to why Abdul needed Viggo and worried for Viggo's safety. They had agreed that it would be unwise for Viggo to reveal his name and background just in case anybody decided he might be worth kidnapping and ransoming. Their story was that Sulamain had been at Ivar's court in Jorvik teaching his nephews and Viggo, as a bright young boy and a friend of the Ragnarssons, was permitted to attend their lessons. He had begged to accompany Sulamain back east so he could learn more about medicine and make his fortune.

Abdul said, 'It is just a matter of translation, really. I have recently remarried and my wife is of Danish heritage.'

Sulaimain recalled that Abdul must have at least three wives already, and a multitude of offspring of varying ages.

Abdul smiled. 'You look shocked, Sulamain?'

'Forgive me sir, but it's not something I would expect. Marriages between different religions are not considered acceptable here unless, of course, she has converted to Islam.'

'No, she hasn't but this is where this young man could be of assistance. I will relate the full story, but I want your absolute discretion in this matter.'

Sulamain nodded his agreement but felt dreadfully uneasy about the role Abdul had in mind for Viggo.

'I assume your travels will have given you knowledge of these Dane warriors – and some understanding of their customs and practices.'

'Yes, sir but I am by no means fluent in their language, which changes dependent upon their specific birthplace. I conversed with Ivar and his family mainly in Latin, although he had knowledge of French and Saxon.'

Abdul said, 'But I thought they are uneducated, cannot read or write and are total pagans?'

Sulamain shook his head. 'Not so, your excellency;

they take their Norse religion as seriously as we take ours. Granted it may be very different in teaching to ours, but never dismiss them as uncultured or uneducated. They are masters of the sea, both as sailors and boat builders, and anyone who contemplates crossing the North Sea in a longboat must have the courage of a lion. They live in the moment and when faced with impossible challenges, they find a way to succeed.'

'I know and that is why I am interested in having Helga as my wife. I don't think she understands that she is married to me and not just my slave.'

'How did she come to you?'

'She lived in a small village on the coast in Denmark with her mother, while her father was over raiding in Northumbria with the local jarl. Unfortunately, her village was attacked by Frisians who had started raiding Denmark in the summer, knowing that most of the Danish men were conveniently raiding in Europe. Her mother was killed hiding her when the village was attacked and she was taken as a slave to be sold overseas. Her captors realised her value as a beautiful virgin far exceeded the price they would get for selling her into slavery and she was sold to an Eastern slave trader in Paris. When he reached Alexandria, he contacted me and I went to see her. She is 16 years old with hair like burnished gold, deep blue eyes and a pale complexion. Christians talk of angels and that's exactly what she looks like.'

Sulamain sighed deeply. 'But Abdul, she is an innocent child who will be well aware of what her future now holds. Danish women are respected by their men and they have their own rights. If a woman marries a Dane and he disrespects her, she can divorce him and retain whatever dowry she brought into the marriage. Danish men know that without the huge contribution women make, rearing their children and keeping their homes running whilst they are away raiding, they would have nothing to come home to. Granted, a lot of them are killed in the process, but it is the community back in Denmark that picks up the pieces when men are killed. Why did you want to marry her instead of keeping her as a slave?'

'Because she is so beautiful. I want to produce children with her courage and beauty.'

'In other words, you want her as a brood mare just like your horses, dogs, falcons and everything else you own. There is one thing I have learnt about Danes and that is they are bonded to the land. They need to be free and in a loving relationship. They do not thrive in excessively warm climates, either. You cannot lock her in a gilded cage and expect her to be eternally grateful to you. To her, your palace is no different from a cell underground – it is still a prison. I assume that if you have taken her as a wife, you have taken her virginity. I can't imagine it was an enjoyable experience for Helga.'

'Look, I did everything possible to ensure she knew what was expected of her as a dutiful wife. I left her with my senior wife to educate her on what was expected of her in the bedroom. I was very gentle with her on our wedding night, but after I demanded more she became demented and very nearly gouged my eye out and then bit me in a very sensitive place; she was like a hellcat. I could not allow such dangerous behaviour, so I restrained her and beat her, just as I would any animal that attacked me.'

'So, you raped her and beat her into submission, but yet purported to love her as your wife.'

'That's why I am here. I don't think she fully understands that I mean her no harm. I want Viggo to explain to her that she is my wife, not my prisoner.'

'Abdul, Viggo will be as mortified as I am to see a young Danish girl in such a perilous state. She is responding exactly as I would expect in this situation. How long have you been married and how is she coping now?'

'We were married eight weeks ago and now she permits intercourse without having to be restrained, but will go no further than that. She has lost weight and when she does eat, she is violently sick. The beautiful girl is disappearing before my very eyes and I don't want to lose her. I am frightened she will starve herself to death.'

Sulamain threw his arms in the air and proclaimed, 'But to her, death is her only way out of this situation. When you try to control the mind and body of someone to this extent and she has come to the conclusion that she would prefer to die than continue this life, then the future is in doubt. Have you thought she may already be pregnant and trying to deprive you of your child?'

Abdul jumped up. 'No, I didn't think of that at all. Please, Sulamain, you have to confirm if she is pregnant and find a way to stop her being so sick.'

'Look, some women do become sickly in response to their hormones when they become pregnant, particularly in the early stages of pregnancy – and others blossom as pregnancy progresses. But if all she has experienced is pain and constant beatings then she knows the only way out is death. Dane warriors fear captivity far more than death. Depriving them of their freedom is to them a life not worth living.'

Abdul sighed. 'She has never once cried out when I have beaten her. Even when I took her virginity, she remained totally silent, although she shed a few tears.'

Sulamain turned on him angrily, 'So where was your love for her then Abdul, when you were raping her body and mind?'

Abdul screamed back at him, 'There is no such thing as rape between man and wife, and you well know it! She is mine to do with exactly as I see fit.'

'Well you shouldn't have taken a Danish girl to your bed. She will never love you and will kill herself rather than remain in captivity. She may have already lost the baby due to your savage beatings.'

'Look, she can have whatever she wants: precious jewels, clothes, gold, silver, even her own palace and servants.'

'She doesn't want any of those things; she wants her freedom. She would marry a goatherd if she loved him; money does not buy happiness! She knows that a life with you will be intolerable. She will probably have a life worse than slavery. No doubt you will take her children from her and raise them as you decree. She is also going to be hated by the other wives in the harem. In fact, they could already be trying to poison her and any children will be targeted by your older sons and may well never make adulthood.'

Abdul gasped with shock. 'You really think she may be poisoned?'

'Yes, especially if she has children. I know what you are like when something becomes too great a problem in your life. You really have not thought through the repercussions of what you have done, but she has and is prepared to face death to get away from it. You will do to her the same as you do to your horses, dogs and wives who don't make the grade – kill her!'

'I would never do that to her!'

'But she will beat you to it! Look, I will examine her and treat her, but I insist on you not being present. The girl is traumatised enough already and much as I would prefer to keep Viggo out of this mess completely, I appreciate that we cannot make any progress until she can communicate. I am appalled at what you have done and want no part of it, but for the girl's sake I am prepared to help her. Whatever obsession you have over her is purely transient; she will never love you. Do you seriously think that she will reproduce blonde, blue-eyed children to you? Genetic makeup is a mixture of 50% from each parent, but some genetic traits are stronger than others. The darker skin, eye and hair colour will be more dominant. We know this is true because we see it in animals. If you are wanting to produce strong courageous fighters then you have chosen the wrong broodmare. I have seen with my own eyes that genetic inheritance in the Ragnarssons.

Not all of them want to be King. Ubba Ragnarsson certainly did not; he was hefted to the land.

'If you really love her then send her back to Denmark, particularly if she is not pregnant. She will struggle to acclimatise to our weather, food and culture. How many slaves from northern climates have died out here already? She comes from a supportive family background and needs to feel safe and loved. You have made her a target for hate and this will break her spirit.'

There was a prolonged silence as Abdul paced the room with a face as black as thunder. 'I will agree to let you see her, on the one condition that you never leave her alone with Viggo. She will see him as her hero and saviour, fall in love with him and try to escape.'

'Why do you think I did not want him to be involved? His future is in medicine and the last thing he needs is any distraction from his studies. I promised his parents he would not marry and when he is suitably competent he will return to Jorvik to practice medicine there. He has already devised treatments for various diseases and is an excellent surgeon. He is highly intelligent, has taught himself astronomy and speaks several languages. He has studied Greek and Roman history and understands politics too.'

'So, not quite the Dane warrior one would expect.'

Sulamain replied, 'Believe me, he may not wish to be hands-on in battle, but he has all the skills necessary to win any war. His ability to devise a winning strategy outshines any Greek or Roman emperor. Try playing chess with him because I can assure you that you will never beat him.'

Just at that moment, Sulamain heard Viggo coming in from the stables and knew he would have seen Abdul's horse. He opened the door and called him in to the room. 'Viggo, may I introduce you to his excellency, Abdul Habib. He has asked us to assist with a problem in his household.' He spoke in Arabic and gave Viggo a warning look.

Viggo immediately stepped forward, bowed to Abdul and replied in perfect Arabic. 'Your excellency, I am delighted to make your acquaintance.'

Abdul replied, 'Sulamain tells me you are a very gifted pupil.'

'I have been very lucky in that Ivar took me under his wing and allowed me to study with his nephews when Sulamain came to Jorvik. He also introduced me to falconry and breeding raptors, and allowed me to care for and hunt them. He had a pair of gyrfalcons that he released in Yorkshire as it was the perfect environment for them. He also taught wild sea eagles to fish for him.'

'But that cannot be possible, how did he manage that?'

'He built a rapport with them and they watched him fly his raptors who returned with differing prey, and then one day just flew off to the River Ouse and returned with a salmon and dropped it at his feet. He had a special relationship with raptors.'

'Do you know who I could purchase gyrfalcons from here?'

'No, your excellency, gyrfalcons would not survive

in this climate and I do not agree with caging birds purely to look at. They need to fly free to hunt and this would not be possible over desert.'

Abdul gave him an appraising look and said, 'So, how have you coped acclimatising to Egypt?'

'With difficulty for sure, but I do not have to do manual outdoor work so I am very lucky. I have learned to adopt Arab dress because it keeps me cool and although I struggle with highly spiced food, particularly with its effects on the stomach and bowels, I have slowly introduced small amounts into my diet now.'

Abdul looked at Sulamain and said, 'So you would be able to advise a diet for a northerner new to this country?'

Viggo looked slightly confused, but said, 'I am sure I could, your excellency.'

'Well, Sulamain will be bringing you to my palace soon and I would be pleased to show you my raptors, hounds, horses and camels.'

'That would be very generous of you, although I have to say I have not taken well to camel riding. I find the rolling gait rather uncomfortable, but I adore your Arab horses and how they have adapted their gait to cope with the sand.'

'Well, Sulamain, I shall enjoy picking Viggo's brain about my livestock. When will you be able to come, as it may take a few visits to ingest all his knowledge?'

'Sir, I need a day to make some of the lotions and potions I think you will need, so probably Thursday. Viggo can do his hospital shift early in the morning so he does not miss his studies. We will be with you around noon.'

Viggo said, 'I will go and fetch your stallion, your excellency.'

After he had gone, Abdul said, 'I am certainly impressed by him, but regrettably, I expect Helga will fall readily for his charm and good looks. You must not let them get too close.'

'May I remind you that had you been less brutal in your domination of this poor girl, I would not need to be treating her at all.'

Abdul did not deign to reply to Sulamain, but gave him a withering look.

After Abdul had left, Sulamain called Viggo back and could tell he was intrigued to know why Abdul wanted them.

He explained as gently as he could exactly what had transpired and as he expected, Viggo went through a series of emotions ranging from anger to tears. He emphasised that he needed Viggo to communicate with Helga so they could ascertain whether she may already be pregnant and to help her cope with her situation. He begged him not to consider trying to remove her from the harem because now she was married, she had become the legal property of Abdul.

When he mentioned that she did not cry out when beaten, Viggo said, 'But it is not our custom to show pain. Women give birth silently and stoically and men never cry out when mortally wounded in battle. We are expected to die an honourable courageous death so we have a chance to go to Valhalla. You will recall

Torri's husband being blood eagled by my grandfather and he never uttered a sound.'

'Viggo, I know you took my advice seriously about restricting your natural sexuality and keeping to bathhouse attendants and prostitutes because of the danger of attracting the wives and daughters of Moslems, but I know you will struggle morally with this situation. Do not let your heart become involved in this case. Every country has different attitudes to women. I know this will affect you, but you must promise me to remain cool, calm and detached as both our lives could be in danger.'

'Sulamain, I have no desire to lose my head over a woman. I promised my father I would not be foolish and marry whilst overseas. I sowed my wild oats very young and sailed very close to the wind many times, but to me it was all part of experimenting and learning. I am a lot wiser now and far more politically astute. I know that Abdul will not tolerate any interference with his wife, but if I can help guide her into understanding the power that she has, it may result in her being able to accept her situation and use it to her advantage. However, I do see the pitfalls and danger she will be in; it depends how strong she is at exploiting his weaknesses. She just may not have the intelligence or even want to play the game.'

THIRTY-FOUR

They left for Abdul's palace on Thursday morning. Sulamain had made up some soothing ointments made of beeswax to heal her external wounds and also internal ones, where he knew she must be feeling very uncomfortable and sore. Viggo had made up two different drinks – one based on oranges and mango and a second based on lemons and vanilla, both containing small amounts of arrowroot – to try and quell the sickness. He had also composed a list of foods with more meat protein and limited spices, to tempt her to eat more. He had been out and bought her some hair ornaments so that she could braid and weave her hair to keep her cooler in the arid heat.

Viggo enjoyed his ride out of the city centre and they both let their horses canter when the footing was suitable. Viggo hated getting sand in his hair, so was wearing a headdress, but thankfully there was little wind to contend with. As the palace came into view it looked like a green oasis surrounded by a tributary of dykes that maintained water flow around the entire area.

At the main gates they were ushered through to the palace and grooms appeared to take the horses. Panniers from both horses were carried by liveried servants as they were shown through to Abdul's office. Viggo was amazed at the luxury of the building and the furnishings. In the centre was a garden full of bright flowers and shady trees, with an undercover swimming pool at one end.

Abdul greeted them politely and dismissed the servants immediately they had brought in refreshments. He offered them cooling mint or fresh orange drinks to assuage their thirst.

He nodded at the panniers and said, 'I will have to inspect those to ensure there are no concealed weapons and I want to know exactly what is in the potions and lotions. I regret this, but I insist on knowing exactly what drugs you are using.'

Sulamain sighed. 'Abdul, there are no drugs in anything I have brought you. If your wife is pregnant then she cannot consume anything that may damage the foetus. I trust you are not giving her anything that could put her at risk.'

Abdul replied, 'Perhaps a glass or two of wine to help her relax occasionally.'

'Why, when you don't drink alcohol? You must stop if she is pregnant.'

'How will you verify the pregnancy? Will you have to examine her internally?'

Sulamain replied, 'The last thing she needs is an internal examination as this would put at risk a potential pregnancy. The only way I can test at this early stage is by taking a urine sample and see if when tested, it changes colour.'

'Very well. Now show me what is in the panniers?'

Sulamain opened the first one and explained what the bottles contained and how they were to be used.

Finally, Abdul personally led them into the harem and Viggo's eyes scanned every corner, amazed at the show of wealth on view. The main door was guarded by two eunuchs holding curved axes. Viggo cringed at the thought of being castrated and vowed not to upset the guards.

They went into a sumptuous bedroom with its own mini pool surrounded by palm trees, and a separate bathroom. The bed was enormous and surrounded by silk hangings, covered with animal skins and numerous pillows. A door opened at the far end and two guards appeared with Helga in between them.

Viggo looked intently at the girl and she looked terrified. She had long blonde hair that was dry and tangled. She had black underneath her eyes and bruised cheekbones. Her arms and legs were very thin and her hip bones protruded through the full-length silk wrap. Her skin was red and inflamed and she looked much younger than seventeen. Her eyes darted from Sulamain to him, and he gave her an encouraging smile. As Abdul approached, she bowed low until he took her hand and led her forward to Sulamain. He introduced her in Arabic and Viggo saw her panic as she did not understand that Sulamain was a healer.

Finally, Abdul led her over to Viggo and introduced him, saying he was a Dane.

Suddenly, her eyes lit up and she stood straight and tall. She spoke quickly in Danish and asked if he had come to rescue her. Viggo interrupted and said he was merely the healer's assistant and was there to translate only. She kept her eyes on Abdul, but lowered her voice, 'Please help me. I have been sold to this man as his sex slave.'

Viggo interrupted, 'No, my lady you are not his slave, you are his wife.'

She looked straight at him with anger in her eyes. 'He claims I am his wife, but no man would do what he does to me, to a woman he loves. I have not willingly agreed to marry him and I never shall.'

Sulamain intervened and suggested Abdul leave so he could carry out the examination, worried he may understand what she had said.

Abdul and the two servants left the room. The panniers were brought in and left by the sumptuous seating area.

Viggo suggested they sit down and she tell them what had happened to her since she had been brought to the palace.

Slowly, peppered with tears, Helga told them what had happened. When she got to the beatings, Viggo desperately wanted to hug her, but Sulamain bade him leave her alone and put his own arm around her and hugged her instead.

He asked her whether she had noticed changes in her body and she confirmed she had been violently sick, maybe because the food was too hot, and that her appetite had gone the longer she had been in captivity. Sulamain turned to Viggo and told him to explain about the urine test and ask her if she would let him examine her body and treat her wounds.

It took some convincing that this was not a trick. Sulamain gave her the bowl and pointed to the bathroom for her to take the test privately. She did as requested and handed it back to Sulamain, who had already set up a table with his equipment on it. He poured some urine into a glass jug and then added the reactive powder. It bubbled furiously and then the colour changed to purple. Sulamain looked at Viggo and saw the sorrow he felt reflected in his eyes.

'Tell her gently and persuade her that I need to examine her.'

Viggo broke the news. As the realisation dawned on her she sobbed and said, 'So he just wanted me for a broodmare and he will take my babies away at birth. I will be trapped in this hell until he tires of me or kills me.'

'Sweetheart, I know this is traumatic for you, but you must stop resisting him and submit to his desires.'

'I can't pleasure him. I find it disgusting and repulsive and it just makes me vomit. I have accepted that I have to permit sexual intercourse – he already owns every part of my body – but I will not kiss him or do that. I will kill myself before my innocent child is born.'

Sulamain intervened, 'Helga, now that you are pregnant I will insist he leaves you alone for fear of losing the baby. The first twelve weeks are when most miscarriages take place. I will also tell him that he must not force you to do anything against your will. If he wants a live child, he must respect your wishes. I have no idea whether it will work, but it is worth a try.

Once you are into the pregnancy he will tire of you, as most men do when their wives are breeding.'

She rounded on him, 'He won't! He is obsessed with my body, my hair, my skin and other private areas. He will not leave me alone.'

Viggo covered the sofa with a sheet from the pannier, as he had dismissed using the bed as he feared it would traumatise her even more. He held her hand and gently said, 'Sweetheart, just slip your wrap off, lie down on your back and let Sulamain examine you. I promise he will not examine you internally; he just wants to make sure there is no infection in any cuts and then he will apply a soothing cream to them. You must tell him where your body hurts in case there are any broken bones.'

She shivered and said, 'Will you hold my hand?'

Viggo looked pleadingly at Sulamain, who said, 'Yes, but do not tell your husband as he insisted Viggo did not touch you at all.'

Viggo helped her take off the wrap and averted his eyes while she lay down. He also covered her with the wrap from her shoulders downwards, to make her feel less exposed.

Sulamain knelt down beside her and put a cushion under her head. He examined her face and although there was some bruising on her cheeks, the skin was unbroken. However, her skin was dry, flaky and inflamed. He asked Viggo to get the moisturising skin cream and then he put some on her face. He took her hand and examined her wrist. There were old marks where her wrists and ankles had been manacled, probably whilst she was on the slave ship. However, there were also new red rope burns that had torn her skin but were partially healed. He used the bee balm to cover her wrists and ankles. She had a sore, weeping rope burn around her neck.

Sulamain asked Viggo to ask her why she had been tied up. She explained that after Abdul had raped her, he wanted her to pleasure him and she would not. He had put his hand over her nose until she had to open her mouth to breathe, forced himself inside her and she bit him. He was demented and tied her down, gagged her and beat her with a leather whip. After that, he tied her and gagged her for the next week convinced she would cease fighting, but she was violently sick every time he tried to force her so he gave up. They came to an agreement that she would tolerate intercourse but nothing further.

Sulamain pulled the wrap down and exposed her breasts. Viggo took in a sharp breath. There were tooth marks on her breasts and her nipples were swollen. Sulamain asked if she would like to put the ointment on herself, which she did.

Sulamain observed that Viggo was holding her hand, but silent tears were dripping down his cheeks. He signalled with his hand for him to go, but he shook his head and told him to carry on. As he pulled the wrap off her and she opened her legs, he saw she was bruised around her thighs and very swollen internally. Sulamain asked Viggo to ask her if she would like to put the ointment on when she was alone and she agreed. Viggo's face was distraught and Sulamain regretted having him witness the scene.

She turned over onto her front and exposed the whip marks to her back and buttocks, which were healing and indicated the beatings had indeed ceased. Sulamain covered them with the ointment and could feel anger emanating from Viggo. He gave her the wrap to cover herself and told her to sit up.

He turned to Viggo and pointed for him to sit next to Helga. 'I want you to ask her what we can do to make her feel well. Ask her about what she would like to eat, and give her a sip of the two drinks, which will help morning sickness. We have to stop her losing weight. We can't prevent him from touching her, but we can insist he stops having sex if he wants a live offspring from her. Ask her about the other wives – are they jealous of her? Do not frighten her by saying that she is at risk of poisoning. I know this is hard for you Viggo, but there is nothing we can do to remove her from this ordeal – only suggest ways in which she can use his obsession with her to gain more freedom and status.'

Viggo chatted to her for a while and then they heard Abdul returning. He removed himself to the panniers and started unloading the contents. To avoid any confusion, each bottle or jar was labelled in Arabic and Danish. He had listed the recipe for the drinks in Arabic, so the kitchen could reproduce them, and prepared a diet sheet. He was slightly concerned that her having separately prepared meals could permit an opportunity for poisoning, but after what he had seen today, surely Helga would be better off dead.

Abdul arrived and looked for some clue on their faces. The black look he received from Viggo gave a positive indication of how he felt. He walked over to Helga and patted her on the head. 'How's my dear wife, Sulamain?'

Sulamain thought before replying. 'Amazingly, still pregnant, despite the state of her abused body.'

Abdul's face was a picture and he knelt down and hugged her to him, kissing her on the cheek. 'Oh, you little beauty, Helga; what a clever girl.'

Sulamain interrupted, 'You do realise that if you wish to maintain this pregnancy, you must leave her body alone. The first three months of pregnancy are crucial whilst the foetus attaches safely in the womb. You cannot continue to beat her or have frequent intercourse with her. She is also suffering from early stage sickness, and unless she eats properly, the baby will die. I have prepared drinks to keep her hydrated and Viggo has prepared a list of high protein foods that she likes to eat. No heavy spices or sauces are to be given at this stage.'

Abdul clapped his hands in joy and said, 'She will have everything you suggest, and more besides.'

Sulamain said, 'I have not finished yet. She must use the ointments I have prescribed for her skin and she must have access to fresh air and outdoor exercise (under a parasol of course) and perhaps a daily ride on a suitable quiet horse. She needs clothes of pure silk to keep her cool and help her wounds heal. She must be bathed in camel milk and encouraged to swim daily. She needs to have an older woman of her choice as her companion to help her through the pregnancy and she needs a woman who can plait and braid hair so that she keeps cool during the day as she tells me you won't allow her to cut her hair shorter.'

Abdul looked perplexed but said, 'I will endeavour to carry out your instructions and will expect you to visit her frequently to ensure the pregnancy is proceeding well, and to oversee the birth.'

Sulamain replied, 'Very well, we will return in two weeks and hope to see much improvement in her condition. If you have any concerns about her health then send for me.'

He turned to Helga and bowed. 'My lady, I hope we have been of good service to you both spiritually and bodily. I implore you to use the ointments I have given you to speed your recovery. We will bring you more stock next time. It is imperative you drink and eat in spite of any sickness. You need to eat an arrowroot biscuit to calm your stomach every morning. Remember, outdoor exercise is vital for your mind, too.'

She said, 'Thank you so much, both of you, for your care and attention.' Her eyes went to Viggo but he kept his back turned to her as he knew Abdul would be watching his reaction.

Viggo stayed silent on the way home, going over what he had seen. His quick brain had already analysed the data and he accepted that he could do nothing more for her; he was not going to lose his head and future over something he could not control.

That evening over dinner, Viggo brought a bottle of wine to the table. Sulamain raised an eyebrow and said, 'I understand today was very hard for you Viggo, but you handled it very well.'

'Helga is a victim of circumstance and was in the wrong place at the wrong time. I am appalled at her treatment by Abdul, but wise enough to know I cannot afford to become involved. You have drummed into me the dangers involved in approving or disapproving of events, religious practices or traditions in foreign countries for fear of offending. I have accepted that I must maintain a discreet silence. Helga is a child plucked from her homeland and her future is now determined by her captors. I have a sister her age and I would be devastated if it happened to Freya, and my mother was kidnapped and raped four years ago, too.

'My culture respects women as individuals and the contribution they make to family life. However, here, many women are very much dominated by men and given no free expression or allowed to live their own life. They become the property of their husband upon marriage. I may disagree with it, but who am I to condemn it? I am not a god. I cannot change it, so if I wish to live here, I have to accept it.'

'Oh Viggo, what a wise head on such young shoulders. You have inherited Ivar's quick intelligence and strategy. You will go far, whatever path in life you take. You have empathy and a social awareness, hence your desire to heal.'

'That is why I don't think Helga has the ability to use Abdul's obsession with her to her advantage. If she goes too far, she risks death, and she just wants her freedom. Neither does she want to be kept in captivity and bred from, either. She is not motivated by anything he can offer her. She has never had unlimited money or lived a luxury lifestyle. She certainly hasn't even seen the political implications and I did not enlighten her. I was appalled that Abdul could do that to her, but then nobody will have ever given him boundaries. He has always been able to have whatever he wants. I am not defending him in any way for what he did; that was pure anger, dominance and aggression. Because she kept silent and continued to deny him, she probably faced more pain than necessary.'

'I like that you understand it from both their perspectives; that demonstrates your lively mind to be able to relate to the cause and effect of both their environments. Tell me, Viggo… Do you think love on both sides is necessary in a marriage?'

'Yes, of course it is, but not having been in love with a girl yet I don't speak from experience. I can only relate to my own family and you know how much love there is between my parents. I hope I can find the same when I am ready. Now, sex for me is just a pleasure, but I can understand how much more it would mean in a long-term relationship. When I find the woman I wish to marry and rear children with, I will do it.'

'But you wouldn't be tempted to marry someone who may come with rich rewards and lands, whom you don't love?'

'Come on, Sulamain. I am not motivated by money and possessions, but if she came with money and land I would have to consider my options. In Europe, marriage between royal offspring from different countries is common as it can bring money, status and power. In Frankia, most royal marriages are purely an alliance and having mistresses is perfectly acceptable. It may be the European way, but it certainly would not suit me. I have been extremely lucky to have my father to guide me and I have seen the joy he has found in rearing his younger children with Serena. He missed out on family time with us because of his duties overseas, but since we moved to Jorvik I have loved every minute of having both my mother and father's love and support. I am also eternally grateful for Ivar's guidance and support. He gave me an education, which allowed me to explore what I wanted to do in life. It may not make me rich, but I hope I can relieve suffering and find ways of fighting diseases.'

'Viggo, you are already producing new cures and treatments and at only 17 years old that is remarkable.'

THIRTY-FIVE

Viggo worked hard at his research over the next two weeks and developed a hair balm from chamomile and coconut oil, which would hopefully restore the shine and lustre to Helga's hair. This gave him a relaxing break from finding a safe substance to use on human hair to kill lice.

They returned to the palace and set off early, as the temperatures were getting higher out in the desert as summer wore on. Viggo flatly refused to travel by camel. He had plaited and weaved his hair and tied it up on top of his head, and wore a white traditional Arab headdress to reduce sweating. He had the thinnest tunic he could find over a long silk shift. To protect his eyes he wore a muslin scarf to lessen the sun's rays and allow him to see where he was going.

They arrived at the palace at 11.00 am and he knew they would be unable to return before 6.00 pm, because of the heat. They both hoped they would find Helga in a better physical state.

Abdul greeted them with enthusiasm and reported an improvement in Helga's health. When they were shown to her room, Viggo was delighted to see her wearing a beautiful blue silk gown and she had also pinned half her hair up and braided the sides. Her face was clear of bruises and her eyes seemed brighter.

Sulamain said, 'Praise to Allah that you look so well. Has he stopped intercourse with you?'

Helga smiled. 'Yes, he has taken your advice on that score. He is still infatuated with my body, and his fingers and tongue are all over me, but at least he is gentler and has still refrained from forcing me to pleasure him. He has to do it himself now!'

Viggo could not stop himself laughing at her explanation.

Sulamain also understood what Helga had said, and he too laughed.

Helga continued, 'Some nights, he brings in one of his wives and pleasures me, then makes her pleasure him and humps her instead of me.'

Viggo laughed loudly. 'Well, for once you are getting the better deal and I am delighted to see you smile again.'

Helga laughed, 'But how long did you tell him to leave me alone for? He's surely not going to deny himself the pleasure for much longer?'

Sulamain replied, 'I told him until you were four months pregnant, but by then his desire should have waned. Most Arab sheikhs have enough wives to satisfy them, and hate signs of pregnancy in their women, so they usually leave them alone until well after the birth.'

Helga said, Well, it's not going to happen with him, I can assure you. He has found another passion. He has taken to drawing me nude in very intimate detail, but at least he doesn't hurt me or have sex with me.'

Sulamain sighed and said, 'Now let's have a look at you and see if I can date this pregnancy yet. I won't examine you internally.'

Viggo helped undo the buttons at the back of her dress and Helga whispered to him, 'I bet you have had plenty of experience of divesting women of their clothes?'

Viggo was shocked and even managed to blush, but chose not to answer.

Helga stood facing them and Sulamain was relieved to see that there were no bite marks on her breasts and the ointment had relieved the inflammation of her skin. He turned her sideways, looking for any thickening of her waist. She had been very thin before, but her hip bones did not appear to stick out as much as they had done. He turned her round to examine her back; most of the whip marks had now healed and some of the early ones were fading to silvery lines. The ointment had definitely helped heal them. She redressed with Viggo's assistance and returned to the sofa.

Sulamain asked her about the morning sickness and she confirmed the drinks and arrowroot biscuits for breakfast had stopped her sickness, provided she ate nothing with spices in all day. The kitchen made her the dishes Viggo had suggested and she was now able to keep food down.

Viggo gave her the balm for her hair and she confirmed that her hair had stopped falling out and was less dry and brittle. He suggested she use this balm after washing her hair and see if it improved the condition further by the next time they came.

They heard footsteps approaching the door and Abdul swept in. 'Gentlemen, do you note the improvement in my wife's health? She has been taking regular exercise, both riding and walking. Your lotions have considerably improved her skin and the drinks do seem to calm her stomach. I am delighted she can ride well and can escort me to social events. Obviously when the baby is visible, then she will retire from public life and become the mother of my son.'

Sulamain replied, 'Let's not get too far ahead; many things can happen during pregnancy and she is young and inexperienced. I told you that the sex of the child is determined by male sperm so you must not rule out that she may be carrying a daughter.'

'I know that, but every man hopes for sons and she will have many years of breeding in her. Beautiful daughters attract attention and make good marriages. Now, I have been summoned to the aviary to see some newborn falcon chicks and if Viggo is free I will show him around.'

Viggo beamed, bowed respectfully and said, 'Your excellency, I would be honoured to see your raptors.'

Sulamain waved his hand. 'Yes, I just wish to discuss diet with your wife, but you can take Viggo now.'

As they left the room, Viggo remembered that it was an unwritten rule that nobody ever walked in front of an Arab sheik and as Abdul was well under six feet tall with short legs and he was over six feet with a long stride and brisk walking pace, he had to severely slow down so as not to outpace Abdul.

They passed the stables, which were built with

the same materials as the house, with marble pillars supporting the entrance. Abdul said he would show him around after they had been to the aviary. Again, no expense had been spared here; it was a large square building with four towers, one at each corner, and the different species of raptors were kept separately.

Abdul showed him the peregrine falcons first and he was fascinated at the attention to detail that provided a perfect environment for the raptors. He was allowed to go outside with Abdul wearing a leather glove and two hawks were released from the tower and flew straight to them for their bait, followed by two falcons, which had to be lured in.

Abdul was impressed with Viggo's handling of the raptors. He had remained calm, was knowledgeable, murmured quiet platitudes to the birds when on his glove, and stroked their heads. He had handled luring the falcon in very confidently.

'I can see Viggo that you are well skilled at managing these birds. Would you like to go with me when I next hunt?'

Viggo's face lit up and he said, 'Nothing would give me greater pleasure, your excellency.'

'I shall let you know when I am having my next official hunt and I shall loan you a raptor to hunt with. Now I will show you my hunting hounds, too.'

Viggo was delighted to see the sleek greyhounds, Salukis and long coated hounds.

Abdul smiled. 'Now I will show you my jaguars and cheetahs, who hunt larger prey. I assume you will not show fear when we go into the pens.'

'No, your excellency. I am used to wolves and powerful livestock guardian dogs at home.'

He went into the cheetah pen and a large male started stalking him. Viggo kept his ground and talked soothingly to the cheetah, which then approached him and allowed him to stroke its head.

Abdul said, 'You have a gift with animals, Viggo.'

'I was taught by Ubba Ragnarsson, the best horseman and animal trainer I have ever seen.'

'Yes, Sulamain told me of Ubba's extraordinary ability to train horses and dogs. He must be very grounded to the earth to be able to communicate so easily with wild animals.'

'He has no fear and the animals accept him as their pack leader.'

Abdul said, 'You must find it very difficult to acclimatise to the heat and humidity here, having lived in the forests and hills of Jorvik.'

'I do miss the hills, trees, rivers, seas and moorland of Yorkshire, but it can be harsh there in winter... although not as harsh as the mountains in Denmark.'

They went to the stables. Abdul showed him his Arab breeding stallions and then had one of his grooms bring another stallion into the paddock. Viggo stared in disbelief at the unusual colour of this horse. Its coat was a combination of chestnut and palomino; it shimmered like burnished gold.

'What breed is he?'

'An Akhal-Teke horse from Turkmenistan. This metallic gold coloured coat appears in some, but not all of them. You even get pure silver looking horses but they tend to have albino traits, such as blue eyes and very pink nostrils, and sometimes they cannot cope with direct sunlight. They are fast horses bred for mountainous and desert regions, but their coat colour is my fascination. I have three mares and this one stallion Grigor.'

Abdul took him over to the kennels to see a litter of six Saluki pups of six weeks old. Viggo made sure he introduced himself to the mother before he touched her pups.

Abdul commented, 'You really must have some power that makes her trust you as she will only let her own kennelman touch her puppies usually.'

Viggo smiled. 'She must know I mean them no harm and have no fear of her.' He sat down and the puppies jumped all over him.

Abdul replied, 'And no doubt you have the same effect on women, too. Many of them are chattering about the young Dane doctor who visits and want to meet you.'

'I do find that some women find me attractive, but I did my sexual experimenting at a young age and Sulamain warned me to keep well away from any relationships with women. I am here to learn medicine and keep my head firmly attached to my body.'

'What is it that makes you Danes such courageous fighters? The stories I have heard about Ragnar raiding in Europe sound almost unbelievable.'

'I think we have been successful invaders because we bring our women with us and they fight alongside us. Plus, Ivar believes that although the Romans tried to conquer the Britons, they underestimated the ethnic makeup of them. They assumed they were all Britons, but many of the early settlers were from Europe and beyond, with their own religions and identities. Ireland is an obvious example as it is made up of feudal tribes that have little in common. When Ivar took over as King of Dublin when Sigtryggr left to invade Jorvik, his reputation gained in Jorvik was a major factor in there being little objection from the Irish. He had transformed Jorvik into an important trading centre, as London and Dublin already has traders from Rus, and he will do the same there. Ivar is famed for his fighting and invading, but he has been a master at creating wealth and trade for the areas he ruled. As he proclaimed, "reputation is all" and in his case, it made men fear him.'

'Are all the horrors Ivar inflicted on his enemies true?'

'It depends who is telling the story. The Saxons will no doubt fabricate his deeds to play down their own inability to fight back. Christianity has had too great an influence by keeping them praying to their God when they should have been fighting to protect their land. King Alfred was to blame for that and learnt the hard way that not having trained warriors to protect from invaders was a disaster. He ended up paying the Danes to teach his Saxons how to fight – and lost all the silver in his monasteries in the process.'

'Do you have any inclination to become a warrior?'

'I know how to wield a sword and an axe to protect myself, but I would not cope well in a shield wall. I prefer to fight in the open, preferably on horseback, but Ivar said I have a natural talent for battle strategy and it was my favourite lesson when Ivar and Ubba taught us how to plan a battle. Bjorn's eldest son Erik and I were usually the winners. Ivar would set up a miniature battle area on a massive table depicting towns, rivers and streams and whether the land was hilly or flat. Then one team were the Britons and the other were Norsemen. Ubba taught us about using the lie of the land to gain advantage, when he was training us to fight. We had such a lot to learn.'

Abdul smiled. 'It must have been a fun way to learn, at the hands of two such legends of war. Wouldn't you prefer to be a king rather than a healer? There would certainly be a lot more money to be gained.'

'I am not unduly motivated by money, and prefer to save someone's life if I can, by finding ways to prevent some of the diseases we see. Sulamain saved Bjorn Ironside from malaria and that is where my passion for healing came from.'

'Well, you certainly picked the right teacher in Sulamain. He also has high praise for your abilities as a doctor and if you are returning to Jorvik then you will be revered for the knowledge you will have gained from him.'

They returned to the palace. Sulamain and Helga were chatting by the outdoor swimming pool. Sulamain had been getting concerned as to whether Viggo had said something to offend Abdul and feared he may have been taken captive, so when he saw them approaching deep in conversation, he breathed a sigh of relief.

They went inside and were offered a meal before they departed. Afterwards, Sulamain asked him how he was getting on with Abdul.

Viggo replied, 'You have taught me that I cannot be a judge of other people's lives in a foreign country, and as much as I deplore his treatment of Helga, I cannot say that a Norseman would never do the same. It happens in a war situation; we have taken many captives into slavery. What I have an objection to is him disrespecting the rights of a woman from my homeland. However, I can do nothing about it, so I have to live with it.

'My father detested the practice of Danes raping women after winning battles, and as troop commander, he was in a position to do something about it and he banned it. As we know, many men take alcohol or mushrooms to bolster their confidence before they fight and raping women after invading is driven by the euphoric effect of success. He declared that anyone who raped hostages would be executed. Now, he was in a position to do something about it. I am not, living here, and so I have to accept it.'

'Wise decision Viggo, spoken like a king. I suppose we have done what we can to make her life more bearable for now, but eventually his passion for her will diminish and who knows what the outcome for Helga will be.'

o0o

Back home that evening, Viggo treated himself to a bottle of wine and they sat outside in the courtyard watching the sun go down. The conversation was mainly about fertility. Viggo asked Sulamain at what age a boy became fertile.

Sulamain said, 'Probably around 14-15 years old.'

Viggo laughed. 'I think I may be able to dispute that, Sulamain. I sired my first child at 12 years old.'

'Impossible! You would have had to be sexually active frequently to produce live sperm.'

'Oh, but I was, Sulamain. The young wife of one of my father's bodyguards had taken me under her wing whilst her husband was in Lincoln, and taught me all I needed to know about sex. Unfortunately, when the baby was born he was definitely a Ragnarsson. My mother knew instantly and shortly after that I went to live with Ivar in Dublin. I don't know whether my father knew about this at the time, but I would have expected an eruption if he had known, and if Ivar did he never raised it with me.'

'You can't be sure as she could already have been carrying to him before he left.'

'Not when she had bled the week before he left. I was anxious to find out what sex was all about. You know I have an enquiring and competitive mind. I could not wait to savour the joy of sex since Erik and Refil had joined us by then and Erik was certainly sowing his wild oats and bragging about it. I didn't want to miss out!'

'Your desire to experience so much of life so young could have serious repercussions, Viggo. I trust you have learnt the difference between sex and love.'

'Absolutely, why do you think I do not wish to be involved with a woman now? I have many areas I want to explore before I consider settling into a relationship. I have the Ragnarsson genes to explore, and I am politically aware. I want to make my own mark in life, but in what capacity, I don't know yet.'

'Viggo, take it from a wise old man. You will be a success whatever path life takes you on, but promise me you will never lose your compassion to heal. It is a gift from the gods that you must not squander. You have a fine brain Viggo, please use it.'

THIRTY-SIX

The next day when Viggo came home from the hospital, Sulamain handed him a letter from Abdul, which had been delivered by messenger. It was a personal invitation to join a large hunting party the following weekend.

Sulamain insisted he must go, as to decline would be an insult. Viggo's desire to enjoy a day's sport was paramount, but he wondered if Abdul just wanted him to handle some of his raptors to show off to his exclusive guests.

On Saturday morning before breakfast, Sulamain was schooling him in etiquette issues when surrounded by several sheiks and warning him to keep out of the harem as no man was allowed into a harem. He feared that as Viggo had been granted access to the harem to treat Helga, he might just think he could wander in unaccompanied, but in Arab terms this could be a death sentence. He promised Sulamain he would not make such a stupid mistake and would be careful what he discussed at the table, too. He knew he must not talk to Helga alone, or to any of Abdul's wives.

Just before he left, Sulamain hugged him and said, 'Be careful, Viggo; treat this invitation with the same caution you would riding onto a battlefield.'

Viggo laughed. 'I didn't know you cared so much about me Sulamain, but I am pleased to know it.'

As he mounted his horse, Sulamain said, 'Now behave yourself and absolutely no flirting with any women... or men, for that matter!'

Viggo spun his horse around. 'Certainly not! I experimented young and found that it is definitely not to my taste. Now stop fussing like a mother hen; even my own mother would not be as concerned as you. I will be back for my Monday morning shift at the hospital.'

As he made his way across the sand dunes, he contemplated what he might expect of a major hunting expedition. Would it be just falcons and hawks, or would they be hunting with jaguars and cheetahs for bigger game? At the highest level he noticed small groups of riders heading on the same track, but miles in front of him.

Within the last mile he spotted an Arab at the top of a distant sand dune. His horse was piebald in colour (black/grey), but it was not an Arab horse. It reminded him of Ivar's Magpie, with similar markings. The rider was in Arab dress, but had a pannier attached to his saddle, so he assumed he was going to join the hunt... but he just stayed where he was and watched from a distance.

When Viggo arrived at the palace gate, Aziz one of the falconers came forward, ushered him in and said, 'His excellency wants you to ride the Akhal-Teke stallion and insists you have one of his best falcons as well. You will be riding up front as an honoured guest with him.'

Viggo was shocked. 'What time are we due to set off? I need to have a school on him before we go out.'

Aziz replied, 'In two hours, sir.'

'I will be back here in an hour and a half. Can you speak to a groom and sort it out for me?'

'Of course, sir. I will take your horse to the stables now, if you wish.'

Viggo dismounted, removed his saddlebag and headed up to the palace entrance. As soon as he came in, one of the servants approached him and said, 'Sir, his excellency wishes me to show you to your room.'

He was whisked up the sweeping marble staircase to the first floor and shown into a beautiful bedroom suite with a balcony overlooking the garden and stables. Laid over the enormous bed was a beautiful silk riding robe with a gold trimmed headdress and soft, thin black leather boots. There was also a navy silk evening dress trimmed in silver.

'His excellency would be honoured if you would accept the clothes as a gift.'

'Please extend my sincere thanks to him for his generosity.'

The servant departed. Viggo ripped off his riding tunic and threw himself onto the bed. He felt so excited that he had been treated with such honour, but he worried it might be a trap. Why did Abdul want him to take centre stage in the hunt? Maybe he just wanted to show off his falcons and horses and realised that he would be an excellent ambassador to promote them.

He had no time to think about it as he knew he had better get showered and his hair washed and braided so he looked respectable in the clothes provided. He made the deadline, although his hair was not fully dry, but it soon would be out in the heat of the desert.

Most guests were in the atrium at a drinks reception, except those who had gone to change to go hunting. He strode across to the stables, intent on finding someone who had ridden Grigor and knew all his foibles. He remembered where his stable was and found his groom saddling him. Grigor knew something exciting was about to happen and he was practically bouncing on the spot even though he was tied up. He asked the groom who normally rode Grigor if he was a safe ride out hunting.

The groom laughed. 'He can play the fool at times, but nothing to worry a Dane warrior like you, I am sure.'

Viggo replied, 'I am not a Dane warrior, just a doctor learning his trade. If he is a bastard to ride I need to know about it now.'

'No, he will be fine – just keep him away from any mares in season – and he is used to having hawks and falcons fly from the saddle.'

'I need to assess him in the schooling paddock to see what his mouth is like and which commands he is used to.'

'Very well, sir. I will show you out to the paddock.'

The groom led Grigor out and he immediately screamed his stallion cry to proclaim his authority. Viggo decided to get him into the paddock before he attempted to mount him, for safety reasons. He had pinched the tiny blocks of sugar used for coffee out of his room to give to Grigor on introduction.

The stallion whickered his appreciation and stood still next to the mounting block. Viggo collected both reins in his left hand, turning his head to the right slightly so Grigor could not whip round and bite him as he mounted. He let him walk out to the track and took no contact on the reins or with his leg. Some horses hated to be held in a vice like grip and he just wanted Grigor to relax and stretch before he took up the contact. Viggo talked quietly and soothingly to the horse and he walked quietly around the school. Viggo then introduced him to his leg and the horse accepted it and moved into trot when asked. Still, he had not taken up the reins. He preferred to let the horse balance himself, rather than forcing him, as the movement would be much more supple.

The groom raised an eyebrow at Viggo having loose reins and no contact; he was sure disaster would ensue. However, Viggo's balance and position in the saddle was so light, the horse never once tried to take off. The speed was being controlled by Viggo's legs, not by the reins. He even risked a canter with no contact and the horse seemed surprised but pleased.

Viggo gently took up a loose contact on the reins, still allowing the horse to stretch through the trot. He changed direction and the stallion was light and relaxed. He increased the contact with his legs and took up the slack on the reins. Grigor accepted his control with no objection. Viggo transitioned to a collected canter and started to ask some questions with his aids to see how much the horse knew.

After ten minutes, he was satisfied the horse was well schooled, but how he would behave in the excitement of a hunt could well be another matter. Viggo spoke to the groom. 'Well, are you surprised to see me still on Grigor and now in full control?'

'Yes sir, I am, but it was beautiful to behold and tales of Danish horsemanship appear to be true.'

'If your life depends on your horse then you have to be a team and ensure that you watch out for each other. Sheer dominance with a savage bit and whip are no substitute for harmony between horse and rider.'

As he rode into the courtyard full of other horses and riders, a silence descended as people took in the vision of the metallic gold horse and the tall elegant rider walking so relaxedly into the noisy environment. Whispers circulated around the courtyard, asking who the rider was, anticipating it would be one of Abdul's sons.

Abdul spoke, 'Gentlemen, may I introduce Viggo Larssen who is the young doctor working with Sulamain in the hospital. He is an accomplished horseman and falconer; I could think of no better stallion than Grigor to show off his skills.'

Viggo was slightly concerned that if anything went wrong, he would look like an idiot, but Grigor was settling under him and was enjoying having a rider with very light hands.

Abdul rode over before they left the courtyard, accompanied by another rider.

'Viggo, may I introduce you to my son Prince Fayed. He is around your age and has been wanting to meet you. He's happy to introduce you to your first hunt. I will see you later when we stop for our first session.'

Prince Fayed was studying how quietly Grigor was standing on a loose rein. His own Arab stallion was already fidgeting to be off.

'How come Grigor is not wandering off when you have practically no contact on his mouth?'

'Because I am holding him with my legs. When I have the falcon on my arm, I need my hands free to see to him. The same would apply if I was going into battle, as I would have my sword and seax to carry.'

Fayed said, 'You don't use your hands to steer the horse. So how do you stop him when you are galloping?'

'I have my voice and I squeeze with my thighs to shorten his stride and collect him and reduce the pace.'

'My father said you have a very different approach with horses than we do.'

'We develop a relationship with them because we are dependent on their cooperation to stay alive. Our battle horses are specially trained to respond to every move of our body so we can change direction very quickly and still fight in the saddle. Eventually, the horse learns to fight with you.'

'How?'

'He will attack the horse your enemy is riding by biting or kicking out and he will also try and push your opponent's horse off balance. He will watch your back for you while you are engaged in a swordfight.'

Fayed smiled. 'How absolutely fascinating, Viggo; you must tell me more.'

After a while, they reached the first stage of the hunt. They were positioned on elevated ground overlooking an oasis where animals and birds were grazing or drinking from a large pond. Viggo's falcon was brought to him and he settled him on his arm with his hood covering his head. He stroked his feathers and crooned quietly to him.

Fayed said, 'Do you Danes talk to all your animals? We only issue commands to ours.'

Viggo laughed. 'Well, believe me, you are missing out on having a beautiful relationship where you can both nurture each other. Most animals love to please, and if you praise them when they do well, they will keep repeating the good things you want them to do. Surely you must have a relationship with your hounds. We do not beat our animals into submission; we reward them with affection and food when they do well and only ever shout at them if they do wrong. They learn very quickly. My brother has a wild wolf as his companion and they go everywhere together. Shadow's hearing and sense of smell are far superior to those of a human and he warns of riders approaching far sooner than Arne would see or hear them.'

The first wave of raptors were returning to their falconers and it was Viggo's turn to fly his falcon. He released her straps on his arm and then undid her hood. He stroked her and gave the command to fly and she flew gracefully up into the air and headed over the oasis to select her prey.

Suddenly, Viggo saw the horse and rider he had seen earlier in the day across on the opposing high ground.

'Fayed, who is that man over there on the piebald horse?' He pointed out the figure in the distance.

Fayed replied, 'I can't see anyone on a black and white horse. You must have eyes as good as a hawk if you can see someone.' Viggo was disconcerted as the figure was very clear to him.

He heard the falcons calling, looked up and saw her swooping low over the oasis. She slowed down and hovered and then swooped down into the long grass and snatched some creature similar to a rabbit. She flew back overhead and waited for him to prepare the lure, swooped to his arm with her prey that was bigger than her, but expertly killed with one bite to the back of the neck.

Viggo was pleased with her kill even though he wasn't quite sure what it was. He dropped it into his saddlebag and hooded her back up.

After a successful few hours of hunting they returned to the palace. Viggo had again seen the man on the piebald horse watching and following the hunt from a distance. He assumed he must be a Bedouin tribesman spying on the hunt.

Viggo thanked Fayed for coaching him through the hunt and Fayed said he would be sitting next to him at dinner and there was to be some entertainment afterwards.

He headed back to his palatial room, anticipating a good snooze before dinner as he was tired. He showered off the sand and sweat, released his hair from the plaits and gave it a good wash. He thought he would show them how long a Dane warrior's hair could be when unbound, as his was shoulder length now and he was pleased with the blond streaks the sun had put into his auburn hair. It would certainly fall below his headdress.

He slept naked on top of the bed with a cool sheet covering his body. He slept for two hours and then woke, startled by his dream. He must have been thinking about the Bedouin horseman before he went to sleep; he woke with a vision of him close up, with a sword in his hand. The hilt was embedded with sapphires and rubies. His headdress covered his hair and he had a scarf around his neck. What would a Bedouin be doing with an expensive sword? Probably stolen. Still, he had better get dressed and go down for dinner.

His hair had dried out and he combed it through. It still retained a curl from being plaited at the sides. He put on the navy silk evening dress and was delighted with the fit. He was finally beginning to appreciate the Arab dress code, but would have preferred it only to fall to the knee, not full length. However, he knew that sunburnt legs would not be pleasant.

He went down to dinner and Fayed came over to him straight away. 'Be thankful you are not on the top table, but with my siblings.'

'Does that mean I get to speak to your sisters?'

'I cannot understand why you would want to speak to my sisters; they are either ugly and boring, or still playing with their dolls.'

He was seated next to Fayed and his younger brother Zahir, who was 16 years old. Dinner went well and he had cleverly selected less spicy dishes so he did not have an upset stomach.

Fayed tried to draw him into conversation about his father and Helga, but he told him very firmly that as a doctor he was bound by the Hippocratic Oath and could not discuss his patients with anybody. Fayed obviously did not approve of his father's obsession with Helga. Viggo dared not ask him how the hierarchy worked in a family with multiple wives. Fayed told him he was third in line to the throne. His eldest brother was Crown Prince, but Viggo wondered what happened to all the other offspring?

After the meal there was some entertainment. He noticed that the female dance troupe was made up of mixed ethnic origin and there was a very pretty petite white girl who stood out from the crowd.

He decided to question Fayed. 'Are the dancing girls a travelling troupe?'

Fayed grinned. 'Some are just local dancers, but there are some slave women who belong to us. Tell me which one has taken your fancy.' They were just taking their final bow.

'The brunette, third from the left.'

Fayed chuckled. 'That my friend is Clotilde from Frankia. I know her well. She is in her late twenties and has been with us for three years.'

Viggo replied, 'I thought she had a certain petite elegance. Ivar adored French girls and swore they made the best lovers. They certainly did when he taught them the art of love.'

'But why would someone as tall as you want a girl at least a foot smaller than you?'

He chuckled. 'To quote Ivar on this, "The most expensive gifts come in small packages!" and he would know.'

Fayed roared with laughter. 'I agree – she is a rather special jewel with those sapphire eyes and I have had the pleasure of her company many times.'

'You lucky bastard. I suppose being a prince gives you many advantages in life.'

Not always Viggo, because you don't have the freedom to do what you want; you have to do as you are told and the expectation is very high. I won't be able to marry Clotilde. I will have no say over who I marry.'

'So perhaps Prince Fayed, you are no freer than the slaves you own.'

Thankfully, guests were retiring after their early start for the hunt. Viggo was quite content to have an early night as the cheetah hunt was set for early the next morning.

Viggo was just on the verge of sleep when he heard footsteps in the corridor and someone knocked on his door. He grabbed a towel from the chair and tied it around his waist. His balcony door was open and there was enough light from outside for him to see his way around. He opened the door to see Fayed and Clotilde and they rushed giggling into the room.

Fayed laughed at his towel and Viggo froze as there

was nothing larger to hand. 'I have brought you the lady you wished to meet and she is just as keen to entertain you.'

Viggo was shocked. 'Whatever do you mean?'

Fayed grinned. 'We have a reputation for keeping our guests happy and I thought you may welcome a night with Clotilde. I have heard that traditionally, Norsemen share their wives and girlfriends with visitors and thought this would be perfect for you.'

Viggo stuttered, 'But I cannot contemplate such a thing without Clotilde's permission… and I thought she was your girlfriend.' Just as he moved forward, the towel caught on the wardrobe handle and fell to the floor. Viggo bent down to grab it, exposing his backside as he turned.

Clotilde laughed. 'Oh, what a beautiful body to explore, Fayed. This gets better and better.'

He gasped. 'Is this some sort of a trap? Are you going to return and accuse me of stealing your woman?'

Fayed shook his head. 'Oh, you Danes, always thinking it's a plot. No it is not, I am giving you a chance to enjoy yourself with a beautiful woman. Don't say you are turning me down!'

Viggo gasped, 'But what if I get her pregnant?'

Fayed replied, 'There's no chance of that; she's already carrying my child.'

'What?!'

Fayed turned to Clotilde. 'She will explain to you shortly. Now, I am away to my bed. Just carry on and enjoy yourself.' With that, he turned and skipped out of the door.

Viggo was speechless and still clutching the offending towel as Clotilde giggled and started undressing. He just stood still, frozen to the spot, watching her closely. When she had disrobed, she moved to the balcony into the light and turned to face him. 'Now, my Danish warrior, do you approve of your Frankian gift?'

'Yes, mademoiselle. I certainly do, but I need to know that you do this entirely of your own free will and not because you are commanded by your master.'

She smiled. 'I am overjoyed to give my body to you, Viggo. Now come and take me to your bed and explore me until your passion is fulfilled.'

Viggo threw away the towel, walked over to her, bent down to kiss her and then swept her into his arms and did exactly as she commanded.

THIRTY-NINE

After very little sleep overnight, Viggo ate a good breakfast and then thanked his hosts profusely – especially Fayed – and started his journey home. The other guests were staying longer, for the cheetah hunt, but he knew that if he did not go home early and get some sleep he would be unfit for duty at the hospital the next morning. Besides, he had lots to think about on the long ride home.

As a Dane, he was used to sexual encounters with women purely to appease his appetite and his tryst with Clotilde should have felt no different. They had both enjoyed the experience immensely and he should just be able to move on and forget it. There was no way either of them could take it any further, but she had intrigued him.

She explained that she was carrying Fayed's baby, but this was purely to prove his fertility for his future father-in-law. It was common both here and in Europe that no royal family marriage would proceed until proof of male fertility was concluded. Dynasties were founded on hereditary succession and should a male be infertile, it could cause a whole bloodline to be wiped out. Divorce was rarely an option and such issues could lead to the death of the infertile husband in some cases.

Clotilde had not only conceived Fayed's child, but had also produced a son to his brother the Crown Prince, soon after she was sold to them as a slave. However, she had assured him that she was perfectly happy doing this as she enjoyed the lifestyle and recognition that came with it. She had come from a poor family in Frankia and she would never have achieved the lifestyle she now had.

Clotilde had asked him whether she was carrying a son for Fayed. He had laughed and told her he was a doctor not a seer and there was no way of confirming the sex until birth. She told him several ways that women used to predict the sex of their babies, but he had laughed and explained that there would always be a 50% chance of being right and not to take too much notice of these fairytales.

Ivar had always liked teaching petite French girls what a man wants in bed. He had always said they were uninhibited in their approach but expected their partner to satisfy them equally. He smiled at the memory of their passionate lovemaking and hoped he had fulfilled Clotilde's fantasies.

His horse stopped dead as the Bedouin tribesman appeared on the crest of a sand dune about 100 metres in front of them, with his horse rearing. He raised his sword in salute and then when his horse stood still, sheathed his sword, blew him a kiss, spun round and galloped off.

Viggo shouted, 'Wait!' in Arabic and cantered after him, but when he reached the top of the sand dune and looked below, there was no sign of horse or rider although there was a trail of hoofmarks in the sand that stopped when he reached the valley bottom. How could he have disappeared when he had seen him so clearly?

Finally, he knew just who the rider was and why he looked so familiar. It had been Ivar on Magpie and the sword was one Ivar had commissioned from Ulfberht when he was in Jorvik.

He had never experienced visions from the past or future like some of his family. He knew Freya had experienced them all her life. His mother had also, and his father occasionally. Realisation dawned that this must mean Ivar was dead and as they had always had a special relationship, he had come to say goodbye. After Ragnar's death at King Aelle's hand, all of his sons had seen visions of his death.

Tears rolled down his cheeks and he sobbed, 'Oh, Ivar, I have loved you as a second father. I hope you go to Valhalla because you deserve it. You have carved your own history on this world and will be remembered forever.' Due to the image in which Ivar appeared to him, he assumed that he had not died in battle, as all Ragnar's sons had seen images of his prolonged death in a viper pit. He prayed Ivar had died peacefully, but he hoped the sword meant he had been accepted into Valhalla by the gods.

He calmed down as he made his way home. He had to remain positive about the vision he had seen and of course he may have been totally wrong. For the first time, he felt homesick for his family and knew the trauma his parents would be feeling if Ivar had died. News from Jorvik had reached them that Sigtryggr had taken the city from Aethelflaed, so he knew that Dublin would be without a king. There was no way Sigtryggr could hold Dublin from Jorvik; he was concerned about Skye and Aralt. He hoped they had joined Sigtryggr in Jorvik before Ivar's death as they could otherwise be a target of the many Irish tribes that would be hungry for power. However, there was nothing he could do.

He reached home by 2.00 pm and a confused Sulamain rushed out to meet him. 'I did not expect you back until midnight. What's happened? You look distraught; have you done something wrong?'

Viggo waved his hand. 'No, just give me chance to speak. I haven't done anything wrong. I came home early because I didn't get much sleep last night and I am exhausted.'

There were no grooms on Sunday so Viggo set to washing his horse down, putting down his bed and filling a hay net for him whilst Sulamain went inside to prepare him a cool drink and some food.

When he came in, he pulled off his headdress and his hair tumbled down as the tie band had come undone.

Sulamain could not resist commenting, 'Goodness Viggo, your hair is so long and thick, surely you need to cut it to keep you cool.'

Viggo shook his head. 'No way! My hair defines my heritage and I am proud of it. I didn't bother plaiting it, just tied it up on my head and unfortunately the 'band snapped.'

Sulamain laughed. 'I am insanely jealous of your lustrous locks Viggo and have always admired the Dane warrior hairstyles. If only I were your age again and brave enough to let my hair grow. Now, tell me what ails you. There is something bothering you.'

Viggo explained the vision that he had seen, knowing that Sulamain would be more than a touch sceptical as his religion did not have this sort of history, although he had been at Bjorn's bedside when Ragnar had appeared to him.

He listened carefully to Viggo's assessment of what he thought he had seen and said, 'I think you may be correct, although you did not get a closeup of him. But hiding his face may well have been a sign of him being deceased. I am sad as I had huge respect for Ivar and what he achieved with the permanent disabilities he was born with. He would have had pain every day of his life and I am just glad I was able to give him something to relieve it when it became unbearable.'

Viggo sighed. 'My mother and father will be devastated and I cannot reach out to them.'

'Both of your parents are intuitive enough to feel that you are aware of the situation and I am sure there will have been a plan in place for Ivar to dictate his own wishes for his funeral. Don't great kings have longboat burials?'

'Yes, but with the political situation in Ireland and the fact that Sigtryggr has only just invaded Jorvik, and my father and brother are fighting for Halfdan over Durham, there is no way they can organise a

Viking burial for Ivar. It would also be impossible for Bjorn's family to attend as his sons were due to sail the Northwest Passage this summer.'

'Viggo, you can do nothing but stay where you are. I am sure your parents will do whatever Ivar has planned. Now, tell me about your hunting weekend.'

He gave Sulamain an outline, but neglected to mention Saturday night's frolics with Clotilde. However, when he had finished Sulamain said, 'Come on, I can tell by your eyes that something very special happened and knowing you, I think it involves a woman, so spill the beans.'

Viggo laughed. 'I daren't tell you; I don't want you to have a heart attack.'

Sulamain raged, 'I knew it would be impossible to keep a Dane away from women and danger. You are just like your father: both so attractive that women of all ages want to bed you.'

Viggo laughed and then told him what he had done and assured him that it had been a simple one-night tumble for both of them. They had been sexually attracted to each other and that was that.

Sulamain calmed down, but said, 'Are you sure, Viggo? I sense you like her, as your eyes light up when you mention her name.'

Viggo laughed. 'Look, you were the one who lectured me on not becoming involved with women. There is no future in a relationship with Clotilde. I just have to accept it. We both have to follow the path destiny carves out for us and they are never going to intertwine.'

'Spoken like a true king. Ivar would be so proud of you and I suspect you will be seeing him again in your dreams now he is watching over you.'

FORTY

Egil was busy in the stables when he came out into the yard and saw a pigeon on the barn roof. It moved to where the entrance to the pigeon loft was and disappeared inside.

The network Viggo had invented meant that homing pigeons were reared in Jorvik and then sent by land or sea to the various bases so that they could communicate with each other very quickly. Messages were carried between all the Ragnarsson bases and even to Winchester for King Edward. Since the family's visit to Frankia where more pigeons were given to Rollo, Bjorn and Sigurd, the network now covered Normandie, Norway, Sweden and Denmark.

Egil assumed this was another message from Ubba, who was in Durham with Halfdan, so he wandered over to the pigeon loft to check. To his surprise, the message had come from Dublin and was addressed to Ubba. He wondered whether to open it or give it to Torri; as he was going to breakfast, he took it with him. Torri was busy in the kitchen, but he went over and mentioned he had a message from Ireland.

Torri turned to him. 'Oh, Egil, you read it out while I dish up the breakfast for the family. It's probably Ivar wanting to know how they are doing in Durham. He asks me because he knows I will always tell him the truth.'

Egil, having been Ivar's Head of Household, could read and write in Latin as he'd had to purchase goods and services for Ivar from all over the globe. He opened the cannister containing the parchment and looked to see who it was from. It had been sent by Skye and she had written in very small handwriting to get as much information on the parchment as possible. He scanned back to the beginning, but on the second line three words jumped out. "Ivar mortuus est" (Ivar is dead). He gasped and read the rest of the note.

Torri said, 'Well come on, Egil; spit it out.'

'My lady, please let one of the servants see to breakfast. I need to speak to you alone.'

Torri looked at Egil and knew it must be bad news. She called the cook to take over and went outside to her rose garden. She motioned to the swing and told Egil to sit down beside her and read her the letter.

'It is with a sad heart that I must inform you of the sudden death of Ivar on Wednesday night. He passed peacefully in his sleep, with Irina by his side. He had been getting weaker gradually over the last few weeks, but had still attended to his duties as King. I was preparing to come over to join Sigtryggr with Aralt, as Sigtryggr thought Jorvik was secure enough now for us to travel. As you know, Ivar wished to be buried in Repton and you agreed to arrange this. I have had his body embalmed and a funeral service will be held in Dublin. He will be "buried" here in the palace grounds. However, he will not reside here. I will bring his body secretly on the longboat to Jorvik. It will be at least a week before we set sail, but as Ivar wished, his burial in Repton must be done in total secrecy. In view of the battles for Jorvik and Durham there is no possibility of any family coming over to Dublin, so I will organise the funeral here.'

Torri sobbed and Egil hugged her to him, with tears pouring down his face.

'I am so sorry, Torri; this is a mighty blow for all of us and you don't even have Ubba here to comfort you. Do you want me to send a rider to Durham? We don't know whether he knows yet, but he will have to come back to Jorvik anyway.'

Torri was so choked, it took her a while to stop sobbing. 'Yes, I suppose so, but I expect Arne will need to stay with Halfdan while everything settles down. Poor Skye and Irina, it sounds like they had no idea his health was deteriorating. Do you know, Ubba told me when we were coming home from visiting him, that he knew he would not see Ivar alive again?'

Suddenly Freya appeared. 'Mama, what on earth is the matter?' She ran and knelt in front of her.

Torri took her hands and said, 'Sweetheart, we have just received a message from Skye in Dublin, advising us that Ivar has died suddenly.'

Freya shouted, 'No, Mama, not Ivar. He was invincible!'

Torri pulled her close. 'Nobody is invincible and for Ivar to reach such an age with his health problems was a miracle in itself.'

'But Mama, he won't go to Valhalla if he did not

die in battle.'

'Freya, we know for a fact that your grandfather Ragnar is in Valhalla and he died in a viper pit with no sword in his hand. The gods will not deny entry to Valhalla for Ivar the Boneless, either.'

Freya stood up and said, 'The gods talk to Thorin and I, so we could pray to them and offer a sacrifice asking them to release his spirit to Valhalla. The gods listened when Ivar prayed for Bjorn Ironside's life, so we can all pray for him in the same way.'

'We can do nothing until your father comes back and takes charge, but you must not discuss with anyone that Ivar's body is coming here for burial. Officially, he will be buried in Ireland.'

o0o

It was late at night when Ubba arrived from Durham, and he went straight to his bedroom, making as little noise as possible. He had been warmly greeted by Caesar, but managed to stop him barking.

He observed his sleeping wife. The overwhelming love he had for her moved him deeply. She looked drawn and pale. He knew that losing Ivar would leave a large gap in her life. They had always had a deep love and understanding of each other, despite their many contentious rows and arguments. Ivar had listened to her because he knew she never shied away from telling him the truth.

He stripped off his clothes and pulled the sheet back. Torri lay naked in the bed. He climbed in quietly, trying not to disturb her, but she sensed him next to her, pulled him close and kissed him longingly.

Ubba laughed. 'How do you know I am your husband and not one of your lovers?'

'I can smell you and feel your presence. I don't have to even open my eyes and when you kiss me, I certainly know it is you.'

He stroked her cheek and kissed her nose. 'And my body recognises you as soon as I touch you; even after 12 hours' hard riding, it wants to possess you. Apologies if I offend your nose with my smell of horses and sweat.'

'Not at all, that is a part of you that is imprinted on my brain because you always smell like that. Can you summon the strength to make love to me? I have missed you so much. I need to be as close to you as possible to convince my mind that you have survived yet another battle.'

He chuckled. 'Well I didn't think I could when I arrived, but something is telling me otherwise now. I didn't get there in time for the battle, but our son equipped himself with honour and we should both be proud parents.'

'Oh, I am so pleased for him. I knew it played on his mind that he may be found wanting at his first attempt.'

'He was one of the first climbing up the ramparts and he killed three men when he climbed up and over. Stefan said he never hesitated, and was so quick with his sword and seax, the guards never got a chance to attack him.'

'Well now he has killed in his first attempt, he

should be a lot more confident about his abilities. Ivar's death was a shock to everyone. Freya took it badly; she thought he was invincible.'

Ubba put a finger to her mouth and said, 'Shush, we will discuss Ivar in the morning. Now I want to concentrate on giving you a memorable reunion!'

oOo

After breakfast, Ubba summoned Freya and Egil to a meeting with him and Torri.

'I know this will have been a shock for you, but Ivar consulted me when we were with him in June and asked a favour of me. He said he was struggling some days to walk. His strength was declining and he knew he was on borrowed time. He did not wish to be buried in Ireland, preferring to be buried in Repton in Derbyshire, where he overwintered on his first visit invading this country. He wanted to be buried secretly, in an unmarked grave. He did not want a longboat funeral as like me, he has always been a landlubber not a sailor. He realised that not being buried in Ireland would cause trouble there, so there will be a funeral in Dublin – except Ivar won't be in the coffin. Skye was already about to leave to join Sigtryggr in Jorvik, so she will bring Ivar's body over here in secret.'

Freya asked, 'Will we be able to attend Ivar's funeral?'

'I have thought about this. It will be impossible for Sigtryggr to leave Jorvik, or Halfdan and Arne Durham... and bearing in mind this is a secret, the fewer people that know about it, the better. I assume

Skye will want to attend and she can leave her son with Gytha and Sigtryggr. I think Skye should have the support of Ralf her father during this difficult time. I don't know whether Irina will come over or not yet. I have made no plans regarding the funeral and burial place yet, but I think we need you Freya, and Thorin, who have a link to the gods, with us – and of course Torri will be there. Egil, I would like you to accompany us both as Ivar's faithful friend and colleague and as a brilliant organiser. There is no hope of contacting Bjorn and his sons, or Sigurd in Zealand. Rollo would not have time to come over from Normandie either. Viggo is the furthest east and much as he was Ivar's favourite nephew, it would not be practical for him to return yet.'

Freya asked, 'How do Thorin and I summon the gods? We don't receive visitations from them.'

Ubba replied, 'I don't know for sure, but in a similar small ceremony to when we were trying to save Bjorn. Ivar was adamant he wanted no big ceremony; he just wants to be buried with his sword and a prayer to the gods to grant him admission to Valhalla as he did not die in battle.'

Freya said, 'I am sure Thorin and I can plead on his behalf and they know how much Ivar the Boneless has done for his country in expanding its empire.'

Ubba said, 'Thorin will join us in Jorvik at the weekend and I suggest we all leave tomorrow so I can have time to consult with Sigtryggr on our plans. I have sent a message to Keir in Hull as I want him to skipper the longboat. He knows the waterways like the back of his hand and we may have to sail at night to avoid detection. The arrival of Skye in Jorvik will make it easier to hide who else is on board and we shall depart at night.'

Freya said, 'Who will be the next King of Dublin?'

Ubba shook his head and said, 'That's up to Sigtryggr and the Irish feudal lords to decide. I suspect there will be bloodshed before it is settled. He cannot be King in two places at once and Aralt is far too young to be considered. Maybe if Halfdan hadn't already taken Durham, he might have wanted to take on Dublin, but I certainly do not.'

Egil asked, 'How far is Repton from Tamworth?'

Ubba responded, 'About 23 miles from the Lady of Mercia's palace, where she is now safely in residence.'

Torri said, 'And what is she likely to think of Ivar the Boneless being buried in Mercia? I can't imagine she will be thrilled at the prospect. Ivar never converted to Christianity and she lost Jorvik to Sigtryggr.'

'Well I wasn't intending to ask her permission, but she and Edward do owe me a favour and if I have to then I will pursue it.'

Egil asked, 'Are you content with leaving your men here to protect the farm and carry on preparing for the Autumn season?'

Ubba considered. 'Well, we didn't have any problems whilst we were away in Ireland and Normandie over the summer, so I don't expect any trouble and if I need to take warriors I will select those who came abroad with us as sailors too. Sigtryggr may insist I take some of his warriors just in case we run into trouble, but until

I get to Jorvik and speak to him about the logistics I can't be sure. Arne is too useful to Halfdan, so I don't want to bring him home, and I am already pinching Thorin from him. Edward is not going to try and seize Jorvik back and Sigtryggr will keep a watchful eye out for any unusual activity in the area. I will ask Serena if she wants to stay in Jorvik with the children, but I don't think she would want to move there with them just for a week or so.'

Egil said, 'Right, I will go and discuss with Josh and sort out anything that needs doing from a logistical angle, as he is in charge of the stud. We can liaise with the shepherds regarding movement of the sheep back up to the hills when the lambs are weaned.'

The meeting broke up and they all hurried to prepare to go to Jorvik the next day.

Ubba sought out Serena as he knew she would not be too pleased about him departing yet again, when he had been away from home since June on his travels. He found her in the dairy with Frank, who was now three years old and full of mischief.

Frank ran up to him shouting, 'Dada, pick me up and swing me round. I have missed you. Where have you been?'

'I know, son. I have been away for most of the summer visiting relatives, but I have come to assure your mama that it won't be too long before I am back home with you all permanently.'

Serena scowled. 'Don't make promises you cannot keep, Ubba.'

'I know. I am sorry. This should be my last trip this year and I will spend autumn and winter at home.'

'Will you teach me to ride, Dada?' Frank started jumping up and down in his arms.

'Whoa, young man, or you will fall. Three is a little early to master riding a pony, but we can give it a try.'

'I don't want to ride a pony. I want to ride Sleipnir or Diablo?'

Ubba laughed, threw him up in the air and caught him. 'You have to learn to ride a pony first, young man. Stallions are for warriors who are skilled enough to ride into battle. You have to earn a horse's respect before you can ride one into battle.'

Frank spotted through the window his brother throwing a ball for the sheepdogs and he shouted, 'Down, Dada! I want to go and play with Theo and the dogs!' Ubba put him down and he ran off as fast as his chubby legs would allow.

Serena was churning butter and he put his arms around her waist and nibbled and kissed the back of her neck. Her hands were covered in butter so she could not object. She said, 'Don't you dare try and flirt with me; you are not in favour after neglecting me all summer. I dread to think how many women you bedded in Ireland and Frankia.'

Ubba continued with his butterfly kisses and then slid his hands round and cupped her breasts. 'I was with Torri and had to behave myself, especially in Normandie. She was not in the best of health in Ireland.'

'Don't tell me you had no trysts, Ubba. You may be

getting older, but your looks and those eyes will always attract women.' She tried to scrape the butter off her hands and turned round to face him.

'Don't waste that lovely butter.' He took her hand, licked the butter off her fingers and pressed her back against the bench.

She laughed and said, 'You wouldn't dare!'

'Oh, but I would, Serena. I want you right here and now!' He pushed the butter dish to one side, pulled up her skirt, lifted her onto the bench and proceeded to do exactly as he pleased.

In their frantic passion, neither of them heard the door open and Theo (aged six) and Frank standing in the doorway speechless, observing their parents. Theo pulled Frank back and shut the door quietly.

Frank said in total amazement, 'What are they doing?'

Theo chuckled. 'Having sex. Something only grown-ups are allowed to do. The same as the stallion does to the mare to get her in foal.'

Frank looked puzzled and said, 'Does that mean Mama might have another baby?'

Theo giggled. 'Probably, knowing our father's excellent fertility rate.'

'But I don't want another brother or sister! I just want Dada to teach me to ride!'

FORTY-ONE

Their party arrived in Jorvik at lunchtime and they were ushered straight to Sigtryggr's office. Already there were Ralf and Gytha, and they all rose to greet them. Gytha hugged Torri and said, 'My commiserations on the loss of Ivar; it must have been as big a shock to you as it was to me.'

Torri replied, 'At least he died peacefully.'

Sigtryggr hugged Ubba. 'I am so sorry. I had no idea he was unwell before I invaded Jorvik, or I would not have left him with the onerous task of being King of Dublin.'

Ubba patted him on the shoulder. 'This is not your fault, Sigtryggr. Ivar would not have had it any other way. When I was over in Ireland he did not indicate his health was deteriorating, but he did tell me he wished to be buried secretly at Repton, not in Dublin, and asked me to organise it.'

Sigtryggr replied, 'So he must have expected it to be when I was over here, which is why he asked you to organise it. Shall we get the meeting finished and then we can have a leisurely lunch.'

They all sat down round the table. Freya seemed delighted to be involved.

Sigtryggr said, I have further news from Dublin.

Axel suggested that they sail on one of his small merchant vessels, which will create less attention and will provide more privacy than on a longboat. He has offered to captain the ship and guarantees his crew's absolute discretion. They will have sailed today, so should be here within three days.'

Ubba added, 'That would make it easier to keep quiet as Axel's boats come through Jorvik once a month at least. I have contacted Keir my boat captain and prepared to use my longboat to go to Repton so that the Irish boat can sail home quickly. If Axel is prepared to sail south with his crew then Keir would still need to be there as he has extensive knowledge of the Mercian river network. I have brought Egil to assist me with the planning of the internment and thought it wise to have Freya and Thorin with us as they have ways of communicating with the gods. Thorin will be here tomorrow from Durham. Torri and I will be Ivar's closest relatives in attendance, as there is no way we can expect my other brothers and family to get here quickly. Halfdan sends his apologies as he feels he can't leave Durham yet and I am sure you Sigtryggr feel the same about Jorvik.'

He replied, 'I think I owe Ivar the respect of being there, but I understand that it is early days since I took the city and accept I need to be here should any counterattacks take place.'

Ralf said, 'I agree with Ubba. I don't think you should leave the city. I am prepared to accompany Skye, and Gytha will happily see to Aralt here as well. He needs to have protection and Jorvik offers fortified walls.'

Sigtryggr said, 'Ubba, have you any idea exactly where Ivar wants burying in Repton? I can't imagine the Mercians will be too pleased if you turn up and want to bury a coffin in some farmer's cornfield.'

I have no idea, but the Lady of Mercia owes me a favour, as does her brother King Edward. Do you think Aethelflaed would grant permission but not inform her brother?'

Torri said, 'No! If she didn't inform Edward and it was found out later, she would be in deep trouble with him.'

Sigtryggr said, 'Surely it could be done at night in an isolated spot?'

Ubba said, 'I will think about it. We may just have to wait until we get there.'

They finished their meeting and went to the dining room for lunch.

Sigtryggr asked Ubba to join him at his table for a private chat.

As Ubba joined him he said, 'I really think I should go. I owe Ivar a great deal and he never asked for anything in return.'

'Look, this is not an official funeral and in similar circumstances Ivar would be telling you exactly what everyone else has told you. Stay put in Jorvik; you cannot risk losing it now, or an issue flaring up in your absence. You did repay him; you took back Jorvik for the Danes when he once lost it. That's what he wanted – revenge.'

'I know, but I would just feel bad not being there. I

408

have put considerable pressure on Skye, having to deal with all this.'

Ubba interrupted, 'Look, you have no control over what the gods throw at us and Skye is a strong woman. She will want to carry out Ivar's last wishes for both of you. She will have her father, me and Torri at her side. You stay here and guard your city and your son, with Gytha's help.'

He sighed. 'Yes, I can see the sense of it, but I wanted to put my plea to the gods to let Ivar into Valhalla.'

'Well, do it here! Make an animal sacrifice and make your own farewell to Ivar. That's why I'm taking Thorin and Freya with me. Ivar was the one who summoned the gods to save Bjorn. I don't know whether I can do it, so taking them for backup is sensible. I only see visions, but they hear the gods speak to them.'

'Not a bad idea, Ubba! Yes, I will do that. But for optimal effect it needs to be when you are performing your ceremony.'

'Well, I will be doing it at night so if I release one of the Jorvik pigeons in Mercia on the morning of the ceremony, you should receive the message back before nightfall and we will all aim for midnight.'

o0o

Three days later, Axel's merchant ship docked just before dawn in Jorvik at his usual trading post. They had been kept informed by Sigtryggr's network of spies, using carrier pigeons to convey messages back to Jorvik whilst en route. Only Sigtryggr, Egil and Ubba met them, riding normal troop horses, with

Egil leading two spare mounts for Irina and Axel and a small farm cart driven by a groom for Skye and the nursemaids.

Sigtryggr was first on board. He hugged Skye and both had tears running down their cheeks. Neither spoke; they were too emotional. He then kissed Aralt, who was in the arms of the nursemaid.

Ubba shook hands with Axel and gave Irina a welcoming hug. 'I am so sorry, Irina; this must be a very difficult time for you, but I will ensure Ivar's wishes are carried out.' She was too overcome to speak.

Egil and the groom transferred the luggage to the cart and settled the entourage on board.

At Sigtryggr's request, he and Ubba were shown down into the hold to where Ivar's coffin was concealed by Axel.

Ubba laid a hand on the coffin and said, 'I'm here now little brother, to carry out your last wishes.'

Sigtryggr did the same, but muttered a silent message to Ivar, with tears still falling down his face.

Axel observed the scene emotionally. Here on his ship were two of the greatest Danish warriors paying homage to the most famous – Ivar the Boneless.

As they reached the palace Torri, Gytha and Freya ran out to meet them and Torri immediately supervised staff to take care of Aralt so that Skye was free to be with Sigtryggr.

Torri was first to greet a very pale, shocked Irina and hugged her tightly. 'I am so sorry. You must be exhausted after your journey.'

Irina patted Torri's arm and said, 'I am just so

relieved to be here amongst family and friends. Axel has been such a support and him bringing us over on his trading ship was an inspired decision. We left Dublin completely unobserved by anybody from his warehouse docks.'

Ubba and Egil ushered them into the dining room, where hot drinks and crusty bread were being served.

Sigtryggr approached Irina and he hugged her tightly. 'I am so sorry. I had no idea Ivar was unwell. Did you know?'

'No, he kept it quiet. I knew he was slowing down because he was less mobile; he couldn't walk very far as he was gasping for breath after only a short distance. He said he had picked up a chest infection, but I honestly think it was his heart that was the problem.'

They all sat round the table and after most had eaten, Sigtryggr said, 'I just want to hear from Irina and Skye about what transpired and then bring you up to date with what we have planned for the funeral. It will be kept short so that you can both go and rest from your journey. Skye, your mother and Torri have organised the nursery so you can accompany Axel and Ubba to Mercia. I will reluctantly be staying here as it would be unwise to leave Jorvik just yet, until matters of governance are finalised.'

Irina said, 'Ivar had been slowing down recently. There was no real indication that it was serious. On Thursday night we went to bed as usual and at about 4.00 am I felt Ivar take my hand and kiss it. As I turned over, he literally took his last breath. So quickly and peacefully, but an absolute shock for me. I knew I

411

could have done nothing to prevent it. It was as if his life just... expired.'

Ubba was visibly shaken. 'When we came over to Ireland in the summer, he asked me to carry out his last wishes and I felt at the time that I would not see him alive again. However, he laughed it off, saying he would be around for years yet. He never even told me why he chose Repton rather than here in Jorvik.'

Irina commented, 'He told me that on his first trip to Mercia he overwintered in Repton, along with 250 Danes and their families. They had King Egbert's blessing, provided they moved on in the spring. It was early March and Ivar was getting restless and he and three other young Danes opted to leave to go north as Danes had taken several strategic cities on northern rivers and they wanted to seek their own fortunes. A week later, Egbert ordered troops to massacre the village and kill every last Dane. Ivar never forgave himself for not being there and vowed to reap revenge on Egbert.'

Ubba commented, 'So that's why Repton! The Saxons must have buried the Danes somewhere. I need to find out where and bury Ivar with them.'

Sigtryggr said, 'It also explains why Ivar committed such cruel and excessive torture on his captives when he was at war. I think the travellers need some rest now. We will prepare for you to sail south within the next couple of days.'

Sigtryggr took the opportunity to whisk Skye off to his room to have some time together, as it was nearly two months since he had left Ireland.

She was exhausted and admitted she was too tired to talk. He suggested she climb into bed with him and they would have a chat, then he would leave her to sleep for as long as she wanted.

He jumped in naked, trying to conceal his ardour as he could not expect his exhausted wife to relish sex after the trauma of the last two weeks.

She did manage to comment, 'Well, at least you are pleased to see me husband, and I have missed you, but my stress levels have gone off the scale.'

He cuddled up to her and held her close to his chest. 'Tell me about it and share it with me. I feel so guilty that you were there alone when all this happened. I know it must have been dreadful.'

'The shock of Ivar dying hit me hard as well as Irina, because we both felt guilty and like we should have known he was unwell, but to be honest it wasn't obvious. I am certain it was a heart problem that took him in the end, but at least it was peaceful.

'My biggest cause for concern was being attacked by someone trying to claim the throne. I feared for our safety. However, the troops you left at home rallied instantly to that possibility and organised their own patrols, looking for potential threats and guarding the palace, closing the gates to everyone to protect us. Your counsellors met and discussed the succession, but I was too busy to attend their meetings as I was organising the funeral and ultimately removing Ivar from Dublin. Axel came straight away to support Irina and she will move back in with him when they return to Dublin. Donal Mcarthy came as soon as he heard and offered to take us to Tara, but as this had happened when I was already about to come over to Jorvik, I felt we would be better protected at the palace.'

'Oh, my sweetheart and brave little queen, you coped admirably under very difficult circumstances; you must have been terrified.'

She pulled his face closer to her and kissed him. 'I did miss having my Viking king beside me. You are so tall and strong and instantly command respect, but I felt like a little lost lamb without you there to take charge.'

Their kissing became more passionate and Sigtryggr smiled, knowing his beloved was safe and well and back in his arms, seeking his body once again. He made love to her gently and reverently and she felt like a huge weight had been lifted from her shoulders.

After their reunion, he insisted she remain in bed until she had caught up on her sleep.

As he left his bedroom Egil approached and said, 'My lord, Axel's men have just brought the luggage, furniture and personal possessions your wife brought over from Dublin. Do you wish me to see to sorting them out and distributing them where I think they belong?'

He patted him on the shoulder. 'Egil, that would be so good of you if you don't mind.'

'Happy to be of use, my lord. I will liaise with Ubba about Ivar's personal possessions as his weapons are in one box and Ubba may want to take some items for his internment. Skye brought Ivar's favourite wolfhound Conan over on the ship, but he refused to leave his coffin to go on the wagon.'

'Oh dear, well best mention this to Ubba straight away as he may think it appropriate to take him with us. He has already had me load two sheep and a goat for sacrifice to the gods. Although I can't see Ubba wanting to sacrifice the dog or leave it in the tomb with Ivar. He does not approve of animals or humans being slaughtered for grave ornaments.'

oOo

Axel's ship moored on the Trent by the village of Repton. Their journey had been uneventful as Axel was a well-known frequent trader in Mercia. Several people expected him to be selling his wares, but he explained his stock was sold and his hold empty, as he was now returning to Ireland.

Ubba had devised a strategy for finding out where the Dane burial ground was. It involved the men drinking frequently in the local tavern and trying to find someone who had been around when the massacre took place. Ubba would claim he had lost an uncle from the encampment and wanted to visit his grave. Surprisingly, on the very first night they were there, this yielded a possible contact. A local farmer informed them of a young man whose father had been a priest at St Wystan's Church at that time. His son Burgred still lived in the area and worked for the church as a grave digger and gardener. He pointed out his house but said he would probably be at the graveyard until the evening.

Ubba and Egil could not believe their luck and

went back to the boat to wait until Burgred was likely to be in. There was no point in visiting the church and creating suspicion amongst the priests and villagers. They agreed that just he and Torri would go, so as not to frighten him or alert the villagers.

Ubba and Torri had discussed the ceremony and planned it based on Ivar's ceremony that was conducted for Bjorn. Thorin had offered to deal with killing the sacrificial animal and collecting blood, whether it be sheep or goat, knowing Ubba's distaste at killing. Ubba would be the lead gothi in the ceremony. Torri would also be involved in the invocations to the gods. Egil had brought the white ceremonial robes that were used in Jorvik for Bjorn's ceremony.

Torri and Ubba set off at about 6.30 pm to go and see Burgred. Ubba agreed they would meet the others in the tavern later. When they reached the cottage, a young man in his twenties was digging vegetables in the garden. He looked up as they came through the gate.

Torri said, 'Are you Burgred? May we have a word with you?'

He looked them both up and down and knew instantly they were wealthy Danes. 'What business would you have with me?'

Ubba realised he was anxious and said, 'I spoke to a man in the tavern who suggested you may be able to point me in the direction of where the Danes' graves are who were massacred here 10 years ago. My uncle was one of them and I would like to pay my respects. He said your father was one of the priests living at St

Wystan's at the time.'

Burgred's face relaxed and he said, 'I was 12 years old when it happened and I still have nightmares about that fateful night. My father and I were told by Egbert's troops to stay locked in the church and they posted guards around it. They attacked at midnight and burned their huts and shelters, then slaughtered them as they tried to escape. There were over 500 Saxon troops and I know for a fact that 250 Danes – men, women and children – died that night. I still have nightmares about their screams and I saw their burned, raped or butchered bodies the day after. My father said the King had not told the priests what he was intending to do. They did not deserve to die like that; they kept to their promises and we lived side by side in harmony throughout that winter.'

Torri said, 'It must have been a huge shock to see that sight at 12 years old.'

Burgred continued, 'The problem was, the bishop would not allow them to be buried in consecrated ground owned by the church, because they were pagans.'

Ubba said, 'So where did they bury them? Egbert would have wanted to keep this as quiet as possible.'

'They buried them in a mass grave in the farmer's field next to the church. The farmer received a good payoff, but he didn't want to have his crops ruined so they dug deep and used as little of the field as possible – just piled them all on top of one another.'

Torri gasped. 'As if murdering them wasn't bad enough, they denied them a proper burial too.'

Burgred replied, 'I am sorry to say so, my lady. My father was deeply affected by the whole thing because he considered it should never have happened in the first place. He died within two years of their death, still traumatised by what he had witnessed. I will willingly show you where they were buried when it's daylight tomorrow, if that is your purpose for coming here.'

Torri replied, 'We would be so grateful if you could do that for us.'

Burgred smiled. 'I will be at the church all day tomorrow; just come when it pleases you.'

Ubba thanked him profusely and they departed. They went to the tavern to report what they had found and plan their next step.

FORTY-TWO

Ubba and Torri went to meet Burgred at midday in the churchyard the next day. They thought if they went at this time, Burgred would probably be having his lunch there, and there would be less chance of any of the priests being around.

He welcomed them pleasantly and took them into the adjacent farmer's field, which fortunately had been growing oats that had been harvested only two weeks ago. The grave was parallel to the graveyard, but separated by a stone wall. Burgred marked out the perimeter as he recalled it.

Ubba explained that he and Torri would like to come back the next day at midnight, to conduct their own vigil and pray to the gods for their uncle's soul, as they feared that due to him not being buried in accordance with Norse traditions his soul may still be earthbound and might not have gone to Valhalla.

Burgred said that provided they conducted this quietly, so as not to disturb the priests, he could not see a problem. After all, it was King Egbert who had committed the massacre in the first place and he as a Christian was appalled at what had taken place. It was the least he could do for the relatives of the dead.

Ubba thanked him and gave him two silver arm

rings for his trouble. He was delighted and confirmed he would not say anything to the priests or the farmer.

They went straight back to the boat to plan their operation in detail. Axel suggested two alternating teams from his crew should carry the wooden coffin to the burial site. Egil said he would release a pigeon that evening informing Sigtryggr of the funeral taking place tomorrow at midnight. It would be Thursday (Thor's day) which should help speed their message to him.

Ubba explained the format of the ceremony. Before the coffin was put in the ground, Ivar's Ulfberht sword and his arm rings would be placed on his body in the hope the gods would grant him entry to Valhalla. The slaughter of the goat would be done at the graveside by Thorin. Ubba would paint the sign of the cross on the chief mourners' faces and after they had prayed to the gods, the lid would be nailed down and the coffin lowered into the grave.

Egil and Axel would take a digging party to the site as soon as darkness fell tomorrow night. It was considered too risky to dig the ground tonight. Ivar's wish was for a secret grave; he did not want disturbing in the afterlife by anybody.

Freya had campaigned for Conan the Wolfhound's life. Irina and Axel agreed that as he was only three years old, they would take him back to Ireland. Freya would accompany him at the ceremony. Ivar had not requested any of his animals to be buried with him. All his hunting birds had travelled with him from Dublin and Sigtryggr had agreed they could stay in the aviary in Jorvik. Irina said Ivar hoped that Viggo would inherit his birds when he returned to Jorvik from his travels.

Ubba hardly slept that night, worrying about the ceremony and what he was going to say. Thorin had been adamant that whatever he said would reach the gods' ears. He had even offered to do his own special tribute to Thor, calling on him to listen. Ubba realised he should have taken more notice when Ivar did the last ceremony. It was ironic that he was conducting this service for Ivar when he personally was the only Ragnarsson that had converted to Christianity. He had visions of being struck by a bolt of lightning for his betrayal of the true gods. He hoped he would be forgiven as Torri, Freya and Thorin were all taking part in the ceremony too. After half an hour trying to sleep, and failing miserably, he quietly extracted himself from Torri's sleeping form and went down to the hold. So as not to wake any of the crew, he did not take a lighted sconce and when he entered the hold he was met with low growling from Conan.

He quickly said, 'Shush, boy. I mean Ivar no harm; I am his beloved brother.'

Conan ceased growling, came over to him and licked his hand. 'Good boy, I know you are just doing your duty by guarding your master, but tomorrow we will be burying him for good. Ivar would not want you to pine away just because he has died; he would want you to live your life in peace. Irina and Axel will take you back to Dublin and you can have a normal life surrounded by plenty of dogs and people.' He sat down on a bench near to Ivar's coffin. Conan came and sat next to him and he hugged him and fondled his ears.

'Oh, Ivar, I hope this is what you wanted. I expected you to choose Jorvik but I can understand why you would choose here and want total anonymity. All your life, your infamous reputation has been your driving force and I know it pleased you to be the most feared Dane warrior. But you and I both know that wasn't really true. Living every day in constant pain would drive anybody else to kill themselves. But you chose to prove that you can triumph over adversity and handicap and be whoever you want. Nobody was going to dismiss you as a cripple even though father sought to end your life shortly after birth. Mother rescued you from the mountain, but I don't think she realised how tough life would be for both of you.

'I know you appreciated the time I spent with you back in Jormund during the winters and I am happy that it helped you forge your own path to being the ultimate warrior. As you know, I forced myself to do it out of sheer fear of dying in pain or being captured and tortured. We both did it for entirely different motives, but had that Ragnarsson reputation hanging over our heads.

'I shall miss your political flair and war strategy. You reinvented the game as far as invading new territories. You found ways of winning that confounded belief and left your enemies traumatised, if not already dead! I shall miss your constant spying and interfering in my love life and encouraging me to breed. I hope the six children I have now produced will make their own marks in life and I am sure there are plenty of unknown children that I have sired that will keep the Danes in this country that Alfred wanted to unite as England. I have to admit it is beautiful and the land so bountiful; everything that I want is available in Yorkshire.'

oOo

The digging party returned to the boat at around 10.30 pm, with the grave dug. Egil had made sure they took the top layer of turf off in one piece so they could cover it up until the service began and then roll it back. The night was cloudy and muggy with no moon and Ubba expected rain would come at some point.

He had remained on the boat to prepare for the ceremony. When going through Ivar's possessions he had discovered a leather bag containing large solid silver coin replicas that Ivar had struck when he first introduced coinage in his own right. These large coins were double the size of the original coins, but worth more than double the value. He had shown them to Torri and suggested that all Axel's crew should be given one for their part in the funeral. This would make them feel honoured and would also help secure their bond of secrecy, as if they broke it then they would fear Ivar's wrath from beyond the grave. Torri insisted that the men left guarding the boat were not left out and they agreed Ubba would present them afterwards.

The procession left the boat at 11.45 pm with Ubba and Torri leading, followed by Axel and Irina, and then the family group all wearing the ceremonial white robes. Freya held Conan on the lead as he had panicked when the coffin was raised from the hold. She had her father's empathy with animals, and once he realised he was going to accompany the coffin on land, he settled down. The second bearer group lit the way with blazing torches. They swapped over halfway to the site so they could keep a good pace.

When they reached the grave, Egil and Axel rolled back the turf and Thorin prepared to slay the goat, assisted by Egil. He wielded the axe and followed up quickly with a knife to the throat to collect the blood. He was so quick the goat never uttered a sound. Thorin presented Ubba with the ceremonial bowl of blood and he marked himself first and then one by one, approached each member of the group offering a continuous prayer to the gods for Ivar's admission to Valhalla.

Torri then made her plea to the gods, followed by Thorin and Freya.

Meanwhile, Egil assisted Ubba in opening the coffin lid. Ivar's body had been embalmed, which made him look as if he was asleep. There was no sign of him having fought death at all. He had been laid to rest in a red tunic covered by a blue velvet cloak scrolled in silver around the edges, which was trimmed in ermine. Ubba and Egil put his arm rings on and then Ubba laid the Ulfberht sword on his chest and pulled his replica necklace of Thor's silver hammer out to touch the hilt of the sword. The sapphires and rubies reflected in the torchlight. Ubba then kissed his cold cheek and said, 'Go, little brother, to Valhalla. Our father is waiting for you to fight and feast with him.' Tears were running down his cheeks, but he stepped back as Egil bowed to him, said goodbye and moved to invite Torri and Freya to approach the coffin.

They each made their final kisses and comforting words. Freya, although tearful, allowed Conan to lick Ivar's cheek and he whined. This small act caused Ubba to let out one sob, but he fought hard to contain himself as his job was not over yet. Irina and Axel were next and she was calm and in complete control. She had done all her crying after his death and his Irish funeral. Thorin followed, placing his hand over the hilt of the sword and praying to the gods.

Egil and Thorin closed the coffin lid as Ubba needed a moment to compose himself for the final address. Torri squeezed his hand in support and muttered, 'You are doing fine, Ubba; showing your emotion only proves how much you care.'

Ubba then listed the names of his family and friends who were unable to be present and, apart from a stumble when he named Arne and Viggo, he remembered everyone.

For the invocation to the gods he, Torri, Freya and Thorin linked hands in a circle and each one made their own prayer aloud. During this, the weather started to change. A strong breeze started to blow and thunder could be heard in the distance.

Afterwards, the bearer party began to lower the coffin into the grave. Conan started to get stressed and was pulling at the lead. Ubba took the lead from Freya as she was in danger of being pulled over. He bent down and hugged Conan, murmuring platitudes, and stroked him. He calmed down and sat obediently at Ubba's side while the grave was refilled with soil, but when the turf was rolled back over he jumped up and howled as the thunder and lightning rolled closer. Thorin came to take him from Ubba and the dog was baying, looking up to the sky.

Ubba distributed the silver coins to family, friends and then Axel's crew. He then announced that everyone who had attended was sworn to secrecy and if they broke the oath then they may have to answer to the gods later. The rain started and the sheet lightning lit the entire sky. They moved quickly back to the shelter of the boat while the storm raged. However, within half an hour it subsided completely.

Thorin and Freya had stood in the bow of the boat holding hands, watching the storm. As it subsided, they both hugged each other and Thorin said, 'We did it; the gods have listened and sent the Valkyries to take him on his journey to Valhalla.'

Ubba joined them hastily. 'Did you see anything?'

Thorin smiled. He described what he had seen and Freya confirmed that she had shared exactly the same vision.

The relief Ubba felt was overwhelming and he embraced them both. His biggest fear had been that he would not be able to achieve this mammoth task.

He looked up into the sky as the rain clouds had dispersed and the stars were visible. He prayed, 'Safe journey, Ivar the Boneless, the most feared Dane of all time. I hope to join you in my own good time.'

Milton Keynes UK
Ingram Content Group UK Ltd.
UKHW030516311024
450440UK00001B/6